# A SURRENDERED
HEART

Books by
# Tracie Peterson & Judith Miller

BELLS OF LOWELL
*Daughter of the Loom* • *A Fragile Design*
*These Tangled Threads*

LIGHTS OF LOWELL
*A Tapestry of Hope* • *A Love Woven True*
*The Pattern of Her Heart*

THE BROADMOOR LEGACY
*A Daughter's Inheritance*
*An Unexpected Love*
*A Surrendered Heart*

*www.traciepeterson.com*

*www.judithmccoymiller.com*

THE BROADMOOR

LEGACY      BOOK THREE

# A SURRENDERED HEART

## TRACIE PETERSON
### AND
## JUDITH MILLER

BETHANY HOUSE PUBLISHERS

*Minneapolis, Minnesota*

Published by Bethany House Publishers
11400 Hampshire Avenue South
Bloomington, Minnesota 55438

Bethany House Publishers is a division of
Baker Publishing Group, Grand Rapids, Michigan.

Printed in the United States of America

**Library of Congress Cataloging-in-Publication Data**

Peterson, Tracie.
    A surrendered heart / Tracie Peterson and Judith Miller.
        p.   cm.—  (The Broadmoor legacy ; bk. 3)
     ISBN 978–0–7642–0684–9 (alk. paper) — ISBN 978–0–7642–0366–4 (pbk.) — ISBN 978–0–7642–0685–6 (large-print pbk.)
        1. Thousand Islands (N.Y. and Ont.)—Fiction.  2. United States—History—1865–1898—Fiction.  I. Miller, Judith, 1944–  II. Title.

    PS3566.E7717S87      2009
    813'.54—dc22
                                                                2009007611

# Dedication

To Dale and Frank Hubbell
for their ongoing friendship and
willingness to lend a helping hand
whenever needed.

—Judith Miller

TRACIE PETERSON is the author of over seventy novels, both historical and contemporary. Her avid research resonates in her stories, as seen in her bestselling HEIRS OF MONTANA and ALASKAN QUEST series. Tracie and her family make their home in Montana.

JUDITH MILLER is an award-winning author whose avid research and love for history are reflected in her novels, many of which have appeared on the CBA bestseller lists. Judy and her husband make their home in Topeka, Kansas.

# Broadmoor Family Tree

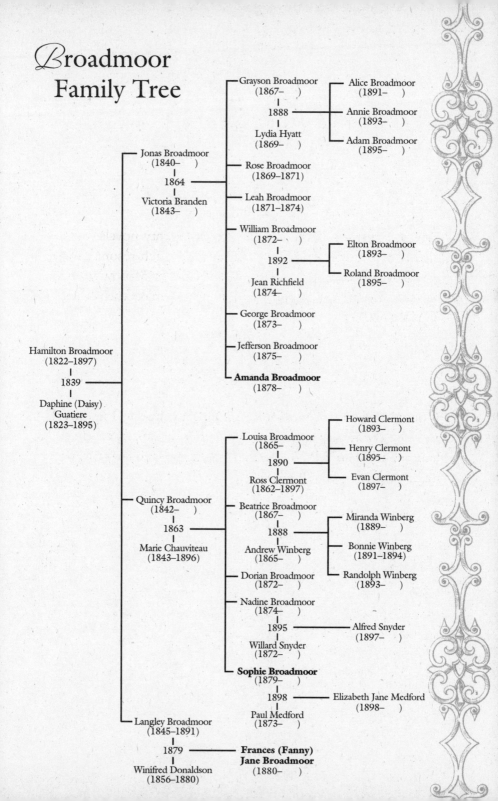

Hamilton Broadmoor
(1822–1897)
|
1839
|
Daphine (Daisy)
Guatiere
(1823–1895)

Jonas Broadmoor
(1840–   )
|
1864
|
Victoria Branden
(1843–   )

Grayson Broadmoor
(1867–   )
|
1888
|
Lydia Hyatt
(1869–   )

Alice Broadmoor
(1891–   )

Annie Broadmoor
(1893–   )

Adam Broadmoor
(1895–   )

Rose Broadmoor
(1869–1871)

Leah Broadmoor
(1871–1874)

William Broadmoor
(1872–   )
|
1892
|
Jean Richfield
(1874–   )

Elton Broadmoor
(1893–   )

Roland Broadmoor
(1895–   )

George Broadmoor
(1873–   )

Jefferson Broadmoor
(1875–   )

**Amanda Broadmoor**
(1878–   )

Quincy Broadmoor
(1842–   )
|
1863
|
Marie Chauviteau
(1843–1896)

Louisa Broadmoor
(1865–   )
|
1890
|
Ross Clermont
(1862–1897)

Howard Clermont
(1893–   )

Henry Clermont
(1895–   )

Evan Clermont
(1897–   )

Beatrice Broadmoor
(1867–   )
|
1888
|
Andrew Winberg
(1865–   )

Miranda Winberg
(1889–   )

Bonnie Winberg
(1891–1894)

Randolph Winberg
(1893–   )

Dorian Broadmoor
(1872–   )

Nadine Broadmoor
(1874–   )
|
1895
|
Willard Snyder
(1872–   )

Alfred Snyder
(1897–   )

**Sophie Broadmoor**
(1879–   )
|
1898
|
Paul Medford
(1873–   )

Elizabeth Jane Medford
(1898–   )

Langley Broadmoor
(1845–1891)
|
1879
|
Winifred Donaldson
(1856–1880)

**Frances (Fanny)
Jane Broadmoor**
(1880–   )

## 1

*Wednesday, April 26, 1899*
*Rochester, New York*

CHOLERA ON THE RISE! EPIDEMIC ANTICIPATED
IN ROCHESTER!

Amanda Broadmoor glanced at the imprudent headline that emblazoned last night's edition of the Rochester *Democrat and Chronicle*. Why must the newspaper exaggerate? People would be frightened into a genuine panic with such ill-advised news reporting. Turning the headline to the inside, she creased the paper and slipped it beneath a stack of mail on the marble-topped table in the lower hallway of her family's fashionable home. Certain this most recent newspaper article would cause yet another family squabble, she had hidden the paper in her bedroom the previous evening.

No doubt the glaring headline had increased sales for the

owner of the press. The paper had been quick to report four recent deaths attributed to the dreaded disease, and with an early spring and unrelenting rains, a number of prominent families had already fled the city. After yesterday's report, more would surely follow. And for those who didn't possess the wherewithal to flee, the report would serve no purpose but to heighten their fear.

Of course the Broadmoors were among the social elite of Rochester, New York. Amanda had never known need or want, and when bad things dared to rear their ugly heads, she had been carefully sheltered from the worst of it. All that had changed, however, when she decided to seek a career in medicine.

At twenty-one, Amanda felt she had the right to make her own way in life, but her father and mother hardly saw it that way. Their attitudes reflected those of their peers and the world around them. Women working in the medical field were highly frowned upon, and a woman of Amanda's social standing was reared to marry and produce heirs, not to tend the sick. Especially not those suffering from cholera.

"And Mama can be such an alarmist."

At the first report Amanda's mother had suggested the entire family take refuge at their summer estate located on Broadmoor Island in the St. Lawrence River. But that idea had been immediately vetoed by her father. Jonas Broadmoor had avowed his work would not permit him to leave Rochester. And Amanda agreed with her father's decision. After devoting much of her time and energy to medical training at Dr. Carstead's side, Amanda couldn't possibly desert her work—not now—not when she was most needed.

Amanda glanced at the clock. Her mother would expect her for breakfast, but remaining any longer would simply ensure a tearful plea for her to cease working with Dr. Carstead. She would then need to offer a lengthy explanation as to why her work was critical, and that in turn would cause a tardy arrival at the Home for the Friendless. Before the matter could be resolved, much valuable time would be wasted, time that could be used to care for those in need of her ministrations. With each newspaper claim, an argument ensued, leaving Amanda to feel she must betray either her mother or Dr. Carstead. She didn't feel up to a quarrel today.

After fastening her cloak, she tucked a strand of blond hair beneath her bonnet and slipped into the kitchen, where the carriage driver was finishing his morning repast. "Do hurry," she said, motioning toward the door. "I'm needed at the Home."

He downed a final gulp of coffee, wiped his mouth with the back of his hand, and nodded. "The carriage is ready and waiting." He quickstepped to the east side of the kitchen and opened the door with a flourish. His broad smile revealed a row of uneven teeth. "You see? Always prepared. That's my motto."

"An excellent motto, though sometimes difficult to achieve," Amanda said, pleased to discover the rain had ceased.

She hurried toward the carriage, the driver close on her heels. Her own attempts to be prepared seemed to fall short far too often. Since beginning her study of medicine with Dr. Carstead, she'd made every effort to anticipate his needs, but it seemed he frequently requested an item she'd never before heard of, a medical instrument other than what she offered, or a bandage of a different width. Amanda was certain her inadequate choices sometimes annoyed him. However, he held his temper in check—at least most of the time.

"Did you read today's headline?" the driver asked before closing the carriage door.

Amanda nodded. "Indeed. That's why we must hurry. I'm

afraid there will be many at the clinic doors this morning. Sometimes simply hearing about an illness causes people to fear they've contracted it." A sense of exhaustion washed over her just thinking about the work ahead.

The driver grimaced. "I know what you mean, miss. I read the article in the paper and then wondered if I was suffering some of the symptoms myself."

"Have you been having difficulty with your digestive organs?"

At the mention of his digestive organs, the color heightened in the driver's cheeks. He glanced away and shook his head. "No, but I had a bit of a headache yesterday, and thought I was a bit thirstier than usual."

"It's likely nothing, but if you begin to experience additional symptoms, be sure to come and see the doctor. Don't wait too long."

Still unable to meet her gaze, he touched his finger to the brim of his hat. "Thank you for your concern, miss. I'll heed your advice."

When they arrived at the Home for the Friendless a short time later, Amanda's prediction proved true. Lines had formed outside the building, and there was little doubt most of those waiting were seeking medical attention. After bidding the driver good day, she hurried around the side of the building and entered through the back door leading into the office Dr. Blake Carstead occupied during his days at the Home.

She stopped short at the sight of the doctor examining a young woman. "You've arrived earlier than usual, I see."

He grunted. "After reading last night's newspaper, I knew we'd have more patients today. I wish someone would place a muzzle on that reporter. He seems to take delight in frightening people. Did you read what he said?"

Amanda removed her cloak and hung it on the peg alongside the doctor's woolen overcoat. "Only the headline," she replied. "I do hope the article was incorrect."

Dr. Carstead continued to examine a cut on his patient's arm. "It was exaggerated. There was one death due to cholera, but a colleague tells me the other deaths occurred when a carriage overturned and crushed two passersby. I don't know why the owner of that paper permits such slipshod reporting. If I practiced medicine the way that newspaper reports the news, I'd have a room filled with dead patients."

The patient's eyes widened at the doctor's last remark.

"He truly does a better job than the newspaper," Amanda said, approaching the woman's side.

Once the woman's arm had been properly bandaged, Amanda showed her to the door and returned to see how she could best assist Blake that day.

"Honestly, I think the newspaper enjoys putting people in a state of panic," Blake said as he washed his hands.

"Trouble sells papers." Amanda held out a towel.

Blake took it and looked at her oddly for a moment. "You look pale. Are you sleeping and eating right?"

She put her hands on her hips. "I might ask you the same thing. You haven't slept in days."

"I didn't know you were keeping track," he said rather sarcastically. "But I don't have the same privilege of going home to a comfortable meal and bed that you have."

"And whose fault is that?" Amanda countered. "You won't go home, and you won't let me stay."

"It wouldn't be proper."

She huffed. "It won't be proper when you collapse from exhaustion, either, but I'm sure I'll think of something to tell the masses of sick people. 'Oh, we're very sorry, but the doctor

13

is a prideful and arrogant man who believes himself immortal.' Even God rested on the seventh day, Dr. Carstead."

"God wasn't dealing with cholera at the time," Blake replied, unmoved by her comments.

Amanda let out an exasperated breath and went to wipe down the examination table.

It was their last opportunity for private banter, as a steady stream of patients kept them working until well past six that evening.

Exhausted but unwilling to let on to how tired she was, Amanda reached for her coat and suppressed a yawn.

"How are you getting home?" Blake asked.

"I'm certain the driver is waiting for me."

"I'll walk you out and make sure he's there."

Amanda didn't argue. She wanted to ask when he planned to leave but knew it would only stir an argument. She had no energy left to partake of such a silly exchange, and Blake seemed to sense this.

Taking hold of her arm, he escorted her out to the street, where the Broadmoor carriage waited. The driver quickly climbed down and opened the door. His coat revealed that it had been raining much of the time he'd been waiting.

"Try to eat a good meal and take a hot bath," Blake instructed as he helped her into the carriage. "You're no good to me if you get sick."

Amanda shook her head and fixed him with a stare. "I was thinking much the same about you. Besides, you stink and need a shave."

He looked at her soberly for a moment and then broke into a smile. "There you go again. Caring about me."

She reached for the door. "I'm not at all concerned about you, Dr. Carstead, but the friendless and sick are beginning to take up a collection for you. I believe they plan to purchase a bar of soap and a razor."

Amanda pulled the door shut even as she heard Blake roar with laughter. She smiled to herself. It was good to hear him laugh. There had been so little worth laughing about these last days.

❖

*Thursday, April 27, 1899*

"You're late," Blake growled out as Amanda entered the examination room the next day. "I know I told you to rest, but I didn't mean all night and all day."

"Oh, hush. I'm only a few minutes late. The driver was delayed this morning." She hung up her coat and immediately pulled on her apron. She gave Blake a cursory glance. "I see you took my advice. Now at least you won't drive people away in fear."

Blake touched his clean-shaven chin before pointing to the door. "The Rochester Health Board has sent examiners to check us out. I didn't want to look shabby for them."

Amanda dropped to a nearby chair. She gasped as a fleeting pain sliced through her midsection. Once again she had hurried out of the house without breakfast in order to avoid a confrontation with her mother. This time, however, she was certain that had she eaten breakfast, she would have embarrassed herself in front of the good doctor. She swallowed and clasped her open palm tight against her waist. "Has there been any further word regarding the quarantine?"

Dr. Carstead nodded toward the crowd gathered outside his door and touched a finger to his pursed lips. "We don't want to cause undue worry." He leaned forward, his dark hazel eyes radiating concern. "You're not getting sick on me, are you?"

"No, of course not. I experienced a brief moment of discomfort, but I'm feeling fine." She stood and brushed a wrinkle from her faded navy blue skirt.

Shortly after beginning her work with Dr. Carstead, she'd acquired a uniform of sorts. The doctor had been quick to advise that if she was serious about learning medicine, she'd best save her expensive silk and satin day dresses for leisure and adopt a more utilitarian form of dress for her days at the clinic. At first she'd been affronted by his remark, but he'd been correct. Even though she had covered her serge skirts and cotton blouses with a canvas apron, the Broadmoor laundress still complained of the stains that required extra scrubbing.

"I'm sure we'll hear of the examiner's decision soon. Why don't you go through the line and separate those who have complaints that suggest they've contracted cholera. Place them in the office at the end of the hallway. When you've completed that, let me know and I'll examine them."

Amanda retrieved a pencil and paper. She preferred keeping notes while she spoke to the patients, especially when there were so many. Otherwise important details could easily be forgotten.

Before exiting the room, Amanda poured a glass of water and quickly downed the contents. The cool liquid slid down her parched throat, but her stomach immediately clenched in a painful spasm. Perhaps she should have eaten breakfast after all. Forcing a smile, she replaced the glass and hurried out of the room with her stomach still violently protesting.

Dr. Carstead waved another patient into his office, and Amanda stopped beside the next person in line. Although the older man appeared disgruntled when she approached, he finally complied when she advised him that he couldn't see the doctor until he'd answered her questions. A brief look at the lump on his head and a view of his scraped knuckles confirmed that today's visit had nothing to do with cholera. After spending too much time at the local tavern last night, he'd challenged another patron to a fight.

Amanda managed to maintain her composure for a while longer but stopped short when she came to the sixth person in the long line. Clutching her stomach, she pointed her finger toward the ceiling. "I'll be back," she promised, then dropped her pencil and paper on a nearby table. Grabbing an enamel basin, she raced into a room at the far end of the hall and divested herself of the water she'd swallowed only minutes earlier. The liquid burned the back of her throat, and her stomach muscles ached in protest, but that was soon forgotten when gripping pains attacked her lower intestines. The intensity sent her running for the bathroom.

When she returned a short time later, Dr. Carstead was waiting. "You're sick. You're as white as a sheet and shaking. Why didn't you tell me earlier? You may have infected all those you came in contact with today."

Amanda clutched her stomach. "You think *I* have cholera?" She shook her head in denial. "I failed to eat breakfast and my stomach is upset—nothing more." Another spasm gripped her midsection, and her knees buckled. Had Blake not held her upright, she would have collapsed at his feet.

Blake Carstead stared at Amanda's pale face while he tucked a heavy blanket over her quivering body. He raked his long fingers through his unruly mass of dark brown hair and turned toward the door. How could he possibly manage without Amanda's help? The crowd continued to increase by the minute.

"Quincy! I need your help," Blake shouted to Amanda's uncle, the proprietor of the Home for the Friendless. If Amanda contracted cholera, her parents would hold him responsible. Neither had encouraged her to pursue medical training. In fact, her father had used every ruse possible to keep her out of medical school. When Blake had suggested she could work with him and receive training, she'd readily accepted.

Amanda stirred and touched his arm. "Water. I'm so thirsty," she whispered.

He offered her only a couple ounces, for he knew what would occur. She clutched the glass and downed the small amount of liquid he offered. Immediately, she pointed to the nearby basin. Fear shone in her eyes as she heaved relentlessly before falling back onto the bed.

Where was Quincy? He rushed to the door and peered into the clamoring crowd of patients. All of them wanted to see a doctor—and none of them wanted to wait in the overflowing room. They all feared the same thing. The person sitting beside them might carry the dreaded disease. When he finally spotted Quincy, he stepped farther into the room and shouted above the din. Two men, neither one appearing particularly happy, stood inside the front entrance. Blake recognized them as officials from the Health Department. They shook their heads, obviously agitated and anxious to be on their way. They pushed a paper into Quincy's hand and hurried from the room.

After Quincy read the paper, he shoved it into his jacket and then cupped his hands to his mouth. "The Home for the Friendless has been placed under quarantine. The authorities have tacked a formal notice to the front gate."

A hum of dissent quickly escalated into angry voices. Quincy retrieved the wrinkled sheet of paper from his pocket and waved it overhead. "This is a letter of explanation. No one is to leave the building."

Blake wasn't surprised when the gathered patients rushed out of the waiting room and onto the streets. They looked like mice fleeing a sinking ship, and there was no one to stop them. Within minutes few remained, and those who did were too infirm to leave under their own power. By the terms of the quarantine, no one should have left the building, but neither Blake nor Quincy possessed the power to hold them prisoner. And the authorities didn't have sufficient time to enforce the orders. They were too busy delivering them.

The behavior of the patients came as no surprise to Dr. Carstead. He'd seen the same reaction in other cities. People understood the need for quarantines, but they refused to be inconvenienced. He'd discovered many were willing to remain within the confines of their own homes, but they didn't want to be held in an unfamiliar institution such as the Home for the Friendless. And he understood their behavior. He, too, would have preferred to be surrounded by the comfort and convenience of his own home, where the downstairs had been converted into a doctor's office with all of the latest equipment to provide care for patients able to afford his medical services.

Recently Blake's volunteer work at the Home was consuming more and more of his time. There was little doubt he would be needed here during the days to come. The living conditions of those who required free medical care made them all the more susceptible to diseases. Besides, there were sufficient doctors within the city of Rochester to care for those patients who could afford to pay for medical treatment.

According to the terms of the notice, they would be quarantined at the Home for the next five days. Further evaluation would be made at that time. And with several patients showing definite signs of cholera, Blake guessed the quarantine would be extended. If they were to stave off the spread of the disease, it would take more than quarantines.

He lifted his gaze upward. "We need you, Lord," he whispered before finally gaining Quincy's attention. When the older man drew near, Blake grasped him by the arm and pulled him closer. "It's Amanda. I'm afraid she's suffering from cholera."

Quincy peered across the threshold. The sight of his niece caused him to pale. "I greeted her when she arrived this morning. She looked fine. When did this . . . How could this . . . Her parents will never forgive me. They'll blame this on me."

"They can't possibly blame you. They—"

Quincy shook his head with a vehemence that caused his hair to settle in unfashionable disarray. "You mark my words. If Amanda doesn't recover, I'll face my brother's wrath for the remainder of my days. Jonas Broadmoor can hold a grudge longer than any man I've ever known."

Both of the men turned when Amanda stirred. "My stomach. I need help," she groaned.

Blake tightened his hold on Quincy's arm. "We must locate a woman to help her. She'll be in further distress if I attempt to assist her while she's in the throes of elimination."

Quincy agreed. They had both assisted one of the men who'd gone through several days of suffering. The poor fellow had died soon thereafter. The episode was an immediate reminder of debilitating scenes of violent vomiting and unrelenting evacuation of the bowels accompanied by gripping pain and spasms that left the victim dehydrated. Nothing good could be said of what lay in store for Amanda.

Blake would oversee her care, but he didn't want to cause her embarrassment. She had been surrounded by wealth all her life. Now she'd be subjected to suffering this terrible illness in pitiable conditions. And all because of him! He should have insisted that she remain at home when the first cases of cholera had been suspected. Instead, he'd encouraged her to continue working alongside him. He'd told himself he was furthering her medical career, while in truth he'd both wanted and needed the caring hands she offered. Only now did he acknowledge his motivation had been borne of selfishness. What had he done?

While Quincy hurried off in search of some willing soul who might lend aid, Blake dragged a wooden screen from across the room and placed it beside Amanda's bed. It would offer a modicum of privacy.

She moaned, and her eyes fluttered open. "Water. Please won't you give me water?"

The result would be the same, but he couldn't refuse. He placed a basin on the table and then poured her a drink.

She'd barely finished drinking when she retched and emptied the contents of her stomach into the basin. Blake brushed the damp strands of hair from her perspiring forehead. Surely she must have had some of these symptoms before she'd come to work this morning. Why hadn't she stayed home where she could be properly cared for?

Before he could ask, Quincy peeked around the screen. "Mrs. Donner has offered to lend a hand."

"But only for a price," the woman said. She tapped her index finger in the opposing palm. "Don't forget you promised to pay me in advance."

Blake met the woman's intense gaze. "You might consider helping for the sake of simply doing good for another, Mrs. Donner."

"Don't you go judging me, Dr. Carstead. If I die from cholera, Miss Broadmoor's father won't take it upon himself to feed my children. I learned a long time ago that God helps them that help themselves."

"If I recall, you and your children have been living in the Home for the Friendless free of charge for well over three months now. Aren't those beds and food worth a speck of charity from you?"

When she shrugged, her tattered shawl slipped from one shoulder, and she yanked it back into place. "You'll not convince me to change my mind. Do you want my help or not?" She turned to face Quincy.

"We want your help."

Blake motioned to a pitcher and water. "You'll need to be careful to wash your hands after you've had contact with Miss Broadmoor." He glanced at the woman's dirt-encrusted fingers. "In fact, I had best teach you the proper method for scrubbing before you begin your new duties."

"Soon as I get my money," she said.

Quincy offered an apologetic look. "She's the only one who would even consider coming back here."

Blake removed several coins from his pocket and placed them in the woman's outstretched hand. "This will have to do for now. We have no way of withdrawing money from the bank. The quarantine, you know."

Her hand remained open. "I'm guessing Mr. Broadmoor can offer a little more."

Quincy withdrew two bills from his pocket and gave them to her.

The older woman grinned and tucked them into her pocket along with the coins. "Now let's have that lesson in hand washing."

While Blake led Mrs. Donner to the washbasin, Quincy

followed along, reciting Scripture. " 'And above all these things put on charity, which is the bond of perfectness.' "

Mrs. Donner squared her shoulders and pointed her finger in Quincy's direction. "I don't need you reciting passages about charity. It's easy to be charitable when you got food on your table and money in the bank." Anger flashed in the woman's eyes. "If you want my help, you'll pay me with money and keep your preaching for them that want to hear it."

Blake sent a warning look in Quincy's direction. If he was left to care for Amanda through this undignified illness, she'd never be able to look him in the eye. He didn't want Mrs. Donner to leave him stranded in such a circumstance.

2

With a mixture of irritation and surprise, Jonas Broadmoor waved Victoria into his office. He was certain his wife had advised him she would be remaining at home all day today. Now here she was distracting him before it was even midmorning. After all these years, Victoria still didn't seem to realize that the business day was exactly that—a time set aside to complete meaningful tasks without interruption.

He dipped his pen into the ink bottle and continued writing in the ledger. "What brings you to the office, Victoria?" A brief glance was enough for him to place the pen in the bronze holder. She was positively pale. "Has something happened?"

Victoria placed her handkerchief to her lips and nodded. "They've quarantined the Home for the Friendless. I sent my maid to pick up that new gown I ordered. The driver passed by the Home, and Veda saw the quarantine sign. She told me they aren't letting anyone in or out of the place."

Jonas shrugged. "I doubt Quincy will be overly inconvenienced. He's at the Home all the time as it is."

Victoria straightened in her chair and slapped her palm on his desk. "Your *daughter* is there, Jonas! Our Amanda is going to be quarantined for five days with those diseased people. Don't you realize what that means?"

Jonas leaned back in his chair. "How does this change anything? I told you months ago I didn't approve of her training with Dr. Carstead. You're the one who agreed with this medical nonsense. You encouraged her when she said she wanted to become a nurse."

"Doctor," Victoria corrected.

Jonas jerked to attention. *"What?"*

"It isn't *nursing* that interests Amanda. She wants to become a *doctor*. There's a vast difference, Jonas."

"Oh, forevermore, Victoria. Why are we quibbling over minute details? Doctor, nurse—it makes little difference. Your decision has subjected Amanda to cholera."

"You know I did everything in my power to stop her from going back to the Home until after the outbreak subsided. If we'd gone to the island as I suggested, she would be safe from harm. Our remaining in Rochester was your doing." She glared across the desk. "And now you dare accuse me of subjecting our daughter to a deadly disease. I'm almost sorry I came here."

"Almost but not quite. Correct?" He arched his brows. They were playing a game of cat and mouse, and he didn't intend to lose. "You expect me to find some way to get her out of that place. That's why you've come here, isn't it?"

Victoria tightened her lips into a thin line and offered only a slight tip of her head. The unanticipated ease of her admission lessened Jonas's thrill of victory. He determined she must be extremely worried—and very likely he should be, too. One of his children had placed herself in danger. He should have insisted that Amanda give up this notion of becoming a doctor. Once he rescued her from his brother's Home for the Friendless, there would be no further discussion. Adult or not, Amanda was going to abide by his rules until she married. And his rules would include the termination of any further medical training with Dr. Carstead!

He closed the ledger and pushed away from his desk. "Before going to the other end of town, let's stop by the house. I do hope Amanda has used her good sense and managed to sneak out after the authorities departed. They're far too busy to guard every home bearing a quarantine notice, and it would be easy enough for her to leave by a back door."

"Jonas! I can't believe you would say such a thing. Those quarantines are in place to help prevent the spread of disease, and Amanda would not ignore such an order."

"She has no difficulty ignoring *my* orders." He shrugged into his black wool topcoat and gathered his hat and cane. "Take us home," he instructed their driver as they exited his office. Victoria didn't argue, and for that he was thankful.

This had been a day he'd set aside to work on his ledgers, and thus far he'd found nothing encouraging in the numbers. His losses appeared even greater than he'd first imagined. The thought was enough to cause perspiration to bead along his forehead in spite of the chilly April breeze. He settled into the thick leather cushion and withdrew his handkerchief from his pocket.

Victoria leaned aside as he swiped his forehead. "Jonas! You're ill. Why didn't you tell me?"

He detected the fear in her eyes. "I don't have cholera, Victoria."

She removed a glove and touched her palm to his forehead. "You feel clammy. That's not a good sign. I've been questioning Amanda regarding the symptoms."

Jonas lightly grasped her hand and lifted it from his forehead. "Please trust me. I am fine."

While keeping her gaze fastened upon him, Victoria worked her fingers back into her glove. "I think your decision to return home before going to check on Amanda is sound. I don't want you going anywhere else if you're ill."

He sighed. No need to argue further. His wife would not heed his words. He dropped back against the seat and stared out the window until the horses came to a halt in front of their East Avenue mansion.

"You sit still, Jonas. I'll have the driver help you down."

Jonas yanked the handle and pushed open the carriage door. "I am not ill, and I do not need assistance out of the carriage. Please stop this foolishness." He extended his hand to help her from inside.

Her furtive glances didn't go unnoticed as they continued up the front steps leading into the house. He wished he'd left his handkerchief in his pocket. "Any word from our daughter?" Jonas inquired of the butler, who helped them with their coats.

"I don't believe so, but you have a visitor waiting in the library, Mr. Broadmoor."

Victoria shot him a warning look. "Do tell whoever it is that we have important business requiring our immediate attention."

Jonas could feel the perspiration beginning to bead across his forehead again, yet he dared not wipe it away. "Please rest easy, my dear. Nothing is going to change regarding the quarantine. We will go there in due time."

Victoria grasped the sleeve of his jacket. "In due time? Amanda needs to be removed from that place as soon as possible. I want her home before nightfall."

"Yes, my dear. And I will see to it that she is." Jonas glanced at the butler, who appeared as rigid and stoic as the statues that adorned their gardens. "I assume you have the name of my visitor?"

With a curt nod the butler retrieved a calling card from the silver tray and handed it to Jonas. He stared at the engraved block letters. *Vincent Fillmore*. The last thing he needed right now was a meeting with his lawyer's son and law partner. And why had Vincent come to the house rather than his office?

"I won't be long," he told his wife before turning down the hallway.

What else could possibly go wrong today? Wasn't it enough that he was suffering these severe financial woes? His stomach clenched into a knot. What if Vincent had come to deliver devastating news regarding a legal issue—something that would send his finances plummeting even further? At the moment he wondered why he'd even gotten out of bed this morning. The day had been filled with enough bad news for at least a month, and it wasn't yet noon!

He opened the library door and motioned for Vincent to remain seated. "What brings you to my home in the middle of the day?" Without waiting for an answer, he dropped to the chair across from the younger man. "Didn't you realize it's a weekday?"

Vincent raked his fingers through his hair. "To be honest, I didn't think at all. My father died just a short time ago."

Jonas gasped. Panic washed over him and seized a tight hold. His mouth went dry.

"Father told me I was to advise you immediately of his death, no matter when it occurred." Vincent slumped forward and shook his head. "I knew this day would arrive, but he'd been feeling better over the past two weeks."

"So it wasn't cholera?"

"No. The doctor said his heart simply gave out. I had feared Father might contract cholera, but the doctor tells me the newspaper reports have been exaggerated."

"Is that so? My wife will be pleased to hear that." Jonas's thoughts whirred as he attempted to maintain his composure. "I am genuinely sorry for your loss, Vincent. Your father was a dear friend and confidant."

"Thank you. He wanted you to say a few words at the gravesite."

"What? Me?" Surely he hadn't heard Vincent correctly. "I think a local preacher would be a better choice, don't you? I mean, it's just not proper. I wouldn't know what to say."

Vincent laced his fingers together. "Whatever you say will be fine. My father was never one to stand on ceremony. You know that better than anyone. He had no use for the church and always thought he'd outwit God. He used to tell me he was going to live like the devil, and at the end he'd ask forgiveness and step into heaven with a smile."

"Let's hope it works that way," Jonas replied. Their conversation was veering off in a strange direction. The last thing he wanted right now was a discussion of right and wrong or of heaven and hell. All he wanted at the moment was to secure his files from Mortimer's office.

He silently chastised himself. He should have transferred his papers to another lawyer long ago. He'd given consideration to the idea several times. Unfortunately, he'd never found anyone else he could trust like he did Mortimer. The two of them had shared the same ideas about making money: There were no rules as long as there was a profit to be made. He had no way of knowing how much of his business and personal information Mortimer had committed to writing. What if he'd maintained files that told of Jonas's business dealings? He couldn't risk anyone discovering such information.

"We must leave immediately and go to your father's office." Jonas pushed up from the chair without giving Vincent an opportunity to disagree.

"What's this?" Victoria entered the room with her coat draping one arm and her hat perched atop her head. "You're not planning on going somewhere other than the Home for the Friendless, are you?"

Jonas stepped forward. "Mortimer passed on this morning. I believe Vincent needs me to assist him with several matters surrounding his father's death."

Victoria hurried to Vincent's side and murmured her condolences. "Exactly how can Jonas be of help at this moment?"

Jonas couldn't hear Vincent's muttered response, but from the hard-edged look in Victoria's eyes, Jonas knew his wife was unhappy.

"Mortimer died this morning and you want to go and retrieve your business files? Jonas Broadmoor! I can't believe you would even *think* of such a thing when Vincent is overcome with grief and mourning the loss of his father." Victoria patted Vincent's arm. "Do let me call for tea."

Vincent shook his head. "No. I really must be on my way. I have much to do."

Jonas forced a smile. "I'm sorry for my lack of tact, Vincent. However, I think you know your father would approve. He was an astute lawyer who always thought of business first." He needed to win Vincent over. Once the younger man departed, there would be little opportunity until after the funeral to retrieve his files. With family members sniffing about, any one of them might go through Mortimer's files. He didn't want to take that chance. "I can have my driver take us to your father's office this very minute. It wouldn't take but a few moments of your time."

The younger man's jaw went slack, and he shook his head. "Not now, Jonas. I must see to the funeral arrangements." Vincent sidestepped around him and strode toward the library door.

"But I truly need those—"

"What you need to do is show some decency and respect," Victoria hissed. "There is nothing that won't keep until after Mortimer is buried." His wife brushed past him and hurried out of the room. "Do keep us advised of the funeral arrangements."

Jonas dropped into a nearby chair and massaged his forehead. The day had gone from bad to worse by the hour. Could anything else possibly go awry this day? If so, he couldn't imagine what it would be.

❖

Paul Medford kissed his daughter's cheek before his wife lifted her from his arms. "Our Elizabeth is the loveliest little girl ever born."

Sophie tucked the soft flannel blanket around her daughter's tiny body. "I couldn't agree more. And she is very fortunate to have you as her papa."

The words warmed him even more than the hearty breakfast Sophie had served him a short time ago. The fact that Wesley

Hedrick had forsaken Sophie and his unborn child had proved to be a blessing for Paul. He daily thanked God for the opportunity to call Sophie his wife and claim Elizabeth as his child.

He pushed away from the kitchen table, and Sophie accompanied him to the door. While he shoved his arms into his warm woolen coat, she retrieved his hat. No doubt this day would be busy, but he'd discovered deep satisfaction in his work at the Home for the Friendless.

He lowered his head and kissed Sophie's lips. "I'll be home as early as possible."

Sophie didn't reply. Instead, she lifted on tiptoe and kissed him again. They both knew that he'd do his best but likely wouldn't return until well after dark. The needs at the Home increased daily, especially since the outbreak of cholera. It seemed that anyone having the slightest symptom came to see the doctor. Most simply wanted reassurance they hadn't contracted the disease. Others had genuine problems: a cut that required stitches or a woman laboring to deliver a newborn. And then there were those looking for a safe place of shelter and a warm meal. Most thought God had no use for them, but Paul knew better. And he did his best to show them God's love through his actions.

Unless asked, he didn't offer advice or sermonize to the strangers who came for help. In fact, he could quickly calculate the number of times he'd preached since receiving his divinity degree. Those who found shelter at the Home were encouraged to attend a church of their choosing on Sunday mornings. Residents were sent out the front doors after breakfast and not permitted to return until after twelve-thirty on Sunday afternoon. Whether they actually attended church was between them and God. Sophie's father, Quincy, thought the residents should be permitted to worship in their own manner. He didn't want anyone to think they must adhere to specific religious beliefs in order to be welcomed into the Home.

Paul grinned at the thought. People flocked to theirs doors in overwhelming numbers, and he doubted any would depart if forced to attend a church service on the premises. Most would probably prefer such an arrangement. They wouldn't be required to go outdoors in the cold or rain. But Paul didn't argue with his father-in-law. Nor did he look for another place to serve the Lord. For now, he believed God wanted him to serve at the Home for the Friendless.

He shoved his hands into his gloves and reached for the doorknob.

"Why don't you invite Amanda and Dr. Carstead to join us for supper this evening?" Sophie suggested. "I see my dear cousin far too seldom. And I'm certain Elizabeth misses her aunt Amanda, too."

"I'll do my best to convince them," he said. "There are so many patients that need their attention, I'm not—"

"Tell Amanda that I insist. They both need to take a little time for pleasure. And so do you. I'll expect all three of you no later than six o'clock."

"You're right. An evening of visiting and good food is just what the doctor ordered. Even if the doctor doesn't know it."

The sound of Sophie's laughter followed him down the front steps. As a harsh wind assailed him from the north, he tucked his head low. Paul believed the walk to work each morning helped him maintain his good health. However, he would have gladly exchanged his morning exercise for a ride in a warm carriage on this brisk morning.

Though a cutting chill remained, the wind subsided as he rounded the final corner. He squinted against the sun. Not one soul stood waiting for admission to the Home. Ever since the first frightening case of cholera had been detected, the medical office had been swarmed with daily visitors. And after the recent newspaper headlines, he'd expected an even larger crowd. He strode forward but stopped short at the front gate.

*Quarantine!* He didn't take time to read the fine print. The one word was enough to explain the absence of the usual morning arrivals.

Paul cupped his hands to his mouth. "Quincy! It's Paul. Can you hear me? Come to the door." He waited a moment and then tried again.

With the windows tightly closed and shuttered against the cold, his voice would never be heard. He glanced at the iron bell used to announce that meals were being served. Without a moment's hesitation, he entered the gate, pulled the worn rope, and waited. The shutters that covered one of the windows in the front of the house opened. Blake! So the doctor had been captured in the quarantine, too.

Paul pointed to the front of the building. "Open the door."

Blake momentarily disappeared before the door opened and he stepped onto the porch. "Didn't you read the notice? You can't come in here, Paul."

"I understand," he said, careful to keep some distance between them. "But what can I do to help?"

Blake rubbed his hands together. "We'll need our food replenished in a couple days. And could you gather medical supplies? Ask John Phillips. He'll help you choose what I need."

Paul had become acquainted with John Phillips when he'd first arrived in Rochester. The man operated a pharmacy nearby. "Anything else?"

Blake stepped down from the porch and drew closer. "Tell Mr. and Mrs. Broadmoor that Amanda has contracted cholera.

I'm doing my best for her. She's young and strong, but I can't say with certainty that she'll make it. She's very sick."

Paul grasped the fence and steadied himself. The news would devastate Sophie. And what of Mr. and Mrs. Broadmoor? Amanda's parents would surely blame themselves for permitting her to work at the Home. The thought of delivering this dreadful report left him speechless.

"Paul! Did you hear me?" Blake shouted.

"Yes, yes. I'll tell them. Do you think . . . I mean . . . should I . . . ?"

"Just tell them exactly what I've said. There's no way of knowing what will happen. If they want to speak to me, tell them to do as you have. Ring the bell and I'll come out."

Paul nodded and turned, too dazed to ask any further questions.

"Don't forget the medicine and food," Blake hollered.

Paul waved in recognition of the request. He couldn't find his voice. The possibility had always existed that one of them would contract some fatal disease from one of the patients, but Paul had always believed God's hand of protection was upon them. They were, after all, doing God's work. He rounded the corner and forced such thoughts from his mind. He'd speak to Sophie first. It would be best if she accompanied him to meet with Amanda's parents. Sophie knew them better than he. Perhaps she could lend some advice on how to best approach them. For the second time this day, he wished he hadn't walked to work.

3

Sophie tied the ribbons of Elizabeth's bonnet beneath the sleeping child's tiny chin while her husband paced in the hallway. Amanda had stitched the bonnet during one of the three cousins' many sewing sessions before Elizabeth's birth. Sophie pictured the three of them—Fanny, Amanda, and herself—sitting in the bedroom at Broadmoor Castle with their sewing baskets and fabric. A smile played at her lips as she remembered her cousins' efforts to help improve her sewing skills. They'd been mostly unsuccessful, and Sophie had accepted the fact that she'd never be an accomplished seamstress—not like Amanda. She traced her finger along the embroidered stems of bluebells with pale green stems and veined leaves that adorned the cap.

The love she held for her cousins was deeper than that which she held for her own siblings. Throughout the years Amanda and Fanny had been her closest friends and confidants. Many had been the occasion when her own sisters had turned away from her in frustration or disgust, but not Amanda and Fanny. They might not always approve of the things she did, but they would never dream of deserting her.

"How can I help?" Paul asked as he continued to pace.

"I'll be just a moment longer. Is the carriage out front?"

"Yes. We really must be on our way."

Sophie turned and frowned at her husband. "I'm doing my best." She lifted Elizabeth from her cradle, careful to keep the blanket tightly tucked around the child. Some said the damp air could cause cholera, and she didn't intend to take her outdoors unless properly protected against the elements. "I want to make certain the baby is warm enough."

"Yes, of course," he replied, shifting his gaze toward the floor.

Her words carried a hint of censure, and Paul had taken note. Sophie immediately regretted her behavior. Paul was worried and needed her support instead of a reprimand. But she was worried, too—about all of them. What if Paul or Elizabeth should fall ill? She couldn't bear the thought of losing either of them.

"I'm sorry for speaking harshly," she said.

Paul smiled and took the baby into his arms. "You're forgiven. We're both worried." He brushed her cheek with a kiss and opened the door.

The carriage ride to her aunt and uncle's home seemed longer than usual, and Sophie fidgeted throughout the ride. Surprisingly, her movement had little effect upon Elizabeth, who continued to sleep. A short time later Paul brought the carriage to a halt in front of her uncle's home, and Elizabeth's eyes popped open. She wriggled in Sophie's arms and whimpered.

"I know. You like riding, but we must stop for a while," she cooed to the baby.

The butler answered the door and, with a nod, bid them enter. He attempted to remain proper, but Sophie noticed his little smile at Elizabeth.

"Are my aunt and uncle at home, Marvin?"

The butler nodded. "I'll inform them that Mr. and Mrs. Medford and baby Elizabeth have come to call."

"Thank you, Marvin." The man was a saint. No wonder her uncle paid him well. "Marvin is the one who helped Amanda, Fanny, and me set up a bucket of whitewash over the kitchen door."

Paul grinned. "I recall your telling me about that incident. I believe it was your uncle Jonas who ended up covered in whitewash rather than Amanda's brothers, Jefferson and George."

Sophie smiled, remembering the sight of her uncle doused in the white concoction. She didn't know who had been more surprised, but she did recall that her uncle's jacket and spectacles had both required a good deal of Marvin's fastidious attention. The entire incident had delighted Jefferson and George, who had promised they'd be on the lookout for any further antics from the three girls.

How the years had changed their circumstances. Sophie missed the times when they would gather at Amanda's or at their grandparents' home to spend the night together. They would giggle and talk late into the night about all their hopes and dreams. Funny how life had taken so many unexpected turns. This was not anything like the dream Sophie once had for herself. Amanda and Fanny had always advised her to marry a wealthy man—for only a man of great resources could keep

Sophie in the style she craved. Paul was anything but financially well off.

Elizabeth wriggled in her arms and burst forth with a lusty cry as Marvin returned to the foyer. "Seems your little girl doesn't enjoy waiting. Must take after her mother," he said with a grin. "Your aunt and uncle will see you in the library." He leaned a bit closer. "They were preparing to depart on some business."

"So they're not particularly happy that we've arrived," Sophie replied while Elizabeth continued to cry.

"I believe that would be correct."

Sophie lifted the baby to her shoulder and hoped she could quiet the child while they delivered the news. She glanced at Paul when they arrived at the library door. "I can't seem to quiet her. Perhaps you should go in and deliver the news while I wait out here with the baby."

"No." He shook his head and clasped her elbow. "They'll receive this better if you're along."

Sophie arched her brows. She didn't think her presence would soften the blow, but she didn't argue. Elizabeth released a high-pitched wail as they crossed the threshold and entered the library. Her uncle furrowed his brow and scowled in their direction.

"She has just now awakened from her nap and is a bit fussy," Sophie explained.

"Well, do something to pacify her." Jonas pulled on his earlobe. "I can't tolerate that squealing. It's enough to shatter a mirror."

Sophie edged closer to Paul. "I think I should take Elizabeth to the other room."

"We won't take but a few minutes of your time, sir." Paul grasped Sophie's sleeve when she attempted to move toward the door. "Sophie and I have the task of bringing you a piece of disheartening news."

Before he could say anything more, the baby screeched, and Jonas jumped up from his chair. "Do *something* to make that child happy, Sophie. You are her mother—I would think you'd know how to stop that incessant crying."

"I'm trying," she apologized, swaying back and forth and patting the baby's back.

"Jonas! The baby is likely suffering from colic. Your angry temperament is not going to do a jot of good. You've likely frightened the child even further." Victoria extended her arms. "Let me try, Sophie."

Sophie willingly handed over the baby, though she doubted her aunt would have success. Elizabeth was like the little girl in Longfellow's poem: When she was good, she was very good indeed, but when she was bad, she was horrid. Though Elizabeth lacked the curl in the middle of her forehead, Sophie thought that, too, would appear over time.

Jonas massaged his forehead. "The three of you continue your visit. I have matters that require my attention."

Before her uncle could reach the door, Paul stepped in front of him. "You can't leave, sir."

Jonas straightened his shoulders and extended his chest forward. "What do you mean, I can't leave? How *dare* you tell me what I can or can't do in my own home! Step out of the way before I am forced to have you removed, young man."

Paul directed a beseeching look at Sophie.

Stepping to her husband's side, Sophie said, "Listen to him, Uncle Jonas. This is very important, or we wouldn't have come here."

The baby silenced her wailing, and the room became eerily quiet. Sophie sat down beside her aunt and peeked at Elizabeth.

Perhaps she should take the child before Paul announced Amanda's illness. Her aunt could faint and drop the baby. "Let me take her, Aunt Victoria."

Jonas turned on his heel. "Don't touch that child. She'll likely begin to squall if you move her." He shifted around toward Paul. "Now, what is it that's so important?"

"The Home for the Friendless has been placed under quarantine, and—"

"Is that what this is about? We already know that. In fact, if the two of you hadn't interrupted us with your unexpected visit, we'd be on our way over there now. I plan to have Amanda sneak out the rear door and come home immediately."

"You can't do that, sir," Paul said.

"Don't preach to me about what I can and can't do. I'm not going to have my daughter remain in that place with all of those dirty homeless people. They're probably all carriers of the disease. I'm going to bring her home. This doctor nonsense has gone far enough. Amanda is going to remain at home and conduct herself in a proper manner until I find a suitable husband for her."

Sophie shook her head, and her uncle glared at her. "You can't bring Amanda home because she has already contracted cholera, Uncle Jonas. That's what Paul has been trying to tell you." Her aunt's gasp was enough to alert Sophie, and she promptly lifted Elizabeth from the older woman's arms. "Don't fret, Aunt Victoria. Blake will do everything possible for Amanda. She'll have constant care. He won't let her . . ." She couldn't utter the word.

"Die?" Jonas snorted. "Dr. Carstead can't control life and death. Not where cholera is concerned."

"But God can," Paul said. "We must be in constant prayer for Amanda and ask God to remove this plague from our city."

"Why pray? If God has already determined to let my daughter die, your prayers won't change a thing."

The harsh words were meant as a rebuke, but Paul grasped her uncle's shoulder. "You're wrong, Mr. Broadmoor. Prayer doesn't always yield the answer we desire, but God *does* hearken to our prayers. Consider Abraham and his pleas to save Sodom. If we expect God to help, we must communicate the desires of our heart."

When her aunt slumped sideways and fell against Sophie's arm, Sophie placed Elizabeth on the settee. With her free hand she motioned to her husband. "Please ask Marvin to bring a damp cloth."

Jonas tapped his wife's shoulder. "If we're going to go and fetch Amanda, you'll need to muster your strength. This is no time for the faint of heart."

Sophie thought Uncle Jonas an insensitive boor, but his words had the desired effect. Before Marvin arrived with a damp cloth, her aunt's color had returned, and under her own strength she'd managed to return to an upright position.

"You're correct, Jonas. I'll get my hat. We must be on our way."

"She can't be released to your care," Paul insisted. "From what Blake tells me, her condition is grave. Even if permitted, any attempt to move her would prove disastrous. Look at the weather. Would you bring her out in this damp air?"

Victoria stood and steadied herself for a moment before she crossed the room. Pushing aside the curtain, she peered out the window and then turned to her husband. "Paul is correct, Jonas. We can't risk the possibility." Victoria withdrew a handkerchief from her pocket and blotted her eyes. "My dear Amanda. This is my fault. I encouraged her to seek a life of fulfillment."

"Don't blame yourself, Aunt Victoria. Amanda was

determined to pursue a medical career. Even if she had remained at home, she might have contracted the disease."

"I doubt that. *We're* all perfectly fine."

" 'Tis true, Aunt Victoria. I'm told Mr. and Mrs. Warford's daughter Jane is one of the recent victims."

Victoria clasped a hand to her throat. "Jane? Oh, her dear mother and father must be distraught. When did you hear this news?"

"Only late last evening. You see, it makes little difference that you granted Amanda permission to work at the Home for the Friendless."

"The Home? I understand it's been placed under quarantine," Fanny said, bursting into the library. She glanced at Paul. "I'm relieved to see that you're not one of those required to remain there. I assume Uncle Quincy has been restricted." She turned to her aunt. "What of Amanda? Where is she?"

Sophie motioned to her cousin. "Come sit down beside me, Fanny." In hushed tones, Sophie related the news of their cousin's illness.

"We must go to her," Fanny said.

"We've already had this discussion. No one is going to go there," Paul said. "Prayer is the answer."

❖

An hour later Fanny and Sophie were the only ones who remained in the library. Paul had helped Jonas get Victoria to bed, hoping a brief nap would help her better cope with the situation, and then had taken Elizabeth for a walk around the house so that Sophie and Fanny might converse in private.

"Do you suppose Amanda is very ill?" Fanny asked.

Sophie shrugged. "She's been exposed to the disease over and over by those she sought to help. I fear she's gravely ill."

"I can't bear it. The very thought of . . . of losing her is more than I can endure. It's bad enough when you expect the death of an older person. I still miss our grandparents terribly."

"I miss my mother," Sophie whispered. "Especially now that I have Elizabeth."

Fanny took hold of her hand. "Of course you do."

"My sisters have never been as dear to me as you and Amanda," Sophie continued, tears in her eyes. "I wish we could be at her side to nurse her." She squeezed Fanny's hand. "I'd just feel better to be near and see for myself that everything possible was being done."

"Or to tell her how much we love her."

Sophie met Fanny's damp eyes. "You do suppose she knows, don't you? I mean, we've often said as much to each other. Haven't we?"

"We certainly could have said it more," Fanny replied. "I don't suppose one ever declares love and admiration for another as much as one should." She paused only a moment before wrapping her arms around Sophie.

"I love you so very much, my dear cousin. You and Amanda are true sisters to me." She sniffed back tears. "I hope you know that I would do anything in my power to help either of you in any way."

Sophie cried softly. "I do know that, Fanny. I feel the same way. I love you and Amanda with all my heart. To lose either of you is . . . well . . . unthinkable."

❖

Blake cradled Amanda's head in the crook of his arm and offered a sip of water. "No," she croaked from between parched lips. She touched her hand to her stomach and he understood. She would only suffer the pain of bringing up the small amount of liquid. He wet a cloth and dampened her lips, hoping it might ease her distress. He'd been by her side as much as possible, doing his best to lend comfort. What good was his medical training when he couldn't do one thing to help this young woman who had willingly sacrificed her own health to help others?

"There are others who need medical attention," Quincy said.

Blake glanced over his shoulder. The older man stood in the doorway, a shaft of light streaming over his shoulder. The sun must have finally made an appearance, but Blake hadn't noticed.

"I'm doing what I can, Quincy. I've worn a path on the floor going back and forth to care for them and Amanda, but I hate to leave Amanda's side." He rested his forehead in his broad palm. "I feel so responsible. I should have forbidden her coming here to work. Instead, I chastised her if she was late and scoffed when she mentioned feeling unwell. What manner of physician does such a thing?" Blake looked at Quincy. "Even worse, what kind of *man* does such a thing?"

"You're being too hard on yourself. These past weeks have been grueling, and you needed all of us to help wherever we could. Amanda understood that. She would never harbor ill feelings toward you. This is where she wanted to be."

"But I knew the risk. I should have protected her."

Quincy clapped him on the shoulder. "Come along. You're needed elsewhere. We've had another death down the hall, and several others are showing symptoms."

Blake nodded. "I'll be there momentarily. You and the others can do as much for the dead as I can."

Quincy didn't argue but instead slipped quietly from the room.

Blake knew his strength would not last much longer. He needed sleep, but he couldn't bring himself to take the time. He rested his elbows on his knees and stared at Amanda. What would he do if she should die? When had she become so important to him? He tried to recall exactly when he'd realized the joy she provided with her quick smile and willing hands. She'd been more help than he'd ever acknowledged. She'd proved to be a bright student, quick to learn, and willing to accept correction and guidance—traits he'd found lacking in any man he'd ever attempted to teach. He should have told her all of these things. Instead, he'd chastised her if she occasionally dropped an instrument or misdiagnosed a patient.

The remembrance of his pomposity shamed him, and he gently lifted Amanda's hand to his lips. "Forgive me," he whispered.

Her eyelids fluttered. She looked at him, her deep brown Broadmoor eyes appearing clear and bright. "For what?" she murmured before slipping back into a semiconscious state.

He wanted her to remain awake so he could ease his feelings of despair. "Selfish man," he muttered. "You should be thankful she's not feeling pain at the moment. Instead you only want to relieve your own guilt."

He released her hand and brushed a damp curl from her forehead. Even in the throes of debilitating illness, she remained lovely. He met with little success as he attempted to recall the first time he'd felt the agonizing ache that occurred when she was absent. She had woven herself into the fabric of his life, and now he couldn't imagine a future without her. He stared at her quiet form and knew without a doubt that he loved her.

"Now what?" he whispered into the silent room. For the first time in his life, he was willing to acknowledge his love for a woman, but he knew she'd likely be dead within a few days—a week at most. He rested his face in his palms and listened to her uneven, rasping breath. "Please spare her, God." He swiped at the tear trickling down his cheek. "I beg of you. Please let her live."

## 4

Jonas sighed and shook his head in disbelief when Marvin hurried into the library at a near run. "Mrs. Andrew Winberg and children," he announced, clasping a palm to his chest and inhaling deeply.

Beatrice glared at the butler as she brushed past him to enter the room, Miranda and Randolph at her heels. "I told him I know my way into the library and it isn't necessary to announce family."

The woman's surly tone and pinched features had become her trademark. Yet today she appeared even more agitated than usual. And Jonas had already tolerated his share of distress for one day. Would he never get out of this house? He must find some way to retrieve his papers from Mortimer's office. A wave of guilt assaulted him. His thoughts should be with his suffering daughter rather than the business files. But if any of his underhanded dealings became known, both friends and family would be harmed. He didn't want to dwell on what might happen to him if such a thing should happen. No doubt he'd be faced with the same difficult decision his brother Langley had made years ago. But taking his own life wasn't something he wanted to consider. He wasn't certain if it was that thought or Beatrice's whining voice that sent a chill racing down his spine, but he wanted to rid himself of both.

"If there's a reason you've come to call, you'll need to cease your histrionics, or we'll never understand you," Jonas barked at his niece.

His wife withdrew her handkerchief and waved it in his direction. "There's no need to shout."

"If I'm going to be heard, there is," he retorted.

Beatrice glared at her uncle but curtailed her affected behavior and dropped into one of the overstuffed chairs.

Victoria turned to the children. "Come sit by your great-aunt, children."

"My father has been quarantined at the Home for the Friendless. Something must be done." Beatrice sniffled and cast a woeful look at Jonas.

"I am well aware of the quarantine. You are the third person who has rushed to tell me the ill-fated news. No one could be more concerned than—"

"Than *you*? When have you *ever* been concerned about my father?" Beatrice whipped her fan back and forth with a ferocity that caused her curls to ripple along her forehead like waves lapping at the shoreline.

Jonas sniffed. "I am not going to enter into an argument with you. Suffice it to say, I am very concerned about your father.

I am even more concerned about my own daughter, who has contracted the illness."

The fan dropped to her lap. "I didn't know," she whispered.

"Of course you didn't. You never consider others." Jonas felt no sympathy for Beatrice. She had been a cantankerous child, and marriage hadn't softened her. Of course, there were those who would say the same of him. On the other hand, churlish behavior was more acceptable from a man. Women were supposed to be malleable creatures.

Victoria leaned over from the sofa and patted Beatrice's hand. "Don't mind your uncle. He's had a difficult morning. Needless to say, we are most distraught over this recent news, but there is nothing to be done regarding the quarantine. I would like to bring Amanda home and care for her, but we must abide by the order or others may be infected with the disease. Paul has agreed to keep us advised of any changes."

Beatrice straightened her shoulders. "Paul? Isn't he under quarantine, also?"

"No. He hadn't yet arrived at the Home when the authorities delivered the quarantine notice. As soon as Dr. Carstead advised him that Amanda had taken ill, he and Sophie came to tell us. They departed only a short time ago," Victoria explained.

"Isn't that just the way of things? If anyone should suffer, it's my sister Sophie. Instead, all has gone well for her. She has Paul at home, and her baby is well. Meanwhile, dear, sweet Amanda is suffering with cholera. I suppose God has dealt lightly with Sophie because her husband is a preacher." Beatrice sighed and once again lifted her fan.

Jonas frowned. "And is her suffering not as great as your own, Beatrice?"

"There is no good that will come from assessing the

individual depth of sorrow or suffering each one of us bear," Victoria said. "We are all family and must care for one another. Our concern is for every member."

"I'm pleased to hear you say that, Aunt Victoria, for I have come to beg your hospitality until this epidemic has passed. Our home is too close to the area most affected by the outbreak, and I believe the children would be safer if we moved in with you."

The children looked wide-eyed from Jonas to Victoria and then to their mother.

"What?" Jonas jumped up from his chair. "Just because you live in close proximity to the area doesn't mean you're in any greater danger than the rest of us. Paul and Sophie don't live all that far from the same area, and they didn't express concern for their circumstances."

"I have heard some discussion that reinforces what Beatrice is saying," Victoria remarked.

Jonas shot a look of irritation in his wife's direction. What was she thinking? Didn't he have enough to contend with in his life? The last thing he wanted was his whining niece and her unruly children underfoot.

He cleared his throat and met Beatrice's beseeching eyes. If he refused her, he'd suffer Victoria's wrath. At the moment he didn't have the energy for an all-out war with his wife. Not now—not with the threat of his personal records being discovered by members of Mortimer's family. He needed a plan.

"Perhaps Beatrice is correct about the threat to family members. I think it would be best if all of you departed for Broadmoor Island as soon as possible."

"What?" Victoria stared at him, her mouth agape. "I suggested we all go to Broadmoor Island weeks ago, but you rejected my suggestion. *Now* you think it's wise?"

"Changes have occurred since that time."

"Indeed they have. Our daughter has been afflicted by the disease, and I'll not leave her in Rochester while I go off to Broadmoor Island. I don't know what you can be thinking, Jonas."

"We need to be practical. There is nothing you can do for Amanda. They won't let you into the Home, and I will keep in touch with Paul regarding her condition. For you to remain and become ill will serve no purpose. And it won't help her."

"But—"

Jonas pointed at his wife. "Hear me out, Victoria. Once Amanda is well enough to be removed from the Home, I will personally accompany her to the island. She'll recuperate more quickly away from the city."

"Oh, do say you'll agree, Aunt Victoria," Beatrice wailed. "It would truly be best for the entire family."

Jonas wouldn't have been surprised if his niece had dropped to her knees and begged. As far as he was concerned, she'd developed into a wretched example of womankind. "Though I am encouraging my wife to take refuge at the island, there is nothing to stop you and your children from going there. Have you discussed that possibility with your husband?"

"I hadn't considered it. I don't think Andrew would object, though I'm certain he'd refuse to accompany us." She nibbled her bottom lip. "I've never been at the island without the family. I don't know the first thing about opening the house. I've never been in charge when we visited."

"I've never noticed you having difficulty issuing orders," Jonas muttered.

Beatrice narrowed her eyes to mere slits. "What did you say, Uncle?"

"Nothing of importance. I'm merely contemplating the

family's departure." That much was true. The thought of having the entire family out of the city buoyed his spirits. He'd have ample time to take care of business matters without any interference.

"I'm still not convinced this is what I should do," Victoria argued. "And I know how you are, Jonas. If something arises at work, you'll conveniently forget your promise to bring Amanda to the island."

"You need not worry, Aunt Victoria. I'll remain in Rochester and bring Amanda when she's released from the quarantine," Fanny announced.

Jonas sighed. Fanny had silently retreated to the bay window with her embroidery, and he'd completely forgotten she was present. His intent was for her to go to Broadmoor Island with the others. Now she'd inserted herself in the middle of his argument with Victoria. He had far too many women interfering in his life.

"But you love the island, and it would be an excellent opportunity for you to visit with Michael's parents," Jonas replied.

Beatrice snickered. "Since when are you concerned about that, Uncle Jonas?"

"Don't try my patience, Beatrice. I was speaking to Fanny."

Fanny set aside her stitching. " 'Tis true I'd enjoy seeing Michael's parents, and I do love the island, but not nearly as much as I love Amanda. I would count it a blessing if you'd permit me to remain and accompany her, Aunt Victoria. Even if Uncle Jonas comes with us, I'm certain she will still be weak and need a woman's touch."

"That's likely true." Victoria sniffed and dabbed her teary eyes.

Jonas could see his wife beginning to waver. He must take

charge of the family's relocation, or they would all remain in Rochester. And most likely in his house. The idea caused an involuntary shudder. Having only Fanny at the house in Rochester would be the better choice. She'd likely keep to her rooms when he was at home.

"Then it's settled!" Ignoring his wife's obvious trepidation, Jonas voiced the announcement in his most authoritative tone.

Fanny appeared surprised, while Beatrice was giddy with relief. "I'll go home and pack. Do you think we'll be gone for more than three weeks?" She didn't await a reply before rattling on. "I'll leave the children here while I start getting things organized at home; you don't mind, do you? If Andrew insists upon staying in Rochester, I'll advise him he should take refuge here with you, Uncle Jonas."

"No!" Jonas barked. Beatrice's wide-eyed stare and his wife's look of displeasure were enough to warn Jonas that further explanation was in order. "I'm going to send the servants with your aunt, so there will be no one here except for me, Fanny, her personal maid, and my butler, of course. Andrew will be much more comfortable under his own roof."

"But he'll be safer here," Beatrice whined.

Jonas frowned. Like the recent weather, Beatrice offered nothing but gloom. He'd be forced to convince her. "Let me talk to Andrew. I'm certain he isn't nearly so concerned for himself. Once he knows you and the children are safe, he'll settle into his usual routine and won't give cholera another thought. Trust me."

Beatrice offered a halfhearted nod.

Jonas could see she wasn't totally convinced, but he didn't let on. Instead, he patted her shoulder and complimented her insight. "I always knew you were an intelligent young woman."

Beatrice beamed. The lie didn't bother Jonas in the least. Such bold exaggerations were necessary if he was going to make any headway. If left to their own devices, these women would drive him mad before he could arrange for their train tickets.

"I'm not totally convinced I should go," Victoria said. Her taffeta gown swished against his pant leg as she slowly paced across the room.

"Nonsense! It's all settled. Instruct the servants to begin packing immediately. I'm going to the railroad station and will purchase tickets on the first train scheduled for Clayton tomorrow morning." He extended his fingers and began to count. "I'm not certain how many tickets you'll need for the family and servants. We should conduct a head count."

Beatrice quickly came to his aid. After seeking a bit of guidance from Victoria, his niece jotted names on a scrap of paper. When she presented the list to him a short time later, Jonas sighed with relief. He would regain control of his life once he had time to think and calculate his options.

❖

Raindrops plunked into a metal pan that Blake had set beneath a newly discovered leak in the ceiling. They'd patched the roof last fall, but after last winter's harsh snows and the ongoing spring rains, the patches were giving out. The Home needed a new roof. Blake had told Quincy as much, although Quincy had opted to expand the kitchen instead.

"We need to feed the starving," he'd insisted.

When Quincy entered the room, Blake pointed to the pan. "Another leak. If it doesn't quit raining, the cooks won't have any kettles left in the kitchen."

"We'll patch the roof once the weather dries out."

"Patch?" Blake snorted. "A new roof is what's needed. I told you that last year."

"And you were right. But there's nothing that can be done about it until the rain lets up." Quincy stooped down beside Amanda's bed. "Is she faring any better?"

Blake shook his head. "Hard to tell at this point. She hasn't taken in any more liquid, so she's not throwing up. I've given her a dose of morphine. When she awakens, I'll see if she can hold down any fluids."

Quincy grasped his arm. "Until then, you need to come and help me with the others. There are few who are willing to lend a hand."

"I can't blame them. Remember to wash your hands after you touch any of the patients," Blake said as he continued to stroke Amanda's brow.

"I need your help with the others. I know you want to remain with Amanda, but I can't do this without you." Quincy tightened his grasp. "Come along and help me."

Blake shook loose of Quincy's hold. "This is where I need to be right now. Amanda needs me. I'd never forgive myself if she awakened and I weren't here to help her."

"We must find some way to balance this or others are going to die. Amanda is my niece, and I am concerned for her welfare, also, but the other patients deserve your help, too."

"Give me time alone to pray; then I'll join you." Blake waited until the older man exited the room and then buried his face in his hands. He believed in God, but he'd seen few miracles during his medical career. Prayer or not, most everyone with debilitating illnesses died. When medicine failed, he had seen little evidence of God's intervention. But Blake now pushed those thoughts from the forefront of his mind and concentrated on Amanda. He needed a miracle, and he was going to trust that God would find Amanda worthy of healing. Medical science had no answers that would save her.

"Amanda is a fine young lady, Lord." Blake stared at her still form. "You created her, and she's developed into this lovely woman who has a heart to help others. Surely that's reason enough for you to allow her to live awhile longer. You know she's not a selfish person—maybe a little prideful from time to time, but underneath she's a good woman." He gently straightened the sheet and then turned his gaze heavenward. "You know my heart, God. I'm begging you to save this woman. I truly think I love her."

"I do believe it's dangerous when you think for yourself, Dr. Carstead."

He blinked away the tears clouding his eyes, but before he could say a word, Amanda had slipped back into unconsciousness. Even in the throes of cholera, she possessed the determination to banter with him. No doubt remained: This was the woman he desired to wed. If only God would spare her life.

❖

"You absolutely *must* get packed, Sophie. We're departing for Broadmoor Island!"

"Good afternoon to you, too, Aunt Victoria," Sophie said as she motioned her aunt inside.

"There's no time for idle chatter." She yanked off her gloves and tucked them into her reticule. "I do wish your uncle would agree to have one of those telephones in our house. It would save a great deal of time. Come, we must talk."

Sophie didn't mention the fact that a telephone wouldn't help unless the people her aunt wished to call had telephones in their homes, too. And Paul and Sophie certainly couldn't afford such a luxury.

"Did I hear someone at the door?" Paul appeared from the kitchen. "What a pleasant surprise."

The older woman waved him forward. "Oh, good. I'm glad you're here, Paul. I've come to advise Sophie she must hurry and pack. With the cholera spreading, Jonas has decided it's best for the family to take refuge at Broadmoor Island."

Sophie bounced Elizabeth in her arms and shook her head. "We're fine right here. Paul and I aren't fearful of contracting cholera, are we, Paul?" She narrowed her eyes and shot her husband a beseeching look. "There's no need to escape the city."

"Jonas insists it is best for all concerned. Besides, Beatrice is traumatized with worry."

Sophie sat down opposite her aunt and rubbed Elizabeth's back. "Good girl," Sophie cooed when Elizabeth presented them with a loud burp. Sophie lifted the child to her shoulder and met her aunt's steady gaze. "You know Beatrice isn't happy unless she's in the midst of turmoil. My sister enjoys nothing more than drawing others into the center of her turbulence. I can't believe Uncle Jonas has succumbed to her antics."

"This cholera epidemic is more than a silly charade. The disease presents danger to all of us." Her aunt traced her fingers through Elizabeth's fine curls. "I would think you'd be concerned for your daughter."

Sophie's stomach muscles tensed at her aunt's recrimination. "And what of Amanda? Are you going to hurry off to the island and leave *your* daughter behind?"

"Sophie!" Paul chided.

Her aunt flashed Paul a tolerant look. "It's all right, Paul. I'm accustomed to Sophie's truculent behavior."

"Why am I considered quarrelsome when I mention

Amanda's needs, yet it's perfectly acceptable for you to intimate that I'm not properly caring for Elizabeth?" Sophie hugged the baby close.

"I am intensely concerned about Amanda's condition, but with the quarantine in place, there is nothing any of us can do for her. I am most thankful Dr. Carstead and your father are present to aid in her recovery. If it were possible, I would tend to her every need, but . . ." Victoria's words trailed into silence.

Sophie noted the tears that had gathered in her aunt's eyes and regret assailed her, yet it didn't change her mind. She didn't want to leave Rochester. "Our homes aren't nearly so close to the area affected. We'll be fine." She glanced at Paul. "Won't we?"

He frowned. "There's no assurance of safety. Perhaps it would be best if you took Elizabeth and went to the island."

She couldn't believe her ears. Paul was going to take her aunt's side. Worse, it sounded as though he intended to send her while he remained in Rochester. That would never do!

Sophie met her husband's intense look with a forced smile. "The minute you've arranged to depart with us, I'll be prepared."

"That's impossible. You know I've promised to deliver food and medical supplies to the Home."

She shrugged. "If you truly think I should leave, then you can arrange for someone else to see to those matters and come with us."

"I have three families who have requested funeral services this week. No doubt there will be others in need during the coming days."

"There are other preachers in Rochester who can bury the dead." Sophie tapped her foot and returned his icy stare.

Paul pushed up from the sofa with a look of determination

on his face. "When will the family depart for Broadmoor Island, Aunt Victoria?"

"The servants will call for Sophie's trunks late this afternoon. We'll depart tomorrow morning. Jonas has gone to purchase the tickets." Her aunt retrieved her gloves from her reticule and stood. "I'm relieved you and Elizabeth will be with us, Sophie. We'll have a delightful time." She leaned over and kissed Elizabeth on the cheek. "I look forward to helping you with her."

Sophie's anger bubbled near the surface, but she maintained a calm façade until her aunt departed. The moment the door closed, she turned on her heel and poked Paul in the chest. "How could you take her side against me?" She didn't wait for his response before marching down the hallway. "I suppose having Elizabeth and me out of your way makes life much simpler for you, doesn't it?" she called over her shoulder.

The sound of Paul's heavy footsteps signaled his anger. "I am doing what a man is supposed to do. I'm seeking protection for my family." His eyes shone with anger when she turned to face him. "How can you accuse me of sending you off in order to simplify my life? The only pleasure I gain from your absence is the knowledge that you and Elizabeth are safe. You know that's true, yet you fault me."

"Strange that you didn't express concern for our welfare until Aunt Victoria presented you with this wondrous opportunity to be rid of us."

"I haven't spoken of my fear because I didn't want to worry you. I have prayed for the safety of our family, and I believe this may be God's answer to my prayer. I won't have you remain in Rochester and run any further risk of becoming infected when there is a safe haven available."

Sophie snorted. His argument didn't hold water. "If you

prayed for the safety of our family and believe this is an answer to prayer, then you should be coming with us. As the head of our house and a servant of God, surely God would expect you to avail yourself of this opportunity." She tapped her foot and waited. Let her husband find some way to argue *that* point.

He clenched his jaw until the tendons in his neck protruded like taut ropes. "I am a patient man, and you know that since we wed I have given consideration to your wishes. However, I will not argue this matter any further. You and Elizabeth will go to Broadmoor Island tomorrow morning, and I will remain in Rochester."

"When you're unable to provide an argument for your case, you simply cease the debate and issue an order." Sophie wheeled around and stomped toward the stairs. "I'll go to Broadmoor Island, but you'll be sorry, Paul."

She ran up the stairs before he could see the hot tears that formed in her eyes. Her actions were angry and measured as she flung dresses, camisoles, and nightgowns across the bed. She expected Paul would follow and tell her he'd had a change of heart. But he didn't.

## 5

*Thursday, May 4, 1899*

Fanny peeked into the mirror and adjusted the navy blue ribbons that streamed from her straw hat like thick kite strings. When she'd bought the hat in March, Aunt Victoria had declared the chapeau a perfect choice. Fanny hadn't been nearly as convinced. She'd purchased it more to please her aunt than herself. Had there been sufficient time this morning, she would have run upstairs and exchanged it for the one she'd purchased last year. Instead, she collected her parasol and reticule.

"Where are you off to so early this morning?"

Fanny startled at her uncle's booming question. "I thought . . . I'm going . . . it's a lovely day, and I decided . . ."

He waved his hat and continued toward the door. "Oh, never mind. I don't have time."

A sense of relief washed over her once her uncle had descended the front steps. Holding the lace curtain aside, she peeked through the narrow window that framed the front door and watched until his carriage departed.

With a determined step she hurried to the kitchen. "I'll need the spindle-back runabout," she told the stableboy who was helping himself to a cup of coffee. She was thankful her uncle hadn't sent the stablehands to the island. Both the cook and his personal butler had remained, as well. Uncle Jonas had said their services wouldn't be needed at Broadmoor Island. Fanny wondered if Mrs. Atwell concurred and had adjusted to the unexpected arrival of the family. Thoughts of the kindly woman who was the head cook at Broadmoor Island and would eventually become her mother-in-law brought a fleeting sense of remorse that she'd remained in Rochester. She hadn't seen Michael's mother since the family departed the island last year at summer's end. Though Fanny had posted several letters to Mr. and Mrs. Atwell, she'd received only one in return. The missive had been brief. Mrs. Atwell had warned she preferred her kitchen duties to writing letters. She'd certainly spoken the truth on that account.

Fanny inhaled deeply as the driver assisted her into the runabout. The rains had ceased over the last three days, and the air smelled of springtime. The lilac bushes at old Broadmoor Mansion would likely be heavy with blooms. The thought of lilacs served as a reminder of childhood days when she and her cousins had played among the lilac bushes and the grape arbors at their grandparents' Rochester estate. She prayed Amanda would soon be well enough to enjoy the pleasures of the changing season. Dr. Carstead had attempted to assure her that Amanda was making progress, but Fanny remained unconvinced. She leaned back in the carriage. Once her business was completed in town, she'd deliver a bouquet of lilacs to the gate outside the Home for the Friendless. Perhaps the fragrance of lilacs would stimulate Amanda's recovery.

"Where to, Miss Broadmoor?" the driver inquired.

Before leaving home, Fanny had decided against giving the driver her exact destination. If Uncle Jonas discovered she'd taken the carriage, he might question the young man. "The corner of West Main and South Fitzhugh streets."

After climbing to his seat, the driver slapped the reins. The horse slowly clopped down the driveway and turned to head down East Avenue. A variety of colorful flowers dotted patches of green along the way. Rain or not, the gardeners of the wealthy had been hard at work keeping the vast gardens and lawns perfectly manicured.

Had the flowers begun to bloom on Broadmoor Island? She doubted the weather had warmed enough, though a wild flower or two could always force itself from beneath a bed of snow. Winter was slow to disappear in the islands, and dear Sophie would be livid if they remained snowbound and restricted to Broadmoor Castle. Her confinement at the island in the months leading up to Elizabeth's birth had been difficult enough. Though she'd not had opportunity to speak with Paul, Fanny doubted Sophie had easily agreed to be isolated on the island. Epidemic or not, Sophie took pleasure in socializing. The lack of parties, coupled with ongoing interaction with Beatrice and the other family members, would cause Sophie no small measure of suffering. Perhaps a letter advising her to take refuge in the kitchen with Mrs. Atwell would be in order. She would pen her cousin a note this afternoon.

The driver pulled back on the reins, and the carriage came to a halt in front of the Rochester Savings Bank. "Shall I wait while you complete your business, Miss Broadmoor?"

She shook her head. "No. I have several matters that need my attention. You may return for me in two hours. I'll meet you here."

He tipped his hat, hoisted himself up, and slapped the reins. Fanny strolled down Main Street as though she had nothing of import to fill her days. The usually busy streets were nearly void of traffic, and few customers entered the shops along the street. She stopped in front of the narrow brick building on her right. Ebony letters had been outlined in gold leaf to boldly announce the names of the lawyers who occupied the space. She pushed open the door and was greeted by a stern-looking clerk who peered over the rim of his spectacles.

"May I be of assistance?" The man's tone spoke volumes: He thought her an annoying intrusion.

"Miss Frances Broadmoor to see Mr. Rosenblume." She met the clerk's unflinching stare. "He requested a ten o'clock meeting with me."

"You may have a seat. I'll ascertain whether Mr. Rosenblume will see you."

The man's manner was impolite, and she wondered why Mr. Rosenblume tolerated such disrespect from his employees. Then again, perhaps Mr. Rosenblume didn't know. She withdrew the lawyer's note from her reticule. The letter had been personally delivered by a messenger several days ago and asked that she keep the appointment a secret. If either Amanda or Sophie had been available, she would have ignored the request and brought one of them along. The fact that Grandfather Broadmoor's lawyer wanted to meet with her secretly was both intriguing and odd. When Uncle Jonas had hired Mortimer Fillmore to handle her grandfather's estate, Mr. Rosenblume had gracefully bowed out of the picture. Though Mr. Rosenblume would have been

Fanny's choice, she'd had no authority in the decision. The judge had approved Mortimer Fillmore.

Perhaps that was why Mr. Rosenblume had summoned her. Another lawyer would be needed now that Mr. Fillmore had died. She had simply assumed Mr. Fillmore's son and law partner, Vincent, would take charge of the remaining legal details for Uncle Jonas.

Upon his return, the clerk was more congenial. "If you'll follow me, Mr. Rosenblume will see you in his office." With a grand sweeping motion, he waved her forward and opened the door to the adjacent office.

She stopped in the doorway. Mr. Rosenblume sat behind a massive mahogany desk that overpowered his small frame. But it wasn't the sight of Mr. Rosenblume that captured her interest as much as seeing Vincent Fillmore, who stood when she entered the room. Her surprise must have been obvious, for he stepped forward and held a chair for her. "It's good to see you, Miss Broadmoor."

She nodded and sat down. What would have brought these two men together? She glanced back and forth between them. "Have you and Mr. Rosenblume combined your law offices?"

Though his dark eyes appeared dulled by either pain or sadness, the younger lawyer smiled and shook his head. "No, but we have united in an effort to protect you, Miss Broadmoor."

The ominous words were more than enough to capture her undivided attention. "Protect me? Whatever from?"

Mr. Rosenblume shifted in his chair. "We don't want to alarm you, my dear. Your life is not in danger. However, I fear your financial future has been severely compromised."

"By my deceased father and your uncle Jonas," Mr. Fillmore added.

She clasped her hand to her chest. "You must be mistaken.

When I spoke with my uncle in February, he assured me that my investments were sound. Had there been any change, I'm certain he would have advised me." Having noted the pitying look the two men exchanged, she hastened to reinforce her position. She didn't want them to think her a complete dolt. "I understand the country continues to suffer with financial woes, but those had begun even before my grandfather's death. Perhaps it would be best if Uncle Jonas attended this meeting with us. He could better explain my—"

"No, it wouldn't be better, my dear." Mr. Rosenblume assumed a grandfatherly tone as he pushed away from his desk. "I know this conversation is going to prove extremely difficult, but I ask that you give us your full attention as we explain what has happened to your inheritance." Mr. Rosenblume circled the desk and held out his hand. "Why don't we move across the room?"

Fanny followed his gaze to the vast library table, where three chairs had been arranged. Neat stacks of paper lined the shiny tabletop. "How long do you anticipate our meeting will take? I have other matters that require my attention, and I told my carriage driver to return for me in two hours." She'd set her mind upon delivering lilacs to Amanda. Thoughts that the spring blooms might aid in her cousin's recovery took precedence over the heaping papers assembled on the table.

"Then we should begin immediately. If necessary, we can schedule a time to meet again tomorrow or next week."

Mr. Rosenblume escorted her across the room and pulled out one of the chairs. She would be seated between the two lawyers. How she wished Michael were here at her side to offer support through what she feared would be an ordeal. She truly didn't want to listen to the facts and figures these men would likely present. Though they'd been nothing but kind, she would feel more comfortable with a family member present—someone who understood finances. Someone like Uncle Jonas. That was why the judge had entrusted him to handle her inheritance.

"Let me begin by telling you that because my own father was involved in this arrangement, it pains me greatly to explain what I've discovered." Mr. Fillmore tapped his fingers on the arm of his chair. "Your uncle and my father share a common bond."

Was Mr. Fillmore going to examine the history of her uncle's friendship with the senior Mr. Fillmore? Fanny understood that the young lawyer was grieving his father's death, but he was using precious time without explaining the details of why she'd been secretly summoned.

"I understand they were dear friends. That's why Uncle Jonas insisted your father handle the estate when Grand-father Broadmoor died. I argued on behalf of Mr. Rosenblume, but because I was only seventeen and a woman, Uncle Jonas wouldn't listen to me."

"And because he wanted to control the money he believed should have been his," Mr. Fillmore added. "He resented the fact that you'd inherited a full third of the estate."

They were covering facts she already knew. Perhaps she should try to move the conversation forward. "But I thought that Uncle Jonas came to accept the terms of Grandfather's will. My financial returns have been excellent. He's told me so. That's why I'm confused by all of this. Why don't you explain." She pointed at the files and papers spread across the table.

"I'm coming to that," Vincent said. "Because both my father and your uncle are devious men who permitted money and power to rule their lives, they devised a plan that would eventually permit your uncle to convert all your assets."

"Convert them into *what*?" This was all very confusing.

Mr. Rosenblume patted her hand. "Convert them to his name, my dear. It appears your uncle and Mortimer Fillmore created a method whereby any financial losses were credited to your portion of the estate and any gains were assigned to your uncle's. It appears to be a complicated accounting scheme that should have been noticed by the court when your uncle filed his financial accounts."

"If you and Mr. Fillmore's son were able to discover what occurred, why didn't the judge?"

Vincent pointed to the table. "These are records and correspondence that my father maintained in his office files, information that wouldn't have been submitted to the judge. However, we have reason to believe my father may have *influenced* the judge to cooperate."

"Influenced? What does that mean?" Fanny looked back and forth between the two men, uncertain which one she should look to for an answer.

"It means the judge may have been bribed to overlook discrepancies in the papers your uncle filed." Mr. Rosenblume hunched his shoulders. "It saddens me to tell you this, but there are occasions when judges succumb to the lure of money, too. Of course, we can't say this is absolute in your case. As Vincent mentioned, we've only completed a cursory review of Mortimer's records."

Fanny turned toward the younger lawyer. "So when you discovered what you thought were discrepancies, you contacted Mr. Rosenblume?"

"Yes." Vincent scooted forward on his chair and rested his forearms across his thighs. He met her gaze with unflinching determination. "Because of my father's involvement in what I believe to be a misrepresentation of your interests, I thought it would be best for you to employ a lawyer who will give you sound legal advice. I believe it would be completely improper for me or any lawyer in my office to represent you. Since Mr. Rosenblume had been your grandfather's attorney, I thought he could lend you the most expertise."

Fanny attempted to digest the scattered information. Was her lack of money the reason Uncle Jonas had argued against the purchase of a home for Sophie and Paul? Although it had taken a bit of prodding, he'd met her request. Had he withdrawn the funds from his own account in order to meet her demand? Would her uncle have stolen from her? Certainly her uncle was a trying and callous man, but she didn't want to believe he'd steal from his own niece.

"So I have no money whatsoever?" she asked.

"Nothing as bleak as that, my dear." Mr. Rosenblume offered her an encouraging smile. "There is some money available. It simply appears your uncle has commingled and transferred many of your financial assets into his own account. Unfortunately, he has made many ill-advised investments and lost a great deal. Once I've gone through all this paper work and discussed the situation with the banks and accountants for the investment companies, I'll have a more substantial answer. That is, if you wish for me to take over as your legal representative."

The need to make an immediate decision left her breathless. If she employed Mr. Rosenblume as her lawyer, what would her uncle say or do? Would he insist she move out of his home? Not that she would mind that idea, of course. She silently prayed for guidance.

"If I should decide to employ Mr. Rosenblume, how would the transfer take place?"

Mr. Fillmore raked his fingers through his thick hair. "You would inform your uncle of employing Mr. Rosenblume as your lawyer. Your uncle has been intent upon removing his files from my office since the day my father died. After a cursory review of the files, I understood his persistence. I immediately removed the files from my office and told your uncle that there is little paper work there." Vincent massaged his furrowed brow. "That much is true. However, he wants to come to the office and review his files."

Fanny was doing her best to digest the information. "Then my uncle doesn't know these records exist?"

Vincent shook his head. "No, not at this time."

"But once I begin to investigate, he will get wind of what is going on," Mr. Rosenblume warned. "It won't take long before he realizes Mortimer left a paper trail and it has fallen into your hands. I must warn you that this could cause no end of trouble for you, Miss Broadmoor. You're the one who must decide if you'll permit your uncle to continue down this path of deceit and thievery. I would strongly urge you not to do so. But you must consider the difficulty this will cause with other family members."

Fanny considered her dear cousins. Sophie would urge her to hire Mr. Rosenblume immediately. But what of Amanda? In spite of his shortcomings, Uncle Jonas was Amanda's father. Once Amanda began to gain her strength, would such news hinder her complete recovery? And what would happen to Aunt Victoria and the rest of the family if proof of his actions came to light? Would they despise her?

Mr. Rosenblume shifted in his chair. "I know this is difficult, Miss Broadmoor, but Mr. Fillmore needs to know what he should do regarding these records."

"Leave the files here. Mr. Rosenblume, I will retain you as my legal representative. At this moment I'm not certain how far I will proceed. I will need time to consider my actions further."

Mr. Fillmore jumped to his feet. The man was obviously delighted to hear her decision and anxious to be on his way. "You have my word that I will cooperate with Mr. Rosenblume in any manner he requests, Miss Broadmoor." He hesitated for a moment. "And I hope I have your word that you won't tell your uncle what I've done."

Fanny nodded. If Uncle Jonas quizzed her at length, she'd simply direct him to speak with Mr. Rosenblume. That was, after all, what lawyers were supposed to do, wasn't it? Moments later, Mr. Fillmore hurried out of the office, leaving her to deal with Mr. Rosenblume and the mountain of paper—a task that didn't appeal to her in the least.

She glanced at the clock on Mr. Rosenblume's mahogany desk. A full forty-five minutes remained until the driver was due to return. Though she understood the importance of the issue at hand, she longed to take her leave and contemplate this unsavory news in private. She longed to walk among the gardens of her grandparents' home and pick lilacs for Amanda.

Before she could excuse herself, Mr. Rosenblume retrieved several papers from one of the files. "There are several things I believe you need to review immediately. Much of this can wait until I've conducted a thorough examination, but this is a matter of import. It appears your uncle has been actively seeking a buyer for the Broadmoor Mansion, and I'm not at all sure you would agree with such a sale."

Fanny frowned. "Broadmoor Mansion has already been sold, Mr. Rosenblume. My uncle sold it without my knowledge. He proposed the sale with the hope I would marry the young man of his choosing. Though I was distraught, the court approved the sale, and there was little I could do. I don't know how he managed the legalities."

"My dear, the entire setup was a sham. Your uncle duped

young Daniel. Still, his plan fell short, for he didn't convince you to marry Mr. Irwin, did he?"

Fanny shook her head. The lawyer's knowledge of Daniel Irwin piqued her interest, and she leaned closer to examine the file's contents. "Exactly what makes you think the house is for sale?"

He handed Fanny a note written on her uncle's stationery and dated only a week prior to Mortimer Fillmore's death. The letter confirmed exactly what Mr. Rosenblume had told her. Uncle Jonas blamed Mortimer for not locating a suitable buyer even though they'd lowered the selling price. How could her uncle do such a thing! He knew how much that house meant to her and how much it had meant to his parents. Indignation assailed her as she read the words scrawled at the bottom of the page. *Burn this letter after you have read the contents.*

Mr. Fillmore hadn't followed her uncle's orders. In addition to the letter, there was an unsigned deed made out to Daniel, together with background information that had been gathered on several men, Daniel included. Fanny recognized the names of the others—all of them men her uncle had invited to Broadmoor Island. With each additional detail, her anger mounted.

"Has your review revealed how my uncle gained permission to sell Broadmoor Mansion?"

"The paper work appears to be in order. The judge signed a document approving the sale. You uncle's motion to the court states that cash was needed to meet unexpected debts. He further declared Broadmoor Mansion could be easily sold and the proceeds used to pay those undisclosed debts. Since your uncle has authority to act on your behalf, notification to you wasn't required. The records reflect your uncle Quincy was notified, but he filed no objection. If he truly received the notice, I doubt he even read the papers. Quincy has never been interested in business matters. I would guess Jonas relied upon that knowledge as well as the fact that Quincy's charity work generally keeps him too busy to worry over issues relating to your grandfather's estate. Like you, Quincy relies upon Jonas."

"Since the court has already granted permission to sell the house, I want to purchase Broadmoor Mansion, Mr. Rosenblume."

Mr. Rosenblume smiled. "I was certain that would be your reaction."

"Can it be arranged without my uncle's knowledge?"

The lawyer hesitated. "I assume your uncle has continued to hold control of your investments and funds even though you've attained your majority?"

"I'm afraid I had little choice. The judge, Mr. Fillmore, and my uncle all advised that it would be imprudent for a woman to attempt managing my vast holdings. The judge indicated he wouldn't approve such an arrangement. Uncle Jonas gives me an allowance each month. Other than that, I don't know if I have access to any of my money or not. I've never made any attempt to withdraw funds. Even when I purchased a house for my cousin, I had my uncle see to the transaction. After what you've told me, I'm doubtful I can access any of the accounts." She silently chided herself for such a grievous error in judgment. "This will ruin my opportunity to purchase Broadmoor Mansion."

"Not necessarily. I could purchase the house for you," Mr. Rosenblume said. "Once we've gained access to your funds, you could repay me."

Fanny stared at the lawyer. No wonder her grandfather had valued Mr. Rosenblume. In addition to his honesty, he was obviously a compassionate man. She didn't want to take advantage of his kindness, but she had little choice. If she didn't agree,

Uncle Jonas would continue to seek a buyer for the house. It might be lost to her forever.

"Please do what you can to secure the title for me," she said.

"I know you may find it difficult to trust anyone right now, Miss Broadmoor, but I hope you will remember my years of faithful service to your grandfather. My intent is to help you in any way possible." Mr. Rosenblume gathered the papers and shoved them inside the file folder. "I will make every effort to secure the mansion at the lowest possible price. The fact that Jonas is anxious to sell should work in your favor."

"Let's hope so," she said. "Is there anything else we must address this morning?"

"I do want you to understand that your uncle has com-mingled funds and it will take time and effort to determine exactly what is yours and what is his. While some of the details are clear-cut, others are clouded."

"If these allegations prove to be true, I want to take every effort to protect my aunt and cousins. They had no part in any of this. It is Uncle Jonas who must answer for his actions."

The lawyer nodded. "I will do what I can to protect both your interests and the family name." He lifted some files from one end of the table. "These files were marked with your name and the word *confidential*. I have not examined their contents." The clock chimed, and he handed her the files. "Take these papers with you. Once you've reviewed them, we can discuss anything you discover that might require my attention."

After bidding Mr. Rosenblume farewell, Fanny tucked the files under her arm and arrived at the Rochester Savings Bank only minutes before the carriage appeared. Instead of stopping to pick lilacs, she instructed the driver to return home. It wouldn't do for Uncle Jonas to be waiting and confront her when she entered the house. What if he spotted the files and inquired? What would she say? Even with the driver's urging, the horse seemed to plod along at an unusually slow pace. She prayed her uncle wouldn't decide to come home for the noonday meal. Since Aunt Victoria's departure, his schedule had become irregular, and Fanny never knew when he might appear. Not that it had mattered much in the past.

Fanny leaned forward and tapped the driver on the shoulder. "Was my uncle at home when you left the house?"

The driver shook his head. "Haven't seen him since early this morning, and he didn't leave any instructions to pick him up until this evening. 'Course you can't never tell about Mr. Jonas. Sometimes he hires a cab to bring him home."

When they neared the house, she once again tapped the driver. "Go around to the back of the house. I'll enter through the kitchen."

The young man glanced over his shoulder and frowned, but he didn't question her. The servants who worked for Jonas Broadmoor knew better.

"Thank you," she said as he helped her down. "After lunch, I'll need you to take me to Broadmoor Mansion and then on to the Home for the Friendless." The driver nodded. Fanny gazed over the driver's shoulder and was pleased to see that her uncle's horses hadn't been hitched to his carriage. She hoped that meant he had remained at his office. The minute she entered the kitchen, she quizzed the cook and was relieved when she heard that her uncle hadn't darkened the doorway.

"When would you like to eat, Miss Fanny?" the cook asked when she continued toward the rear stairway.

"I'll get something a little later. I'm not hungry right now."

The cook nodded. "If you're sure, 'cause I could—"

"I am. I'll be upstairs in my bedroom," she called over her shoulder.

Never before had Fanny locked the bedroom door, but today was different. She placed the files on her bed, removed the key from the top dresser drawer, and slipped it into the lock. One twist of the key and the bolt slipped into place with a soft *clunk*.

Apprehension filled her as she crossed the room and settled in a chair that overlooked the rear garden. She sifted through the papers and then stopped to more closely peruse a letter addressed to Mortimer Fillmore. The missive was written on her uncle's stationery and in his familiar script. More importantly, her inheritance was the subject of the letter.

She clasped her palm to her lips when she read her uncle's directive to falsify the records and deduct his financial losses from her accounts. He set forth a plan that clearly proved what Mr. Rosenblume and Vincent Fillmore had suspected. Her hands shook as she turned to read the final page. *Your fears concerning Fanny are needless. She is a foolish young woman who lacks the intelligence to question her finances. She will never request an examination of the accounts.* He'd signed the letter and added a final caveat instructing Mortimer to burn the letter. Fanny could scarcely believe what she'd read.

She had hoped to find something in the files that would vindicate her uncle. Instead, he had secretly schemed against her. How could someone who professed to love her pledge his loyalty and then betray her? Uncle Jonas had evolved into a Judas Iscariot. She shuddered at the thought.

❖

Amanda struggled to push aside the pile of quilts that enveloped her like a smothering cocoon. Had Blake thought she might freeze to death? She would have inquired, but he appeared to be dozing in a chair near the foot of her bed. The scent of lilacs drifted toward her and momentarily replaced the putrid smells wafting from the bucket by her bed. The quilts landed on the wood floor with a dull thud that immediately startled him awake.

"I'm sorry. I didn't mean to waken you, but I thought I might suffocate under all of these blankets." Amanda forced her dry, cracked lips into a half smile. "I see the rain has stopped." She lifted a shaking hand and pointed to a nearby table. "Lilacs?"

Blake stared at her as though he'd seen a ghost. "Quincy! Quincy! Come in here." He jumped up from his chair and sent it crashing to the floor. Kicking aside the pile of quilts, he rushed to her bed and grasped her hand. "How do you feel?"

"Thirsty, but much better," she said. "May I have a drink?" Her voice was raspy to her ears, and she noted the worried look in his eyes. No doubt he thought she wouldn't manage to keep the liquid down. But the terrible stomach pains had disappeared.

He poured a small amount of water into a glass. Slipping his arm beneath her shoulders, he held her up while she swallowed the contents.

"I must look a wretched sight." She brushed the hair from her forehead.

"Amanda! I can't believe my eyes." Her uncle hurried across the room and positioned himself at the other side of her bed. He touched his hand to his stomach. "Any pain?"

She shook her head while both men stared down at her as though she might disappear if they looked away. "Other than a weak, groggy feeling, I believe I'm fine."

"The weakness is to be expected," Blake said. He squeezed her hand. "I had nearly given up hope."

"I had an excellent doctor caring for me," she whispered.

"My medical ability had nothing to do with your recovery. The fervent prayers of those who love you have been answered."

*Those who love me?* Did Dr. Carstead count himself among that number? She vaguely remembered his sitting by her bedside and praying, but she couldn't recall what he'd said. Yet he had prayed for her. And he'd said those who loved her had been praying. Could *he* possibly love her? Should she harbor such a thought?

# 6

*Wednesday, May 10, 1899*
*Broadmoor Island*

Sophie held Elizabeth close and wrapped the soft blanket tightly around the baby's legs. She pointed at two boats passing on the river. "See the boats, Elizabeth?" The baby cooed, but her gaze followed several of her young cousins romping in the yard rather than the boats. She wriggled in her mother's arms and chortled at the children's antics. "It won't be long until you'll be able to run and play, too." Sophie nuzzled the soft folds of the baby's neck until she squealed in delight.

Elizabeth's antics had provided occasional moments of enjoyment, but the days had passed slowly since their arrival on Broadmoor Island. Beatrice had been like fingernails scratching chalkboard since the day they'd set foot on the island. Sophie decided her sister should be awarded a prize for the most annoying person in God's creation. Though there might be someone who was more irritating than Beatrice, Sophie couldn't begin to imagine the possibility. And the fact that she and Paul had parted on less than good terms didn't help, either.

To make matters worse, she hadn't received even one letter from him. Each afternoon when Mr. Atwell brought the mail to the house, Beatrice noted that fact with great pleasure. When Beatrice had made a huge show of the letter she'd received from Andrew yesterday, Sophie had considered throttling her. Hoping to silence her sister, Sophie had defended Paul's inattentive behavior. "While Andrew whiles away his evenings with nothing to do but write letters, Paul is busy seeing to the welfare of others," she'd said. The comment had led to a nasty exchange between the sisters and had heightened Sophie's discontent. Surely there must be some escape from this place. Although she could move about the island at will, she felt as though she'd go mad from the enforced captivity. At least she'd had Fanny to keep her company during the months before Elizabeth's birth.

Veda rounded the corner and waved at Sophie. "Are you ready for me to take Elizabeth upstairs for her nap, Miss Sophie?"

"I suppose it is that time, isn't it?" She kissed Elizabeth's cheek before handing her to the maid. "Make certain you or Minnie remains upstairs while she naps. It's impossible to hear her cry when you're downstairs."

"Yes, Miss Sophie."

Sophie didn't miss the sullen tone. The maid had likely grown weary of hearing the cautionary instruction every day. She wondered if Veda and Minnie hated being tied to the same wearisome duties each day. There must be something good to be said for such a life, but she couldn't think what it might be. It would be similar to living on this island with nothing new or different, each day the same as the last. She tugged at her skirt and sighed. Her tiny waist hadn't returned as quickly as she'd hoped after Elizabeth's birth. Most of her clothing remained snug and uncomfortable. She'd need to either pass on desserts in the future or purchase new gowns. Paul wouldn't be pleased with that option. He hoped to save enough money to reimburse Fanny one day for the cost of their house. Sophie held out little hope for that plan—not with her husband's meager wages.

Perhaps a stroll would lighten her spirits. She downed the last of her tea and meandered along the path that led to the side of the house.

With an old woolen shawl pulled tight around her shoulders, Mrs. Atwell was stooped over, tending a small herb garden. The older woman glanced up as she approached. "Hello, Miss Sophie. Another gorgeous day, don't you think?"

Sophie nodded. "I wouldn't mind a little more warmth to the days. And the company of someone I enjoyed spending them with. Don't you grow lonely during the winter when you and Mr. Atwell are out here by yourselves?"

Mrs. Atwell prodded the ground, pulling a weed here and there as she checked the plants. "Being alone for a time can be a good thing, Sophie. It gives us time to reflect and commune with God. I look forward to each season as it arrives, and I'm never disappointed. I enjoy having your family arrive at the beginning of each summer, but I'm equally pleased to see them depart." She stood and arched her back. "Each year my back protests the gardening chores a bit more."

"Having us arrive so early this year must have taken you by surprise."

Mrs. Atwell shook her head and trudged toward the side of the house. "No, I can't say I was surprised in the least." She picked up an old milking stool from alongside the kitchen door and brought it back to the small patch of garden. "Mr.

Atwell had heard that some of the families were fleeing to the islands to escape the cholera epidemic." She sat down on the small stool. Her chin appeared to touch her knees as she bent forward to continue weeding. "I had expected the entire family to come."

Sophie hadn't considered the possibility that no one had explained to Mr. and Mrs. Atwell why some members of the family had remained in Rochester. She should have realized her aunt wouldn't feel the need to provide details. Even though Michael's parents were soon to become members of Fanny's family, they were still Broadmoor servants. And servants weren't entitled to know why. They were simply expected to perform their duties and not ask questions. Mrs. Atwell had probably been beside herself, privately questioning why Fanny hadn't come with them. Yet she dared not inquire.

"You're wondering about Fanny?" Sophie asked.

Mrs. Atwell sat upright on the stool. "Yes. Please tell me she hasn't contracted cholera."

"No. Fanny is fine—at least she was when we left Rochester. It's Amanda who contracted cholera. Fanny asked to remain in Rochester so that she could accompany Amanda here once she's well enough to travel. Although Amanda has shown some slight improvement recently, she is still very ill."

The weeds dropped from Mrs. Atwell's hand and fluttered to the ground. "Dear me, that is sad news. I'm surprised Mrs. Broadmoor didn't stay in Rochester with her daughter."

"She wanted to, but Uncle Jonas insisted all of us come here. Amanda fell ill while working at the Home for the Friendless, and the entire Home was placed under quarantine," Sophie said. "I'm sorry, Mrs. Atwell. I didn't even think—"

Mrs. Atwell waved as if to silence her. "Don't you concern yourself, Miss Sophie. It's not your job to keep me updated on your family. I received a letter from Fanny a week before you arrived. I'm certain she'll be sending another letter soon. Fact is, it's none of my business."

"But it *is* your business. Fanny is soon to be your daughter-in-law—she'll soon be *your* family, too." Sophie settled her gaze on the horizon. "Each day I hope that Amanda and Fanny will be on the train from Rochester. I miss them very much. The island isn't the same without them."

"You girls have been inseparable since you were little," Mrs. Atwell said with a smile. "I always teased that you were three girls sharing one heart."

Sophie smiled. "Yes. I remember." She sighed. "Life would not be the same without them."

"Mr. Atwell and I will be praying for Amanda's speedy recovery and for Fanny's continued good health." The older woman pointed at a boat speeding down the river. "Appears some of the Pullmans have returned to the islands. Mr. Atwell tells me that folks have been arriving every day. Some say they'll not be going home before the end of summer. Others say they'll go home the end of May and then return the end of June."

Sophie perked to attention. "Has he heard if any socials have been scheduled at the Frontenac Hotel?" She didn't await an answer. "Do you have a copy of the paper? In the summertime they list the parties on the society page. With folks returning early, perhaps they've already begun."

"The paper should be in that stack near the kitchen door. To tell you the truth, I don't look at the social page, so I don't know what they've listed in there."

Sophie bounded off toward the kitchen and shuffled through the papers until she located the latest edition. She spread it on the worktable and quickly turned the pages of the meager weekly offering. The social news had dwindled from the full page of last year's summertime news to half a column of winter offerings. Disappointed, she flapped the pages together and was about to shove the paper back in place when she noticed a small article on the front page.

"Wonderful!" she whispered. A party had been scheduled for Saturday evening at the Frontenac Hotel. All who were seeking refuge in the islands were invited to attend.

Of course, those who read the article knew not *everyone* was invited. The party was being hosted by Mr. and Mrs. Edward Oosterman. Certainly they weren't Sophie's favorite host and hostess, for they generally catered to an older crowd. All the same, it was a party. Perhaps Georgie and Sanger Pullman would be there to add some fun. Both Jefferson and George, Amanda's unmarried brothers, had booked passage for Europe when threatened with banishment to the island for several months. Not that Sophie blamed them, but she was jealous of the freedom and wealth that permitted them such an escape.

She hastened back outdoors. Mrs. Atwell had disappeared, but Sophie didn't bother to seek her out. Right now she was more concerned about what she would wear to the party. The better question was what *could* she wear? Stones skittered beneath her slippers as she quickened her step and returned to the house. She'd packed several gowns, but none of them fit. The green silk might have adequate fabric to release the seams. Yet even if the alterations permitted an extra half inch, she'd need her corset laced as tight as possible. Minnie would be the best choice to alter the dress, but Veda was far superior at squeezing her into a tight corset.

Veda looked up from her sewing when Sophie entered the nursery. She crooked her finger at the maid. "Come here," she whispered.

The maid tiptoed across the room and followed Sophie into

the hallway. "I have need of a dress that will fit me for a party Saturday evening. Where is Minnie?"

"Minnie doesn't have a party dress," Veda replied.

Sophie sighed. Sometimes Veda didn't have the sense God gave a goose. "I don't want to *borrow* a dress from Minnie. I want her to *alter* one of mine."

"Oh, I see." Veda's head bobbled like a worn-out spring. "You might look in the servants' quarters. She was going to—"

With a brief wave Sophie turned and hurried off. Veda had a way of explaining things that took forever, and Sophie didn't have forever. She had only a few short days. The thick hallway carpet muffled her footsteps—and those of her aunt Victoria, as well. They had a near collision when Sophie rounded the corner.

Her aunt gasped and took a backward step. "Where are you off to in such a hurry?"

"Oh, Aunt Victoria, you startled me. I was going to look for Minnie."

"Whatever for? Isn't Veda looking after Elizabeth?"

"Yes, but I wanted to see if Minnie had time to alter one of my gowns. There's going to be a dance at the Frontenac Hotel on Saturday evening."

"I've heard nothing of a party. Did you receive an invitation?"

Sophie did her best to remain patient while she described the article in the paper. "I knew you'd approve since Mr. and Mrs. Oosterman are hosting the event."

Her aunt frowned. "I'm not certain you should be attending unescorted. I wonder if Andrew will be coming to see Beatrice and the children this weekend. If Beatrice wants to attend, you could accompany them."

The thought of Beatrice and Andrew acting as her chaperones

was enough to cause Sophie to rethink her plan. If she had to spend the evening under Beatrice's watchful eye, she didn't want to attend. "Wouldn't *you* like to go? Mrs. Oosterman will be disappointed if you don't attend, and you could act as my chaperone if you truly think I am in need of one. Since I'm now married, an escort shouldn't be required, but I'd be delighted to attend with you."

"Being married doesn't permit you to overlook the proper rules of etiquette, Sophie. I realize many of you young married women have decided you can attend formal gatherings without a proper escort. However, you'll find such behavior is still frowned upon." Her aunt looped arms with her. "Let's see what Minnie can do about altering your dress; then we'll decide upon the matter of an escort."

Escort, chaperone, someone to watch over her behavior— how was she to have any fun? Aunt Victoria wouldn't have blinked an eye if Beatrice had divulged plans to attend the dance without Andrew. Of course, Beatrice wouldn't want to attend the party with or without Andrew, especially if she knew that remaining at home would prevent Sophie from attending.

They discovered Minnie polishing silver in the dining room, and Sophie presented her idea. The maid shrugged while she continued to polish a silver platter. "Until I look at the seams and measure you, I can't say it will work. Even so, such refashioning will take time."

"Then let's be off," Sophie said. "I'll have Veda finish polishing the silver when Elizabeth wakens."

Once they'd arrived in Sophie's bedroom, Minnie made a cursory examination of the seams before Sophie wriggled into the dress. "Turn," Minnie commanded while she poked and prodded the fabric.

Her aunt maintained a watchful eye throughout the process.

While Sophie removed the dress, her aunt nudged Minnie. "What do you think? Can you make it work?"

"If her corset is tightly laced, it should fit. I could use lace overlays to hide the fact that the seams have been let out," Minnie suggested.

Sophie clapped her hands. "That is a wonderful idea, Minnie. You have saved my life."

"I don't believe refashioning a dress constitutes a life-saving event," her aunt said. "And there is still the matter of an escort."

"Do say you'll come with me, Aunt Victoria. You know Beatrice won't want to attend."

Her aunt tapped her fingers on the dresser. "I would enjoy visiting with the Oostermans. . . ."

"Then it's settled." Sophie hugged her aunt around the shoulders. "I can't thank you enough."

❖

*Saturday, May 13, 1899*

After numerous fittings and hours of stitching, Minnie completed the alterations to Sophie's satisfaction. "It looks lovely," her aunt remarked as the two of them descended the stairs Saturday evening. "No one would ever guess that your dress has been refashioned. You look absolutely lovely."

"I would think you'd consider it more important to remain here and care for Elizabeth than go off to a party without your husband," Beatrice said. She was sitting in the front parlor where she had a view of the staircase, obviously lying in wait.

Sophie forced a smile. "My daughter is being well cared for, and I don't believe I asked for your opinion. If you prefer to sit at home, I don't question your choice. I would appreciate the same courtesy."

"Marriage to a fine man and the birth of a healthy baby girl would be enough to satisfy most women, but you're never happy. You can't wait to go to the hotel ballroom and become the center of attention. What would Paul think of your behavior?"

Sophie clenched her hands into tight fists. "My behavior is beyond reproach. It's your evil thoughts that make this anything more than an evening with friends."

"I want the two of you to cease your bickering." Victoria pointed her fan toward Beatrice. "I would not escort your sister on this outing if I believed our attendance overstepped proper etiquette or protocol. Whether it was your intent or not, you've also insulted me, Beatrice."

Sophie grinned at her older sister as Beatrice hastened to offer an apology to their aunt. Though she had doubts, Sophie wondered if the reprimand would put an end to Beatrice's constant criticism.

"Is this the final menu for the weekend meals, Mrs. Broadmoor?" Mrs. Atwell asked as she hurried toward them waving a piece of paper in one hand.

While her aunt and Mrs. Atwell stepped aside, Beatrice drew near to Sophie. "You don't fool me, Sophie. You were an unruly child, and you've grown into an ill-behaved woman. Though you won't admit it, we both know your intentions aren't to sip punch and visit with the old dowagers. You plan to flirt with the men and pretend you're a young debutante."

"You have no idea what I plan to do this evening," Sophie hissed.

An evil glint shone in Beatrice's dark eyes. "Perhaps I shall spend my evening penning a letter to your husband. Does that prospect remove the smirk from your lips?"

"Do what you will, Beatrice. A letter to my husband doesn't concern me in the least." Sophie hoped the response sounded more assured than she felt, for there was no telling what Paul would think if he received such a letter from Beatrice.

She took a deep breath as she and her aunt walked onto the veranda and down the path to the boat. Let Beatrice write her letter if she wanted. Paul had insisted she come out here against her wishes. She'd pleaded to remain in Rochester; it was Paul who had pushed her away. She had wanted to stay by his side, not on this horrid island with nothing to do but miss him. Instead of honoring her wishes, he'd given her no say. She wanted a husband who would listen as well as talk, one who would truly consider her wishes before issuing ultimatums. Perhaps Paul needed to learn a lesson.

## 7

*Monday, May 15, 1899*
*Rochester, New York*

"Vincent! This is a surprise. I was beginning to wonder if you were ever going to meet with me. But I had hoped to meet in your office so that I could examine my files."

Mortimer's son patted his leather satchel and a box he'd placed on the floor. "They're right here. I apologize for the delay, but as I explained on several occasions, it was necessary for me to address issues with all of my father's clients."

"As his dear friend, client, and business associate, I think he would have wanted you to attend to *my* files first," Jonas said. "And wouldn't it have been easier for me to go there to review the contents?"

Vincent shook his head. "I've delivered your files to you because I have come to the conclusion that you need a lawyer who can devote a great deal of time to your legal matters—much more time than I can spare."

"Don't be ridiculous, Vincent. Your father was a much busier man than you, and he found ample time to represent my interests. Once you have a better understanding of my files and investments, you'll discover you can complete them with ease. I'll lend you the assistance you need to gain that understanding."

"That won't be necessary, Mr. Broadmoor. You see, I've conducted a cursory review of the files myself. It didn't take long to realize that you and my father went beyond the boundaries of the law in handling many of your business matters." Vincent reached into his leather satchel and withdrew a stack of files. "I can't be a part of this." The files landed on Jonas's desk with a dull thud.

Jonas massaged his forehead. "I don't know what you're talking about, Vincent. If your father and I hadn't been dear friends, I would throw you out of my office for making such an appalling accusation." Though his stomach roiled at Vincent's revelation, Jonas hoped the young lawyer would believe his feigned indignation and surprise. "How can you stand here and disparage your dear deceased father? What a disappointment you must be to the rest of your family."

"You need not concern yourself with how my family will react to this news, Mr. Broadmoor. You have more than enough right here to worry about." Vincent tapped the files. "Once you review these files as well as those in the box, you'll clearly understand why I have adopted this position."

Jonas leaned back in his chair, his mind suddenly reeling at what the files might contain. Surely Mortimer had followed his orders and burned all the incriminating documents. The man wouldn't have been foolish enough to retain records of their misdeeds. Mortimer knew any leak of their actions would ruin both their power and reputations among their peers—not to mention the possibility of criminal proceedings. Of course, Mortimer didn't need to worry about any of that now. But Jonas did. Fingers trembling, he reached across the desk and glanced at the folders.

"Put that box up on my desk," he commanded.

Vincent lifted the box and slid it across the desk. "I have other things that require my attention this morning." He picked up his coat and hat while Jonas riffled through the box of files.

"I don't see any files regarding my niece. Did you locate any files with the name Frances Jane Broadmoor?"

"Indeed, there were a number of files with her name. They have been delivered to her," Vincent replied. "Good day, Mr. Broadmoor."

Jonas didn't look up. There was little doubt Vincent would detect his fear. He wanted to flail the man for giving any of the files to Fanny, but he dared not object. Besides, it wouldn't change anything. The files were already in her possession.

He removed the files from the box. One by one he opened the folders, each one revealing far more information than the last. Information that Mortimer had been instructed to destroy. And what if Vincent had retained some of the incriminating records? How would Jonas know until it was too late? He couldn't recall even a portion of the paper work he had passed along to his lawyer. He could burn the records, but the thought gave Jonas no reassurance. Vincent could have shown the files to someone before turning them over.

He silently chastised himself. In spite of Vincent's protests, Jonas should have insisted upon retrieving his files the day Mortimer died. In his younger years, Jonas never would have permitted anyone to hold him at bay. Now he would suffer for his kindness. For that's what his agreement had been: a simple act of kindness. What a fool he'd become in his old age!

Strange how he'd believed that Mortimer had begun to lose his edge and bordered on senility. Under his façade of memory lapses, Mortimer had been intensely shrewd. There was little doubt he'd saved all these documents as insurance against any attempt at betrayal. The old man had safely maintained every record that could implicate Jonas and prove that he'd been the one to initiate the plan to use Fanny's money. *Use.* Jonas liked the word *use* much better than *steal* or *convert* or *embezzle.* *Use* didn't sound as though he'd intended any real harm to his niece or her assets. And if his financial hunches had been solid, her accounts wouldn't have suffered. At least that's what he told himself.

Now Mortimer was dead, and Jonas was left to wrestle through this treachery. He would be the one who would suffer the loss of reputation, power, and money. Well, he wouldn't give up easily. The Broadmoors weren't among those who had only recently become rich. They were old money. That fact alone granted immense power and prestige. Power and prestige that Jonas wouldn't relinquish—no matter the cost.

For now, he must direct his attention to Fanny and those records Vincent had given her. How much did those files contain, and did she go through them? Surely Mortimer had heeded the instructions to destroy those incriminating records. But given what he'd found thus far, his doubts continued to rise. If Fanny had discovered his less-than-legitimate handling of her affairs, he needed the assurance of available cash to set things aright. Or at least to appease her until he could develop some story to convince her that none of this had been his doing. He yanked his coat from the chair where he'd tossed it earlier that morning. A visit with Jonathan Canby at the Profit Loan Association bank was in order.

Jonas wasn't going to beg, but he'd certainly remind Jonathan of the loyalty and preference he'd given his bank since it had opened its doors for business. Had it not been for Jonas, their father would have never considered moving his accounts from the Rochester Savings Bank. Jonas had argued at great length with his father, but he'd finally won his confidence. When his father had made the change, many of his business associates eventually followed. Once the transfers had been completed, Jonathan had shown his appreciation with any number of loans at lowered interest rates or without proper security. Of late, the banker hadn't been as agreeable when Jonas had requested financial aid. There was no way to know whether Jonathan would be amenable to this request. But Jonas was prepared to remind the banker of past favors. He had no choice. He needed help, a fact he didn't like to admit, even to himself.

Head bowed against a stiff wind, Jonas didn't notice the bulky white-thatched man until they collided near the front door of the bank. He mumbled a quick apology, but the thick fingers digging into his upper arms caused him to look up and twist away from the hold.

"Jonas! It *is* you, isn't it? Jonas Broadmoor. How long has it been?"

Jonas stared into the intense blue eyes for a moment before realization slowly washed over him. "Ellert Jackson. Where did you come from?"

Ellert clapped him on the back and, with a hearty laugh, pointed over his shoulder. "The hotel. I'm here for only a few more hours. I was going to have lunch at the men's club. Do you have time to join me?"

"Of course, of course," Jonas replied. "I was going to take

care of some banking business, but it can wait. Friends are more important than work."

Ellert gave him a sideways glance. "Since when?" He guffawed and nudged Jonas in the ribs. "If you've changed that much, it may take more than one lunch to hear what's been happening in your life."

From time to time Jonas had heard mention of Ellert's continued success in New York City, but the two men hadn't seen each other in years. While living in Rochester, Ellert and Jonas had invested in several of the same business enterprises, though they'd never been close friends. Ellert had never been accepted in fashionable social circles. He'd belonged to the gentlemen's club, of course, but his name failed to be included on the Rochester social register. When Ellert later joined forces with some foreign investors and moved to New York City, the two men lost contact. Some years ago Victoria had mentioned reading an obituary for Ellert's wife. Or had one of his wife's gossipy friends mentioned the death? He couldn't remember, but he did recall there had been no children born to the union. Jonas had expected Ellert to meet with failure and return home, but that hadn't occurred.

They walked side by side the short distance to the club. "It appears life has treated you well in spite of the country's bleak economy," Jonas said.

Ellert smiled and nodded. "I can't complain. Life has been good since moving to New York City."

Ellert's words seeped into Jonas's consciousness like a soothing balm. His old acquaintance who could access financial resources had appeared after years of absence. Was this simply a fortuitous encounter, or was God looking out for him? Jonas smiled at the thought. Even though he attended church services on Sunday mornings, it had been a long time since he'd truly considered the possibility that God might be interested in his life.

❋

Mr. Rosenblume welcomed Fanny with a kind smile. Perhaps because he had been her grandfather's trusted lawyer for years, Fanny felt a sense of comfort whenever she entered his office. He escorted her to the library table, where he'd arranged papers for her review.

Fanny handed him the private files he'd given her at their last meeting. "I thought I should bring these back to you for safekeeping."

He nodded and accepted the folders from her, setting them aside. "It is probably for the best. I hope the information was useful to you." He offered her a seat. "I wanted to go over a few details regarding the purchase of your grandparents' home."

Fanny's pulse quickened as she settled into one of the leather chairs. "So I still have an opportunity to purchase it?"

The old lawyer nodded.

"I was afraid my uncle had located a buyer and hadn't passed along the details to Mr. Fillmore." She clasped her palm to her bodice. "I can't begin to tell you my relief."

"I've been using another party, one I trust, as an intermediary in this transaction. I don't want to tip our hand and have Jonas discover you're involved. I've been told that your uncle is desperate for a quick sale. He's apparently in need of cash, but real estate sales are nearly nonexistent at this time. To my knowledge he's not had any offers. We can't be absolutely certain, but I believe that if we offer him less than the asking price, he'll accept out of desperation."

This talk of finances and sales gave rise to an important question. "Have you examined the records closely enough to know if there are any funds maintained solely in my name? I'd prefer to pay for the house myself rather than rely upon your personal funds."

"I haven't visited the bank, as I didn't want to alert Jonas. However, in going through the papers, it appears there are some funds that he hasn't attached." The lawyer tugged at his starched collar. "But I fear if you attempt to withdraw any of it, the bank will notify your uncle. Since you've never before attempted to access your inheritance, the bank would feel obligated to make an inquiry."

"Even though I've attained legal age?"

The lawyer offered a sympathetic nod. "You've never notified the bank to withdraw his authority to act as your representative, have you?"

"No," Fanny murmured. Mr. Rosenblume was likely correct. The bank officers wouldn't permit her to withdraw money without notifying her uncle. "If you pay for the house from your own funds, how can my name be placed on the deed?"

"If you trust me, I have a proposal for you."

Fanny gave the old lawyer her full attention. "I'm willing to listen to any idea you have."

"The intermediary will act as our agent to purchase the house. Jonas will be told that the purchaser wishes to remain anonymous. He won't care, as long as he gets his money," Mr. Rosenblume explained. "I will pay for the house. You and I will enter into a contract. Once we manage to release any of your inheritance that your uncle hasn't converted to his own use, you can reimburse me and the house will be yours."

"But what if there isn't enough . . . ?" She couldn't bring herself to say the words.

Mr. Rosenblume patted her hand. "There will be enough.

From all appearances he didn't commingle all of the funds. He and Mr. Fillmore had a fairly detailed plan."

"So you've completed your review of the files?"

"All but a stack of personal notes. Still, additional time will be needed to complete my findings." He retrieved a stack of papers and pushed them toward Fanny. "If you have time, you could review these in the adjacent office before you leave."

"Of course." She followed Mr. Rosenblume into a small office that adjoined his. She wondered if this was where he escaped when he didn't want to be bothered by the worries of the world. Though the room contained a small desk, it was the overstuffed brocade chair that captured Fanny's attention. Situated alongside a large window that offered excellent light, it provided a perfect place to read a book. She strode toward the chair. "I believe I'll sit here."

"An excellent choice." He padded back across the thick carpet, and a click of the door announced his departure.

Fanny settled into the chair, the bright rays of afternoon sun warming her as she sifted through the papers. An ivory envelope with a gold and blue seal in the corner captured her attention. Holding the corner between her finger and thumb, she gently pulled it from the center of the stack. The envelope was addressed to her uncle Jonas, but one glance revealed the fact that it was from the medical school where Amanda had applied for training. She withdrew the letter and scanned the contents.

"How *could* he?" She tried to grasp the full impact of what she'd read. Her uncle had bargained with the president of the school and had gotten what he wanted. In return for a letter rejecting Amanda's admittance, Uncle Jonas had donated money. Lies and betrayal. Was there no end to what the man would do in order to have his way? In spite of the sun's warmth, an unexpected shiver coursed through her body. She tucked the letter into her skirt pocket and hurried out of the room.

Mr. Rosenblume looked up from his desk. "Done so soon?"

"I'm suddenly not feeling well and believe I had best go home and rest. I'll finish going through the papers tomorrow or the next day."

He pushed to his feet and came to her side. "You are pale, my dear. I'll have my driver bring the carriage around and take you home."

She apologized for her early departure, thanked Mr. Rosenblume for the use of his carriage, and bid him good-bye. Her thoughts raced in circles during the ride home. Even though Uncle Jonas had voiced his disapproval of Amanda's medical training, Fanny had never considered he would go to such lengths. And if he would commit such an odious act against his own daughter, how much more might he do to her?

❖

Jonas paced in front of the library fireplace considering where his niece might be. No one seemed to know where Fanny had gone. Neither her personal maid nor the cook could offer a scrap of information. He'd used the last hour to advantage and searched her room, but to no avail. Either she'd hidden the files somewhere else in the house, or she'd taken them and gone in search of a lawyer. It was the latter thought that caused his head to ache. If those files contained incriminating information, his life would be ruined. He attempted to calm himself with the thought that she wouldn't be interested in the contents of the files. Or that a woman wouldn't understand what they contained.

The familiar click of footsteps on the hallway tile brought

his pacing to an immediate halt. Fanny was home. He hurried out of the room. Had his niece not stopped midstep, they would have collided. "I'm sorry. I didn't realize you were right outside my door." Her complexion was pale. "Where have you been, my dear? You don't look well."

"Since when have you concerned yourself over my health, Uncle Jonas?"

He took a backward step. Clearly, she was upset—and suspicious. If he was going to gain any information, he needed to adopt his usual attitude or she'd become even more guarded. "Vincent Fillmore mentioned that he had given you some files regarding your grandfather's estate. Poor fellow is simply too busy with his other work to handle anything as large as the Broadmoor estate." He straightened his shoulders and hoped he was exuding an air of confidence. "And now he's burdened you with a portion of the files. I'm uncertain of his reasoning, but I wanted to assure you that you can depend upon me to continue handling all matters regarding your inheritance."

"Truly?" She folded her arms across her chest.

"Indeed. Why don't you tell me where you've stored the files, and I'll see to them this very minute."

"That won't be necessary, Uncle Jonas. I have already employed a lawyer. Mr. Rosenblume has agreed to act as my legal representative and ease me of the *burden*."

His stomach clenched in a tight knot. Under any other circumstance, he would have been tempted to throttle the girl. But not now—not today. He must maintain his decorum and continue to try to win her over. "Mr. Rosenblume will understand if you advise him you've changed your mind. Women are permitted that concession."

"I feel quite confident that Mr. Rosenblume will be a perfect representative for my interests. After all, Grandfather thought him to be the best lawyer in all of Rochester."

She flashed a smile, though her complexion remained pale. How much did she know, he wondered. "In that case, I'd be more than willing to deliver the files to Mr. Rosenblume. I can drop them off tomorrow morning."

"That won't be necessary. They're already in his office."

His head throbbed as she headed off toward the kitchen without a backward glance. He touched his fingers to his temples. This encounter had not gone at all as he had hoped. If he didn't devise a plan, his life would be a shambles. While Mortimer lay cold in his grave, Jonas could be prosecuted for their criminal actions. To the world it would appear otherwise, but Jonas decided he had drawn the short straw. Death would have been easier than facing disgrace.

He dropped into his chair and continued to massage his temples while misery threatened a tighter hold. "I'm alone, with no one who would understand," he whispered.

Had his brother Langley felt this same sense of despair and loneliness during the ten years following Winifred's death? Had the possibility of a future filled with pain and solitude provided the impetus for Langley to take his own life? A vision of his brother slumped beneath a tree on Broadmoor Island flashed through his mind. When Jonas had arrived on the scene that day, he'd discovered the empty bottle of laudanum and a grief-stricken young Fanny. Jonas had thought Langley a coward—a man afraid to face life. Now he wondered if he might sink to that same depth of hopelessness.

"No," he muttered, silently vowing to save himself at all cost.

❖

Ellert hadn't planned to see Jonas Broadmoor. In fact, he hadn't thought about him in years. Even his journey back to Rochester hadn't brought his former acquaintance to mind. Had they not run into each other outside the bank, Ellert would have left town that same afternoon. Jonas hadn't been himself during their luncheon. At first Ellert thought it simply the span of time between visits. But as their conversation continued, he knew there was more to it. His years of dealing with shrewd businessmen had instilled an ability to know when something was amiss, and something was very wrong with Jonas Broadmoor.

It hadn't taken much time or effort to discover that Jonas had recently suffered some significant financial losses, although he managed to keep the details to himself. The most Ellert could gather was vague information about Jonas's investments. Since the entire country was suffering through a financial downturn, perhaps that was the sum total of his old acquaintance's problem. But Ellert sensed there was something more than bad investments. Jonas had been far too careful with his answers during lunch. And although Jonas had alluded to the possibility of needing to locate financial backing, Ellert hadn't responded. First, he'd wanted to conduct his own research.

The two men had parted outside the men's club, but Ellert returned a short time later. Discovering exactly what had happened with Jonas's finances had proved a costly endeavor. Ellert had crossed the palms of more greedy men than he cared to recall, but the end result had been worth the effort—and the money. Mortimer's clerk had been easily persuaded. On the other hand, Judge Webster had turned out to be the most difficult piece of the puzzle—and the most expensive. But in the end Ellert had succeeded. Money spoke volumes to men at the top of the ladder, and even more so to those like Judge Webster, who teetered near the bottom rung with only a powerful position to make him acceptable. The judge had upped the ante, and Ellert had complied. The information he'd gained had been more than he could have ever hoped for—enough to bring Jonas Broadmoor to his knees.

A feeling of self-satisfaction washed over him. He would be more than pleased to speak with Jonas about a loan or investment. After the many social snubs he'd endured from the entire Broadmoor family, nothing would give him more satisfaction than to bring Jonas to ruin. There had also been the incident when Ellert had wanted to invest in a silver mine. He'd attempted to secure a loan through every means possible before he'd gone to Jonas Broadmoor. After a great deal of cajoling, Jonas had finally agreed—but at a huge cost to Ellert. He had repaid the loan and the exorbitant interest, but Jonas never knew that it was the silver mine that had set Ellert on his path toward financial security.

He raked his fingers through his thick white hair. Indeed, he would be very pleased to offer Jonas help in his time of need—the same way Jonas had helped him—at a very dear price.

8

*Friday, May 19, 1899*

"What are you doing out of bed?"

Amanda whirled around. Seized by a bout of dizziness, she dropped to the side of the bed. "You startled me!" She pressed her fingertips to her temples in a futile attempt to ward off the sickening feeling. Would she never regain her strength?

While the room continued to swirl in a tilting motion, Blake drew near. "What must I do? Shall I be forced to tie you to that bed in order to keep you there?"

"Don't you dare think such a thing!" She shouldn't have shouted. The dizziness returned with a vengeance, and she was forced to lie back on her pillow. Exactly what Blake wanted. He stood peering down at her. "Are you happy now?" she whispered.

"I'm not pleased if you're feeling worse, but it's good to see you back in bed." He placed his palm across her forehead. "No fever. That's good."

"I know I don't have a fever. And I wouldn't have experienced the dizziness if you hadn't startled me."

He chuckled. "So my voice alone is enough to cause you to swoon. Is that what you're saying, Miss Broadmoor?"

"I didn't *swoon*. I am not one of those young women who swoon in order to gain a man's attention. And I see no reason why I must remain abed. Only yesterday you said I was much improved. Can I not trust your medical opinion, Dr. Carstead?"

"I'm ashamed of you, Miss Broadmoor. You are twisting my words in order to achieve what you want. However, your little game is not going to work. I said you were coming along nicely. I did *not* say you could or should be out of bed."

Now that she was lying down, the dizziness had subsided, and she continued to wage her argument. "You obviously need my help. Do you not think I know how many patients are in those adjoining rooms? Uncle Quincy is worn to a frazzle, and you look like you haven't slept or taken a razor to your face in days," she said, pointing at the several days' growth that covered his jawline. Though she'd never reveal such a thought, Amanda found his unshaven appearance somewhat appealing. "I am bored with nothing to do but stare at the paint chipping from the ceiling."

Blake looked up and then grinned. "The ceiling does appear to need some repair, doesn't it? I'll mention that to your uncle. I'm certain he'll want to have it repainted once—"

"Don't attempt to turn this conversation into a discussion of building repairs. We are discussing the fact that I am well enough to help you with the patients."

"You are having a memory lapse, my dear. We were discussing the fact that you need to remain in bed."

*My dear?* Had she heard him correctly? She'd not mentioned the memory that had lingered since the turning point in her recovery when she'd rallied and been awake for nearly five minutes. Even now the picture of Blake sitting at her beside and declaring his love remained vivid. As she'd continued her period of recuperation, she'd thought the memory genuine. During those first days, Blake had been nothing but attentive and kind. But as she had continued to gain strength, he'd been provoking her at every turn. The remembrance of his declaration couldn't be real. If he loved her, he wouldn't be such a disagreeable boor now.

She could only assume that the words *my dear* had been nothing more than a calculated plan. Clearly he hoped she would embrace his decision. Well, it would take more than a few words of endearment to convince her that she should remain abed while others suffered without proper care. "I suggest we strike a bargain. If I am able to carry out my normal duties for the remainder of the day, then you will admit that I am well and permit my return to work. I assume you will prove you have confidence in your medical opinion by agreeing to my terms." She pushed herself upright and held her breath. Her words had been full of false bravado. She could only hope he would take the bait she'd dangled in front of him.

"I'm not one to pass up a wager so easily won." He gestured for her to remain still a moment longer. "Your duties will be what I assign. I don't want you fainting atop one of the patients."

"I see. You plan to wear me down scrubbing floors and emptying pails of—"

"I will not assign any duties you didn't perform before you contracted cholera. Do you still wish to bargain with me?"

"Indeed." A quick nod created another wave of dizziness, but she forced herself to remain upright and smile. If she was to win this contest of wills, she must remember to make all movements in a slow and determined fashion.

"Come along, then. And remember that when I win this wager, you must follow my orders without question. I have a great need for bandages. You can tear and roll the old sheets in between your other duties. Fortunately for you, the sheets have already been laundered." His lopsided grin was enough to lend added resolve.

"If they weren't, I'm sure I could accomplish the task," she countered.

His hazel eyes sparkled from beneath thick dark brows. "Then you should have no difficulty preparing the necessary medicines for my patients. You may place the individual doses on the trays, and I'll deliver them. Don't hesitate to call me if you have any questions or need any assistance."

The patronizing offer set her teeth on edge, but Amanda resisted the urge to tell him so. He might withdraw his proposition and send her back to bed. Blake followed her into the small room adjacent to his office and pointed at the cabinet lined with jars of medicinal remedies. She opened one of the glass doors and peered inside. There was little evidence of powders or liquids in the bottles. "How could you permit the supply to fall so low? I trust we'll receive more today."

"Let me refresh your memory, Amanda. There has been sickness throughout the city. Even though the entire city has not been placed on quarantine, many people fear doing business in Rochester. Supplies of every variety are in high demand. I have placed orders with all three pharmacies. They bring what they have to the front gate."

"Then I suppose we must make do." She looked about the small room. "Where is the chair?"

"In the women's quarters. We're housing more people than usual, and they had need of additional seating." He narrowed his eyes. "Are you feeling too weak to stand and complete the task?"

"Not at all. I was merely inquiring." She waved him from the room. "I don't require supervision."

He returned to his office but reappeared minutes later with a small brass bell. "Ring this if you need me." The clapper bounced against the bell with a soft *clunk* when he set it on the table. "Don't let your pride get in the way of your good sense, Amanda."

Before she could reply, he strode out of the room. She heard his soft footfalls on the carpet and then the louder click of his shoes on the wooden floor of the hallway. She peeked into his office to make certain he was gone before she scanned the room for a chair. Blake's large chair remained, but she couldn't possibly move it from behind the desk and through the small entrance to the adjacent room.

After reading the names of the patients and the list of medications, she began the process. She placed the powders on tiny squares of paper until only two names remained. The jar of medicine she needed was nowhere to be found. Could Blake have used the last and forgotten? Resting her hands on her hips, she stepped back and surveyed the cabinet one final time. *There!* On the bottom shelf at the very back, a dark blue bottle—exactly what she'd been searching for.

Bending at the waist, she leaned forward and immediately knew she'd made a mistake. "I should have crouched down instead," she whispered as she lunged for the brass bell.

The bell was the last thing she remembered until she forced

her eyes open to stare into Blake's frowning face. "You are a stubborn woman, Amanda Broadmoor. Why didn't you ring the bell?"

"I couldn't reach it," she whispered.

He gently lifted her into his arms and carried her back to bed. "I believe we had an agreement. You will remain here until I declare you well enough to be up and about."

"But what am I to do? Can you not understand my boredom?" Thoughts of Sophie during her months of confinement came to mind. No wonder she had complained so arduously about remaining abed for all that time. "At least bring me something to read and some paper so that I may write to my family."

"If all of my patients were as demanding as you, I'd accomplish very little," he called over his shoulder as he strode back toward his office.

Moments later he returned with an article he'd clipped from a medical journal. "Read this. I found it quite interesting."

"This won't keep me busy for long," she grumbled.

He ignored her complaint, not even offering so much as a good-bye before leaving the room.

She propped herself up in bed, slapped the article on the small table beside her bed, and stared across the room. She must regain her strength and get out of this bed or she'd go mad.

"What's this I hear about my niece being a difficult patient?" Her uncle entered the room carrying a tray laden with two plates and two cups. "I thought a bit of company while you ate your lunch might be in order."

"I would be delighted to have lunch with you. I am starving for both food and civil conversation."

Quincy laughed and set the tray atop the small table. "Are you implying that Dr. Carstead is boring?"

"He does nothing but issue the same orders over and over. I'm to remain in bed until he deems me fit to return to my duties. Surely you would agree I'm strong enough to be of some help around here."

"I'm not a physician, so I can't offer any opinion about your recovery, but I can offer you some chicken and dumplings that smell quite delectable." He handed her a napkin. "I thought you might be interested in hearing about the family. Your father received a letter from your mother, and it seems all is going well at the island. She included this note for you." He handed her the paper, and she tucked it under her pillow.

"I'll read it after I finish my lunch." Amanda swallowed a bite of chicken and sighed with approval. "This is as good as it smells." She poured a cup of tea for each of them. "Has Sophie adjusted to being on the island without Fanny or me? I'm certain she must be lonely."

He patted her arm. "She knows it's best for Elizabeth that they remain out of the city, and I imagine caring for the baby fills most of her waking hours. Your mother mentioned some of the other families have also escaped to the islands."

"Others who live in Rochester?"

"Yes, but also families from other cities. I think most of them thought it prudent to escape earlier than usual, although I think the idea rather silly. Mr. and Mrs. Oosterman are there and have already hosted a gathering at the Frontenac Hotel."

Amanda ate the final bite of her lunch and wiped her mouth. "I can't say I'm surprised. Mrs. Oosterman wouldn't be happy without some sort of soirée where she can gather the latest gossip."

"That seems a bit harsh. I think she's lonely when she's in the islands, and social gatherings are her way of helping pass the time."

Amanda didn't argue. Let her uncle think what he would. But he wouldn't convince her that Mrs. Oosterman simply wanted to while away the hours. As far as Amanda was concerned, Mrs. Oosterman had more interest in the lives of others than in her own.

Her uncle returned her plate and utensils to the tray. "I could bring you some writing paper and a pen if you'd like to post a letter to Sophie. I'm certain she'd enjoy hearing from you, and it would help pass the time."

She nodded. "I asked Dr. Carstead to bring me writing supplies, but he hasn't done so. I would be most appreciative."

He kissed her cheek, and after a promise to return with paper and pen later in the day, he left. She withdrew her mother's letter from beneath her pillow and perused the contents. Except for a few additional details regarding the Oostermans' party, there was little more than what Uncle Quincy had related. She tucked the letter back into the envelope. Now what?

She folded her arms across her chest and then remembered the article Blake had given her a short time ago. She took it from the bedside table and read the headline. *Infant Mortality Rate Approaches Twenty-Five Percent in Largest Cities in the United States.* Amanda immediately considered little Elizabeth and was thankful Sophie had taken her to Broadmoor Island. The article commended some progress where tent cities had been erected for infants during the summer months.

Amanda was familiar with the concept. Though she'd never visited any of the facilities, she'd heard about the Infant Summer Hospital near Rochester. It had been established along the shores of Lake Ontario several years ago. The doctors professed that lake breezes blowing through the tent community were believed to be healthful for the babies during the hot summer months. They also quoted statistics showing a reduced number of deaths among those children afforded the opportunity to spend their days in such an environment.

She was nearing the end of the article when Blake arrived and dropped a stack of books, newspapers, and magazines onto her bed. "What's all of this? Do you expect me to complete a research project?"

"You said the article wouldn't occupy you for long, so I located a few more items to keep you busy for the remainder of the day."

"Are they all medical books? If so, you may find I'm more knowledgeable than you by the time I return to my duties."

He reached for one of the publications and held up a copy of the *Delineator*. "I believe this should keep you from learning enough to take over my medical practice."

"Did you wish to discuss the article regarding the Infant Summer Hospital?"

He shook his head. "I haven't time to stay."

"I'm willing to help you," she called after him, but he didn't acknowledge her offer. At least now she had some excellent reading material to help pass the time.

She finished reading the article on the Infant Summer Hospital and then thumbed through the newspapers. She wondered where Blake had found such a variety. Surely he didn't subscribe to all these newspapers. Many of them were several months old, but she continued her quick review. Out-of-date news was better than no news at all. She snapped open a copy of the *New York Journal* and turned to the social columns. She scanned the page but stopped short when she saw Wesley Hedrick's name.

The article stated that Wesley Hedrick had been the host at a number of grand parties attended by many dignitaries. Wesley was described as the sole beneficiary of Lord and Lady Illiff, who had been lost at sea when their ship went down off the coast of France. The newspaper fluttered to her lap. How could this be possible? The man who had fathered Sophie's child and then run off like a thief in the night had inherited a vast fortune and was dividing his time between London and New York City.

What if he should decide to reenter Sophie's life? Surely he wouldn't do such a thing. He'd have far too much to explain. Should she tell Sophie? Would it be best to prepare her cousin for such a happenstance, or would such a revelation only open old wounds and create more pain? She considered writing Fanny to seek her advice, but there was the possibility the letter would be seen by someone other than Fanny. She best not take such a chance. If only they would lift the quarantine, she could talk with Fanny. Together they could come to a sound decision. She looked to the bedside table for scissors but seeing none decided to simply tear the article from the paper. It might come in handy later when she tried to explain her concerns.

Fanny stood outside the gate at the Home for the Friendless and pulled the rope attached to the metal bell. She hoped the noise wouldn't disturb any patients who might be resting. Her uncle waved from the doorway and then hurried down the path to greet her. "Fanny!" he said, stopping a few feet from her. "I do hope you've brought some of the supplies from the pharmacy."

She nodded and set the basket down in front of her. "Yes, but not the amount requested by Dr. Carstead. The pharmacist said to tell him that he's running low on supplies but expects another shipment next week."

"Next week? Some of our patients can't wait that long.

Perhaps Paul could take the train to Syracuse. Surely he could purchase drugs at one of the pharmacies there."

"I'll give him your message and tell him it's important he leave as soon as possible." She dug her toe in the dirt. "I brought these things for Amanda. There's also a note for her," she added.

"Why so downcast? Is something amiss?"

"Nothing that can be easily remedied, and nothing that I can't learn to accept, I suppose."

Her uncle frowned. "Are you ill?"

"No, but I do feel pain."

"What kind of pain? In your stomach? You should see a doctor immediately. We don't want you coming down with cholera."

She shook her head. "My pain isn't caused by illness. Have you ever felt betrayed by someone you care about? Someone you trusted and thought loved you and cared for you?"

"Does this have something to do with Michael? Has he written and said he no longer intends to marry you?"

Tears welled in her eyes. "No. I haven't had a letter from Michael in months."

"Tell me what's happened, Fanny. I'll help in any way I can."

She longed to tell him that Uncle Jonas had betrayed her trust and deceived Amanda. Yet she didn't want to be the cause of another rift between the two brothers. There had been enough harsh words among family members in the past. Better to remain silent than say something that couldn't be taken back. What was the Bible verse that Michael's mother had quoted to her? It was from Proverbs. Something about the tongue and power. "The tongue has the power of life and death, and they that love it will eat the fruit," she muttered.

That was close, anyway. Better to keep Uncle Jonas's name out of the conversation. "I'm simply disappointed because someone I thought I could trust has let me down."

His brow furrowed. "What has Jonas done now?"

## 9

*Monday, June 12, 1899*

Amanda folded her hands in her lap. "This is entirely unfair. My parents can't continue to order me from pillar to post because it suits their whims. I'm no longer a child."

"They are doing what they believe is best for your full recovery. Besides, it's June and the weather is quite lovely. In times past we would already be at the island for our annual summer stay. And when your mother departed, I promised I would escort you to the island." Fanny had been trying to reason with her cousin for well over an hour before Dr. Carstead and Uncle Quincy joined them.

"In the future, you should refrain from making promises you can't keep." Amanda tightened her lips into a sullen pout.

After more than six weeks the quarantine had finally been

lifted the preceding day. Immediately after breakfast Fanny had arrived at the Home and announced she planned to escort Amanda to Broadmoor Island. Amanda had promptly refused. She planned to remain in Rochester and work at the Home. Though their train would leave the station in only two hours, Amanda continued to wage a battle.

"Tell my cousin that I am needed here to assist you with your duties," Amanda said, waving Blake forward.

"I'll do no such thing. I plan to escort you to the train station and make certain you board the train." He sat down in a vacant chair beside her. "In fact, I'm going to wait until the train leaves the station to make sure you don't attempt an escape."

His chuckle didn't ward off her feelings of betrayal. How *could* he? Until stricken with cholera, she'd worked alongside him without complaint. There had been days when her back ached and she longed for a few minutes' rest, but she'd continued to do his bidding. Now he sided against her. "So this is my reward? What did my father promise you in order to gain your complicity in this plan?"

Blake's jaw twitched. "I have not had contact with your father, and I have not sided against you. But I am intent upon seeing you attain a full recovery."

"I *am* well. Why don't you offer me that wager again, and we shall see who will win this time?"

He shook his head. "That kind of talk is exactly why you must leave Rochester. If you stayed here, you'd work too hard. No matter what you say, I will not change my mind."

"You don't control me, Blake Carstead. If I want to remain in Rochester, you can't force me to go to Broadmoor Island."

He shrugged. "You're right. But if you don't go, I'll no longer teach you. If you want to continue with your medical career, you'll have to enroll in medical college or find another physician willing to train you."

Amanda extended her neck. "Do you have a collar and leash you'd like to place around my neck so you may control my every step?"

Fanny nudged Amanda and shook her head. "What has come over you?"

"Nothing has come over me. I'm simply weary of others controlling my life."

Blake leaned forward and rested his forearms across his thighs. "You're exaggerating in an attempt to gain a toehold in this argument. You know that your plans to remain in Rochester are faulty." Blake raked his fingers through his unruly dark hair. "I don't want to part on unpleasant terms. Surely you know that my concern for you is well founded and has nothing to do with any edict you've received from your parents. You have my word that you can continue your training with me once your family returns. I hope you'll get plenty of rest and avail yourself of the fresh air."

"I'll have little choice, will I?" Her behavior was no better than that of a petulant child, but Amanda didn't care. "And we'll see whether I'm still interested in working with you when I return." She shrugged her shoulders. "I may very well decide to move to Syracuse or New York City. I'm certain I'll find a physician who will be pleased to continue my training there."

"Please give that matter considerable thought, Amanda." He stood and held out his hand. "I believe we should be on our way. I assume you'd like to stop at home and put some things in a trunk before we head to the depot."

Amanda huffed but took his hand nevertheless.

"We'd better make haste. I don't want you ladies to miss your train."

❖

Throughout the ride to the train station, Amanda stared out the carriage window. Fanny and Blake discussed the cathartic effect the fresh air at Broadmoor Island would have upon Amanda during the next weeks, but she steadfastly ignored their conversation. Let them attempt to win her over by expounding upon the beneficial and invigorating effects she would experience while languishing in the fresh air and strolling along the St. Lawrence River—she'd not be swayed by their talk.

Blake didn't budge from the strategy he'd laid out to her. He accompanied them through the station and out the heavy wooden door that led to the platform. "Once Amanda ceases her pouting, you might ask her to tell you about the healing effects of fresh air upon infants who have been transported to live near the water during the heat of summer. She read a lengthy article on the topic, didn't you, Amanda?"

Amanda decided against breaking her silence, but she did offer a slight nod.

Fanny grasped her arm. "Oh, I do hope you'll tell me all about what you've learned. It sounds fascinating."

The hissing and clanging of the arriving train mixed with shouts from the porters, crying children, and passengers bidding their loved ones farewell. Amanda was thankful the noise prevented further conversation. While Blake assisted Fanny up the steps to the train, Amanda stared longingly at the door leading back inside the station. She could make a run for it—but to where and for what purpose? She'd still be unable to tend to the ill. Blake would make certain of that. No need to dwell on thoughts of escape.

"Come along, Amanda," Blake said.

The toe of her shoe caught on a heavy baggage cart as

she stepped toward the train. Like a bird attempting to take flight, her arms spread and flapped while she lunged to gain her footing.

Blake charged toward her and captured her in his arms. "Are you all right?" His dark hazel eyes glistened with concern.

Her pulse quickened as she stared into his eyes. "I th-think so," she stammered.

He pulled her close to his chest. "I was so worried. I thought you were going to fall and injure yourself."

She took a backward step. "Did you worry for my safety, or was your concern that if I suffered injury you wouldn't be able to send me off to Broadmoor Island?"

His eyes turned darker. "Think what you will, Amanda. Whether you wish to believe me or not, my concern is for your welfare."

"Are you injured, Amanda?" Concern edged Fanny's voice.

Her cousin's words were enough to bring her back to the present. One glance at his hands resting on her hips was enough for Blake to release his hold. He escorted her to the train and bid her a formal good-bye. As promised, he waited on the platform while their train departed the station.

Once the train had begun to gain speed, Fanny nudged her. "I believe Dr. Carstead cares for you."

"I had thought the same thing. But what man who truly cares does everything in his power to rid himself of the woman he loves?" Amanda settled against the dark green upholstered seat. "Now let us speak of something else. I don't wish to dwell upon Dr. Carstead."

"As you wish, but I'm not convinced you're correct." Fanny adjusted her skirts around her. "Do tell me about the report you read on the infant hospitals."

At Fanny's mention of the article, Amanda's thoughts returned to the piece she'd seen in the paper regarding Wesley Hedrick. "I'll tell you about the summer hospitals later. First I must tell you about something else I read while I was in confinement." She reached into her reticule and handed the now neatly trimmed piece of newspaper to Fanny.

Fanny quickly scanned the piece and looked up in disbelief. "Instead of simply a ne'er-do-well, Wesley has become a wealthy ne'er-do-well. I cannot imagine why Lord and Lady Illiff would leave their vast fortune to the likes of Wesley Hedrick." She handed the article back to Amanda.

Amanda shrugged and slipped the paper between the pages of a book she'd brought along. "They had no other family."

"He wasn't a blood relative. I'm not certain he was married to Lady Illiff's cousin for more than a few years before she died. I would think they could have found someone more deserving of their wealth. A charity would have been a better choice. I can only imagine the women who must be flocking around him."

"Like hens scratching for feed." Amanda giggled, then stopped short and clapped her hand to her lips. "I shouldn't be making light of the situation, for this bit of news could upset Sophie. What if someone should read the news and mention it to her? I have been weighing whether to tell her since the day I picked up that newspaper. What do you think?"

"I don't believe it would serve any good purpose to tell her. And few people were acquainted with Wesley."

"Few people? Do you forget that Uncle Quincy announced at the Home for the Friendless fund-raising event that Wesley had pledged a huge donation? I would think those who attended would remember his name."

"You give the local gossips far too much credit, Amanda.

They would have discovered more recent fodder long ago."
Fanny tapped her finger on the armrest. "On the other hand,
a wealthy eligible man does stir up a great deal of interest. How
long ago was the piece in the newspaper?"

"I don't remember the exact date, but all the out-of-town
papers were at least three months old."

Fanny gave an affirmative nod. "You see? No one gave notice
to the news. If anyone had remembered Wesley, we would have
heard something by now. I don't think we should mention any
of this to Sophie. Wesley is but a bad memory in her life."

"I suppose you're correct, but Uncle Quincy told me Mr.
and Mrs. Oosterman have arrived at the islands. And you know
Mrs. Oosterman doesn't forget even the tiniest morsel of information. What if she's heard something? I would rather Sophie
hear the news from us than from someone such as Mrs. Oosterman." Amanda scooted sideways in her seat. "And what if
Sophie should discover we knew and didn't tell her. Would she
think we'd betrayed her?"

"You worry overmuch about something that isn't likely to
occur. Even if she should find out, Sophie would understand
our reticence to tell her. She would know our decision was made
with her best interests in mind. Unlike others, the three of us
would never intentionally hurt one another." Fanny turned and
stared out the train window.

"I suppose you're correct," Amanda replied.

Her cousin appeared lost in thought. Amanda studied Fanny
and decided that she hadn't been herself since they'd boarded
the train. No. It was before that. Even back when Fanny had
first arrived at the Home, she hadn't had much to say. Not that
she'd been rude. Fanny would never be impolite. But she'd barely
entered into the conversation before their departure. Of course,

Fanny had been polite to Blake during the carriage ride, but that was likely to offset her own ill-mannered behavior.

Amanda tapped her cousin on the arm. "Are you feeling unwell, Fanny?"

"I'm fine," she said without turning away from the window.

"We've been separated for weeks with only a few letters exchanged between us, yet you have nothing of interest to tell me? Come now, Cousin, what ails you?"

"Truly, I am fine. Don't worry yourself over me."

Amanda slapped her gloves on the leather seat. "You are not fooling me in the least. I know you as well as I know anyone in this world, and I can certainly tell when something is amiss. You may as well tell me, for I'll not give you a minute's peace until you do."

"Ever the persistent one, aren't you! Sometimes it's best to let sleeping dogs lie. I can't talk about what is bothering me just yet."

"I *knew* it! You're keeping a secret from me. We've never kept secrets, Fanny."

Fanny arched her brows. "We're going to keep a secret from Sophie."

"Because it's for her own good."

"Then you must consider this the same thing. If and when the time is right, I will tell you. For now, you must trust my decision to remain silent." Fanny squeezed Amanda's hand.

Though she longed to know what bothered her cousin, Amanda said no more. They conversed little during the remainder of the journey. Fanny appeared lost in her own thoughts while Amanda contemplated whether Dr. Carstead might hire someone to help at the Home during her convalescence.

Although she knew he needed help, the very thought annoyed her.

❖

"Wake up, we're here." Fanny's words were followed by a gentle nudge.

Amanda forced herself awake as the train hissed and jarred to a stop in the Clayton train station. "I didn't realize I was so tired."

Fanny smiled. "Dr. Carstead would say that you've proved his point and that you've not fully recuperated."

"Well, he would be incorrect. I didn't sleep well last night." Amanda peered out the train window. "I suppose Father notified Mr. Atwell to come and meet us." She glanced over her shoulder. "Or did you write to Michael's parents?"

"I believe your father sent our arrival information to the Clayton telegraph office. He said Mr. Broomfield would pass along the information."

Amanda didn't doubt Mr. Broomfield would do exactly as her father wished. Years ago the old telegrapher had forgotten to deliver a message that her father had wired from Rochester for delivery to his father on Broadmoor Island. Mr. Broomfield had suffered the wrath of Jonas Broadmoor and had never again made the same mistake. She imagined if necessary, the poor man would row to the island to ensure that the message arrived.

A stiff breeze greeted them when they stepped down from the train. Amanda grasped her hat with one hand and pointed to the *DaisyBee* with the other. "There's the boat. Mr. Atwell must be inside."

Fanny locked arms with her cousin, and the two of them bowed their heads against the wind as they hurried inside the train station.

"Fanny! Amanda!" Sophie rushed forward and grabbed them around the shoulders in a giant hug. "I am so excited to see you. Now that the two of you have arrived, it's going to be just like old times."

Amanda took a backward step and glanced around the station. "Where's the baby? I'm anxious to see how much she's grown."

"Elizabeth is with her nanny. Aunt Victoria found a wonderful lady who lives here in Clayton, and she's come to stay at the island to take care of Elizabeth. Both Veda and Minnie complained they had too many other chores to accomplish now that there are so many parties taking place." Sophie glanced outside and then motioned to her cousins. "Mr. Atwell has your trunks loaded. You're both going to think it's the height of the summer season once you get settled at the island. It is absolutely amazing how many dinner parties and dances have taken place since shortly after we arrived." She winked at Amanda. "There are several fine bachelors among the attendees, and all of them are capable dance partners."

Amanda shot a glance at Fanny. In the past Sophie had been unwilling to leave Elizabeth in the care of anyone but Paul or one of them. Now it appeared she'd relegated the baby's care to a stranger. The change seemed inexplicable, but before Amanda could gauge Fanny's reaction, Sophie stepped between them. She continued to regale them with the details of a dinner party she'd attended Saturday while they walked across the train tracks to the dock and boarded the *DaisyBee*.

When Sophie finally stopped long enough to take a breath, Amanda leaned forward. "What do you hear from Paul?"

"He says he's busy helping several churches that are without preachers. He doesn't know when he'll be coming to the island for a visit." Sophie shrugged. "I don't mind in the least. There have been more than enough social gatherings to keep me occupied, and there are even more in the offing. Now that the two of you have arrived, it's going to be completely grand."

"I brought only two gowns that would be appropriate for such festivities," Amanda said. "And you were complaining before you departed Rochester that you hadn't been able to fit into your gowns since Elizabeth's birth. Exactly what have you been wearing to all of these galas?"

"Your mother has been ever so kind in that regard. Once she realized the state of my wardrobe, she enlisted the help of a seamstress in Clayton. Thankfully, the woman has several others who work in the shop with her. Minnie and Veda have been called upon to lend occasional help, as well." Sophie's eyes sparkled with excitement as she told them of the various fabrics she'd chosen for her dresses.

"And with a nanny to care for Elizabeth, that leaves you free to attend as many parties as you desire," Amanda remarked.

Sophie's smile disappeared. "You disapprove?"

Amanda nodded. "I can't comprehend the change that has taken place since I last saw you. Back in Rochester you were content with your life and found joy in your marriage to Paul and caring for Elizabeth. There was no mention of parties or fancy dresses. What has come over you?"

Sophie glared at Amanda. "You're always finding fault with me—isn't she, Fanny?"

"I don't think that's true. Unfortunately, what Amanda says is true. You do seem like a different person."

"I don't want to talk about this anymore. You've only just arrived, and we shouldn't have an argument before we even arrive at the island."

Before Fanny could respond, Mr. Atwell waved an envelope

overhead and smiled. "Would you be interested in what arrived just yesterday, Fanny?" he called.

Fanny clasped her hand over her heart. "A letter! From Michael?" She jumped to her feet and dropped back down as the boat lurched through the choppy water.

"Stay there," he called. "I'll bring it to you."

With the ease of a practiced sea captain, Mr. Atwell arrived at her side and handed her the missive. "This one was tucked inside the letter he sent to us." He pointed to the seal and grinned down at her. "As you can see, we didn't open it."

Fanny nodded. "He's doing well?"

"I think you'll be pleased to hear his news." He tipped his hat and returned to his post.

She slipped her finger beneath the seal and carefully opened the envelope. She was now sandwiched between her cousins, who were peering over her shoulders as she withdrew the pages. Fanny waved them away. "Do move back a little. I promise to tell you what he says, but I'd like to read it first."

Amanda leaned back, though she wasn't certain Sophie paid heed to Fanny's request. She waited what seemed an eternity before nudging her cousin. "Well, what does he say?"

The pages crackled as she held them to her bodice. "He's coming home in June, and he says to plan the wedding." Her broad smile seemed to stretch from ear to ear. "Finally! Can you believe it?"

Amanda shook her head. "No! He obviously doesn't realize how long it takes to prepare for a wedding. We'll need to begin immediately. I do think we should enlist Mother's help, too."

"You must choose the perfect wedding gown, Fanny. With all your money you'll be able to afford the finest wedding Rochester has ever seen," Sophie said.

"Michael and I plan to be married on Broadmoor Island,"

Fanny told them. "Still, there will be much to accomplish before we are wed, and I will need help from both of you."

"You know you can depend upon us," Amanda said. She extended her fingers and the three of them joined hands. "Together always."

"Together always," the three repeated in unison.

❖

Jonas folded his hands atop his desk and did his best to remain calm. Ellert Jackson was a shrewd man, and he'd sniff out any hint of fear. Several days earlier Ellert had confirmed he would stop by and discuss the possibility of a loan. Jonas had expected him to appear that very day. When he hadn't arrived by the next morning, Jonas had gone to the hotel and discovered Jackson had checked out. The news had rendered him despondent. But today his spirits had buoyed.

He'd received word that Ellert had returned to Rochester. And when the man had entered Jonas's office only a few minutes ago, his heart had pounded with renewed hope. Ellert could help him escape from his financial woes, but Jonas must play his hand with finesse.

"I'm surprised to see you back in Rochester," Jonas said.

Ellert guffawed. "You're *relieved* to see me. Isn't that what you truly mean, Jonas?" He didn't await a reply. "They tell me at the hotel that you came looking for me after I'd checked out the last time I was in town."

Jonas silently chided himself. He should have tipped the hotel clerk and told him to keep his mouth shut. Too late now. Ellert had gained first advantage in this game of cat and mouse. "Yes. I stopped by to extend an invitation to supper."

Ellert tapped his walking stick on the floor. "You came to

the hotel because you were worried I had forgotten about your loan." He stared across the desk, his eyes unwavering.

There was no doubt Ellert expected Jonas to acknowledge his assessment was correct. Jonas could read it in his eyes. Though he longed to remain silent, Jonas didn't hold the advantage. He gave a half nod. "Because I wanted to invite you to join me for supper and discuss the loan."

Like a cat preparing to pounce on its prey, Ellert leaned across the desk. "You are in no position to play games with me, Jonas. I know what you've been up to with your niece's inheritance."

Jonas willed himself to remain calm, but perspiration covered his palms and a sudden weakness assailed him. He'd never fainted in his life. Was this how women felt when they swooned? He fought to bolster himself with a deep breath—and then another. How could Ellert possibly know what he'd done?

"I don't know what you're—"

"Stop!" Ellert slapped his palm on the desk. "I will not play games with you. The only way you will receive a loan from me is on my terms. I know you are in dire financial straits. And my terms require a full disclosure of your finances and those of your niece." He removed a sheet of paper from his pocket and pushed it across the desk. "This is only a small portion of what I know. If you want my help, you'll tell me the rest—all of it."

Jonas scanned the page and felt the blood rush from his head. Ellert had been digging, and he'd excavated far more information than Jonas would have thought possible.

"How did you come by this knowledge?"

Ellert smiled and crossed his arms casually against his chest. "Come now, Jonas. You above all men should know what a well-placed dollar or two can do for a man. I have my sources—

friends, if you will. Surely you wouldn't expect me to divulge such information."

Jonas forced himself to concentrate. Who would have had access to the records? Possibly one of the clerks in Mortimer's office had snooped in the files before his death. That had to be it. If only Mortimer would have done as instructed and kept no written documentation of their dealings. If only he would have realized the harm it could cause in the days to come.

Jonas dropped back against his chair and stared into Ellert's gleaming eyes. The man was taking great pleasure in seeing him squirm. "It appears I have little choice," Jonas said.

Ellert had won—at least this round.

## 10

*Thursday, June 15, 1899*

Jonas sighed at the sight of his brother entering the outer office. He should have closed his door and told Mr. Fryer to send any visitors on their way. Though he truly couldn't afford the services of an office clerk any longer, Jonas couldn't imagine his office without Mr. Fryer. The man had worked for him for nearly twenty years and could be trusted to do Jonas's bidding without question, a trait that had long ago endeared the man to Jonas.

His brother nodded at Mr. Fryer but continued past the clerk's desk and strode into Jonas's office. "We need to talk." He closed the door and dropped his hat atop Jonas's massive desk before sitting down.

Jonas straightened in his chair. Without the slightest show

of manners or greeting, his brother had entered his office and made himself quite comfortable. "Good morning to you, too, Quincy."

"Good morning!" Quincy shot back.

Jonas didn't miss the irritation in Quincy's voice. "Looks as though we're going to have some nice weather today."

"I didn't come here to discuss the weather. I came here to ask what you've done to aggrieve Fanny. I spoke with her shortly before she and Amanda departed for Broadmoor Island, and she wasn't herself."

"You know women. Their moods are as changeable as the weather—perhaps even more so." He chuckled, though he gripped the arms of his chair in a fierce hold. What had Fanny been up to now? How much had she divulged to Quincy? His brother didn't act as though he knew anything, but he'd not fall into a trap. "I have no idea why Fanny is upset. Did you not inquire yourself?"

"Yes, of course, but she wasn't as forthcoming as I had hoped. She simply said someone had betrayed her."

Jonas rubbed his jaw. "Probably that useless Michael Atwell. Let's hope he's found another woman and doesn't plan to marry Fanny."

"No. I specifically asked her about Michael. She denied he was the cause of her despair. Naturally I could only think something had gone amiss in regard to her inheritance." Quincy arched his brows and waited.

Jonas shook his head and feigned ignorance for a moment before acting as though he'd had a sudden flash of genius. "She must be unhappy over the sale of Broadmoor Mansion—that must be what has caused her despondency."

"What are you talking about? You sold the mansion to

Daniel Irwin long ago." Quincy frowned. "I'm beginning to worry about your memory, Jonas."

"I did sell it to Daniel, but once Fanny refused to marry him, he no longer wanted the house. He petitioned the court to withdraw from the agreement and was granted permission."

"Why didn't I know anything about this?"

"If you'll recall, you told me that unless the Home for the Friendless would be adversely impacted, you didn't want to be bothered with matters related to the estate."

"That's true," Quincy mumbled. "So you've sold the mansion to another purchaser?"

"Yes, but at a loss. The maintenance expense on the place was costing us more and more, so it was better to sell at a loss than continue the upkeep. The court agreed. Unfortunately, I think Fanny felt betrayed by my action."

"Because she wanted to buy it for herself?"

"Yes, but I couldn't permit a young single woman to live alone in that place. It wouldn't be prudent or proper. I was looking out for her best interests, but you know how young people are—they simply want their way in everything." Jonas loosened his grip on the chair arms. From all appearances, his efforts to convince Quincy were meeting with success.

"I wonder why she didn't mention that. Selling the house doesn't seem like something she'd be reluctant to tell me."

There was a question lurking in his brother's comment. Had he misjudged him? Did Quincy know more than he'd revealed? His confidence waned. Best to meet the situation with a direct question of his own. "Did Fanny mention me specifically or any problem she's had with me?"

"No, but I assumed that since she's been living in your house, you would be the cause of her unhappiness—or at least know what the problem might be."

"Your assumptions are unfounded on both accounts. Fanny and I have had little contact over the last weeks. We didn't take our meals together, and I saw her only in passing on one or two occasions. She didn't appear unhappy or troubled on those brief encounters. And now that she's left for Broadmoor Island with Amanda, I'm certain she's in good spirits."

Quincy leaned back in his chair and stared out the window as if contemplating the explanation. "No," he said, shaking his head. "I believe something of greater import than a change of mood has occurred with our Fanny."

*Our* Fanny. Jonas winced at the affectionate expression. When had Quincy become so worried about the girl's welfare? And why? Normally he couldn't be pried away from the Home for the Friendless long enough for a family gathering. Suddenly he sounded like a protective father rather than a disengaged uncle. Jonas needed to shift his brother's focus.

"What do you hear from Sophie and Beatrice? In her most recent letter, Victoria mentioned that Beatrice seems to be out of sorts most of the time. Strange, don't you think, since she was the one most interested in fleeing the city? Perhaps she's suffering from some mental ailment and should see a physician."

Quincy scooted to the edge of his chair. "Is that what Victoria thinks? If so, I shall ask Dr. Carstead if there's a doctor he can recommend. Of course, Beatrice has always been somewhat antagonistic. I believe she bears a good deal of anger and jealousy, though I don't know why."

Jonas guffawed. "Truly? Perhaps because you devote all your time to everyone except your immediate family."

"That's not true. I've done my best since Marie's death. Besides, Marie encouraged my work with the underprivileged."

Pleased that he'd managed to redirect their conversation, Jonas didn't retreat. "No one would disagree that Marie offered her support to your work. I never quite understood why, for it surely placed an undue burden upon your family, though there are many things I don't profess to understand."

Using the desk for leverage, Quincy pushed up from his chair. "I promised Dr. Carstead I would stop at the pharmacy. He's likely wondering what happened to me."

"Don't let me keep you from your duties." Jonas tapped the stack of papers on his desk. "I have many matters needing my attention, as well."

Without further comment, Quincy picked up his hat and strode to the door. He waved his walking stick in a farewell gesture as he departed.

Jonas exhaled a low whistle and leaned back in his chair. By the time Quincy had exited the office, he'd clearly forgotten why he'd come calling. Jonas reached into his humidor and removed one of the two remaining cigars. He'd given up purchasing the expensive Cubans—a self-imposed punishment for being lax and overlooking details in his business dealings with Mortimer. He passed the roll of thick brown tobacco beneath his nose and inhaled the fragrant odor before returning it to the box. There wasn't time to indulge at the moment.

He stood and looked down to the street below. Quincy was nowhere in sight. He'd likely departed by carriage. Jonas removed his hat from the hook by the door and stepped through the doorway. "I have errands to complete, Mr. Fryer. I'm not certain what time I'll return."

The clerk glanced up from his journal. "I'll lock up if you haven't returned by six o'clock, sir."

Jonas could always depend upon Mr. Fryer. No matter the task, Mr. Fryer never asked questions. He faithfully appeared each morning and disappeared like a vapor ten hours later. Jonas had no idea if the man had a wife or family. They never discussed anything unrelated to business. Yet another reason Jonas was grateful for Mr. Fryer.

Jonas walked the four-block distance to the courthouse. By the time he rounded the side of the brick structure, he was puffing for air. He entered a side door that would take him through a private corridor that led directly to each of the judges' chambers. It was Mortimer who had originally shown Jonas the entrance used by the lawyers to conduct business with the judges. The side door provided easy access. And if one was fortunate, one could slip in and out without ever being seen. Jonas hoped he could accomplish such an entrance and exit today.

Before rapping on the door, he glanced over his shoulder. Not a soul in sight. He sighed with relief and tapped on the door where the name *Harlan G. Webster, Probate Judge* had been painted in black. Proper etiquette dictated he await a response, but Jonas wouldn't chance being seen, so he turned the knob and stepped inside. The clerk's desk was empty. "Judge Webster?" Jonas called.

"Who's there?" A drawer slammed. "Make yourself known!"

"It's Jonas Broadmoor." He crossed the room at a near run and stood in the doorway to the judge's inner sanctum.

The judge traced his finger down a list on his desk. "I don't have you on my calendar for today."

"I don't have an appointment, but it's urgent that we talk. Can you spare me a few minutes right now?" Jonas felt like a sniveling child. Judges! They took absolute delight in wielding their power. A year or two ago, Jonas could have bought and sold every judge in the state. Now he was relegated to begging for a few minutes of this pompous man's time.

Judge Webster waved at one of the threadbare upholstered

chairs. "Sit down, but don't get comfortable. I have another appointment in half an hour."

*Don't get comfortable?* How did the foolish man think anyone could find a scrap of comfort in this shabby office? "There have been some problems since Mortimer's death."

"And?" The judge arched his bushy brows.

"Mortimer maintained far too many records of our business dealings regarding my father's estate." In a rush of words, Jonas detailed the plethora of events that had unfolded since his lawyer's death. Judge Webster stared out the window, seemingly bored by the tale. When he had revealed all of the facts, Jonas edged forward on the chair. "Well, what do you think I should do?"

The judge shrugged his bony shoulders. "I suggest you get your books in order and hire an excellent lawyer to represent you." His glasses slipped down on his nose as he leaned across the desk. "Mr. Rosenblume has already been here to meet with me on behalf of his client. He has expressed a deep concern for what he considers inappropriate handling of estate funds."

Jonas grasped the judge's thin arm. "You're a part of this. You must help me."

With a steely glare, the judge nodded toward his arm. "Remove your hold."

"Yes, of course. I didn't mean to—"

"Now, you listen carefully, Jonas. I am no longer a party to this. This plan was developed by you and Mortimer. I will deny any knowledge of what has transpired. I've already told Mr. Rosenblume I am shocked and appalled by the very idea that Mortimer, a lawyer sworn to uphold the law, may have presented falsified records to the court."

Jonas slapped the desk with his palm. "That's it! We can blame all of this on Mortimer, and both of us will be free from any liability. Frankly, it does appear Mortimer didn't keep me completely apprised of matters, and my financial condition is much worse than even I had imagined."

The judge didn't appear completely convinced. Jonas would be forced to use his trump card. "I thought you might be interested to know that when I was reviewing the files, I came upon a note you wrote to Mortimer."

The judge wrinkled his forehead in a frown. "I don't have the slightest idea what you're talking about."

So the judge wanted to play coy and see if Jonas was bluffing. Well, he could certainly understand that tack. Hadn't he done the same thing countless times? Jonas couldn't fault the man for being suspicious.

Jonas tapped his pocket. "Your note tells Mortimer to deposit funds into an account at a Syracuse bank prior to the date of our hearing regarding the estate inventory and appraisal. Does that help jog your memory?"

The judge narrowed his eyes. "Mortimer told me all correspondence between us would be destroyed."

Jonas took a modicum of pleasure watching the judge squirm. The old man didn't appear quite so supercilious at the moment. "Obviously Mortimer lied to both of us."

"I suppose there is merit to joining forces and placing all of the blame on Mortimer. If we both disavow knowledge of what he was doing, we should be able to avoid being drawn into the fray. The fact that your finances are in worse condition than you thought will help substantiate our claims to lack any knowledge regarding Mortimer's wrongdoing." The judge leaned back in his chair and stared into the distance. "Yes. This is perfect. Who will doubt us?"

"Then if we've agreed, I'll be on my way. I don't want to further interfere with your busy schedule."

The judge pointed to Jonas's pocket. "I would be grateful if you'd give me that note I wrote to Mortimer."

Jonas withdrew an envelope from his coat pocket. "Oh, *this*? This is a letter from my wife. Surely you didn't think I would carry your note on my person."

The judge gripped his pencil with a fury that caused it to snap. He stared at the two pieces of wood as though he couldn't determine how they'd come into his possession. "You may bring it to me the next time you pay me a visit."

Jonas forced a smile. "Of course." If the judge thought he would gain possession of that note before all of the legal proceedings had been completed, he was a fool. And Jonas didn't think the man a fool. "I do hope the rest of your day passes without interruption."

The judge's obvious irritation created a warm feeling of self-satisfaction that lasted until he returned to his office. He settled at his desk and reviewed the ledgers and bank accounts. Their plan would cause little difficulty for the judge. But Jonas realized he would be faced with an onslaught of questions from both Quincy and Fanny. They would make prying inquiries that would require both precise and consistent responses. Before any of their questions arose, he must be prepared with answers that would nip any thought of wrongdoing in the bud. If he was to succeed in his ploy, he must appear shocked and surprised by Mortimer's mishandling of the estate.

Jonas hoped the files Vincent had given to Fanny held nothing that would incriminate him.

## 11

*Monday, June 19, 1899*

As the train came to a hissing, jerking stop at the Rochester train station, the three cousins stood and then edged down the aisle. Sophie grasped Amanda's arm when they stepped onto the platform. "Do you think Dr. Carstead will be surprised to see you?"

"I imagine he will. And what of Paul? Did you tell him that we were coming to Rochester to shop for Fanny's wedding gown?"

The fashionable feathers on Sophie's hat waved back and forth as she shook her head. "No. He would have insisted I bring Elizabeth with me. Had the baby accompanied us, we would get little shopping completed."

"I wouldn't have minded in the least. She's a good baby,

and I'm sure Paul would have been willing to look after her while we shopped," Fanny said.

Sophie stopped in the middle of the depot and planted her hands on her hips. "Whose side are you on, Fanny? I came along to help you, and you are taking Paul's side against me."

Fanny sighed. "I'm not taking sides, but I imagine Paul misses the baby and will be sad that you didn't bring her."

"From his lack of attention, I doubt he misses either of us overmuch. He hasn't yet come to Broadmoor Island for a visit." Sophie tipped her head to the side as if to challenge anyone who might defy her. "Here's a cab. Come along."

"But ever since you wrote to him, he's been writing with regularity. And you said he was needed to help with several of the churches in town, didn't you?" Fanny truly couldn't understand Sophie's recent behavior. The only things that now evoked any excitement in her cousin were the mention of shopping or the latest invitation to a dinner dance at one of the island hotels. She was acting like a silly debutante seeking a husband instead of a married woman with a delightful infant daughter.

Sophie shrugged. "If his work is of greater import than his family, so be it. He's become much like my father, tending to the needs of others instead of his own family. I'm capable of being occupied without him." She clasped Fanny's arm. "I do need to stop by the house and retrieve a piece of jewelry that I forgot to pack."

"Your mother's necklace?" Fanny asked.

"Yes. The amber stones match my gold satin gown. And now that Aunt Victoria has had it altered for me—"

"You'll suffer Beatrice's wrath if you wear the necklace in her presence," Amanda said.

"I don't care if she becomes angry. Father gave the necklace to me, and Beatrice can complain all she likes. Jewelry shouldn't be stored away; it should be worn. Don't you agree?"

Amanda peeked around Fanny's flower-bedecked hat. "Why don't the two of you go to Sophie's house while I stop by the Home for the Friendless? Blake is always there on Monday, and I'd like to speak to him. Then we can begin our shopping in earnest."

Fanny hesitated. "I suppose that would be acceptable, but we do want to reserve enough time to choose fabric and flowers."

"We will not leave Rochester until we've made the perfect selections for you. Even if we must remain several days." Amanda tapped on the window and gave the driver Sophie's address.

Sophie shook her head. "We need to complete our shopping by Friday at the very latest. The Armbrusters are hosting a party at the Crossman House on Alexandria Bay. I do enjoy parties at the Crossman, don't you?"

Amanda made a *tsk*ing sound and shook her head. "I should think you'd refrain from attending *all* of the parties, Sophie. It gives the wrong impression."

"Oh, do cease your chiding, Amanda. I'll begin to think Beatrice is at my side rather than one of my favorite cousins. Besides, your mother has given her approval to every party I've attended."

"That's because she doesn't know that you disengage yourself from the couples she's arranged to act as your escorts."

Sophie giggled. "Well, you had best not tell your mother, or I'll be slow to forgive you. I've done nothing improper. A few dances and a bit of conversation with a gentleman or two mean absolutely nothing."

Fanny didn't wish to enter into the fray between Sophie and Amanda, but Sophie's comment was a sudden reminder of how easily she had been enchanted by Wesley Hedrick not so long ago. There was little doubt Sophie could be easily swayed by the charms of a smooth-talking man. But surely she'd never do anything to threaten her marriage to Paul.

Worry loomed in Fanny's mind as their carriage came to a halt in front of Sophie's house. Fanny and Sophie stepped down. "Once you've seen Dr. Carstead," Fanny said to Amanda, "why don't you return and then we'll go shopping." Fanny drew close to the carriage window and lowered her voice. "If Paul is at the Home, you might tell him Sophie is here."

Sophie nudged her cousin in the side. "I can take care of arrangements for meeting my own husband, Fanny. Didn't you say you wanted to allow ample time for shopping?"

Amanda leaned forward and pointed at the runabout sitting near the side entrance to Sophie's house. "I think you two may stop arguing. I'll return shortly."

The carriage driver slapped the leather reins against the horse's backside. Once the carriage had pulled away, Fanny turned her attention to Sophie. "I didn't mean to anger you, but I do find your lack of concern toward Paul disturbing. You *do* love him, don't you?"

Sophie frowned, her displeasure obvious. "Of course I love him, but he's the one who banished me to the island. I wanted to remain in Rochester, and he wouldn't even consider my wishes. I could have been a great deal of help to him. That's what I wanted to do—assist him with his work. It is Paul who decided on this separation." She strutted toward the front door as though she'd sufficiently defended her behavior.

Fanny quickened her pace and came alongside her cousin. "He didn't want you or Elizabeth to contract cholera. And I believe he hasn't come to visit because he didn't want to take the chance he might carry the disease to any of us. Neither your father nor Uncle Jonas has set foot on the island, either."

"And none of them have become infected with cholera. There was no reason to send Elizabeth and me to the island."

"I disagree, but now I realize that you're behaving badly to teach Paul a lesson." Fanny tugged on her cousin's arm. "I'm correct, aren't I?"

"That was my intent at first, but now I'm simply enjoying the parties. And I'm *not* behaving badly."

"By whose standards?" Fanny followed her cousin up the porch steps.

Sophie glanced over her shoulder as she turned the doorknob. "Do stop these tiresome questions. You're beginning to sound like Amanda." She stepped across the threshold. "Paul! Are you here?"

From the kitchen the sound of a chair scraping across the floor preceded Paul's appearance. He stepped into the hallway, his eyes wide with surprise. "Sophie! I can't believe you're here. Why didn't you tell me you were coming? And where's Elizabeth?"

"She's at Broadmoor Island, of course. If you're disappointed she isn't with me, I suppose you can blame yourself for sending us away—or you can blame Fanny, if you prefer. We've come to shop for her wedding gown, and it would have been difficult to bring Elizabeth along when we have so much to accomplish. And I thought you would be busy with your many charitable duties."

Fanny didn't miss the sarcasm in Sophie's curt response or the pain that shone in Paul's eyes. She longed to remove herself from this awkward situation.

❖

Amanda's stomach tightened into a knot when she caught sight of the Home for the Friendless. She clasped a hand to her midsection, hoping to ease her anxiety. Would Blake be pleased to see her? She hoped he would regard her unexpected visit a welcome surprise.

The carriage driver assisted her down. "Please wait for me. I shouldn't be more than fifteen minutes."

He nodded his agreement, and Amanda inhaled a deep breath as she approached the front gate. It seemed an eternity since she'd departed. How she had missed caring for the ill. Perhaps Blake would reconsider and permit her to stay. Before entering the gate, she pinched her cheeks. If she hoped to convince him that she should remain and work, she'd need to look like the picture of health. She hoped a rosy complexion would help. After a quick adjustment to her hat, she entered the front door and tiptoed down the hallway to the medical office.

She instantly smiled at the sight. Blake sat at his desk hunched over a medical book. He didn't even know she was around. "Could you spare a few minutes for someone who isn't ill?"

Blake snapped to attention. Instead of the bright smile she'd expected, he pinned her with an icy look that immediately wilted her resolve.

"Amanda! What are you doing here? I gave you explicit medical orders. You of all people should be willing to follow orders. Surely you realize you're risking your recovery."

She folded her arms across her waist. "May I say that it's a genuine pleasure to see you, too, Dr. Carstead."

He pushed away from the desk. "No need to mock me. I doubt you thought I'd be pleased to see you here."

"Frankly, that's exactly what I thought," she said, before dropping to one of the chairs opposite his desk. "I do believe you are the man who made declarations of love while I lay dying." She touched her index finger to her lips. "Or was that some other doctor who ventured in and sat vigil by my bedside?" She settled in her chair and smiled. How she had missed bantering with Blake. He always had an excellent riposte for her.

"No other doctors were in the infirmary during your illness, but I fear you were suffering from delusions if you believe I declared my love for you, Miss Broadmoor."

"You're not fooling me in the least. I know what I heard. You're simply unwilling to declare the truth to me because you fear rejection."

"Rejection? Whatever are you talking about? Perhaps I should take your temperature. I fear you are once again suffering from hallucinations."

Amanda chuckled. "You fear my only interest in you is your medical knowledge and that if you declare your love, I will surely reject you." She held up her hand to ward off his reply. "I haven't time to sit and argue the depth of your affection for me, Doctor. I've come to Rochester to assist my cousin in her choice of a wedding gown."

"Michael has returned?" Blake asked as he rounded the desk.

"No, but she received a letter. He'll be back soon, and he's instructed her to begin preparations for a summer wedding at Broadmoor Island. *Some* men are anxious to declare their love and marry," she teased while he walked alongside her to the front door.

"And some *women* are far too anxious to hear a man declare his love and then move along to another. I believe some refer to it as the excitement of the conquest."

"I believe you're the one suffering from hallucinations, Dr. Carstead. It's men who enjoy the conquest and then move along to another woman." Amanda chuckled as she slipped her hands into her lace gloves.

Blake joined in her laughter, but as the front door opened, his smile was replaced by a look of utter disbelief. "Julia," he whispered.

A striking dark-haired woman clothed in the latest fashion brushed by Amanda and pulled Blake into an embrace. "I've come to say yes, my darling."

"Yes to *what?*" Blake attempted a backward step, but the woman held him close.

"Yes, I will marry you, dear boy."

*Marry?* Amanda turned on her heel and rushed from the room.

❖

Jonas waved his brother into the library. "I thought you would be here hours ago. It's nearly one o'clock."

"There was work at the Home that needed my attention, and then I decided to partake of my noonday meal. You weren't expecting me for lunch, were you?"

"No. I was expecting you *before* the noonday meal. My note said I had an urgent matter to discuss with you. I thought you would realize that *urgent* meant you should arrive as early as possible."

Quincy nodded. "I understand the meaning of the word, Jonas. And I came as quickly as possible. Your sense of urgency doesn't always align with my own."

"Oh, do sit down. We don't have time to quibble over such nonsense." His voice held a sharp tone, and Jonas silently reminded himself he didn't want to alienate Quincy. "I apologize for my impatience, but I find myself involved in a tumultuous situation."

"Does this have something to do with Sophie, Amanda, and Fanny returning to Rochester today?"

"What? I didn't know any of them had returned home. For what purpose?" A burning sensation crept from the pit of his stomach and deposited hot bile in the back of his throat. He swallowed hard. Why had Fanny returned to Rochester? Had she discovered something and come to talk to Quincy? Worse yet, had Mr. Rosenblume summoned her back to Rochester?

"Fanny received a letter from Michael. He is returning to Broadmoor Island and has told her to make plans for a summer wedding. The girls are in Rochester to help her choose a wedding gown." Quincy scratched his head. "At least that's what Sophie told me. I saw the three of them only briefly. Amanda stopped by the Home to speak with Blake. I assumed Amanda and Fanny would be staying here overnight."

"I know nothing of their plans." Jonas could barely gather his thoughts. He needed to convey his concerns to Quincy before the girls walked in on them. But before he could regain his momentum, Quincy interrupted.

"I was surprised Victoria wasn't with the girls. Amanda said you'd written Victoria that you planned to come for a visit next week. Your wife decided to remain at the island to ensure you kept your word." Quincy appeared somewhat bemused. "I didn't know you'd made arrangements for a trip to the island."

Jonas sighed. "You don't know my plans because we seldom see each other. If we could get back to the matter at hand, I have an issue of greater concern than a visit to Broadmoor Island or the purchase of a wedding gown." He leaned across the desk. "I've been in meetings with Judge Webster regarding the estate, and we have combed through all of Mortimer's records."

"I'm sure that proved to be terribly boring."

"Quite the contrary. We discovered that Mortimer had deceived me and falsified the records he presented to the court as true and factual documents." Jonas didn't need to force himself to appear distressed. He worried that the girls would walk in the house at any minute, and he wasn't prepared to include Fanny in their discussion just yet.

Quincy frowned and shook his head. "How is that possible? Did you give Mortimer free rein? You're the man who prides himself upon keeping abreast of details. How did this slip by you?"

The questions and comments were not what Jonas had expected. He'd thought Quincy would simply acknowledge the oversight and ask for financial details. Instead, his brother appeared unconvinced that Mortimer could have accomplished such a feat without his knowledge.

"You may recall that I have had my own business matters to handle. I didn't have time to oversee all of the issues surrounding the estate. That's what a lawyer is hired to do. Rest assured that if I'd been checking on Mortimer, I wouldn't have suffered such huge losses myself. His actions have created problems for all of us."

With the revelation that Jonas had been financially affected, his brother appeared at least partially convinced. "Exactly how did Mortimer commit these transgressions?"

"From what the judge and I have unraveled thus far, it appears Mortimer commingled the money and skimmed a healthy portion off the top for himself."

"Why would he commingle the funds?"

"To make his crime more difficult to discover. It appears he'd been converting assets for his personal use for some time. Now that he's dead, we're unable to locate any of those funds. This is a financial disaster. And to think that I trusted Mortimer!"

Quincy visibly paled as he digested the unwelcome news. "This affects all of Father's estate? *All* of the Broadmoor holdings?"

"I won't be able to say with absolute certainty until we've completed our audit of all the records, but I assure you that Judge Webster has been assisting me with a plan to secure the estate from further losses."

"This is tragic news." Quincy massaged his forehead. "We ought not to tell Fanny just yet. There's no need to upset the girl with this news when she's in the midst of making plans for her wedding. However, I do hope that you've retained a reputable lawyer to help you work through this muddle."

"I haven't had sufficient time to decide upon a lawyer. I thought my first obligation was to talk to you."

"I appreciate that, Jonas. But now that we've talked, I think you must make your priority hiring a lawyer who will protect all of our interests. If you'd like me to assist you in finding someone, I'd be happy to request references from several of my acquaintances."

"No, no—that's not necessary. You're busy enough with your duties at the Home. I can make inquiries at the men's club. I'm sure one of the businessmen there can offer an excellent recommendation."

Quincy appeared shaken by the revelation, but at least he'd accepted Jonas's explanation that it was Mortimer who was at fault.

"I suppose you're correct. The men at the club could furnish an excellent recommendation."

"You do understand none of this is my fault, don't you? I hope I can count on your support."

Quincy nodded. "I know you would never intentionally do anything that would cause the family to lose any of our assets. We'll get this all worked out. Who knows, perhaps something good will come from all of this."

Jonas arched his brows. How like his brother to think

something good could come from having his inheritance stolen from beneath his nose. He wanted to tell his brother he was a fool. But he remained silent. For now, Jonas needed Quincy as his ally.

"I know you'll manage to find the proper attorney to help us through this maze. You have my every confidence," Quincy continued as the men walked toward the front door.

"And we're agreed that we'll say nothing of this to anyone else," Jonas said.

"Yes. I would especially urge you to remain silent where Fanny is concerned. We don't want her unduly upset."

"You need not worry yourself in that regard. I'll not say a word."

# 12

While still in the arms of the carriage driver, Amanda glanced over her shoulder to make certain no one had observed her. She'd let out a high-pitched yelp that should have wakened the dead. But from all appearances, no one had noticed. Or if they had, they obviously weren't concerned over her distress. In her haste to escape Blake and his beautiful visitor, she'd forgotten to lift her skirts and had snagged her hem on the toe of her shoe. Had the carriage driver not been standing nearby, she would have been thrown headlong into the front wheel of his cab.

After righting herself, she showered the driver with profuse thanks. Unfortunately she'd likely overdone it, for the poor man's face had turned the shade of a ripe tomato by the time he closed the carriage door. Once they were on their way, Amanda leaned forward and lifted the edge of her skirt to examine the stitching. She hadn't torn the fabric, but the hem would require repair before she went shopping with her cousins. Otherwise she would likely once again become tangled in the hem and end up flat on the sidewalk before day's end. A disgusted sigh escaped her lips as she dropped her skirt back into place. What had begun as an enjoyable few minutes of banter with Blake had ended in disaster.

She stared out the window and tried to convince herself she'd gone to the Home to check on the progress of ailing patients. In truth, she'd wanted to know how Blake was faring without her. She had hoped Blake would tell her he'd been rendered useless without her and beg her to remain at his side. Before going to bed last night, she'd played the scene over and over in her mind. But instead of being implored to stay, Amanda had been forced to witness a strange woman rushing into Blake's arms and accepting his marriage proposal. Tears pooled in the corners of her eyes. She batted her lashes, but to no avail. The tears trickled down her cheeks. No wonder Blake had disavowed he'd ever proclaimed his love for her. He was engaged to marry. What a fool she'd made of herself!

When they arrived at the small house belonging to Paul and Sophie, the driver jumped down and opened the door. Amanda withdrew a coin from her reticule. "For your excellent service," she said, placing the coin in his hand.

He tipped his hat. "Thank you and a good day to you, ma'am."

"I don't think it can get any worse," Amanda muttered, holding her skirts high. She climbed the front steps to Sophie's house and tapped on the door.

Within moments Sophie opened the front door. "What has happened? You look like a thundercloud about to burst."

"*I'm* not the thundercloud, but you're right about one thing. A dark cloud arrived in Rochester, and it has dumped a bucketful of cold water on my entire future." Amanda brushed past Sophie and strode into the parlor while still holding her skirt above her ankles.

"Was that Amanda I heard?" Fanny brightened when she entered the room. "I'm so pleased you've returned. We do need to be on our way."

"We can't go anywhere until I st-stitch my . . ." She waved the hem of her skirt in the air and broke into heaving sobs.

Amanda sat down and both Fanny and Sophie rushed forward. The two of them surrounded Amanda, and Fanny gathered her into a warm embrace. "Do tell us what has happened. Did you fall and injure yourself?"

"N-n-no," she sniffled. "It's B-b-blake." She accepted the handkerchief Sophie offered and wiped her eyes.

"Take a deep breath and then tell us," Fanny instructed.

After several restorative breaths, Amanda gave an affirming nod. "I think I'm better now." In between occasional sniffles, she related the unexpected and harrowing events. "Then, as I rushed down the path and through the gate, I caught my hem on the toe of my shoe and lost my balance."

Sophie straightened her shoulders. "Exactly who is this Julia woman?"

"I've told you everything I know. Blake has never mentioned her to me, but from all appearances they are very well acquainted."

Sophie's eyebrows pinched together in a frown. "Who does this Julia think she is, coming to Rochester and interfering with the man you want to marry? I've half a mind to go over there and have a long talk with her. I could set matters aright in no time."

"Sophie Medford, you'll do no such thing! Remember, you're a lady." Fanny tapped Amanda on the arm. "When did you decide you wanted to marry Dr. Carstead? The last I recall hearing, you said you wanted only to become a doctor and that he was too old for you."

"I never said he was too old." How could Fanny say such a thing? Amanda had always considered Blake quite perfect—his age, at least—if not his actions. "He is less than ten years my senior."

"If he's not ten years older, then he's nine and three-quarters," Fanny replied. "I care little about his age. It is you who took issue with his age when he first arrived."

"I don't recall any such thing. Sophie, do you remember me ever saying Dr. Carstead was too old for me to consider a suitor?"

Sophie shrugged. "As I recall, you've never wanted a suitor, no matter his age."

Amanda sighed. Their conversation was hardly relevant. It seemed Blake Carstead was a fraud. He'd never so much as hinted that he already had plans to marry. She sniffled and wiped her eyes.

"I'm sorry, Amanda. Instead of showing you proper sympathy, I've been busy asking questions." Fanny grasped Amanda's hand. "Please forgive me for my insensitivity. I think we should put aside today's shopping expedition and wait until tomorrow. The two of us should take our bags and get settled at your house, Amanda."

"I want to come along, too," Sophie put in.

Amanda blinked away her tears and glanced toward the kitchen. "What about Paul? Don't you want to remain here with him?"

"He's not very happy with me," Sophie whispered.

"All the more reason you should stay," Amanda replied. "If Paul must return to work later, you can come and join us at the house. We promise that we'll not do anything fun without you."

"I doubt the two of you would ever do anything fun or exciting if you didn't have me to urge you along." Sophie grinned. "I suppose you're correct. I'd best stay here for a while."

Fanny leaned close to Sophie's ear. "See what you can do to resolve your difficulties with Paul."

Sophie turned her gaze toward the staircase. "I will."

❖

A sense of relief washed over Fanny once they arrived at Broadmoor Mansion and the butler informed them the master of the house had departed only a few minutes earlier. "A shame that you missed him, for he'll likely be out the remainder of the afternoon."

Fanny hoped that would be the case. The one thing she'd dreaded about this trip back to Rochester was seeing her uncle and living under his roof. If she had her way, she'd spend the majority of her time at Broadmoor Island until Michael returned. Of course, legal matters with Mr. Rosenblume might require a return to Rochester, but she hoped any such legal proceedings could be conducted without her.

"Shall we have tea prepared?" Amanda inquired.

The question pulled Fanny from her thoughts. "Yes, of course. Tea would be lovely. After today's events, we would both benefit from refreshments. I'll go to the kitchen and ask to have tea served in half an hour. That way we can go upstairs and freshen up beforehand."

"An excellent idea," Amanda said as she peered into the

mirror above the mantel. "My hair is a fright and my eyes are puffy."

Fanny chuckled. "Your eyes are not puffy. You didn't cry enough to cause puffy eyes. Go on—I'll join you upstairs shortly."

The two of them parted in the foyer, Amanda turning toward the front staircase and Fanny toward the kitchen. Once Fanny had greeted the cook, she requested tea and hurried up the back staircase to her bedroom. The maid had already unpacked the few belongings she'd brought along. She had hoped they would need to stay under Uncle Jonas's roof only one night, but with Amanda's tears and the angry exchange between Paul and Sophie, they would likely be here longer than expected. She removed a dark brown gored skirt and fawn silk blouse from the wardrobe. These would do nicely for a quiet afternoon.

She was adjusting the last pin in her hair when Amanda tapped on the bedroom door and called, "Are you ready for tea?"

With a determined push, she stuck the pin into her hair, took one final look in the mirror, and hurried to the door. "I am refreshed and eager to have a cup of tea." She looped arms with her cousin. "I do hope the cook put a few of her wonderful lemon cookies on the tray. I saw she'd been baking earlier in the day."

Amanda chuckled. "If she didn't, we'll have to go in and demand our fair share."

Fanny had poured tea in both of their cups when the front doorbell rang. Marvin hastened through the hallway, and moments later Sophie appeared in the parlor doorway. "I see my timing is impeccable. I'm just in time for tea."

"Sophie! I thought you were going to spend the afternoon

with Paul." Amanda set her cup and saucer on the marble-topped table and leaned forward to peek around Fanny.

"That was my intention, but soon after you departed, he told me he had an appointment at one of the local churches and then was needed at the Home for the Friendless." She took a seat across from her two cousins. "Once he left, I decided to join you two."

Paul couldn't have been at home for long, as Sophie had refashioned her hair and changed into a different dress, one that appeared brand-new. "Was Paul in good humor when you two parted?" Fanny asked.

"I believe he was rather preoccupied. He said he would call for me when he had completed his duties." Sophie helped herself to one of the lemon cookies. "If he forgets, then I may spend the night here. Are you feeling better, Amanda?"

"I suppose, but I am shocked by this secret life Blake has been leading."

"I wouldn't make any hasty judgments," Fanny cautioned. "There may be an explanation."

Sophie chortled. "An explanation? How does a man explain a woman rushing into his arms and accepting his marriage proposal? Amanda's already told us that Blake knew her. After all, he said her name, did he not?"

"I suppose there's some merit to what you're saying, but—"

"Then you do think he's an ill-bred cad," Amanda cried as she removed a handkerchief from her skirt pocket and dabbed her eyes.

"I don't think I would consider him ill bred, but perhaps a cad," Fanny said. "Of course, I knew nothing of this romance you indicate existed between the two of you, so I find it difficult to judge the man or his actions."

"Indicate? He said he loved me. I heard him when I was lying on my sickbed near death. He was praying. I know what I heard."

"This discussion is doing nothing but causing distress. I suggest we formulate our plans for tomorrow's shopping," Fanny said. "I think if we begin—"

"Good afternoon, Mr. Broadmoor." At the sound of the butler's greeting, the three cousins turned toward the foyer. "Your daughter and two of your nieces are taking tea in the front parlor."

When Jonas appeared in the doorway, Fanny met her uncle's intense stare with what she hoped was a hard look. She was determined that he would be the one to turn away first. Silly, perhaps, but she didn't want her uncle to think he frightened her. Let him worry that his disloyal behavior would cause him no end of difficulty.

"I had heard the three of you were in Rochester. I do hope you don't plan to remain here for any length of time." He set his gaze on Amanda. "I have much I need to accomplish before going to the island to visit your mother and don't need any added inconvenience."

He turned and walked off before any of them could respond to his curt announcement.

"That was certainly a fine welcome for his daughter and nieces," Fanny said. "Your father appears to have set aside all civility and love of family since your mother has departed." She glared after her uncle. "In fact, long before Aunt Victoria departed."

"There's no need for harsh words, Fanny. Father is pre-occupied with his business. From what Mother tells me, he worries overmuch since the financial downturn. He doesn't want the family to suffer any losses."

Fanny attempted to shake off her feelings of disgust. The only person her uncle worried about was himself. Yet she couldn't say that to his daughter. What would Amanda think if she knew her father had thwarted her plans to attend medical school? Fanny doubted Amanda would think him such a fine patriarch if she knew he had no more character than a rotted turnip.

Jonas closed the door to his library and removed a bottle of scotch from the bottom drawer of his desk. Of late he'd taken to drinking during the afternoon, especially when he couldn't control the circumstances of his life. And that lack of control seemed to occur more and more frequently. Of all days, why had his nieces and daughter appeared in Rochester today?

He glanced at the clock. Ellert Jackson would be arriving for dinner, and he didn't want anything to go amiss. Just as the return of his daughter and nieces had come as an unwelcome surprise, Ellert's arrival in town had managed to catch him off guard. Though there should be no cause for worry, the very fact that Ellert wanted to see him caused a sense of apprehension. The liquor would quiet the demons that danced in his mind nowadays.

He tipped the glass against his lower lip and then savored the burning sensation the amber liquid created as it slid over his tongue and trickled down his throat. He finished the glass and then poured another. What could Ellert want? Their agreement had been completed, the papers had been signed, and Ellert's bank draft had been deposited in Jonas's bank account. Did Ellert call upon all the men who owed him money? Jonas attempted to quiet his fears with some simple explanation. Perhaps Ellert had other business in Rochester that required his attention. Yes, that must be it. He was paying a simple social call since he was in the city. Jonas threw back the contents of his glass and swallowed hard before returning the bottle to its hiding place. Instead of worrying, he should be pleased that Ellert had requested a social appointment.

There was nothing to fear. He had five years before his note to Ellert would come due. Granted, he had no formal plan for how he would repay the funds, but Jonas had to trust that eventually everything would work out for the best. The liquor warmed his belly, and his hands relaxed as he leaned his head against the leather chair. Everything would be fine.

Jonas didn't know how long he'd been napping in his chair when sounds of an argument interrupted his sleep. He strained to listen but couldn't hear well enough to discern the voices. He pushed away from the desk, raked his fingers through his hair, and plodded to the door.

"What's all the commotion out here?" he called. Was it Sophie? "Yes, of course," he muttered. That girl was always creating havoc. When no one responded, he used the noisy sounds to direct him. He came to a halt outside the parlor doors. Paul and Sophie were in the midst of a disagreement, and it seemed Fanny and Amanda were spectators for the event. "Exactly *what* is going on in here?"

Sophie turned on her uncle and sent an icy glare in his direction. "This has nothing to do with you, Uncle Jonas. I am having a discussion with my husband."

"If you don't want my interference, I suggest you keep your voices down. I would think you could control your wife, Paul."

"*Control* his wife?" Sophie fired. "I am not a servant that is employed to do his bidding, Uncle Jonas. I am a woman with a mind of my own."

"Yes, we all realize you insist upon making your own choices, even when they're to your own detriment."

"I believe I can deal with Sophie without your interference, Jonas."

"Deal with me?" Sophie stomped her foot and glared at Paul. "What is that—"

The doorbell rang and interrupted Sophie's response. Jonas waved at his relatives. "If we could please maintain a modicum of dignity, it would be appreciated. Before I knew all of you would be here this evening, I invited a business associate and old friend to join me for supper."

Paul beckoned to Sophie. "Perhaps we should leave. We can continue this discussion at home."

"There is nothing to discuss. If you want to see Elizabeth, you can come to the island."

Jonas sighed. He had better things to worry over than where Paul would visit his child. "Answer the door!" Jonas called to the butler when the doorbell rang for the second time. "And I expect all of you to be on your best behavior. Amanda, you can act as hostess since your mother is absent." Jonas didn't fail to note Fanny and Sophie glaring at him before he exited the room to greet Ellert.

Jonas hastened to explain as he led Ellert into the parlor. "Some members of my family arrived home unexpectedly earlier today. I'm certain you'll enjoy the pleasure of their company while we dine."

"Why, I'd be delighted. During the years I lived in Rochester, I don't believe I ever had the pleasure of meeting any members of your family. This is a genuine pleasure."

An undeniable hint of satisfaction shone in his guest's eyes as Jonas introduced him. Though Jonas couldn't guess why, Ellert appeared inordinately interested in chatting with Paul as well as the three young women. Thankfully, the butler entered and announced dinner before any of them made an inappropriate remark. Now, if they would simply eat their meal in silence, all would go well. The effects of his scotch had worn off, and his nerves were on edge. He could have downed another drink before Ellert's arrival if Sophie hadn't been in the parlor squabbling like a fishwife.

"And where did you purchase yet another new gown?" Paul inquired as they prepared to exit the parlor.

"You need not worry. I didn't spend any of your money," Sophie rebutted.

While Mr. Jackson escorted Amanda into the dining room, Jonas stepped between Paul and Sophie. "Would the two of you *please* cease this bickering for the duration of the meal? I care little what you do once you are out of my house. But I am entertaining a guest and expect your cooperation. Now, go in there and act like civilized adults."

"I'll not say a word," Sophie hissed in return.

Jonas tugged on the corner of his vest as he made his way to the head of the dining table. Amanda was seated to the right of Jonas; Paul took the seat to his left. Sophie sat between Paul and Fanny. Mr. Jackson had taken the chair beside Amanda and was making an unsuccessful attempt to engage her in conversation.

The silence around the table was deafening. Jonas was accustomed to his wife leading the dinner conversation while he simply enjoyed the food. Tonight, however, it appeared he'd be required to perform this social duty. "Do tell us what brings you to Rochester, Ellert."

"I had a few business matters that required my attention, but let's not discuss business during this fine meal." He smiled at Amanda. "Perhaps your daughter could regale us with a story or two. Won't you tell me about your plans, Miss Broadmoor?"

His gaze settled on Amanda's left ring finger. "I don't see any evidence that an immediate wedding is in your future."

Amanda stiffened. "I have no interest in discussing that particular topic, Mr. Jackson."

Jonas chuckled, hoping his laughter would lessen the impact of his daughter's strident response. "Amanda envisions becoming a doctor." Jonas grinned. "Her application for medical school wasn't approved, so she's been helping one of the local doctors at the Home for the Friendless."

Ellert shook his head as if in disbelief. "Why, I would think any university would be pleased, even proud, to have such a beautiful and intelligent woman in their numbers."

"I'm certain the school would have been delighted to have such a brilliant student if her application had been received in a timely manner." Fanny leaned forward and flashed a look of hatred at her uncle.

Jonas flinched at his niece's tone and her angry stare. Did she have knowledge about what he'd done? Foolish thought! He'd burned that letter from the school. Hadn't he? He attempted to recall exactly what he'd done with that missive.

Ellert's attention remained fixed upon Amanda. "So you're training with another doctor, but you'd prefer medical school. Is that correct?"

"I don't wish to discuss my education at the moment, Mr. Jackson. You and my father must have far more interesting topics you'd like to discuss."

"My daughter and nieces have been at Broadmoor Island. They left during the cholera epidemic and have returned to Rochester for a shopping trip. They'll be leaving in a day or two. Isn't that correct, Amanda?"

"That's correct. However, the outbreak of cholera here wasn't a true epidemic, Father. In truth, Rochester lost few lives. There is no comparison to the epidemic of 1852. Uncle Quincy said that epidemic was a genuine tragedy. If the city would enforce the sanitation codes, we'd have far fewer worries of disease."

Mr. Jackson chuckled. "You have a daughter who is intelligent beyond her years." He turned toward Amanda. "I will tell you why those codes aren't enforced, Miss Broadmoor. It is because high-powered men are willing to grease the palms of those in authority in order to bypass the rules."

Amanda arched her brows. "Men such as yourself, Mr. Jackson?"

Mr. Jackson placed his palm against his chest. "*Me?* No, Miss Broadmoor. I don't even own property in Rochester. But your father could affirm that I speak the truth. Couldn't you, Jonas?"

Jonas shifted in his chair, annoyed by Ellert's snide remark and irritated that the conversation had taken a turn he didn't like. "I'm sure there is truth in Mr. Jackson's comment. However, I don't believe I could produce a list for you, Amanda. Now, if we could discuss something of greater interest to all of us, I think that would be wise."

"There's always the weather," Fanny remarked while feigning a yawn.

A stifling quiet hovered over the dining room like the stillness before a storm. With each bite, Jonas worried that Amanda or Fanny would say something to irritate Ellert. Fortunately, Sophie had maintained her vow of silence—out of anger either at Paul or at him. Jonas cared little as long as she didn't speak.

The moment they'd completed their final course, Jonas pushed away from the table and suggested Ellert join him in the library for brandy and a cigar. The sooner he could get Jackson away from family members, the better. Although Ellert gave only a nod to the other guests at the table, he kissed the back of Amanda's hand and said he hoped they'd soon meet again. He couldn't hear his daughter's response or the rest of what was said, but Ellert chuckled when he finally stood and followed Jonas from the room. Jonas hoped his laughter was a good sign and that Amanda hadn't offended the man. She certainly hadn't been herself at supper this evening. He'd need to speak to Victoria. Obviously their daughter needed further training in proper etiquette.

After Ellert lit his cigar, Jonas poured two snifters of brandy and handed one to his guest, who sat down in one of the leather chairs near the library fireplace. Jonas held a match to his cigar and puffed until the tip fired bright orange. "I do hope you enjoyed dinner. My family can sometimes be . . . shall we say, less than affable."

"No need to apologize, Jonas. I'm not easily offended by the social set. You'll recollect I was generally snubbed by Rochester society during the years I lived here."

"Were you? I don't seem to recall." Jonas took a sip of his brandy and hoped it would calm his nerves. "So have you come to Rochester to invest in a new business?"

"No. Merely checking on a few of my holdings, and I thought I'd see if you were taking steps toward repayment of your loan by Christmas."

Jonas startled and met Ellert's intense gaze. "Christmas? When we discussed the contract, we both agreed that it would be five years from this Christmas—Christmas of 1904 was what we said."

"You're right. We did mention a date that was in 1904, but if you'll read your contract, I believe you'll see that your loan comes due this Christmas."

"That's impossible!" Jonas said, jumping to his feet. He set his brandy on the corner of his desk. With his cigar clenched between his teeth, Jonas pulled open his desk drawer and retrieved a file. With trembling fingers, he dropped the file onto his desk and riffled through the papers. When he'd finally located the contract, he pulled it from the pile and waved the white pages in the air. "Here it is!" He dropped to the large leather chair behind his desk and traced his index finger down the page.

When he reached the middle of the second page, Jonas ceased reading and looked up. A gleam of satisfaction shone in Ellert's eyes. How had this happened? In the past, Mortimer had reviewed Jonas's contracts. But Mortimer was dead, and Jonas had quickly perused the pages. He'd had no reason to doubt the terms would be exactly as they'd discussed.

"But you knew I thought it said 1904," Jonas croaked. "What would you have done if I'd noticed the incorrect date?"

Ellert shrugged. "If you'd objected or if you'd had a lawyer read the terms and protested the provision, I would have been required to reassess the terms. However, you didn't, and the contract is valid."

"I can't possibly pay you by Christmas. Why, I won't even have the issues surrounding Fanny's inheritance settled by Christmas. Be reasonable, Jackson."

"You owe the money, and I intend to collect in a timely manner and according to the terms of the contract."

"Surely you understand I'm in an extremely difficult place right now."

"Indeed, I do. I understand difficult situations better than most, Jonas. You played a large part in one of the most harrowing times in my life."

Jonas picked up the glass of brandy and downed the contents before returning to the chair beside Ellert. "I don't know what you're talking about." He waited for the brandy to quiet his fears.

"Don't you?" Ellert took a puff on his cigar and blew a smoke ring into the air. "Then it was completely insignificant to you that I was forced to sell my family home in order to repay a debt I owed you years ago?"

Jonas raked his fingers through his hair and forced himself to think back to the loan he'd made to Ellert, but he couldn't recall ever forcing any man to sell his home in order to repay a loan. He shook his head. "You have me confused with someone else."

"No. It was *you*, Jonas. I sold my family's home to pay your debt."

"But I didn't force you to sell. I didn't know—"

"Of course you didn't. I wasn't about to let you know!" He sipped the brandy and placed the glass on the table between them. "Selling my family's home caused me a great deal of pain, Jonas. I believe it is only fair that you suffer the way I have suffered. You'll have to part with something you love in order to meet your obligation to me."

"But I can't let anyone know the details of the situation," Jonas protested. "Not only that, but I can't touch any of my properties."

"What of the Broadmoor Island estate?"

"It's bound by legal terms to remain in the family. Currently there are other members who hold shares in the property, but none of whom could afford to buy out my portion."

"And what of your home—your business affairs?"

"As I stated, I cannot let anyone know what has happened, or my reputation will be ruined and there will be no hope of me reclaiming my fortune. I can't even suggest selling this place for a smaller home without my wife and sons questioning me. Besides, you know full well it wouldn't come close to paying off what I owe you."

Ellert smiled in a smug manner. "I suppose it wouldn't, but

mark my words, Jonas. I care little for your reputation or good standing with your family. You owe me, and you will pay me."

"But I can't do it by Christmas. Surely it is in your own best interest to give me an extension. That way at least you will receive regular payments and eventually the entire note will be redeemed."

"Father?" Jonas turned to see Amanda standing in the library doorway.

He waved her forward, glad for the momentary reprieve. "What is it, my dear?"

"I've had a tiresome day, and tomorrow will be filled with shopping. If you have no need of me, I'm going to retire for the night."

"Of course. You go upstairs, and I'll see you at breakfast."

She leaned down and placed a kiss on his cheek and then glanced toward her father's guest. "Good night, Mr. Jackson. I trust you'll have an enjoyable visit in Rochester."

He smiled broadly. "I already have. I had the pleasure of meeting *you*, Miss Broadmoor." Ellert stared after Jonas's daughter and then shifted in his chair. "Now what was it we were talking about? Oh yes, an extension. Perhaps if you had something of value to offer me, I might be convinced that extending your note terms would be of benefit to us both."

Jonas shook his head. "I have nothing."

Ellert glanced at the door through which Amanda had just exited. "I believe you have something of great value, Jonas. Something you can give me that will cause me to reconsider the terms of our agreement."

Amanda's shoes clicked on the tile and echoed through the hallway as she strode toward the staircase. When she neared the foyer, a knock at the front door surprised her. The butler had gone upstairs to turn down her father's bed. "Who could that be?" she muttered.

She opened the door and took a backward step. Hat in hand, Blake Carstead stood in front of her. Before she could close the door, he stepped over the threshold. "We need to talk. From your hasty departure earlier today, I fear you formed some incorrect assumptions."

"I made some assumptions, but I doubt they are incorrect, Dr. Carstead."

He pointed toward the parlor. "Could we sit down and talk for just a moment? I can explain if you'll only give me the opportunity."

Although she desperately wanted to hear how he could possibly explain this afternoon's happenings, she didn't want him to think her overly interested. Nor did she want him to know how deeply he'd hurt her. She'd not let that happen again. "I was preparing to go upstairs to bed. I've already bid my father good-night."

"I promise to be brief. Please?"

In spite of her best intentions, there was a longing in his voice she couldn't deny. "We can't go into the parlor. My father has a business associate meeting with him in the library. Their visit may end shortly, and I wouldn't want my father to find you with me this late at night and without a proper chaperone. Whatever you have to say must be said right here." Blake didn't argue. He was probably surprised that she'd even speak to him. And after what she'd observed, he should be!

"I know you were both surprised and shocked when Julia appeared this afternoon. However, your surprise can't begin to match my own."

Amanda tapped her foot. "I don't intend to argue about which of us was more surprised. Go on with your story."

He pressed the brim of his hat between his fingers. "When I was living in California, I met Julia. She was an important part of my life. I fell deeply in love with her and asked her to be my wife."

Amanda sucked in a breath of air. *So Julia* was *his fiancée!*

"Julia said yes, but a few weeks later, she told me she'd chosen to marry someone else. A man who'd be able to provide for her in much better fashion than a doctor could. After she gave me her decision, I left California." He took a step closer. "Now, after nearly two years, she has shown up to tell me that she made the wrong decision and that she loves me and wants to marry me."

"I don't know why you're telling me all of this. You don't owe *me* any explanation. Go ahead and marry Julia. I don't care one bit."

She turned on her heel and started toward the stairs, but before she had taken more than a step, Blake grasped her by the hand, pulled her into his arms, and captured her lips in a passionate kiss.

Amanda melted into Blake's arms and felt her lips form perfectly to his. Her heart pounded an erratic beat, and his kiss sent shivers of excitement racing through her body. She'd never experienced such a feeling.

She drew even closer, but he pulled away from her and looked deep into her eyes. "*Now* tell me that you don't care." Without another word, he released her and walked out the door.

## 13

*Monday, June 26, 1899*
*Broadmoor Island*

A few days after the cousins returned to Broadmoor Island, the door to Amanda's room creaked open, startling her. She clasped a hand over her heart. "Sophie! You should knock before you enter."

"I'm sorry. I shouldn't laugh, but the look on your face . . ." She clapped her hand over her mouth and burst into a fit of giggles. Tears rolled down her cheeks as she crossed the room and dropped into a chair near the window.

"I don't believe I looked *that* funny." Amanda yanked a handkerchief from the top drawer of her chest and tossed it at her cousin. "Did you come here for a purpose or simply to see if you could frighten me?"

Sophie wiped her eyes. "I'm sorry. I shouldn't have laughed."

A loud snort followed the apology, and she clapped a hand over her mouth again.

"Somehow it's difficult to believe you're truly sorry when your words are laced with laughter." Amanda dropped to the edge of the bed. "Are you enjoying Paul's visit?"

Amanda hoped her cousin would answer in the affirmative, for Sophie had been less than pleased when Paul had unexpectedly arrived at the island with Amanda's father Friday evening. The tension between the young couple was obvious.

"Enjoying? Haven't you noticed how he's put a damper on every suggestion I make? I was so looking forward to the party at the Frontenac Hotel, but Paul won't even consider attending." She shook her head and a hairpin dropped to the floor. A rich coffee-colored tress fell across her forehead.

"No doubt he simply desires time alone with you and Elizabeth. After being away from you and the baby, you can understand his feelings." Amanda arched her brows, hoping for a positive response from her cousin. It seemed the young couple had been quarreling ever since Paul's arrival. Amanda hoped she could somehow smooth the waters.

"Oh, *pshaw*! Quit defending him, Amanda. You've done nothing but come to his defense since he set foot on the island. He's the one who banished me to this place, but now that I'm enjoying myself, he thinks I should return home."

"And you disagreed?" Amanda couldn't withhold her alarm. "You need to reconsider, Sophie."

"We're in the midst of planning Fanny's wedding. I can't possibly go back to Rochester while the two of you are here. Absolutely not! I told Paul that once we've completed all of the arrangements, I'll return." She picked up the hairpin and walked to the mirror. "Of course, that may not be until after Fanny's wedding." With a deft hand, she refashioned the fallen tress and jabbed the hairpin into the wayward curl. "There! That should hold it in place."

"I'm not certain your decision is wise."

Sophie shrugged. "And I don't believe your assessment of Paul's reasoning is correct. Elizabeth was in bed for the night long before we would have left Broadmoor Island to attend the party." Sophie returned to the chair and picked up one of Amanda's books from the small table. "He said he was too tired from all his work these past weeks. You may recall that while we were playing charades, he retired early Saturday night. Is that the picture of a man who desires his wife's company?"

The question brought a vision of Blake's unabashed kiss to mind. Amanda felt the heat rise in her cheeks as she remembered how thoroughly she had enjoyed the feel of his body next to her own and the surprising softness of his lips as they'd taken command over hers. Yet she dared not think of a future with Blake. He'd stunned her with his kiss and walked out the door without a word.

Even though Blake had told her of his past with Julia, he hadn't admitted he no longer loved the woman. Why, he'd not even asked her to remain in Rochester. She had hoped he would send word or reappear and tell her of his love, but he hadn't. Now she decided the best thing was to erase any feelings for Blake Carstead from her mind and concentrate on Fanny's wedding plans.

Amanda forced her thoughts back to the present. "Perhaps you should reconsider your decision and tell Paul you'll return to Rochester. You've helped choose the fabric for our dresses and Fanny's gown, and I believe Fanny would concur that you belong at home with Paul." Amanda turned toward her cousin. "Did you hear what—"

Sophie dangled a newspaper clipping between her index

finger and thumb. "Exactly *when* did you plan to tell me about this?"

"What?" Amanda paled as she focused upon the news clipping. Her stomach lurched as she attempted to gather her thoughts.

Sophie held the clipping at arm's length and waved it back and forth as she walked toward Amanda. "How long have you been hiding this from me?"

"Hiding? I wasn't hiding it from you. Frankly, I didn't believe it was anything that would be of interest now that you're happily married with a family." Amanda fervently hoped the word *happily* still applied to her cousin's marriage.

"If you didn't think it was important, why did you cut it out of the newspaper? And how long have you known about Wesley's inheritance?"

"I can't recall exactly." Choosing her words carefully, Amanda explained how she'd happened upon the item in one of the many stacks of reading material Blake had given her to read while she was recuperating. "I was surprised by the information and cut it out. I wish I'd never seen it, yet I don't see how it should matter in the least."

"Not matter? Wesley Hedrick has inherited a vast fortune and you think I wouldn't be interested?"

"Tell me, Sophie, exactly *why* would news of Wesley interest you?" Amanda walked to the window. "Look down there at your husband playing with Elizabeth." She grasped Sophie by the arm. "Come here. Look at them and tell me why you should care about Wesley Hedrick or his inheritance."

Sophie jerked free and turned on her heel. Her shoes pounded across the carpet. She yanked open the door and then slammed it behind her, the bedroom window rattling in the quake.

When had life become so complicated? Back when Amanda and her cousins had been young girls, life had been so simple and problem free. Now it seemed there was upheaval at every turn.

Amanda opened her bedroom door, and as if on cue, she heard her parents arguing. Was there no peace to be found anywhere in this house? She did a quick turnaround and proceeded to the rear stairway, where she could avoid the possibility of being drawn into the dissension. Careful to avoid Paul and the other relatives on the front lawn, she took the path leading from the rear door to the north end of the island. Only a short distance down the path, she heard the crackle of branches and looked overhead. The wind had picked up, but the sky remained a cloudless azure blue. No storm in sight. Not unless she counted the storms that raged among her relatives.

She turned toward a rustling of leaves, took a backward step, and inhaled a deep breath. "Fanny! I didn't know you were out here."

"I was at the outcropping overlooking the water. I find it a good place to gather my thoughts."

"You're not having second thoughts about the wedding, are you?"

"No, of course not. I love Michael with all my heart and can't wait for his return. I only wish he were here now."

"Be careful what you wish for. We've not yet completed your wedding preparations." Amanda observed the brooding look in Fanny's eyes. Even *she* was unhappy. "Do tell me what's wrong. You don't seem yourself. Ever since Father and Paul arrived, you've distanced yourself from the rest of us."

"To be honest, I don't want to be around your father."

"Whyever not? I know he can be brusque and unapproachable at times, but—"

"I don't think we should discuss this any further. I don't want to say anything that will cause a rift between us."

"You know that could never occur. No matter what happens, you and Sophie will always remain dear to me. I believe I could tell you anything and you would understand. I only wish you felt the same way about me." Amanda didn't know which she found more distressing: the fact that Fanny wouldn't confide in her or the idea that her cousin believed there was something that could cause a breach in their relationship. "I *want* you to tell me what's wrong. I promise whatever you have to say will not change how I feel about you."

Fanny sighed. "I truly need to talk to someone, if you're certain you want to hear. But be forewarned, what I say about him will not be pleasant to hear."

"My mother has probably said worse. Don't you recall her anger when Father didn't accompany us on our voyage to England?"

"I believe this goes far beyond anything any member of your family might imagine." Fanny paused and gave another sigh. "I don't want to go into all of the details, but I have ample proof that you father has cheated me out of a great deal of my inheritance. Your father betrayed me. I shouldn't have given him the authority to continue managing my inheritance." Fanny reached forward and grasped Amanda's arm. "I'm sorry to tell you this, but now you know why I find it difficult to be in his presence."

Amanda swallowed the lump that had quickly formed in her throat. How could her father do such a thing? Didn't he have enough money without stealing from Fanny? It seemed his greed knew no boundaries. "Have you confronted him? How did this come to light?"

"When his lawyer died, the situation was brought to my

attention. Your father is aware of the fact that I have hired Grandfather's former attorney, Mr. Rosenblume, to act on my behalf."

Amanda dropped to the ground and stared across the grassy expanse toward the distant horizon, where water and sky met in melding shades of blue. She wondered if her mother knew of her father's treacherous behavior. Was this the cause of the argument she'd heard when she departed the house?

❖

Jonas placed a firm hand along the center of his wife's back and moved her toward the parlor. "I don't believe we should be having this discussion in the foyer. If you want to talk, I suggest we go into the other room."

Once they'd entered the parlor, Jonas closed the pocket doors. Of late, Victoria seemed determined to discuss everything in detail. He sighed. No wonder he stayed in Rochester as much as possible when the family was on the island. He didn't want to hear trivial details about the fabric for Fanny's wedding dress or the fact that Victoria didn't like the china or glassware Fanny had chosen. He'd done his best to avoid any wedding talk, but Victoria had been insistent they must talk. Thus far, it seemed Amanda, Sophie, and Fanny were his wife's favored topics.

"I am concerned about all three of the girls. Sophie and Paul appear to be having a disagreement, Amanda has been despondent since her return from Rochester, and Fanny has avoided the entire family since you and Paul arrived."

"First of all, they are not *girls*, Victoria. All three of them are young women, and you should cease your ongoing attempts to coddle them."

"Coddle them? I'm doing no such thing. I'm simply

attempting to find out what is causing all the discord among the family of late."

"Of late? When has there been anything but dissension in this family?" Jonas glanced about the room. With a grunt he sat down on the divan. "Why isn't there one comfortable chair in this parlor?" He felt like an oversized bird perched on a fragile branch.

"I'm especially concerned about Amanda. Something happened with Dr. Carstead while she was in Rochester, but that's as much as I've been able to learn from her. When I've pressed her for more information, she refuses to confide in me."

While his entire financial world was tumbling down around his ears and his contractual obligations to Ellert Jackson were resulting in disaster, Victoria was worried about nothing more important than Amanda's preoccupied state of mind. What would Victoria do if she were faced with a genuine problem? He felt the perspiration bead along his forehead. No doubt he would soon discover the answer to that question.

"Did you hear me, Jonas? I believe she's in love with him, and they had a spat while she was in Rochester. Did you notice anything while she was at home?"

Jonas pulled his handkerchief from his pocket and wiped his forehead. "No, Victoria. I had concerns of greater import that required my attention."

"I'm sure it was something that had to do with business— that seems to be the only thing of importance to you anymore. I want you to speak with Dr. Carstead and see if—"

"Whether or not she's had an argument with Dr. Carstead does not matter. Amanda has no future with him."

"Please, Jonas. Don't bring up the topic of an arranged marriage again. You know that I truly do not approve. Dr. Carstead is a fine man, and even though he isn't wealthy, he is well educated and is esteemed in the community. I believe he would make a fine husband for Amanda."

Jonas pushed himself up from his uncomfortable perch and began pacing the carpet. "Another man has requested Amanda's hand in marriage."

For a moment Jonas thought his wife had been struck dumb. But then she jumped up, grabbed the sleeve of his jacket, and shouted, "*Whaaat*? That's impossible. Amanda hasn't had a gentleman caller of any sort. Who could be asking for her hand?"

Jonas led her to the divan. "Do sit down. You look as though you may faint."

She permitted him to assist her to the couch, but she pulled on his sleeve until he sat down beside her. "Tell me this is your attempt at humor, Jonas."

"I'm afraid not, my dear. The truth is, Ellert Jackson has professed his love for Amanda and has requested permission to marry her."

The color returned to Victoria's cheeks. "Amanda doesn't even know him. It's inconceivable that you would mention his name as a possible suitor for our daughter. Even if Amanda loved him, I would expect you to refuse his offer of marriage. And the fact that you would force her to consider such a marriage is beyond my belief. Why, they would have little in common."

"He's a successful businessman who respects Amanda's interests in medicine. He would be a good match."

"A good match? She doesn't know him. That fact aside, he's nearly your age, Jonas. He's far too old for Amanda. She's young and vibrant and deserves a husband her own age. Amanda doesn't want to marry someone who reminds her of her father."

"Nonsense. Ellert's hair has turned prematurely white. He is only forty-five, which is an acceptable age for Amanda."

"No! I will not allow it. If you attempt to proceed with this ridiculous match, I'll do everything in my power to stop you, Jonas. I want our daughter to marry for love, and I am certain she loves Dr. Carstead."

Pain shot up the tendons at the base of his skull, and Jonas massaged his neck. He had foolishly hoped that Victoria would easily acquiesce to this arrangement and he wouldn't be forced to lay out the brutal facts of their finances. He'd known that he'd be required to admit the truth to Victoria eventually, for there was no doubt Ellert would be quick to tell Amanda that she had been given in marriage as payment of her father's debt. The words sounded harsh, but Jonas salved his conscience with the fact that such marriage arrangements had been an accepted practice for many years. Amanda would be happy once she reconciled herself to the idea.

Victoria rose to her feet and folded her arms across her waist. "I mean what I say, Jonas. I will not agree."

"Sit down, Victoria." She had left him no choice: He must tell her. "I want you to listen to me carefully. This is not a decision I have made lightly. However, it is a decision that must be followed. We are in dire financial straits. I don't mean that we are suffering a slight problem, Victoria. I owe Ellert Jackson a great deal of money. If Amanda does not marry him, everything we own will be at risk. *Everything!* Do I make myself clear?"

## 14

*Saturday, July 1, 1899*

Amanda picked her way along the path following Fanny's footsteps. The sunshine filtered through the trees, creating a splotchy patchwork along the trail. The day was beautiful, but she couldn't put aside thoughts of what her father had done to Fanny—to all of them. How could he be so deceiving?

"This shortcut will take us directly to the kitchen," Fanny called over her shoulder. They'd been finishing their picnic lunch when Fanny announced that she needed to return to talk with Mrs. Atwell.

"I do wish you would have told me you'd made plans for this afternoon before we arranged for our picnic. I had hoped to spend the entire afternoon away from the house. I told Mother we wouldn't return until supper."

"I'm sorry, but you're welcome to join me. I promised to discuss some of the wedding plans with Michael's mother. I don't want her to feel excluded. She's insisting on preparing much of the food, and she's going to bake our wedding cake." Fanny's eyes sparkled with excitement.

"I don't know how you can just go on as if nothing has happened. Fanny, I can't even begin to understand what my father has done."

Fanny stopped and took hold of Amanda's hands. "It cuts me deeply to know the pain I've caused you in revealing the truth. I should never have said anything."

"No. You were right to tell me everything. I can't help but wonder how many other lies have been told."

Fanny frowned and looked away. "I've been praying about such things. I know that nothing can be gained by dwelling on the bad. We must think of the good." She smiled. "That's why I choose to think of Michael and how much I love him. When I think of him and that we'll be married very shortly, nothing else seems as important."

The feelings of envy that filled Amanda's heart surprised her. She loved Fanny and wanted Michael to return and marry her cousin. There was nothing she desired any more than to see Fanny and Michael happily wed—or was there? The sudden stab of jealousy stopped her in her tracks. She forced herself to trudge onward. She didn't want Fanny to question her. Not now. Not when she couldn't understand these strange, unwelcome feelings.

Amanda spotted Mrs. Atwell's skirt and shoes below the line of damp clothes hanging on the line. As they drew closer, the older woman leaned down, lifted a towel from the basket, and flipped it in the air with a loud snap. A bright smile creased her face the moment she spotted them. "Just in time for tea," she called.

"Don't tell her we've just finished our picnic," Fanny whispered.

"I'm not a dolt. I wouldn't refuse her hospitality." There was a sharpness to her words that she hadn't intended.

Fanny spun around. "I've hurt your feelings. I'm so sorry. That wasn't my intent."

A rush of guilt washed over Amanda. "No need to apologize. I'm the one who was short with you. Forgive me. I want to choose better things to dwell on, but my father's actions have grieved me in a way I cannot explain. He has wronged you, Fanny. I would rather he had wronged me a hundred times than to have hurt you."

"Don't say such things," Fanny said, shaking her head. "There is pain enough to go around."

"But I needn't add to it. I'm sorry."

Fanny smiled and grasped Amanda's hand. "Then all is well. I'm so thankful to have you. Life wouldn't be the same without you and Sophie."

Mrs. Atwell gathered up the empty clothes basket and joined them. "Come along, you two. I have the tea brewing, and I've made some special tea cakes." Her gaze settled on the picnic basket dangling from Amanda's arm. "You're probably not hungry right now, but if you come down later, I'll be sure and save some for you."

While Fanny followed the older woman inside, Amanda set the picnic basket beside the back door and then joined them. Mrs. Atwell scooted close to Fanny with a list of items she'd already prepared for Fanny's review.

"I believe the wedding cake should be the bride's choice, so you tell me what you have in mind."

"Both Michael and I have a special fondness for your lemon pound cake. Do you think that would be appropriate?"

Mrs. Atwell beamed. "I don't know. You two know far more about fancy weddings than I do. What do you think, Amanda?"

"I'm not certain—"

Before she could complete her reply, Fanny jabbed her elbow into Amanda's side. "But that's exactly why we're having the wedding here at Broadmoor Island. We don't want to conform to what everyone else does. We want a wedding that is special and meaningful to both of us. And I think a lemon pound cake will be perfect." Fanny patted the older woman's work-worn hand. "If it will make you feel better, we'll ask Michael. He should be home any day now."

"That's fine by me," the older woman said. "We'll have time to decide once he's home."

"What if he doesn't come home?" The words had slipped from Amanda's thoughts to her lips, and now it was too late to take them back. Both Fanny and Mrs. Atwell stared at her, gape-mouthed. You would have thought she'd uttered a sacrilege. "That is a possibility, isn't it? After all, he didn't come home last year when he was expected. And now it's July and he said he'd be home in June. . . . He could be delayed again."

"I have faith he'll be home," Mrs. Atwood replied. "Mr. Atwood, Fanny, and I have been fervently praying that nothing will stand in the way of his expected return. We're trusting God will bring Michael home to us."

Amanda didn't argue. Perhaps God would answer their prayers. Yet she remembered Fanny's praying for that same thing last year, and God hadn't seen fit to send Michael back to her then. "I believe I'll go and see if there are any plans being made for this evening."

She thought Fanny would protest her departure, but when she didn't, Amanda slipped out of the room unnoticed. All this talk of weddings served as an ongoing reminder of Blake and Julia. Had the woman remained in Rochester and managed to convince Blake that she would be the perfect wife for him? Since she'd heard nothing from him, Amanda could only assume they had resumed their relationship. A woman wouldn't come all the way from California and then give up easily. Especially not a woman as forward as Julia. Why, she was probably planning their wedding this very minute.

"*There* you are!" Her father's voice boomed from the lower porch. Startled, Amanda looked up to see him waving her forward. "Come into the house. I need to talk with you."

She couldn't imagine why her father would want to talk to her. He seldom said more than a few words in passing, and now knowing what he had done to Fanny, she really didn't want to speak to him at all. "Is something wrong? Mother hasn't taken ill, has she?"

He shook his head. "Your mother is fine. She's waiting for us in the library."

What possible reason could her parents have to join together and speak to her? Her heart skipped a beat. Had her mother managed to convince her father to use his influence so that she could be enrolled in medical school during the next year? Surely not. He'd been adamant that he'd never agree. What then? Had Blake spoken to her father and asked permission to court her? The very thought caused her mouth to go dry. That must be it! Why else would they want to speak with her?

Hurrying her step, she followed behind her father like a small child expecting a treat. She stopped short at the sight of her mother. From her mother's appearance, this would not be a pleasant conversation. Her complexion was pale, and her red puffy eyes were evidence she'd been crying.

Amanda rushed over to her mother's side. "What's happened?"

The question was enough to release a floodgate of tears. They spilled down her mother's cheeks unchecked. She pointed to Amanda's father. "Y-y-your f-father will t-t-tell you. I ca-ca-can't." Her mother dabbed her eyes and then pinned Amanda's father with any icy stare.

"All these tears are frightening me. Exactly what is this about?" In spite of the warmness of the room, Amanda's hands were now trembling. A part of her was afraid to hear, while another part of her felt an urgent need to know exactly what had caused her mother's tears.

"Sit down, Amanda." Her father closed the library door. He waited until she had taken a seat beside her mother. "Our family has a critical problem, and you are the only one who can resolve it for us."

She thought of the things Fanny had told her. Was there something more to this than her cousin had confessed? "I can hardly believe there is anything I can do or say to help in matters so desperate that my mother is left in tears."

"Just hear me out," her father replied. "You'll understand soon enough."

Amanda sat in stunned silence while her father told her of the plan that would save the entire family from financial ruin. When he finished, he stared at her with an intensity that made her look away.

"Well? Will you do it? Will you marry Ellert Jackson?"

"Surely you don't expect an answer this very minute, Father. You've only just told me of a plan—your plan—that will completely alter my life, and you want me to give it no thought?"

His eyes burned her like hot coals. "You realize I could have agreed to the arrangement without speaking to you. However, I wanted you to understand the seriousness of our financial situation."

"I do understand, but that doesn't change the fact that I need time to make my decision. I don't even know Mr. Jackson, and he's old enough to be my father. He's not a man I would choose to marry under normal circumstances, so please permit me time to weigh a decision that will affect the remainder of my life."

"She's right, Jonas. Go along upstairs, Amanda. I'll be up shortly, and we'll talk."

She bolted from her chair and hurried out of the room without giving her father the opportunity to object. Once inside the sanctuary of her room, she threw herself across the bed and considered what her father had done in light of what Fanny had already told her. There had been a brief moment when she'd considered confronting her father, but what purpose would it serve? Her mother was already devastated beyond belief. No need to create further havoc.

Her thoughts raced back to the supper shared with Ellert Jackson at her home. Had the idea of marriage been discussed in her father's library that evening in Rochester? She forced herself to recall every detail of that meeting. Mr. Jackson had done his best to draw her into conversation during supper, but she'd been preoccupied with thoughts of Blake and Julia. She hadn't given the man any indication that she held any interest in him. Instead, she'd been rather rude. In retrospect, she recalled his lingering gaze when she had entered the library to bid her father good-night. He seemed pleasant enough, but the idea of courtship had never even been discussed. How could she possibly consider marriage to the man? Did Ellert Jackson truly hold regard for her after one simple meeting?

*"People often marry without being in love,"* her father had told her at one point in their conversation that evening.

Amanda thought of Blake and the pain she felt in misunderstanding his feelings for her. Maybe emotional love was not at all what she had believed it to be. Perhaps her father's idea of an arranged marriage truly merited consideration. After all, letting her heart choose for her had done Amanda little good.

❖

*July 4, 1899*

Amanda descended the staircase carrying three thin ribbons between her fingers. She was determined to put aside her sorrow and concerns and enjoy the Independence Day celebration. Spotting Fanny and Sophie on the front porch, she walked outside and waved the red, white, and blue strands overhead. "Look what I've found. Now Elizabeth can join our Fourth of July tradition and wear ribbons that match ours."

Sophie ran her fingers through the baby's thin fluff of hair and giggled. "I don't believe she has enough hair to keep the ribbons in place."

Undeterred, Amanda twisted the ribbons together and tied them around Elizabeth's waist. "There! That will do. Everyone will know she's one of us." She stood back and gave an approving nod.

Fanny waved toward the dock. "There's Mr. Atwell. Come on, Sophie."

"Where are you two going?"

"Your mother volunteered Sophie and me to greet guests as they arrive at Round Island for the celebration. We're supposed to be there early to receive our instructions," Fanny said. "Mrs. Oosterman's orders."

There would be no Fourth of July celebration on Broadmoor Island this year. The family would attend the huge gala being hosted by the Oostermans on Round Island. Amanda's father had announced it would be a nice change for the family, but Amanda wondered if it was his way of avoiding the expense of their usual festivities.

"Wait a moment and I'll go with you," Amanda said.

Sophie shook her head. "Your mother wants you to go with them."

"But why?"

"I'm sure I don't know, but she was insistent you remain here." Sophie nuzzled Elizabeth's neck until the baby chortled with delight. "Would you mind taking Elizabeth upstairs to her nanny? Paul said he would bring her with him. We have a long day ahead of us, and she'll be in better humor if she has a nap."

Amanda lifted Elizabeth from Sophie's arms and watched her cousins stroll down the path to the dock, still uncertain why her mother should want her to remain behind. She kissed Elizabeth's plump cheek and carried her inside. "Let's go upstairs. As soon as you take your nap, you can go on the boat and have fun." The baby gurgled and smiled. How simple life was for babies. No cares or worries. They had only to cry and their needs were met. "Your life will become more difficult with each passing day, dear girl. You had better enjoy this simple life while you can."

After leaving the baby with her nanny, Amanda went in search of her mother. She made a stop on each floor of the house and inquired of the servants, but none of them were any help. Even her father seemed to have disappeared. When she wanted to speak to her parents, they were nowhere in sight. After a half hour of searching, she gave up. She'd return to the front porch and wait.

"Uncle Quincy! When did you get here?" Her uncle was sitting on the lower veranda watching Beatrice's children play a game of croquet.

He looked up and smiled. "I arrived only a few minutes ago. Managed to jump on board with Captain Visegar and save Mr. Atwell a trip to Clayton."

"Mr. Atwell's off to Round Island at the moment." She pulled a chair close. "I'm glad to have a few moments alone with you. I wanted to know how work is faring at the Home since I've been gone. Have you been able to meet all of the necessary needs?"

He shook his head. "I doubt we'd ever be able to do that, my dear. However, I will tell you that it has been much more difficult without you. I didn't realize what a load you must have been carrying. And now . . ." His voice trailed off as he stared at the river.

"Now what? I pray there hasn't been any further outbreak of the cholera."

"No, but there are always those in need of medical attention. And with no one to care for them . . ." Once again his sentence remained incomplete.

"What do you mean no one to care for them? Dr. Carstead is capable. He managed quite well before I came to train with him."

"He managed. Though not as well as when he had you working by his side. But now that Blake is gone, it leaves us without anyone to tend to the needy."

"Gone?" She hadn't meant to shout. "Where? Why? I don't understand."

"I can't give you many answers. I only know that he left town with a young woman. I don't know where they went or if they're ever coming back."

Amanda wasn't certain if it was fear or fury that propelled her out of her chair. "Why didn't you ask him?"

Her uncle raised his brows, obviously startled by her brusque behavior. "If I'd had an opportunity, I would have done so. He left a note. I've told you everything he wrote in his message."

"That's it? *Dear Mr. Broadmoor, I'm leaving town with Julia?*" Amanda couldn't believe he wouldn't say something more.

"Well, something like that. He did apologize for his abrupt departure."

As her anger dissipated into an overpowering sadness, she dropped back into her chair. How could Blake leave without a word? Then again, why would he feel the need to tell her? He'd obviously decided he still loved Julia. The two of them were likely married and settling into a beautiful home in California. Her lips trembled as she struggled to keep her tears in check. Perhaps she *had* only imagined those words of love being whispered by her bedside. There was no hope for a marriage filled with love and laughter in her future.

As if on cue, her father stepped onto the veranda. "There you are. Look who's come for a visit."

Amanda swiveled around and looked directly into the eyes of Ellert Jackson. This was the reason she'd been told to remain on Broadmoor Island. Her parents had invited Mr. Jackson.

Her stomach churned at the sight of him.

Though he offered a smile, Amanda was unable to clearly gauge his mood. His expression seemed almost guarded, but his words were affable. "It's a pleasure once again to be in your company, Miss Broadmoor. Or may I address you as Amanda?"

Her father patted Mr. Jackson's shoulder. "Of course you may. You'd welcome that, wouldn't you, Amanda?"

Her throat felt as though it had been stuffed with cotton. Her lips moved, but not a word came out.

Mr. Jackson chuckled. "I do believe she's so overcome with joy at the sight of me that she can't even speak." He pulled a chair close and sat down beside her. "I hope you will be pleased to know that your father especially invited me to be your escort to the festivities at Round Island." Resting his left ankle across his right knee, he tapped his finger on the arm of her chair. "I trust that bit of news is agreeable."

Her father stood behind Mr. Jackson's chair with a beseeching look in his eyes. He appeared to be holding his breath. She cleared her throat. "I accept your invitation, Mr. Jackson." Her brief acceptance would have to suffice, for she couldn't bring herself to say the idea of spending the afternoon and evening in Mr. Jackson's company gave her any joy. "If you gentlemen will excuse me, I believe I'll go upstairs and fetch my hat."

"Don't be long," her father called after her. "The boat is leaving in fifteen minutes."

Chin tucked, she raced up the steps and into her bedroom. Slamming the door behind her, she leaned against the cool wood and wrapped her arms around her waist. For a short time her breath heaved in short rapid bursts and then slowed to a more normal rate. Her dreams of love collided with the reality of Ellert Jackson, and she wondered if she could possibly marry him. Perhaps he would be willing to wait until they gained a better understanding of each other. If she didn't love him, she would at least want to become better acquainted prior to their marriage. She pressed her knuckles to her mouth at the thought of marriage to someone so old—a complete stranger. They would have nothing in common.

A knock sounded on the door, and she jumped in surprise. "Who is it?" The quiver in her voice was obvious.

"It's your mother. May I come in?" Her mother didn't wait for a response. Instead, she was across the threshold and into the room before Amanda could object. "I know this is more than you should be required to bear, and I'm so very sorry." She wrapped Amanda in a warm embrace and then stepped back and looked her directly in the eyes. "Not all marriages that begin as arrangements are unhappy. If you work at pleasing Ellert, I believe he will treat you with kindness and generosity. After our talk the other night, I had hoped you had begun to accept the arrangement. Who can say? You may even grow to love him."

"Mother! How can you ever imagine I could love that old man? We have nothing in common. I won't even have the comfort of my family close at hand, for you know he won't want to live in Rochester."

"Your father tells me he admires your interest in medicine. Perhaps he would allow you to get the proper education you desire. Maybe in time the age difference won't seem that great."

"But I had hoped to marry for love. To truly desire to spend my life with my husband has always been my dream."

Her mother held up her palm. "You know I have never liked this idea of arranged marriages. In the past I've opposed your father on every front. But I fear I can be of little help to you now. Too much hangs in the balance for your father—for all of us." She clasped Amanda's hand within her own. "Spend some time with Ellert and give him a chance to woo you. A spark may unexpectedly ignite if you give yourself over to the idea that you could care for him."

There was nothing to say. She wouldn't argue with her

mother, but she couldn't deny the foreboding weight that had settled in her heart.

Ellert Jackson waited impatiently for Amanda's return. She was as beautiful as he remembered her, and he desired to be in her presence. He desired something infinitely more intimate but knew that would have to wait.

He smiled to himself. How marvelous that things should have worked out so well in his favor. Not only was Jonas Broadmoor in his debt, but he was in a most desperate bind that left the simpleton forced to barter his own daughter to keep out of the poorhouse. The man's social standing and financial reputation were still the only things that mattered to him.

"And people believe me to be the cold and calculating one," Ellert mused.

"Mr. Jackson, it was a pleasant surprise to hear of your arrival."

He looked up to find Victoria Broadmoor standing before him. He gave a polite bow and beamed a smile. "The pleasure, I assure you, is mine. Why, this island is positively blooming with beauty."

She blushed. "I wonder if I might speak frankly."

"But of course. I would have it no other way."

"My husband has told me of your desire to marry our daughter."

Ellert nodded. "It was love at first sight. Your Amanda is the most radiant and beautiful woman I have ever laid eyes upon. Her intelligence and charm far surpass all others."

Victoria looked at him oddly for a moment. "You love her?"

"But of course. Would a man propose marriage for any other reason?"

"I thought . . . well, that is . . . I presumed this was a type of financial arrangement," Victoria replied.

"My dear woman, I know there are those who would consider such an arrangement acceptable, but I cannot be counted among their numbers. My heart's desire is to marry your daughter and give her the love she deserves."

Victoria's expression seemed to change almost in an instant. The worried countenance softened to a look of pleasant surprise. "I must say, hearing you say that does my heart good."

"I'm so glad I could assuage your fears, madam. I would hate for us to get off on the wrong foot. Especially if you are to become my mother-in-law, although with such a youthful and beautiful woman as yourself, we would be better considered siblings than mother and son."

She laughed nervously at the comment, as Ellert had hoped she would. Women of her ilk were so easily persuaded by a few flattering words. He would charm her and win her over. While Jonas might know the truth of his choosing Amanda to wed, Ellert believed the man would never confide such a thing to his wife. To tell her he'd all but sold their daughter to save his hide and beloved reputation would surely have killed Jonas Broadmoor.

# 15

Mr. Jackson didn't appear pleased when Amanda lifted Elizabeth from Paul's arms and carried her to the boat.

"I believe the baby would be happier with her father or her nanny," he said when Amanda settled Elizabeth on her lap.

"She's perfectly content right here," Amanda said, clutching the child closer. She had hoped the baby's presence would deter him, but Mr. Jackson sat down beside her.

"I'm pleased to see you are fond of children, Amanda. I hope to have a son—perhaps by this time next year." He winked and slid closer. "Of course, I wouldn't want it to interfere with your passion for medicine. But with my money, we could afford the best help. I believe it would be entirely possible for you and me to have a family, even while you completed your medical training."

Amanda didn't know quite what to say. Ellert Jackson was clearly indicating his approval of her interest in medicine. "Your comment surprises me, sir."

He leaned close. "And why is that?"

His breath tickled her ear, and she drew away. "Most men would not desire their wives to seek employment, much less to take an interest in something so controversial as medicine."

He straightened and squared his shoulders. "You will learn quickly that I am unlike most men. I respect intelligence, and I equally desire a family."

"You were married before, were you not? Did you not desire children then?"

"My wife suffered certain . . ." He hesitated a moment before continuing. "Difficulties. She suffered difficulties throughout her life that prevented her from bearing children."

Heat rose in Amanda cheeks. She shouldn't have pursued such a delicate subject.

"I'm sure you'll have no such problems, my dear Amanda." He patted her hand. "I hope I have not embarrassed you, my dear. I would like to think we could speak openly about anything."

Amanda looked up and nodded. He was clearly doing his best to be kind and considerate of her feelings. Perhaps she could bear this arrangement better than she'd originally thought. Still, there was something about the man that made her uneasy. Maybe it was her inexperience in courtship and matters of the heart. Mr. Jackson had been married before and knew what it was to share such intimacy. That might have explained why he seemed rather . . . possessive. Yes, that was it. He seemed as if he already knew what her answer to his proposal would be. His confidence in the situation made Amanda feel very uncomfortable.

The water churned alongside the boat as they pulled up to the dock. When Paul extended his arms to Elizabeth, the baby chortled and lurched forward. Amanda watched Paul step onto the dock with Elizabeth in his arms. Silly, but she felt as though she'd lost a semblance of security when she'd handed the infant over to her father. Now there would be no escaping Mr. Jackson.

"Do you plan to remain on the boat, Amanda?" Mr. Jackson stood in front of her and offered his arm.

She shook her head. "I was lost in thought."

With a firm stance, he offered his arm when she approached his side. Amanda ignored his authoritarian attitude and tucked her hand inside the crook of his arm but was taken aback when he placed his hand atop hers in a far too possessive manner.

With a jerk she attempted to withdraw from his grasp. He squeezed her hand tight against his arm. "The ground here is quite rocky. I would not want you to fall, dear Amanda."

She forced herself to relax. "You are very kind."

"I can be kind in many ways," he said in a low husky voice. "I can hardly wait to show you."

"It's very inappropriate for you to whisper, Mr. Jackson. I wouldn't want others to get the wrong idea."

He laughed. "But we are engaged. Surely they will understand."

Amanda frowned and looked away. She hadn't agreed to marry him, but already Ellert Jackson presumed everything was settled. "Oh, there are my brothers. I'd like to say hello."

She tried again to pull away, but he would not release her. "I would be happy to meet your brothers. Why don't you introduce us?"

Just then the boys linked arms with their companions and headed toward the hotel. "We should hurry or we'll never catch up with them. I don't want to lose them in the crowd."

"It appears they are engaged with a group of their friends. Why don't you wait until later when they aren't otherwise occupied."

The tight grasp he maintained was enough to alert her that his remark was a command rather than a suggestion. A command he meant for her to heed. There was no need to argue. She could see from the set of his jaw that she'd not win.

When amplified bullhorns announced the horse races would soon begin, Ellert said, "Come along. I have a horse and rider participating in the race. I want to place a wager with some of the owners."

"You wager on the horses?"

Ellert guffawed. "Yes, my dear. So does your father, as well as every other wealthy businessman who attends or has a horse in the running. I'd guess that your brothers have even been known to place a wager or two on an animal. A well-placed wager has proved an enormous help to many a man."

"And an enormous loss to others, I would guess," Amanda said. "I don't think the risk is worthwhile. And I've been told it can become addictive—just like strong spirits."

Once again he laughed. "Forgive me. I forget your youth and how much you have to learn." He pulled her close to his side. "I will take great pleasure in teaching you how to become a woman."

"I *am* a woman," Amanda said.

"According to the year of your birth, but you are not a woman in the true sense of the word. Not yet." When they neared the edge of the racing track, Ellert said, "Wait here while I go and speak to my rider and place my wager."

A shiver ran up her spine. What manner of man was this that he would speak so intimately of things proper people never discussed in public? She thought to leave, to go in search of her brothers, but knew it wouldn't please Ellert. She supposed there was no sense in appearing unkind or disrespectful, so she remained in her assigned spot and watched the horses prancing and snorting while their riders led them toward track. The animals held their heads high, seeming to anticipate the attention that would soon be centered upon them.

"Here you are!"

Before Amanda could turn around, she was being hauled into the air. She twisted and stretched her toes toward the ground. "Jefferson! You look so much older."

He set her on her feet and then held her at arm's length. "And you look far too thin. Your bout with cholera has taken a toll on you, sister. I think an extra portion at each meal is called for."

"Enough about how I look. Do tell me when you arrived home." She peered over his shoulder. "And where is George?"

"He'll be here soon." Her brother chuckled and leaned closer. "He's gone to place a wager on a horse. He's hoping to help save the family from complete financial disaster, although I've been advised that you have been charged with that duty."

She took a backward step. "Who told you?"

"Mother. She's none too happy over the turn of events, but she tells me she holds out hope that all will be well, since your suitor is quite smitten with you. George and I arrived only a short time ago, and we didn't have time for a long talk with her."

"And why did I not know of your return?"

"We wanted it to be a surprise. Our way of adding to the

holiday celebration. We haven't even been home to Rochester yet. We came directly to Clayton, where Mr. Atwell met us at the train station and brought us directly here. He'd been sworn to secrecy."

Amanda grasped his arm. "Well, having you and George home has certainly added pleasure to my holiday. Otherwise I would find this day totally gloomy."

"What? When you're here with a man who adores you and has asked for your hand?" He nodded toward a clump of trees not far away. "The shade of those trees would be preferable to standing out here in the sun." He grinned. "I don't have the protection of a parasol."

After quickly scanning the area and seeing no sign of Ellert, Amanda agreed. "Based upon your earlier remark, I assume you've learned that Father is headed for financial ruin. At least that's what he and Mother have told me."

"Frankly, George and I had knowledge of the difficulties before we sailed. Father had us look into some possible investments overseas, but once we'd located a few high-yielding prospects, he couldn't raise sufficient capital." They located an unoccupied bench, which Jefferson swiped with his handkerchief. "I don't want to see that lovely dress ruined."

She stared at him for a moment, remembering the mischievous young brother who had taken pleasure in teasing her throughout the years. When had he evolved into this considerate young man their father now trusted for investment advice? How had she missed the transformation?

Jefferson sat down beside her and peered into the distance. "Of course we didn't realize the depth of Father's difficulty." He covered her hand with his own. "Father speaks highly of this man you are to marry. I hope he will prove to be deserving of you." He smiled and the dimple in his left cheek appeared.

She reached up and touched the small indention. "There's that dimple I love," she said.

He laughed. "As I recall, you always took great pleasure in teasing me because of that dimple. Now tell me about this man of yours. Mother says we've never met him—that he lived in Rochester some years ago."

"Many years ago would be a more accurate statement. His first wife is deceased and—"

"Amanda! I thought we agreed you would remain near the race track? And who is this?" Ellert asked, focusing upon her brother.

Jefferson stood and extended his hand. "I am Jefferson Broadmoor, Amanda's brother. And *you* are?"

Amanda stood up and grasped Jefferson's arm. "This is Ellert Jackson. The man to whom Father has pledged me in marriage."

Jefferson let out a snort. "Do cease your teasing, Amanda."

"I do not consider our betrothal a matter of jest, Mr. Broadmoor. Perhaps you could enlighten me as to why you find our engagement so astonishing."

The gleam in Jefferson's eyes faded, and his smile disappeared. "Forgive me, Mr. Jackson. I merely expected Amanda's suitor would be a man who was not so, so . . . A man closer to her own age."

"I believe Amanda is convinced the advantages of marrying a mature man far outweigh any benefit of marriage to someone her own age. Isn't that correct, my dear?" Ellert turned sideways and edged between Amanda and her brother. "Nice to meet you, Jefferson. If you'll excuse us, we're going over to the races."

"I'm sure Jefferson would be pleased to join us," Amanda said.

"On the contrary, my dear. I imagine your brother would be much more comfortable with his *young* friends—boys with whom he has more in common." Ellert grasped her elbow with a force that caused her to flinch and propelled her forward. "Do come along. We don't want to miss the first race."

In spite of Ellert's remark, Amanda hoped her beseeching look would persuade Jefferson to join them. But as they walked away, her brother remained near the bench, staring at them. While she hastened to keep pace with Ellert, she glanced over her shoulder at Jefferson. They locked gazes, and he mouthed the word *later*. Her spirits soared. He understood she needed him.

The remainder of the afternoon passed in a blur. The races, the polo matches, games of horseshoes and lawn tennis. Ellert kept her close by his side but refused to participate in any of the fun. "Games are for children," he'd said, and she didn't argue. Since losing wagers on the races earlier in the afternoon, he'd become a bit ill-tempered. She supposed it was to be expected, but she didn't want to provoke him further. He thwarted her efforts to visit with friends or family at every turn. Even during the picnic supper, he'd arranged for them to maintain a distance, insisting to her mother that they needed time to become better acquainted without family interference. He gained her mother's approval with honey-laced words and an engaging smile.

Amanda supposed he was right. They didn't know each other at all, and it would benefit their arrangement to spend time together. Still, there was a side of Ellert Jackson that Amanda couldn't quite explain or understand. It was as if just beneath the exterior of his charm and wit, a monster was waiting to be unleashed.

Ellert maintained his hold on her arm as the musicians began to play for the first dance of the evening. Jefferson was working his way through the crowd, but before he could approach, Ellert insisted they take to the dance floor.

The second dance had begun when Jefferson tapped Ellert on the shoulder. "I'd like to cut in, Mr. Jackson." Ellert frowned as he stepped back and handed her over to Jefferson.

"I believe I've angered him," Jefferson said, grasping her around the waist.

"I'm confident he will recover," Amanda said with a grin.

The dance ended all too soon, and before she knew it, Ellert reappeared to claim her. "I wonder if you wouldn't enjoy a walk with me. I would like very much to discuss our plans."

Amanda thought to reply in the negative but changed her mind. Given all that had happened—the things her father had done to Fanny and others in the family, she really needed to do her best to make this work. "Of course."

Leaving the dance behind, Ellert led Amanda down to the river walk.

"I've decided that we will be married immediately."

His words startled Amanda. She looked at him and found his fixed expression betrayed determination. "But that's impossible. The family is in the midst of making arrangements for Fanny's wedding, and that must come first."

His eyes shone with lust. "Unless her wedding is to take place in the immediate future, I'll not wait. I have my needs and desires, and I plan to have them met—by you."

Fanny spread a blanket a short distance from where Paul and Sophie had settled. Under most circumstances she would have joined them, but they'd been in a state of disagreement for most of the evening. Paul had protested when he discovered Elizabeth had returned to Broadmoor Island with her nanny. Although Sophie explained that the damp night air would have worsened the baby's case of the sniffles, Paul dismissed the explanation as an excuse for his wife to be free of any responsibility. Their voices drifted across the short expanse, and Fanny wanted to chide them for their behavior. Neither was completely correct.

The band struck up a lively march, and the young children paraded across the grass, keeping time to the music. When Paul stood and started wending his way through the young marchers, Sophie scooted over to Fanny's blanket.

"Can you believe the way he's acting?" Sophie asked.

"I think I can."

"What? You're taking *his* side?" Anger flashed in Sophie's dark eyes. "You know the night air doesn't agree with Elizabeth."

"I'm not taking sides. I think you are both wrong. Paul is jealous because you've been attracting a lot of interest from the single men. He believes you've sent Elizabeth back home so that you will have total freedom to do as you please without the hindrance of a baby or her nanny. And you, dear Cousin, still want to punish him for sending you to Broadmoor Island when you wanted to remain in Rochester."

Sophie peeked from beneath the brim of her straw hat. "When did you become so wise?"

"I'm not wise. I can be objective because I'm not involved. I do think you're both squandering time that could be put to better use." Fanny looked toward the sun setting on the distant horizon. An edge of the orange globe touched the water and sent rays of light shimmering across the dark ripples. "You love each other. Why not replace your childish anger with joy and thankfulness that you have the pleasure of his company? I'm sure you'll find that Paul will respond with the same spirit."

Sophie appeared lost in thoughtful consideration for several moments. "You're right," she finally said, grinning. "But it's difficult to be the first to extend the olive branch, don't you think?"

"Yes, but it appears Paul is trying, too."

Sophie followed Fanny's gaze across the lawn, where she spotted Paul returning with two tall glasses of lemonade. "Thank you," Sophie whispered as she brushed a quick kiss against Fanny's cheek. "Why don't you move your blanket and sit with us. You look far too lonely over here by yourself."

"I'm quite content. You need to be alone with Paul. I think Amanda may join me a little later."

Sophie wrinkled her nose. "If she can get away from Mr. Jackson. I can't imagine why she accepted his invitation to escort her."

"I'm uncertain, as well, but there isn't enough time for us to discuss her reasons right now. You'd better return to your spot or Paul will think you've deserted him."

As the sky began to darken, Fanny leaned against the trunk of a giant pine tree and waited for the first explosion of color in the sky. How she longed for Michael's return. He'd promised a June return, but June had now turned to July. Each morning she and Mrs. Atwell prayed for Michael's safe and speedy return. And when their spirits waned, they did their best to encourage each other. Now that the last day of June had passed, keeping faith that Michael would soon return proved increasingly difficult. This was the Fourth of July celebration that she and Michael should be attending together—at least that had been Fanny's dream. Now she simply longed to know he would return before summer's end.

Seeing the many couples happily settled on the blankets that dotted the grass did little to keep her jealousy in check. "Be happy for them," she muttered in an effort to tamp down her feelings of envy. The first explosion boomed overhead, and a proliferation of color streaked the sky in a showy display. The crowd responded with thunderous applause and appreciative *ooh*s and *ah*s.

When the second blast exploded and the overhead illumination offered a silhouette of Paul and Sophie locked in a warm embrace, she could feel her resolve begin to vanish. "Why hasn't he returned? I'm trying to trust, but . . ." Words failed her. She did want to believe all would be well. But how did one continue to cling to hope in spite of disappointment?

"May I join you?"

The grass had muffled the sound of approaching footsteps, and Fanny twisted around. She jumped to her feet, unable to believe her eyes. "Michael!" She was certain her squeal of delight could be heard above the sound of the fireworks, but she didn't care in the least. "When did you arrive? Let me look at you! Have you been back to the island yet? Are you well? I can't believe it's you!" She clasped his face between her hands to assure herself he was truly standing before her.

He pulled her into a warm embrace and tipped her chin with his finger. "Before I have the strength to answer all of those questions, I believe I need a kiss." He claimed her lips with a long and passionate kiss that set her heart racing. "I love you, Fanny, and I promise I'll never leave you again. Tell me that the wedding plans have been made and we'll be married soon."

"We can be married in only a few days from now." She breathed his name and returned his kiss with reckless abandon.

16

*Wednesday, July 5, 1899*

After removing a cigar from the humidor, Jonas settled into the leather chair situated behind the desk in the library of Broadmoor Castle. He was never quite comfortable at this desk— probably because the chair had been a better fit for his father's lanky frame. Jonas was required to stuff his portly figure into the chair at an angle. "Most uncomfortable chair in the house," he mumbled while he clipped the end from his cigar. Not a Cuban cigar, but a cheaper, less aromatic replacement.

Michael's return during yesterday's Fourth of July celebration had caught Jonas unaware. He first thought Fanny had withheld information regarding the young man's return, but apparently she had been as surprised as the rest of the family. Now Jonas was eager to discover the profitability of Michael's sojourn to the Yukon. He'd set up an appointment to meet with Michael at one o'clock, and the clock had struck the hour several minutes earlier. Jonas puffed on his cigar, growing more annoyed as each minute ticked by. Who did Michael Atwell think he was to exhibit such disrespect? His time in the North had apparently numbed his good manners.

When a knock sounded at the library door, Jonas first looked at the clock before calling, "Come in." The moment the door cracked open, Jonas leaned across the desk. "You're late, Michael."

"Yes, I know. Fanny and I were discussing our wedding plans."

Jonas couldn't believe his ears. No apology or request to be forgiven for his breach of etiquette? Not only had Michael forgotten his manners, he'd also forgotten his place in this household. "I'm accustomed to servants following orders."

Michael met his gaze with an air of indifference. "So you are, but I am no longer your servant, Mr. Broadmoor. I have been providing for myself since my departure to the Klondike."

"Technically that's correct. But let's don't forget that your parents are dependent upon me for their positions in my household." The comment didn't have the desired effect, for the young man had developed an air of confidence he'd lacked prior to his departure. "Sit down, Michael. We need to talk." Jonas took a long draw on the cigar. "I'm sure you recall we had an agreement before you departed."

"How could I forget."

The statement dripped with sarcasm, and Jonas arched his brows. Michael had best watch his tongue or he'd find himself off the island and out of Fanny's life before nightfall. "Since you've already made yourself comfortable, why don't you tell me about your travels. I'm anxious to learn of your success—or failure, whichever the case may be."

"I suppose you could say I experienced some of both. I was blessed with the friendship of two men and joined with them in prospecting. I think Zeb and Sherman were the greatest blessing I received. Their friendship and what I learned from them are more valuable than the gold we discovered."

Jonas perked to attention. "What could be more valuable than gold? What is it they told you about? If you've come upon some other discovery, you must permit me the opportunity to invest."

Michael laughed and shook his head. "What they taught me is free, Mr. Broadmoor. While I was with them, I experienced the love that Jesus taught about. They shared with me as though I were their brother, and they willingly made me a partner in their claim. Best of all, they taught me what it means to be a true follower of Christ."

Jonas pushed away from the desk and flicked his ashes into the fireplace. "I don't want a Bible lesson, boy. I want an accounting of your finances. We had an agreement that if you attained enough wealth that I could be certain you weren't after Fanny's inheritance, I'd permit the two of you to wed."

"You can demand whatever you wish, but Fanny and I intend to be married in three days. I doubt I could ever offer an accounting that would convince you Fanny's wealth isn't of importance to me."

Jonas narrowed his eyes, convinced Michael was toying with him. The younger man didn't want to divulge the depth of his fortune, or lack thereof, and Jonas wasn't enjoying their game of cat and mouse. "You owe me repayment of the funds that I advanced for your journey. Are you able to pay me?"

Michael withdrew a leather pouch from his pocket and

dropped it in front of Jonas. "I believe this will cover my obligation to you."

"There's interest due on the loan."

Michael nodded. "If you look inside, you'll find that your interest has been included with my payment."

Jonas picked up the bag and arched his brows. He'd expected the bag to be heavy with gold nuggets. Instead, it felt empty. He tossed the bag at Michael. "Is this a joke?"

With a swipe of his hand, Michael grabbed the bag and yanked open the top. He withdrew a bank draft and pushed it across the desk to Jonas. "I believe a bank draft is still considered negotiable tender."

Jonas lifted the draft and examined the amount. "This will do, but there's still the issue of how well you fared financially while you were gone. You have a responsibility to convince me, as Fanny's guardian, that you can care for her in a proper fashion."

"I'm not required to convince you of anything, Mr. Broadmoor. You're no longer Fanny's legal guardian, and we intend to be married—with or without your blessing."

"Don't you raise your voice at me, Michael! You're nothing but—"

"Jonas! What is going on in here?" Victoria pushed open the library door and stepped inside. "I could hear the two of you the moment I entered the hallway." She continued to stare at him. "Well? What seems to be the problem?"

"Michael is unwilling or unable to fulfill an agreement we made before he went to the Yukon. Therefore, I've told him it will be impossible for him to marry Fanny."

"Oh, pshaw! Cease your nonsense, Jonas. Fanny and Michael will be married on Saturday. The plans are made." She smiled at Michael. "You and Fanny have our blessing, Michael. We will be pleased to welcome you into the family." She patted the young man's hand. "Now, if you will excuse us, I need to speak with my husband privately for a few moments."

"Yes, of course. Thank you, Mrs. Broadmoor." He stood and nodded at Jonas. "Good day, Mr. Broadmoor."

The moment Michael had exited the room and closed the door, Victoria wagged her finger at him. "Refrain from any further meddling in this wedding, Jonas. They will be married on Saturday, and we will be happy for them or you will suffer the consequences."

His anger mounted, and Jonas tugged at the starched white collar that surrounded his thick neck. "I have tolerated your outbursts from time to time, Victoria, but I do not like being threatened."

"And I do not like having my daughter forced to marry for other than love." She stepped closer, her face contorted by pain. "Mr. Jackson may be a fine man, and indeed he has proven himself to be of the best manners and expression; however, Amanda should be allowed to choose her own husband, and I cannot abide that we are forcing her to do otherwise. If I can't, I will at least see Fanny happily wed. And if you can't wish her well in this marriage, you had best appear genuinely pleased to walk her down the aisle and offer her hand to Michael on Saturday. Otherwise you may not find the consequences to your liking."

His wife didn't present him with an opportunity to respond. Not that he had the words to put Victoria in her place without forcing her hand. He couldn't risk the possibility that she would find some way to destroy the marriage arrangement with Ellert. Women! If only the world could exist without them. He leaned to the right and pulled open the bottom drawer of the desk. He needed a drink.

❖

Fanny worried that it might rain but proceeded down the path nevertheless. She had received a note from Michael suggesting they meet in one of their favorite secluded spots. It was a place where they often enjoyed fishing and whiling away an afternoon, and Fanny thrilled at the thought of once again sharing it with her beloved.

"I thought you might not come."

Fanny looked through the dark shadows of the trees but couldn't see Michael. "Where are you?"

He laughed. "I'm right here." He moved forward into the fading light.

Fanny rushed into his arms. "I can't believe you've really come home. I've longed for this more than words can say."

"I know," he replied, combing back her unruly curls with his fingers. "There were so many times when I thought I might never see you again."

She touched his cheek. "I tried to imagine you up in your frozen North. I read everything I could find about the area. There really isn't much to be had."

He laughed. "I don't doubt it. There weren't many folks up that way prior to the rush—at least not folks who might want to write a book about it. There were some very interesting native people in the area. I found their culture and ways so different from ours."

"Tell me about them," Fanny urged.

"I'd rather talk about us—about you."

He kissed her gently and then hugged her close. "Every time I lit a fire, I'd see your hair in the dancing flames." He kissed her ear. "I thought of you every night before I went to sleep." He kissed her neck, letting his lips linger for just a moment.

Fanny melted against him. She had no words for what she was experiencing, but at last her heart felt as though she'd truly come home.

"Every morning I woke up with thoughts of you. I could see your smiling face and very nearly hear your voice. It was all that got me through our time apart—that and the Lord. God gave me a comfort that compared to nothing else."

"I know. He gave it to me, as well. All the times Uncle Jonas tried to marry me off to someone else, God was there to sustain me with memories of you."

The light was gone from the sky, but overhead the stars glittered like diamonds. Michael took hold of Fanny's hand and led her to a clearing. "Look, see there? It's the North Star. Remember how we used to wish upon it when you were a little girl?"

Fanny nodded, but she wasn't sure Michael could see her. "When you were gone, I'd find it and think of you. I imagined that it shone right over the place where you were living. I made so many wishes on that star." She stopped and put her head on his shoulder. "And they've all come true."

He held her close and sighed. "I love you, Fanny."

She snuggled against him and smiled. "I love you, Michael. I will always love only you."

❖

*Saturday, July 8, 1899*

Although clouds had loomed overhead Friday evening, Saturday dawned without a hint of rain in the offing. Both Amanda and Sophie had come to assist Fanny with her gown and veil. Amanda fastened the final button on the gown. "You are an absolutely beautiful bride. Michael is fortunate to have you."

"I am the one who is fortunate. Had I searched the world, I know I could never have found a man who loves me any more than Michael does. He is a perfect match for me. We place importance on the same things."

"Like what?" Sophie asked as she wound a strand of Fanny's hair and tamed her curls.

"We both love the islands. Don't tell anyone, but he's purchased one of the islands for me as a wedding gift." She grinned with excitement. "He didn't want to wait to see if we'd be able to buy Broadmoor Island."

"I'd be willing to sell you any share I might have in this place," Sophie said. "Unfortunately, I don't think I have any, but perhaps I can convince my father to sign over his share and then Amanda can talk to Uncle Jonas."

"I doubt my father would listen to anything I'd ask. I have little sway over what he decides. If so, I wouldn't be—" Amanda clamped her lips. No need to ruin Fanny's wedding day with her own problems.

"I do hope that Ellert Jackson isn't going to act as your escort," Sophie said. "I don't like him in the least. The way he clings to you and won't let you out of his sight is most annoying. Why, he wouldn't let any of us near you at the Fourth of July festivities. You need to tell your father that you want another suitor."

"I don't think that's possible, Sophie. Father believes Ellert would be a perfect husband for me."

Sophie clasped her bodice and dropped to the nearby rocking chair. "You jest! Surely you haven't agreed to the match."

"I have no say. It has been arranged. In fact, we will be wed very soon. Had it not been for Fanny's wedding, I'd already be his wife. I managed to convince him we had to wait until after her marriage." She locked eyes with Fanny. "Forgive me,

Cousin, but I had hoped Michael wouldn't return until August. I thought I might be able to convince Ellert that he didn't want to marry me. He can be pleasant enough, but there is something quite demanding about him."

Fanny swiveled around on the chair. "Oh, Amanda. You need not apologize. I understand how you must feel. When your father was trying to force me to wed Daniel or one of those other young men he thought to be perfect, I became panic-stricken. I understand your plight. There must be something Sophie and I can do to help."

"It's best neither of you interfere. Father and Ellert would be angered, and it would do no good. We won't be making our home in Rochester, and my one hope is that I'll be permitted to return and visit with both of you from time to time. If Ellert thinks you've done anything to hinder his plans, I fear he won't allow me to come back to visit."

Her mother entered the room before her cousins could respond, but Amanda didn't fail to see the pity in their eyes. Even though Sophie hadn't been in love with Paul when they married, his kindness and love had won her heart. Both of her cousins were in love with their husbands, but Amanda doubted she could ever love Ellert. Her heart had room for only one love, and that, unfortunately, was Blake Carstead. If only she could have realized it in time, she might have been willing to fight for his affection. She had considered telling Ellert about Blake, but something told her it wouldn't change his mind. He wouldn't care that she loved another.

"Do hurry along, Fanny. Few though they be, your guests are waiting."

Fanny stood and twirled in front of the mirror, examining her gown from all angles. "We wanted only close friends and family to attend. And Uncle Jonas seemed relieved when

I told him I wouldn't need a large sum to prepare for the wedding."

Amanda stepped aside as her mother reached to smooth the folds of Fanny's veil. "There, that's perfect. I'm sure your uncle Jonas would have agreed to a large wedding at the church in Rochester if that's what you'd asked for, dear. Personally, I would have preferred a church rather than sitting in chairs out on the lawn, but it's your wedding." She handed Fanny a lace handkerchief. "This is the handkerchief your grandmother carried at her wedding. I know she would be pleased to have you carry it. Now, come along. I'll go down and take my seat. Listen to the music and come out on cue."

Along with the help of two servants, Jefferson and George had managed to move the piano to the veranda earlier in the day. "I do wish you had contacted the pianist from the church in Clayton," Fanny whispered to Amanda. "I hadn't even planned to *invite* Mr. and Mrs. Oosterman, much less have her play the piano."

"I know, but Mother asked her before I had an opportunity to go into Clayton. I believe Mother invited several other guests who weren't on your list, too. She didn't want me to tell you, but I think it's better if you're prepared."

Fanny's veil fluttered as she spun around to face Amanda. "Why would she do such a thing?"

"You know how Mother is. She didn't want anyone to feel slighted or to do anything that might give rise to gossip." The reply was Amanda's best guess. She couldn't be absolutely certain of her mother's motivation. Perhaps it was her father who had insisted that the social set be invited. She could never be completely sure what prompted her parents' decisions.

Fanny pulled aside the lace curtain and peeked outside.

"This isn't what I expected. Your mother said my *few* guests had arrived, when all the while she knew—"

A crescendo of three piano chords interrupted, and Amanda stepped to the door. "We can discuss this later. That's my signal."

Fanny shot her a look of frustration.

Amanda glanced over the crowd that had gathered to witness the couple's nuptials. More than a verdant aisle separated the attendees. The Broadmoor guests were clothed in fine attire and bore looks of disdain for the guests who sat on the other side of the grassy division. This would be quite an afternoon and evening—an integration of social classes. She uttered a prayer that this day wouldn't turn into a disaster for Fanny.

Throughout the ceremony Ellert's gaze felt like a hot poker boring through to her soul. Amanda had hoped he wouldn't appear, that some business or personal matter would keep him away from the wedding so that she could enjoy this time with her family. But he had arrived. And he'd taken possession of her from the very first moment he set foot on the island. He'd even voiced an objection when she'd excused herself to prepare for the ceremony. Amanda had prayed this day would create many happy memories for Fanny. However, Ellert's presence affirmed that her own recollections of this day wouldn't be so pleasant.

She knew he could be charming, but his lustful nature frightened her. He seemed to think it completely appropriate to discuss topics of a most intimate nature. He alluded to the things they would experience together—some appropriate subjects for discussion and others quite inappropriate.

But she really had no choice in the matter, Amanda realized. She had talked at length with her mother and father, and the situation was quite grave. Every idea for helping the family had failed to move her father toward a change of mind. All he would say was that this was the best solution to the situation if their family was to maintain its position in society. When they had been alone, her father had told her quite simply that it would kill her mother if they were to lose their home and standing. Amanda was starting to believe that he was right. Her mother had always loved her status among Rochester's elite. To take that from her now would be cruel.

Once the ceremony ended, Ellert pulled her aside. "I've been lonely for your company," he whispered. "Hearing your cousin repeat her vows pleased me, for I knew you would soon be promising to love and obey me. You can't imagine how much I'm going to enjoy being loved and obeyed."

She didn't want to discuss Ellert's marital expectations. The thought caused her stomach to lurch. "Why don't we go and join the other guests? Fanny may need my help."

"*I* need you far more than Fanny does. She has a husband who can assist her if she has need of help. I haven't had a tour of the island, and this would be a perfect time for you to show me about."

"You want me to escort you around the island? *Now?*"

"Now!"

"But the wedding guests—"

"If I didn't know better, I'd think you were attempting to avoid me, my dear." Ellert pulled her close. "Come along and show me the wonders of Broadmoor Island. Who knows? I may find that the seclusion of island living appeals to me."

Amanda cast a glance toward the crowd. She had hoped to locate someone who would save her from Ellert, but no one came to her rescue. They walked to the rear of the house and continued along the path leading to the north side of the island. When they reached a small grove below the overhanging rocks, Amanda said, "The view of the water is excellent from this vantage point, but if you'd care to climb the rocks, you'll need to continue on your own. My shoes won't withstand the jagged rocks."

"I find the view from here quite lovely," he said, pulling her into his arms.

Without further warning, he crushed her lips in a bruising kiss. She pushed against his chest, but her attempt to escape his hold only spurred him on. He pulled her to the ground, his hands now groping her body. Frightened, she clawed at his back, but his jacket offered him too much protection. His cruel laughter mocked her, and she yanked at his hair. "Stop or I shall refuse to honor the agreement you made with my father."

His hands stilled and he stared into her eyes.

"I mean it, Mr. Jackson. If you take advantage before we wed, I will *never* be your wife. I am of legal age and care little if my father disowns me."

His anger was evident for only a moment before his expression turned contrite. "I apologize, my dear Amanda. It's just that your beauty—your very presence—is intoxicating. I could not help myself. I desire you more than anything else."

Amanda thought his apology less than sincere, but she couldn't for the life of her explain why. He helped her up and quickly let go his hold. She dusted off her dress, hoping there would be no grass or dirt stains to reveal her shame to others.

"You are so innocent of the power you have over a man," he said, his voice seductive and low. "I promise you will enjoy our wedding night. I only insist that it come very soon. I cannot say that I will be able to control my desires for you much longer. Do you understand?"

Amanda swallowed the lump in her throat. "We can

announce the engagement next week. If my parents' reputation is to be protected, we must follow the rules of propriety."

Ellert chuckled. "A few minutes ago, you didn't care if your father disowned you, but now you worry over his reputation?" Wedging her chin between his thumb and forefinger, he tipped her head upward. "The wedding will take place before the end of August. Agreed?"

"You have my word." Her voice quivered, and he smiled.

He traced his fingers down the nape of her neck and then leaned close as his fingers returned to her cheek. "You'll soon learn not to refuse me anything."

## 17

*Saturday, July 15, 1899*

Blake bounded up the steps of the Home for the Friendless, glad to be back in Rochester and the life he'd come to enjoy. The contentment and challenges he'd found in this community had come as a surprise to him, but he now felt at home in Rochester. He'd stopped at home only long enough to clean up after his journey. Now he was anxious to see his patients and visit with Quincy and Paul. He hoped all had gone well during his absence.

He yanked open the door and nearly collided headlong with Paul. "Whoa! Sorry, Paul. I didn't see you." He grinned.

"No apology needed. I'm running late and wasn't watching where I was going. It's good to see you've returned, Blake. We were afraid you might not come back."

Blake laughed. "You'll not get rid of me quite so easily." He cocked his head to one side. "Where are you rushing off to?"

"I have to catch the train. I was supposed to be at Broadmoor Island by noon. If I don't board the next train, I'll miss Amanda's party, and Sophie will never forgive me." He chuckled. "I'm certain she's going to be unhappy when I don't arrive by noon, so I had better be there by the time the festivities begin."

Blake stood in the doorway, blocking Paul's exit. "What kind of party are they having for Amanda? I know it's not her birthday."

"Oh, I forgot. You don't know. While you were gone, Amanda was betrothed. The engagement party is this afternoon at Broadmoor Island. I fear you'll need to find a new medical assistant. Amanda and her husband won't be living in Rochester. Although I have heard it said he intends to send her to university for proper medical training."

Blake leaned against the doorjamb to maintain his balance. He felt as though Paul had plunged a two-by-four into his midsection. "Did you say Amanda is engaged?"

"Exactly. Now, if you'll step aside, I need to be on my way."

Blake grabbed the sleeve of Paul's dark suit jacket and jerked him to a halt. "Wait! Could I . . . Is there any way . . . What I'm trying to say is that Amanda and I are . . . were close friends. I'd like to go to the party if you think it wouldn't be overstepping proper etiquette to show up."

Paul smoothed his hair into place before donning his hat. "I don't know why anyone would *want* to go to one of these things, but I imagine the family would be happy to have you attend." He clapped Blake on the shoulder. "Having you there will be a nice surprise for Amanda."

Obviously Amanda hadn't been overly distressed by his disappearance. Otherwise Paul would have refused his request. Blake didn't know whether to be pleased or displeased that Paul had so readily agreed, but there would be time enough for questions later.

"Will your wife be joining us?" Paul asked.

Blake shook his head. "Whatever gave you the idea that I was married?"

"I suppose it was something Sophie said."

Blake let out an exasperated breath. Maybe that was the reason for Amanda's sudden engagement. If she thought he'd left to marry Julia . . . "Come on, let's hurry," he said, pushing the thought aside.

After a hasty carriage ride during which the carriage came far too close to colliding with several pedestrians, the two men stepped down, paid the cab driver, and hurried inside the train station. "That was exciting," Paul called over his shoulder while racing toward the ticket counter.

Determined to keep pace, Blake ran to catch up with him. The train was slowly chugging out of the station even before they'd arrived at their seats. "I'd say we didn't have a minute to spare," Blake said, settling into the upholstered seat of the Pullman car. "At least we'll travel in comfort."

"Let's hope the train remains on schedule. I'd rather not have an argument with Sophie the minute I set foot on the island." He chuckled. "You don't have to worry about such things, but one day . . ."

Blake forced a smile. "Yes, one day." He turned to look out the window. How had all of this happened so quickly? Amanda had never mentioned another man. She'd given every indication that she cared for him. He'd expected her to be angry over the incident with Julia and his sudden disappearance, but marriage to another man? The idea was beyond his comprehension. Perhaps it was a man she'd known for years.

When Blake knew he could make no sense of it without help, he turned to Paul. "Who is this man that Amanda plans to marry?"

Paul glanced up from his magazine. "Who? Oh, his name is Ellert Jackson. I can't tell you much about him except that he seems an odd match for Amanda. He's much older. From what I've gathered, Jonas is the only one who is well acquainted with the man. They had business dealings of some sort years ago when Mr. Jackson lived in Rochester."

"And this man suddenly appeared in Rochester and he's already proposed to Amanda? How much older?"

Paul shrugged. "I'd say he's near Jonas's age. Could be a few years younger."

Blake's jaw went slack. He couldn't believe his ears. "Did Amanda consent to this marriage?"

"I imagine she agreed, don't you? She is of legal age. I know her father can be overbearing, but Amanda is a strong-willed young lady. When I consider how she defied her father in order to learn medicine, I find it difficult to believe she would have accepted Mr. Jackson's proposal unless she wanted to marry him." Paul closed his magazine and placed it on the seat. "I hope you won't think me intrusive, but I'd be interested in hearing about your hasty departure. Sophie told me you left town to marry someone named Julia."

"I don't want to offend you, Paul, but I think I should first discuss that matter with Amanda. I assure you, it's not what it might have seemed."

"Of late, nothing in this family is what it seems," Paul said, shaking his head.

❖

"This engagement is a mistake, Amanda. I think you should march downstairs and tell your parents that you've decided you aren't going to marry Ellert Jackson." Sophie folded her arms and gave a single nod for emphasis. She and Fanny had been doing their best to prevent the party, but thus far they'd met with failure.

"Sophie's right. It's clear that you don't have anything in common."

"He's not even as nice as he was at first" Sophie added. "He doesn't seem to care what people think of him."

"You don't understand, and I'm not at liberty to explain," Amanda said, her expression clearly one of distress.

"Why are you being so stubborn? You've made it quite clear to us that you love Dr. Carstead, so why are you permitting your parents to announce your engagement to someone else?"

Fanny sat down on the bed beside Sophie. "She's right, Amanda. You're old enough to refuse your father's demands in this matter. You can come and live with Michael and me. I know he would understand and welcome you."

Amanda sighed. "You and Michael won't be living in Rochester. I want to continue with my medical training, and I can't do that if I'm living out here on an island."

"You can't do that if you're married to Mr. Jackson, either. You'll not be living in Rochester, where you can return to your work at the Home for the Friendless," Sophie put in. "Even if you are able to locate a doctor who will agree to continue your training, do you think Ellert is going to tolerate such an idea?"

"He said he would."

"And you believed him?" Sophie asked. "I can't see that man allowing you to go to a party, much less become a doctor."

"I can't, either. Amanda, he doesn't at all seem the type to want a wife working for any reason. He's much too controlling. Surely you see that."

"But if I prove to be a loving wife, perhaps he will allow me to do the things that are important to me."

Sophie clucked her tongue. "You don't really believe that, do you? Men like Uncle Jonas and Ellert Jackson don't change their attitudes when they take a wife. After you're married, he'll have no more respect for you than he does now."

"Probably less," Fanny said. "Once you're married, there will be no opportunity to refuse his decisions for you. He'll make you miserable, and there will be no escape. You know you couldn't divorce him."

Her cousin appeared to be wavering, and Sophie stepped closer. She knelt down beside Amanda and clasped her hand. "Don't do this, Amanda. There are other choices available. I know you're grieving the loss of Blake, but this man is no replacement for him. From my observations, the man has no admirable qualities. Save for your father, it seems no one I've talked to has anything good to say about the man."

Minnie knocked on the open door. She held Amanda's freshly pressed gown draped across her arms. Ellert had purchased the dress, and although it had been a poor fit, he'd insisted she wear the gown. Minnie had devoted painstaking hours to ripping out seams and restitching the garment. "I hope it will please you, Miss Amanda," she said.

"Has my husband arrived, Minnie?" Sophie stepped to the window overlooking the lawn.

"I haven't seen him. Mr. Atwell picked up a number of guests at the train station two hours ago, but there haven't been any arrivals since that time."

"Thank you, Minnie." The party would begin at two, and Paul had promised to arrive by noon. Her father had conveyed the message when he'd arrived last evening. Had something happened at the Home or at one of the churches he was serving? Surely he would tell them he had a family commitment that required his attention. "When does the last train arrive?"

The flounces of yellow taffeta rustled as Minnie walked across the room and placed the gown atop the bed. "I believe Mr. Atwell said he would make one final pickup in Clayton at one o'clock. Everyone should be here by then," she said.

"Paul will be here. Don't fret," Fanny said. "He probably lost track of time and had to rush to catch a later train."

"You're right. He likely became preoccupied."

"You've done an excellent job, Minnie. Thank you for all your hard work. I know you've been stitching until very late each night to make certain the dress was ready. I appreciate your help," Amanda said.

A blush of color tinged Minnie's cheeks. "Thank you, ma'am. I wish you every happiness in your future."

The moment the maid exited the room, Sophie jumped to her feet. "Did you see the look in Minnie's eyes? Even she knows this isn't a good idea."

"Oh, forevermore." Amanda gazed heavenward. "Minnie didn't appear any different than she normally does. You're simply looking for evidence."

"Don't fool yourself. The servants see and hear things, Amanda. You know that's true. And they talk about us, too. They know as much about what's going on in this house as we do—probably more." Sophie paced back and forth. "Why don't you go and ask Mrs. Atwell what she's heard." She stopped in her tracks. "Better yet, why don't all three of us go downstairs and have a chat with her. She won't lie to us."

"There isn't time for a conversation with Mrs. Atwell." Amanda picked up the gown and motioned to Fanny. She was thankful her cousin had delayed her wedding trip until after Amanda's wedding. Even though Fanny disapproved of her marriage to Ellert, her presence remained a comfort. "Will you help me with my dress?"

"So you're going to ignore my suggestion? Sometimes I do know what's best, even if the two of you don't think so."

Dropping the dress back onto the bed, Amanda turned to Sophie. "You're correct. I don't love him. But not everyone has the privilege of marrying for love. I'm truly happy that you and Fanny have married honorable men who love you. If circumstances were different, I'd refuse to marry Ellert. But this is something I must do. The future of my family hinges upon this decision."

Fanny slipped the dress over Amanda's head. "Your father is the one who created all of this financial difficulty. Shouldn't he be the one to find a resolution to his problem?"

"He has found a solution; it's me."

"That's not what I meant," Fanny said. "I know I can't make your decision for you, but I think this idea is deplorable and you should refuse to go through with it."

Sophie peered out the window and shook her head. "Look at him down there. Puffed up like a rooster with the run of the barnyard."

"Who?" Fanny and Amanda asked in unison.

"Mr. Jackson. He's strutting around smoking his cigar." She turned and shuddered. "How can you possibly think about marriage to that man?"

"Do stop, Sophie. All this talk has become wearisome and changes nothing."

"Then let's make a plan!" Unable to bridle her enthusiasm, Sophie hastened across the room and pulled a sheet of paper from Amanda's writing desk. "I'll write down our ideas."

Amanda followed her cousin across the room and removed the sheet of paper from her hand. "I've told you that I must marry Ellert. Please stop trying to find a way out for me."

Amanda gathered the taffeta skirt in her hand and descended the staircase. Sophie and Fanny followed. Even with all of Minnie's hard work, they all three agreed the dress was ugly. Styles had changed, but evidently Ellert's taste in women's fashion had not. The color washed out Amanda's complexion. Even with extra color on her cheeks, she looked far too pale. The topaz and diamond necklace and earrings Ellert insisted that she wear were gaudy. The color of the large topaz stones didn't match the dress and made her appear garish. She'd mentioned the differing shades of yellow didn't complement each other, but Ellert had been insistent.

She stepped onto the porch and was immediately besieged by Mrs. Oosterman. The old woman frowned and *tsk*ed several times. She leaned close to Amanda's ear. "What were you thinking when you chose that gown? This isn't a costume party, is it?" She touched a bent finger to the necklace. "Although I'm certain this necklace was costly, it looks frightful with your gown. What's come over you, my dear? You have impeccable taste."

"Oh, it's not Amanda who has flawless taste, Mrs. Oosterman. It's me." Ellert had silently approached and obviously had heard only Mrs. Oosterman's final statement. "I chose her gown and jewelry. I'm pleased to hear you approve. Amanda wasn't quite so convinced." There was reproach in his voice.

"To be honest, Mr. Jackson, the ensemble doesn't enhance Amanda's beauty. It might work for someone else, but her complexion is far too pale for this color. She should be wearing a vivid color. I was, in fact, chiding her for this choice when you interrupted our conversation."

Ellert appeared momentarily taken aback but quickly regained his poise. "In the future I shall listen more closely to Amanda's suggestions," he said. He'd managed to keep an even tone, but his fingers were now digging into the folds of Amanda's dress. There was little doubt the woman had angered him.

"I do believe I see Mrs. Pullman across the way," Mrs. Oosterman said. "If you two will excuse me, I want to say hello."

"By all means." Ellert glared after the older woman. The moment she was out of earshot, he said, "I detest that old woman. She has a wagging tongue and an evil heart."

"Truly? I'm surprised then that you didn't put her in her place." Everything had changed between Amanda and Ellert after his attack on her. Amanda no longer even tried to pretend she was happy with their arrangement.

"I was not born into wealth, Amanda. Therefore, I lie in wait for people who either take advantage or treat me with disdain. Eventually I have the pleasure of turning the tables, and it always gives me great satisfaction." His eyes turned dark with hatred. "One day Mrs. Oosterman will be sorry. She doesn't realize that through my silent partnership in many companies, I control many of her husband's assets. If she isn't careful, she may soon discover her husband isn't nearly as wealthy as she thinks."

Amanda sucked in a breath of air. How could one man harbor such deep hatred and disdain? Instead of banning Sophie's idea, perhaps they should have used that final half hour upstairs to formulate a plan to prevent her engagement and marriage to this despicable man.

"I've frightened you. I can see it in your eyes." He pulled her close. "I enjoy the look of fear. It arouses me," he whispered in a hoarse voice.

Her mother caught sight of them and crossed the lawn at a near sprint. She grasped Amanda's hand. "The two of you are supposed to be over here to greet your guests," she said. There was concern in her eyes, but she maintained a smile. "Come along."

"I'd rather have you to myself," Ellert whispered. "I shouldn't have agreed to this large party. None of these people like me."

"An astute observation," Amanda murmured while weaving through the throng of guests.

18

While Amanda and Ellert greeted their guests, Sophie returned
to the quiet of her upstairs bedroom. The window from her
room would provide a good vantage point to watch for the
return of the *DaisyBee*. Mr. Atwell had departed over an hour
ago to pick up the final guests due to arrive at the Clayton depot.
He should have returned before now. Sophie sat down in the
floral upholstered chair beside the window. With no sign of the
boat, a knot of fear formed in her stomach. Could something
have happened? A train wreck or some other mishap back in
Rochester before Paul departed? Perspiration formed on her
palms, and she uttered a prayer for Paul's safety. Observing
Mr. Jackson's behavior over the past days had served to deepen
Sophie's love for Paul and his gentle, caring manner.

Only moments before returning upstairs, Sophie had stood in the shadows of the veranda and overheard Ellert issuing angry orders to Amanda. Sophie hadn't heard the content of his commands, but from his tone of voice and contorted features, there had been little doubt he was enraged. She shivered at the thought of being married to such a man. Although she'd tested Paul's patience on several occasions, he had never been cruel or unkind. He had steadfastly loved her and Elizabeth. From the moment the babe had been born, Paul had accepted her as his own.

"Elizabeth is his child," she murmured. "Perhaps not by blood, but in every other way. Wesley Hedrick was never Elizabeth's father." She removed the clipping she'd shoved inside the book on her bedside table. All of Wesley's wealth could never make him a good man or a good father. Having a man like Paul was worth more than all the money Wesley Hedrick could ever offer.

Shading her eyes against the bright afternoon sun that streamed through the window, Sophie recognized the *DaisyBee* cutting across the water toward the dock. Her heart skipped a beat at the thought of seeing Paul. She dropped the newspaper clipping to the table and rushed down the stairs. "Paul has arrived," she called to Fanny while running down the path leading to the dock. Her shoes thumped against the hard dirt, and she slowed her pace a modicum when she neared the steepest portion of the path.

Paul waved his hat overhead as she reached the dock. The moment he stepped off the boat, she rushed to embrace him. "Oh, Paul, I have missed you so much." She raised on tiptoe to kiss him.

He chuckled and cocked his head to one side. "And here I expected you to be angry with me for my late arrival. What a wonderful greeting." Pulling her close, he covered her lips with a warm kiss.

"I've missed you, and I love you very much," she replied. "I don't tell you often enough."

"Thank you, my dear. Here I have been dreading this engagement party, but you've already made my journey worthwhile."

She took a backward step and stared at the boat. "Is that Blake Carstead?"

"Yes. As a matter of fact it is."

"What's he doing here?"

Paul shrugged. "He appeared at the Home just as I was leaving. I told him about Amanda's engagement party, and he asked if he could come along."

"Hello!" Blake called while stepping onto the dock.

Sophie tapped her foot on the wood planks. "*Now* you return!" She glanced around to see if anyone was within earshot. "What's wrong with you, taking off like that? And where's that Julia woman? Did you marry her?" Her calm demeanor had evaporated at the sight of Dr. Carstead. "Don't you realize Amanda is about to marry a man she doesn't love, and it's all because of you!" She wanted to shake him until his teeth fell out.

Blake ignored her and looked at Paul. "It appears your wife is somewhat disturbed by my arrival."

"Don't you take a condescending attitude with me, Doctor. I am *disturbed* because you've ruined Amanda's life. She is going to marry Ellert Jackson. A man she clearly does not love."

"If she doesn't love Mr. Jackson, why has she agreed to marry him?"

"She refuses to give me all of the details, but it has something to do with the family. I can't believe you ran out of town to marry that other woman. You are a disappointment, and had my husband known all of these details, you can be sure he wouldn't have invited you to join us. Did you not consider Amanda's feelings? While her father announces her engagement to a man she doesn't love, you reappear—now a happily married man."

"*Sophie*, do mind your manners," Paul whispered. "Dr. Carstead is here at my invitation."

Sophie didn't know who appeared more perplexed by her behavior, Paul or Blake. But at the moment she didn't care if she'd offended the fine doctor. She wanted him to suffer for his abrupt departure with that other woman.

Blake was the first to regain his composure. "Where is Amanda? I need to speak to her."

"I wish you well with that prospect. I'm not certain of her whereabouts, but you can be sure that if you locate her, Ellert Jackson won't be far from her side."

Once Blake was out of earshot, Sophie turned to her husband. "I truly do not understand Amanda's agreement to marry Mr. Jackson. She seemingly feels a sense of obligation to marry him, but he's a dreadful man. You should hear the way he speaks to her. He treats her as though she's a servant who must do his bidding." Sophie grasped Paul's arm as the two of them meandered up the path.

Paul frowned. "If what you say is true, something must be done."

Sophie shook her head. "There's nothing we can do. Fanny and I have exhausted all possibilities. Even when I attempted to develop a plan, Amanda wouldn't join in. She said she must marry him or the family will suffer—whatever that means. I'm certain Uncle Jonas is behind all of this. Aunt Victoria doesn't appear overly pleased by the match, but if Uncle Jonas has made the decision, she'll have no say in the matter."

"Then we must hope that Blake will be able to sway her."

"Why would his words count for anything? He never told me if he married that woman. Did you inquire?"

"I did, but he said he didn't want to discuss it until he'd first talked to Amanda."

"You should have insisted." She yanked him to a stop. "Did you see her?"

"See who?"

"Julia!" How could men be so blind to the important things in life? "Was Julia with him?"

"No, but he did mention he had stopped at home to refresh himself before coming to the Home. Perhaps Julia is at his house."

"Or perhaps he isn't married at all." Would a recently married man return to his home and immediately depart to see another woman? "Did he stop at home before the two of you departed Rochester?"

"No. He didn't mention the need to do so. Even if he'd wanted to, there wouldn't have been time. As it was, we had to travel at breakneck speed to arrive at the depot before the train pulled out."

Sophie weighed the possibilities and then steered Paul toward a secluded grove of trees a short distance off the path. "I think we should pray for Amanda and her future. I don't believe God would want her to marry a man she doesn't love."

Paul cupped her chin in his palm. "You're absolutely correct. We must pray about Amanda's future."

Amanda's cheeks ached from forcing herself to smile for the past hour. If only she could escape this madness. Ellert had maintained a tight hold on her elbow while they worked their way through the crowd. She didn't fail to note the women staring at her. Nor did Ellert. He was pleased by the attention, for he thought their stares were in admiration of her dress.

"Look at them. They're jealous," Ellert said with obvious delight.

But Amanda knew the unsightly flounces of yellow taffeta had elicited looks of horror rather than envy. The hideous frock had created fodder that would fuel the gossip mill for weeks to come, but she permitted him to gloat over a dress that made her look like a wilted dandelion.

She managed to free herself from Ellert for a moment and glanced over the crowd, hoping to spot Fanny or Sophie. "Blake," she whispered, her gaze settling on him as he made his way through the crowd and headed in her direction. She glanced over her shoulder. Although Ellert wasn't far off, Mr. Oosterman had engaged him in conversation. Perhaps he wouldn't notice if she slipped away. Fear and panic mixed to form a knot in her stomach. Her temples throbbed like beating drums. She must speak to Blake but not where Ellert might overhear.

Taking several determined strides, she reached Ellert's side and touched his arm. "If you'll excuse me, I'm going inside to powder my nose."

"Don't be long or I'll be forced to come looking for you." He glanced at Mr. Oosterman. "She's a beauty, isn't she?"

His remark annoyed her, and Amanda didn't wait to hear Mr. Oosterman's response. Turning, she hurried toward the house. She could feel Ellert's burning stare until she rounded the corner and was out of sight. Moments later, a strong hand clamped her arm in a tight hold and she let out a gasp. "Ell— Blake!" She swallowed hard in an attempt to remain calm.

Instead of Ellert's cold stare, she was now looking into Blake's questioning eyes.

"Exactly what is going on, Amanda?"

The sharpness in his voice surprised her, and she took a backward step. "Good afternoon, Blake. I don't recall having seen your name on the guest list. Aunt Victoria must have added it after I perused it." She fought to maintain her composure. "I must say that I'm surprised to see you here. I heard that you'd left town with Julia and the two of you wed."

"I don't know how you could have heard such a thing because there's not an ounce of truth in anything you've said."

She arched her brows. "So you didn't leave town?"

"Yes. I left town, but—"

"Amanda!" Ellert's voice boomed from alongside the house. Before he could observe Blake at her side, she hurried off. Better to have her questions go unanswered than have Ellert discover she'd been engaged in a private conversation with Dr. Carstead. No matter what explanation she gave, he'd believe the worst. She didn't want Ellert creating havoc in Blake's life. Her betrothed had already wreaked enough devastation for a lifetime.

❖

Paul cradled Elizabeth in his arms and carried her upstairs to the bedroom. She'd been awake for most of the afternoon's festivities, and he'd marveled at her sweet disposition as she'd been cuddled and fawned over by so many strangers. He nuzzled her neck and silently thanked God for bringing Sophie and Elizabeth into his life. Although he'd felt complete in his service to God before he met Sophie, she and Elizabeth had added a whole new dimension that continued to amaze him.

Elizabeth wiggled in his arms. He sat on the edge of the bed, holding her until she once again settled into a peaceful sleep. Carefully he stood and then laid her down in the cradle. Her tiny lips formed a moue. Her whisper-soft snoring caused him to smile. With a gentle touch, he placed the delicate white cover across her tiny form. So young and innocent she was, and he'd been charged with the privilege of helping to shape her into a fine young woman. He touched a finger to her soft cap of hair. "I'll do my best for you, sweet Elizabeth."

He straightened, walked to the window, and peered down at the milling guests. The party consisted of the usual food, beverages, and boring conversation. Given a choice, he'd remain up here with Elizabeth. He looked longingly at the bed. A nap would be wonderful, but propriety wouldn't permit such a luxury. As he turned back toward the window, a newspaper clipping lying atop the nearby table captured his attention.

At first glance the clipping appeared to be no more than the report of social gatherings in New York City, but as he continued to read, his lungs deflated, and a whoosh of air escaped his lips. Wesley Hedrick was the sole beneficiary of Lord and Lady Illiff, who had been lost at sea when a ship went down off the coast of France. There were words of praise for the magnificent parties he'd recently hosted at his home in New York City.

Could Sophie still be in love with Wesley? Paul dropped to the chair. Certainly Wesley could now provide a better life for Sophie and Elizabeth. Yet Sophie had greeted Paul with great warmth and affection only a few hours ago. Had her loving kiss been merely the expected behavior of a dutiful wife? Surely not. But during her months on the island without him, Sophie had certainly proved she missed the parties as well as the expensive clothing that he could never afford to purchase for her. Had her earlier behavior been no more than an attempt to ease her guilt? Without warning, his joy and contentment evaporated like the morning mist.

# 19

Amanda maintained a watchful eye the remainder of the afternoon. She had hoped for an opportunity to steal away and speak privately with Blake, but Ellert had not given her a moment of solitude. At every turn he was at her side, clasping her elbow or placing a proprietary hold along the small of her back. She edged away every time she had a chance, but he wouldn't be deterred. He appeared to find her attempts to withdraw amusing, and that further annoyed her. When she noticed Blake stop and speak to Paul and then head off toward the dock with a group of departing guests, her spirits plummeted.

A short time ago the guests had congregated to hear the formal announcement of her engagement to Ellert and had offered congratulations, but Blake had remained at a distance.

Though she'd hoped at least to discern his reaction to the announcement, there had been little opportunity. The crowd had gathered around and blocked her view. How she longed for a few minutes alone with him to ask why he had appeared at her engagement party. Even more, she had hoped to discover why he'd left Rochester without a word.

"Ellert!" Her father strode toward them with a satisfied look on his face. "Some of the men wondered if you'd like to join us in the library." He managed to make himself understood while holding his cigar clamped between his teeth, a practice Amanda thought disgusting.

For the first time since she'd come downstairs, Ellert appeared to weigh the idea of leaving her alone for a time. She momentarily considered encouraging him to join the men but then thought better of the idea. It would be wiser to remain silent and let him think his decision was of little interest to her.

"Do you think you can survive without me for a short time, my dear?" His eyes shone with perverse delight.

"I'll do my best," she said, forcing herself to maintain an even tone lest he think her overly anxious to be rid of him.

The moment Ellert entered the house with the other men, Amanda waved to Paul as he returned from the docks. At the very least, Paul should be able to provide some insight into Blake's reappearance. She hastened down the sloping lawn. "Finally I have a few minutes to myself." She glanced over her shoulder. "Ellert has joined my father and some of the men inside. I was wondering if you could tell me when Blake returned to Rochester and who invited him to the party."

Paul gave her a sheepish grin as he described Blake's surprise return to the Home for the Friendless. "I do hope you're not angry. He asked to come along, and I thought—"

"It's quite all right, Paul. I did want to talk to him, but except for a very few minutes, we had little opportunity. And now he's departed without answering the questions I had for him."

Paul gazed toward the river. "Unless he changed his plans, he's not far away. He told me he was going to stay at the Frontenac Hotel tonight, since he'd missed the last train to Rochester."

"I see." Amanda considered this news for a moment, but Paul interrupted her thoughts.

"Might I ask you something?"

Amanda nodded, hoping it wasn't a question about her feelings for Blake. "What would you like to know?"

"It's . . . well . . . Sophie. Do you think she's happy? I mean I know she didn't want to come here, but do you think she's otherwise happy?"

Amanda looked at Paul and considered his sad countenance. "I believe she is content. She loves being a mother and wife. I think this is probably the happiest I've seen her in years. Why do you ask?"

He shook his head. "I don't know. I suppose I just worry that she . . . well . . . perhaps regrets marrying a poor preacher."

Amanda smiled. "You two might have married under strained circumstances, but I honestly think Sophie is happy. I don't think she'd change anything even if she could."

"Amanda! Oh, Paul!" Sophie called as she made her way down the path. "Good, you're both here. I didn't know where you'd gotten off to."

"I was just asking Paul about Blake. I wanted to talk to him."

"Where is he?" Sophie asked, looking around.

"He's gone to the Frontenac Hotel," Paul replied.

Before Amanda could say a word, Sophie eagerly spouted,

"You must go and talk with him before you go through with these wedding plans, Amanda. Paul and I would be happy to accompany you, wouldn't we, Paul?" Sophie tugged on Paul's sleeve, her eyes dancing with excitement.

"I wouldn't want you to enter into a marriage to Mr. Jackson if you harbor feelings for another man, Amanda." Paul's voice held a hint of melancholy. "Such a marriage would eventually prove painful for both of you."

"Well, the only feeling she has for Mr. Jackson is a deep loathing, so I believe a visit to Dr. Carstead is in order," Sophie said without missing a beat. "This will be such an exciting adventure. Do you think we should ask Fanny and Michael to come along, too?"

Apparently Sophie hadn't perceived her husband's dejected tone. Or perhaps Amanda had misinterpreted. Sophie surely would be aware of a change in Paul's demeanor, wouldn't she?

"I think it may be wise to keep the number of people to a minimum. I wouldn't want to attract unwanted attention."

"Oh, of course," Sophie giggled. "I do enjoy plotting clandestine meetings."

Paul looked at his wife. "And how many have you planned recently?"

Sophie batted her lashes. "I'll never tell."

"Truly?" Without waiting for a response, he motioned toward the house. "I believe I'll go and see if there's any of that punch left from the party."

"Wait a minute, Paul. We need to decide the details of—"

He glanced over his shoulder and appeared even sadder to Amanda. "I'll leave the plans to you, Sophie."

"But you will come with us?" she called after him.

He nodded and waved. "You can furnish me the details later."

A SURRENDERED HEART

"I don't know what's wrong with Paul. We were having such a wonderful time earlier in the day, but he suddenly seems despondent." Sophie glanced at Amanda. "Did you notice?"

Amanda nodded, thinking about Paul's question as to whether or not Sophie was happy. Perhaps that question had come about because Paul wasn't happy. Amanda prayed that wasn't the reason. "He didn't seem quite himself. Do you suppose he's tired?"

Sophie bobbed her head. "That's likely all it is. Now, let's decide on the arrangements. When do you think we should go to Round Island? This evening or tomorrow?"

"I can't possibly escape Ellert this evening. I think early tomorrow morning would be my best opportunity. If no one sees us depart, Ellert will think I've decided to sleep late."

"And if he sees us return, I'll tell him we awakened early and decided to try our hand at fishing. We can toss in our fishing lines along the way so we won't be telling him a lie." Sophie clasped her hand over her mouth. "This is such fun. Just like when we were young. Remember those detailed schemes we used to make in order to annoy Jefferson and George?"

"I remember. But tomorrow will be different. I won't be laughing if Ellert discovers I've gone to talk to another man. We need to be very careful," Amanda said.

Sophie nodded and looped arms with her. "No need to worry. Ellert will never know."

❖

*Sunday, July 16, 1899*

As the sun peeked over the horizon the following morning, Sophie tiptoed to Amanda's bedroom and lightly tapped on the door before entering. She grinned when she saw the mound of

255

pillows tucked beneath the coverlet. "Hoping the servants will report you are still sleeping, I see."

"Hoping to keep Ellert fooled for as long as possible," Amanda whispered.

Carrying their shoes in their hands, they silently padded across the carpeted hall and down the back stairs. After slipping outdoors, they sat down and put on their shoes. Neither spoke a word until they were secluded in the trees alongside the house.

"Where is Paul?" Amanda hissed.

Sophie pointed at the river. "Follow me," she whispered.

The sun hadn't yet forced its way through the heavy pines, and once they'd taken to the woods, they clasped hands to keep from becoming separated in the dim light. Pinecones and tree branches spiked with pine needles crunched beneath their feet. Sophie waved Amanda to a halt several times in order to stop and listen for footsteps. They didn't want to arrive at the river and discover they'd been followed. When they reached the clearing, Sophie could see Paul waiting in one of the skiffs from the boathouse.

"How did he manage to get the skiff without alerting Mr. Atwell?"

"He went down to the boathouse last evening and told Mr. Atwell he wanted to take a boat out early this morning. When Mr. Atwell told Paul that he would get up early and meet him, Paul refused. He suggested they tie the boat to the lower dock last evening. Mr. Atwell assumed Paul was going fishing this morning. He even put fishing poles and bait in the boat before they took it to the dock."

A blanket of dew glistened across the sloping grass leading down to the dock. "Careful you don't slip," Sophie warned.

She smiled broadly and waved to Paul. He lifted his cap to

signal he'd seen her, but there was only a faint smile in return. He'd brooded all last evening, avoiding her at every turn. She had hoped a good night's sleep would improve his disposition. Thus far it didn't appear it had helped. What in the world had caused such a mood?

After assisting Amanda into the skiff, Paul offered his hand to Sophie. Holding tightly to his hand, she carefully stepped into the bobbing skiff.

When he didn't offer even the slightest acknowledgment, she leaned forward and kissed his cheek. "Thank you," she whispered.

He didn't acknowledge the kiss or her thanks. Not so much as a smile or a twinkle in his eyes. What was wrong with him! "Did you have any problems when you left the house this morning?" she asked.

Paul shook his head. "I think it's best if we remain silent. There's fog, and you never know who might be out here fishing. We don't want to draw attention to ourselves."

Sophie could feel the heat rise in her cheeks. She didn't believe Paul's admonition had anything to do with other fishermen overhearing her comment. He simply did not want to talk to her. She'd done everything in her power to prove she was sorry for acting badly when he'd sent her to Broadmoor Island, yet he now ignored her and spoke in an abrupt, hurtful manner. Was he attempting to show her how deeply she'd wounded him? She had hoped this would be a time of mending their differences. Instead, it seemed he was unwilling to forgive her.

Paul manned the oars with remarkable ease, and their silent journey soon ended with the three of them stepping onto the pier at Round Island. Several fishermen sat on the dock in their collapsible chairs, tossing their lines into the water. Paul stopped long enough to exchange a few words with one of the men before they proceeded to the hotel.

"Do you know that man?" Sophie inquired.

Paul shook his head. "No. I told him to spread the word that if they caught any fish they didn't want, I would purchase them when we returned."

Sophie patted his arm. "An excellent idea. I should have thought of that! I'm usually the one who comes up with the best way to make our schemes work."

"Indeed," Paul replied.

Normally Sophie would have considered the remark a compliment, but Paul's frown canceled that thought. When they arrived at the steps to the veranda that surrounded the hotel, Paul stopped. "Sophie and I will have coffee at one of the tables here on the veranda, Amanda. You go inside and have a message delivered to Blake's room that you'd like to meet with him in the lobby." He offered her a gentle smile. "There will be no appearance of impropriety if you remain in public view while you speak to him."

"Thank you, Paul. Say a prayer that all goes well."

"I will," he said.

"*We* will," Sophie added. She waited until Amanda disappeared from sight and then followed Paul to one of the tables that lined the veranda. Once they were seated, a waiter hurried to take their order.

"Just coffee," Paul said.

Sophie glanced across the table, but Paul had turned away from her and was staring into the distance. He hadn't even asked if she'd like something to eat. Not that she was hungry, but he could have at least inquired.

The waiter returned with their coffee and disappeared as silently as he'd arrived. Sophie poured a dollop of cream into her coffee and stirred with a vengeance. "Exactly what is wrong with you, Paul? You've been in a foul humor since late yesterday afternoon. Have I offended you?"

"Have you done something that should offend me?" he asked in a manner that seemed guarded yet hostile.

Sophie looked at him intently. "I know I was awful in the way I acted about coming to the island during the epidemic, but surely you have accepted my apology and we can let that be behind us."

"Are you happy with me?"

"What a silly question," Sophie said, trying to make light of the matter. "Of course I'm happy with you."

He swiveled around in his chair. "When did you plan to tell me about this?" He slapped the newspaper clipping onto the table.

Confusion combined with fear to form a tight knot in her stomach. She should have told him about the article. "Is that clipping the reason you've been so irritable?"

"I have been both confused and concerned. I can never provide you and Elizabeth with the way of life you deserve, but it appears Wesley Hedrick can now do so." Paul slapped his palm on the table and sent the piece of paper floating to the wood floor of the veranda.

Sophie reached to clasp his hand, but he withdrew it. There was a time when his actions would have made her angry, but this time was different. Sophie could see the doubt and fear in his eyes. She softened her voice. "Surely you know better than that, Paul. I love you dearly. You are all that I desire."

He shifted in his chair and leaned down to pick up the clipping. Crumpling it in his hand, he stared at her. "Am I? I can't give you expensive things. I can't buy you new gowns and furnish our home with beautiful furniture. I'm a simple man of God. I'll never be wealthy."

"That isn't important to me." Sophie realized the depth of just how true that statement was. It was freeing to know that she loved and cherished her husband far more than the things money could buy.

"I couldn't help but wonder if you would consider taking Elizabeth and running off to be with Wesley."

She could see the sadness in his eyes. "I would never do such a thing, Paul. You have been a loving husband and father. I have no desire for anyone except you."

"I want to believe you, but . . ."

Disbelief shone in his eyes. How could she convince him of her love? "I know I exhibited dreadful behavior when I first arrived at Broadmoor Island. And I won't deny that I was quickly wooed by the new gowns and parties. I was lured back into my old habits far too easily. I admit that. But after seeing the barrier it created between the two of us, I understood that what I truly wanted was a life with you and Elizabeth."

He unclenched his fist. The balled-up clipping rested in his palm, a silent accusation. "Then why do you have this?"

"Amanda read the article in a New York newspaper while she was recuperating from the cholera. She clipped it out and wasn't even going to tell me about it, but I found it when I was looking at one of her books." She wanted to hold his hand but feared he would again withdraw, so she folded her hands in her lap. "In truth, reading that piece helped me to see that money wasn't as important as I'd previously thought. I realize that even though Wesley may have enough money to buy gowns and jewels, he would never cherish or love me as you do. I understand that money is not a key to happiness. In fact, it seems frequently to have quite the opposite effect. It is you

I love, Paul, and I am most content to be your wife, even if I never have another new dress."

"Yet you failed to mention Wesley or the newspaper article to me," he murmured.

"Because Wesley Hedrick is of no importance to me." She cupped his jaw in her palm. "I realize how blessed I am to have you as my husband. You are a good man, and I will always be thankful that you came to my rescue. Without you, I would have thrown myself from those rocks and taken Elizabeth with me." Her voice cracked at the remembrance that she'd been only minutes away from destroying her own life and that of her unborn child. Only Paul's gentle, pleading words had saved her from a crushing death upon those jagged rocks below. "Recently I've acted badly, and I apologize for my churlish behavior. I know that you have our best interests and protection in mind whenever you make a decision."

With the tip of his finger, Paul raised her chin and stared into her eyes. "I'm thankful for your kind words, but I know it was my uncompromising decision to send you and Elizabeth to Broadmoor Island that caused you such unhappiness."

Sophie lifted his hand to her lips and kissed his palm. "That's true enough. Yet I never doubted your love. In my heart I knew you made that decision in order to protect us. Now, seeing the distress Amanda has suffered since agreeing to marry Mr. Jackson, I truly realize how fortunate I am to be married to the man I love."

"And I to the only woman I could ever love." He leaned down and captured her lips in a lingering kiss.

Sophie pulled away. "Let's never allow these kind of things to come between us again. I love you, and that will never change. I do not want Wesley and his money. I want you and your love."

Amanda paced the length of the lobby while she waited for Blake. The bellboy had delivered her message and returned to say Blake would join her in a moment and to please wait. The gossamer curtains that shaded the lobby windows fluttered in the morning breeze and made her long to run outside. She shouldn't have come here. What if Ellert should discover she'd left the house? And what if Blake told her he'd been joking and he and Julia were husband and wife? Worse yet, what if Julia descended the staircase at his side?

There was still time to escape. She turned. "Blake," she gasped.

Obviously perplexed, he tipped his head to the side and arched his brows. "You did ask me to meet you in the lobby, didn't you?" He held her note between his fingers.

"Yes, of course." She cleared her throat, hoping to quiet the tremor in her voice.

"Shall we go for a walk?"

She recalled Paul's earlier comment about proper decorum, but the lobby was filled with guests and who could know what might be overheard. Any number of people might recognize her. She had no idea if any of their other guests had elected to remain in the islands throughout the weekend. What if one of them told Ellert he'd seen her in the hotel lobby visiting with a young man? Without further consideration, she nodded to a door leading to the east side of the veranda. Their departure wouldn't be visible to Paul and Sophie.

"It's good to see you. I had hoped we'd have another opportunity to visit before I left your en-en-gagement party, but Mr. Jackson seemed to be constantly keeping you by his side."

Amanda noted that Blake had stumbled over the word *engagement*. "Mr. Jackson tends to be somewhat possessive," she replied.

"I'm surprised you would choose such a man, since you are such an independent young woman. But I suppose you know what type of man appeals to you."

Amanda led him toward the river, choosing a spot where guests couldn't see them from the veranda. "I don't have time for banter or stilted conversation. I can't be away from Broadmoor Island much longer before I'll be missed. I came here to ask exactly what happened between you and Julia."

"Absolutely nothing happened between us. It's true that I had proposed to Julia before I moved to Rochester. I thought we loved each other, and I asked her to be my wife. As I told you before, she accepted the engagement ring but returned it a short time later. She'd found another prospect more appealing— or so she told me. But things didn't work out with him, so she came to Rochester thinking I would be delighted to pick up where we'd left off."

"But you weren't?"

He cupped her chin in his palm. "No, I wasn't. When I told her I wouldn't marry her, she begged me to accompany her back to California to explain to her parents that I was in love with someone else. She said they would never believe her. I offered to write a letter, but she cried until I finally agreed."

"So that's why you departed in such a hurry?"

"Yes. I knew my explanation wouldn't sound plausible. But I've known Julia for years. Even though she'd broken our engagement to be with another man, I felt an obligation to her and to her parents."

"She probably wanted the time with you, hoping to change your mind."

"You may be correct, but I knew that wouldn't happen. After you left that day, I realized the feelings I'd had for Julia were nothing compared to my love for you. I admired her and considered her a friend, but it's you I desire to have by my side for the rest of my life. I never experienced that intense desire for Julia—only for you."

His words made it difficult for Amanda to breathe. "You truly love me?"

"You know I do. I don't want you to marry Ellert Jackson. You belong with me. Surely you know that's true."

"But that can't happen. The future of my family depends upon my marriage to Ellert."

"I don't understand. How can a family's future depend upon a marriage?"

"My father owes Mr. Jackson a great deal of money. If I refuse to marry him, our family will lose what's left of our assets, not to mention the loss of social position. I am not aware of all the details or arrangements Ellert made with my father, but I do know that my family will be ruined if I don't go through with the wedding."

"But you don't love him. Knowing you'll be subjecting yourself to a life of misery in a loveless marriage, how can you agree?"

"Love doesn't matter. This marriage is required of me."

Blake pulled her into his arms and covered her lips with a fierce and passionate kiss and then pulled away from her. "Tell me again that it doesn't matter." Before she could gain enough breath to speak, he devoured her with another fervent and unyielding kiss. "Tell me you don't love me."

"What I feel isn't important," Amanda said, tears blurring her sight.

Blake wiped one tear away and placed his hand against her cheek. "It's important to me." He lifted her chin, forcing her eyes to meet his. "Tell me that you don't love me, and I will go away and leave you alone."

Amanda did her best to stifle a sob. "I'm already alone, Blake. I will be for the rest of my life."

Ellert had quietly inquired about the young man who'd been speaking to Amanda near the back door yesterday afternoon. In all likelihood Amanda didn't think he'd observed her little tête-à-tête, but she'd soon learn very little escaped his scrutiny. The clueless girl didn't understand that it took only a few coins placed in the proper hand to loosen tongues.

He wasn't all that comfortable around the water, but he was thankful for the rowing experience he'd acquired in his younger years. His muscles would ache by evening, but it would be worth it. If the fisherman who'd watched the threesome depart from the dock a short time ago was correct, he'd locate Amanda at Round Island. Instead of rowing toward the dock where guests might see him and wonder at the sight of Ellert Jackson rowing himself to the island, he approached from the other side. If necessary, he should be able to pull the skiff onto dry land without much difficulty.

He spotted a young couple near the water's edge—young lovers clinging to each other in a passionate kiss. There was something oddly familiar about the woman. He lifted a pair of binoculars to his eyes. Amanda!

She clung to the man—the same man he'd seen her talking to the day before. How comfortable she appeared in his arms. The man touched her face with such familiarity that Ellert wanted to shout across the water and demand he release her. She certainly had never allowed him such liberties.

Ellert shoved the binoculars into the leather case and turned the boat back toward Broadmoor Island. The tightness in his chest caused his breath to come in a strained pant. How dare Amanda toy with him this way? She knew what was at stake. Ellert gripped the handles of the oars until he felt the muscles in his arms spasm in protest. She would pay dearly for this indiscretion. They both would pay.

## 20

*Tuesday, July 18, 1899*

"You are the most beautiful woman in the world," Michael whispered against Fanny's ear.

Fanny opened her eyes to find Michael watching her while she slept. She smiled and reached out for him. "I still can't quite get used to your being here."

He pulled her into his arms and kissed her soundly. "I dreamed of this every night while in the Yukon."

"Was it horrible?" Fanny asked.

"Dreaming of you?" He looked at her oddly. "What would make you think such a thing?"

"No, silly, I meant the Yukon. I heard such horrible stories. The newspapers were full of accounts of tragedy and death. You've hardly told me anything about it."

"It was some of the most beautiful and deadly country I've ever experienced. You would like it there, I'm quite sure. The mountains are incredible, and the vast size of the country is unbelievable." He kissed her again. "But right now I'd rather talk about how much I love you."

Fanny sighed and put her arms around his neck. "And right now I'd love to hear you tell me how much you love me."

"Oh, I nearly forgot," he said, pulling away slightly. "The paper work arrived. We now have the deed to our own island."

"How wonderful. How soon can we move there?"

He laughed. "Well, there's hardly more than a shack on it at present. We'll need to build a better house first."

"I suppose in the meantime we can live here or at Broadmoor Mansion in Rochester."

"I'm so glad you were able to lay claim to it. I know how much your grandparents' place meant to you. I fear, however, there would be very little I'd be able to do in Rochester to make a living."

"Between the gold you mined in the Yukon and whatever I have left of my fortune, we hardly need to be so concerned about that."

"I can't sit idle," Michael countered. "At least out here I can work with the boats. On our little island I plan to set up the finest shop to make and repair boats."

"And I shall cook and clean for you and raise our beautiful children."

He kissed her and pulled her close again. "I really don't care where we live, my sweet wife, so long as you are by my side."

"I feel the same way, Michael. I pray God never allows us to be separated again."

❖

Later that morning Fanny bid Michael good-bye as he headed out to help his father in the boathouse. The house seemed strangely quiet until Fanny recalled that some of the family had departed for Canada earlier in the day. Her cousin Beatrice had decided a trip to Brockville would provide an opportunity for all of the young children to become better acquainted with their Canadian ancestry. Fanny thought Beatrice simply wanted an excuse to go shopping, for she'd made certain that nannies were included among those slated for the daylong adventure.

If all went according to plan, Fanny would locate Uncle Jonas in the library. For some time she'd waited for an opportunity to speak with him in private. She inhaled a deep breath before tapping on the door. When her uncle responded, she opened the door while offering a quick prayer for strength.

"Good morning, Uncle Jonas. I'm glad to find you alone."

"Why?" He didn't look up.

She continued into the room and stood directly in front of the expansive mahogany desk. "Because we need to talk."

"I'm not aware of anything that requires my attention," he said, dipping his pen into the ink.

Not once did he make eye contact, yet she refused to be deterred by his boorish behavior. "Why don't we discuss Amanda's betrothal to a man she doesn't love, a man who bears a terrible reputation and is known throughout Rochester as cruel and heartless. And then why don't you explain to me why you would force your daughter to marry such a man."

Finally her uncle looked up. His angry stare seared like a hot poker, and she took a backward step.

"My daughter and her marriage are none of your business,

but I know that Ellert loves her. You are like so many foolish women who harbor a romantic notion that you must be in love with a man before you wed. Love can grow after marriage. You will see. Once Amanda is married to Ellert, she will learn to love him. Your aunt Victoria didn't profess to love me before we married."

Fanny wondered if her aunt had *ever* professed to love this cold and uncaring man, but she dared not ask such a personal question. "Even if one sets aside the age difference between Mr. Jackson and Amanda, it is obvious they have nothing in common. How can she possibly build a life with him?"

"You have nothing in common with a boatswain, yet you profess to love him. Tell me, how is this different?"

"You would dare to compare Michael to the likes of Ellert Jackson? Unlike your Mr. Jackson, Michael is a kind and generous man." Anger welled within her, and she pointed at her uncle. "Mark my words: I will not stand by and watch you force Amanda into a loveless marriage with that despicable man."

Her uncle scratched the nib of his pen across the writing paper. "I find it amazing that you think you have the ability to influence decisions regarding *my* daughter." He lifted the pen into the air and aimed it at the door. "Go on with you. I have work that requires my attention."

"I will not leave this room!" Fanny considered stomping her foot but decided her uncle would laugh at such behavior. Instead, she folded her arms tight against her chest, hoping the defiant stance underscored her determination. One look proved she'd failed. Her uncle appeared unmoved.

"Suit yourself, but I've given my final word on the matter." Her uncle stood up. "If you won't leave the room, then I will."

She had hoped it wouldn't come to this, but he'd given her

no choice. "I think not, Uncle Jonas." Before he could step from behind the desk, she said, "If you don't release Amanda from this preposterous arrangement, I shall be forced to tell everyone that you stole a great deal of my inheritance, and I will also make it known that Amanda's rejection to medical college was due to your interference. I know that you sent money to the school in exchange for a letter rejecting her application."

He collapsed into the large leather chair. His complexion turned as gray as yesterday's ashes. "None of what you tell Amanda or other members of the family can change the arrangement that I've made with Ellert."

"Your bluff won't work."

"This is no bluff." A shadow of defeat darkened his eyes.

Fanny maintained a steely look. She'd seen her uncle manipulate far too many people in the past. He'd not make a fool of her again—not after stealing her inheritance and lying to Amanda. Uncle Jonas wouldn't win her trust so easily this time. "If you expect me to believe what you say, then I need further explanation."

He closed his eyes and leaned his head against the back of the chair. "Sit down, Fanny. This will take a while."

With her hands clenched into tight knots, she followed his instruction and waited for him to begin. It seemed an eternity before he finally struggled through the first sentence. She considered his words before stopping him. "I don't know what you mean when you say Mr. Jackson bailed you out and you owe him. You owe him *what*? Amanda? Is that what you're saying? You used your own flesh and blood as a guarantee for money?"

Her uncle sighed and hung his head forward. "Mr. Rosenblume is an excellent lawyer. I knew it would be only a matter of time before he pieced together all that had happened. He's obviously revealed many details to you." He shook his head in dismay. "Mortimer was instructed to destroy all of those incriminating papers. Since his death, it's given me pause to wonder if there's any man who can be trusted."

"I had hoped you would say that these circumstances have caused you to reflect upon your own deceitful behavior and you have begged God's forgiveness. Instead, you place blame on a dead man because he maintained a record of your misdeeds."

"He was a partner in my transgressions. They were his misdeeds, as well. Keeping such records was stupidity."

"Was it? I think Mr. Fillmore may have been protecting himself. He likely feared you would attempt to place all of the blame on him if accusations arose in regard to handling the estate. Maintaining the records provided him with proof that you were involved." She shook her head in disgust. "The bards of old wrote that there is no honor among thieves. You and Mr. Fillmore certainly followed that dictate."

"Have you no pity? Had I not been faced with financial ruin, I wouldn't have touched your inheritance. I needed to save the family from disaster. My plan was to borrow from your funds and repay you when my investments improved." His voice faltered.

"But they didn't improve," she said. "And when you could think of nothing else to save the Broadmoor financial empire, you decided Amanda could be sacrificed."

"You make it sound so . . . so . . ."

"Cold and calculating?" She unfolded her hands and leaned forward. "That's exactly what it is, Uncle Jonas. You care little if Amanda spends the rest of her life with a man who is cruel and uncaring. I daresay, he's a man not unlike yourself."

"No! I could never be as ruthless as Ellert Jackson," he defended.

Fanny shook her head in disbelief. "You've just now admitted you know Mr. Jackson to be a heartless man, yet earlier you professed him to be a man Amanda could someday love. How is that possible? You think only of yourself, Uncle Jonas."

"That's not true. I was seeking a way to cover my wrong-doings—that much is correct. But my actions were to protect the family. I knew how they would suffer if the truth came out. Ellert's proposition was my only recourse. Unfortunately, he now holds all the cards. There is nothing I can do to change things."

Her uncle appeared to be telling the truth, yet one could never be certain with him. Had he truly explored every possible option? Fanny tapped her finger atop the desk until an idea occurred. With newfound energy, she jumped up from the chair. "I know! I'll pay Ellert's loan with what remains of my inheritance. Then you'll be free to break your agreement with him." She folded her arms across her chest, pleased with her solution.

Her smile faded as he guffawed and waved away her suggestion. "Don't you think that if there had been enough money remaining in *either* of our accounts I would have used it to save the family?"

"Michael has money now. Perhaps if we pool our efforts."

Desperate to find an answer to Amanda's dilemma, Fanny sat down. She peered across the desk at her uncle. "Do you think Uncle Quincy saved any of his inheritance? Surely he hasn't placed all of it in the Home for the Friendless. With his share he could have built a much more lavish place. If you ask him, perhaps you'll discover that he's invested some of his funds."

"Quincy? He'll be no help. I'm sure he used most of his fortune to pay past debts. You'll recall that Wesley Hedrick's huge pledge never came through as promised. When pledges failed to be paid, I imagine he used his inheritance to cover his losses. No doubt he's given a good deal to several other charities. He never could give his money away quickly enough."

"I'll sell Broadmoor Mansion. Combined with what is left of my inheritance, there should be adequate funds, shouldn't there?"

His brow furrowed, and he swiped at the air as if to brush away her question. "You own Broadmoor Mansion? How is that possible?"

"Mr. Rosenblume handled the details for me. I'm not certain what transpired, but he received permission from the judge before making the acquisition." She took a modicum of pleasure seeing him pale. He was momentarily struck speechless by what she'd accomplished without his knowledge.

He massaged his temples. "Even if you sold the house, there would be insufficient funds to pay off Ellert, and he will agree to nothing less than what he is owed, plus interest. You may take my word for that or ask him yourself. He is set upon this marriage. Believe me, I tried to change his mind." Her uncle laced his fingers together and bowed his head. "You can tell Amanda about the college situation if that's your desire. But I believe hearing such information will only cause her undue anguish. There's no way I can alter the past."

Were Amanda not the one who would suffer, Fanny knew she would shout her uncle's selfish offenses from the rooftop. She cared little if the revelation would embarrass Uncle Jonas, but Fanny would not inflict further pain upon her cousin. "At the moment there is no good that can come from telling her," Fanny said. "Tell me, was Broadmoor Island included in your bargain with Mr. Jackson, or does it still belong to the family?"

"It remains with the family by the dictates of my father's will. Please understand, Fanny. Ellert Jackson knows too much—he can ruin our family even if I had a way to pay him back. At least this way, he will forgive a portion of my loan and grant me an extension to repay the remainder. This will allow your aunt to go on in society as she has before and will see that my sons' good names continue to be respected. Their futures are at stake as much as Amanda's. I've done nothing but cause pain and misfortune to all those I love."

Uncle Jonas covered his face with the palms of his hands and turned away from her. He made no sound, but his quaking shoulders were proof he'd finally been touched by remorse. Fanny stood and quietly crossed the room. After a quick glance over her shoulder, she pulled the door closed behind her. She had no desire to watch her uncle collapse in defeat. Though he'd brought this upon himself, it was Ellert Jackson who now controlled all of their lives. How could Mr. Jackson so easily take advantage of her uncle when he was in dire circumstances? Then again, Uncle Jonas had done the same thing to Ellert years ago. Though two wrongs would not set things aright, Fanny knew Ellert would take great pleasure in watching her uncle suffer.

A tear trickled down her cheek, and she swiped it away with the back of her hand. If only she could think of some way to help Amanda. Keeping to the path leading from the front of the house, she followed the trail until she neared the water's edge. Gathering her skirts in one hand, she picked her way toward a large flat rock, where she could stare at the water and contemplate a solution. Although she normally did her best thinking while near the river, her remedy didn't work today. Not one single idea came to mind. She longed to help Amanda escape before it was too late. But how?

Fanny now understood why her cousin had agreed to marry Ellert, but that wouldn't save Amanda from a lifetime of cruelty. Why did Amanda feel compelled to save the family? Had Uncle Jonas presented such an idea to George or Jefferson, they would have laughed at him. Neither of the young men would willingly agree to such an arrangement. Amanda deserved to make her own choice. It seemed Fanny's marital happiness only served to underscore Amanda's tragic plight all the more. Her tears flowed unchecked as she stared across the water.

"Here you are!"

Fanny swiped at her eyes before turning to look up at Michael.

"What's happened? Why are you crying?" Concern shone in his eyes as he dropped down beside her. He reached around her waist and pulled her close. "Tell me what has made you cry, my love."

She rested her head against his chest and described the exchange with her uncle. "I cannot bear to think of Amanda spending her life with a man like Ellert Jackson. There must be something we can do. I've been sitting here for well over an hour trying to devise a plan, but I can think of nothing." She straightened and looked into Michael's eyes. "Have you any idea how we can help?"

Michael gently wiped away her tears. "No matter what, I believe things will work out for Amanda. We must pray that God will protect her from both her father and from Ellert Jackson." Michael tipped her chin upward until their eyes met. "God knows what's happening. None of this has taken Him by surprise. Right now we don't understand, but I believe good will prevail."

"I know you're right, but it appears it will take nothing

short of a miracle to save Amanda from being sentenced to a lifetime of misery with Ellert Jackson."

"Then you must pray for that miracle, dear Fanny, and I will do the same."

## 21

*Saturday, July 22, 1899*

After a final look in the mirror, Amanda walked to the bedroom window and glanced outside. The sight of Ellert standing near a large pine in the front yard was enough to send her scurrying toward the bedroom door. He appeared none too happy. She hoped that during their tour of the island today she could summon up some sort of feelings, something other than intense distaste, for the man she would soon wed. Ellert could be nice enough when he wanted to gain favor, but he could also be demanding. His passion and lust frightened Amanda more than she could say. Blake's kisses had stirred feelings of desire within her heart, but when Ellert so much as touched her, she wanted to run.

"Amanda! Where are you rushing off to?" Fanny asked. "I told Sophie we would join her for a picnic today."

Amanda glanced over her shoulder. "I can't. I'm late meeting Ellert. I promised him a walk around the island." She could hear Fanny's muffled footsteps on the carpeted hallway and knew her cousin was hurrying after her. She twisted around at the top of the stairs and waved her cousin to a halt. "I'm sorry, but I simply cannot go with you."

"I don't understand why you want to spend time with that despicable man. If we don't find a solution, you'll be tied to him for the rest of your life. I'd think you would want to stay away from him while you can."

"There isn't going to be any miraculous solution, Fanny. If I spend time with Ellert, I may find that he actually possesses a few redeeming qualities—that we are compatible. At least that's my hope."

Fanny sighed. "I don't think you'll be successful, but I wish you well. We'll miss having you with us."

Amanda pulled her cousin into a fleeting embrace. "And I shall miss being at the picnic. More than you can imagine." She released her hold and nodded toward the door. "I must be on my way."

"Do promise to give me a full report later today. I'll want to hear if you discover any admirable qualities in the man."

With a sense of foreboding Amanda ran down the steps and out the front door. Like her cousin, she doubted Ellert would exhibit any admirable qualities. But refusing his request for a full tour of the island had been impossible. The thought of being alone with him caused a tremor. His cruel assault during their previous excursion remained a frightening memory. She slowed to a ladylike gait as she crossed the lower veranda and strolled to Ellert's side. "I do hope I haven't kept you waiting long."

He tapped his watch pocket. "As I recall, we agreed to meet at ten o'clock."

She offered what she hoped was a demure smile. "That's correct."

"You're seven minutes late. I don't tolerate tardiness. Don't let it happen again." Then he smiled and extended his arm. "Tardiness causes so many problems in life. If I sound harsh, it's because I know the damage that can be done in not dealing with matters in a timely manner."

Her stomach lurched, but she managed to maintain her smile. "I'm generally not late, so rest assured I'll give heed to your desires for promptness."

He smiled. "See. It's not all that difficult to please me."

Amanda nodded. "I'll do my very best. Shall we begin our tour?" He offered his arm, and though she accepted, she would have preferred to maintain a greater distance between them. Mr. Jackson's angry, immediate rebuke had increased both her fear and dislike of the older man. "The house sits two-thirds of the way between the furthermost tips of the island. Do you have a preference for which way we begin?"

"I thought you were in charge of this tour. Surely you know which way is best to proceed, don't you? I thought you wanted to be an independent thinker."

She looked at him rather confused. "I do enjoy that privilege, but you've made it clear to me that you would have it otherwise."

"My dear Amanda, there are things I will not tolerate in our marriage, be certain of that." He narrowed his eyes. "Betrayal of my trust in any form will be punished swiftly and without mercy."

She frowned. "But doesn't everyone deserve mercy? Surely

you are a godly man. Does not Jesus ask us to practice mercy and forgiveness, even to those who do not deserve it?"

Ellert laughed. "I am amused that you presume me to care one ounce what godly men might think or do. I serve no master but myself." He looked around. "Now are we to take that walk, or would you prefer to further discuss my supposed shortcomings where spiritual matters are concerned?"

The man was rude, but she'd already known that. "We'll take the path leading south," she said.

Mr. Jackson made no comment on the beauty of the island or the amazing views of the river as they headed southward. Instead, he maintained a downward focus. Perhaps he feared tripping on a branch or a rock. She did her best to draw him into conversation, but it seemed he had no interest in the magnificence of the island. Her attempt to provide him with a brief history had been met with a quick silencing glare.

Curling his fingers into his palm and using his thumb to point back toward the island mansion, he asked, "Who owns the house and this island? The entire family? Your father? Who?"

She hesitated, uncertain why he would ask and not sure she had an answer. "My grandparents owned this island. I'm not sure what distribution has been made since my grandfather's death. I believe there was some stipulation in the will that it remain in the family. Why do you ask?"

"Because I want to know."

His curt response annoyed her. "There are several islands currently for sale. Several have homes even larger than—"

"I don't want to buy an island. And if I did want to purchase property, I *wouldn't* seek the *advice* of a *woman*."

He emphasized the final words as though he intended each one to deliver a fatal blow. And they had—to her ego. If she didn't change the topic, she might tell him exactly what she thought of him.

"I've been completing the wedding plans and thought you might want to offer some suggestions. Other than insisting the wedding take place at the church on Round Island, you've not indicated your preferences."

"I don't care a whit about the wedding plans. The wedding is simply something I will abide for your sake. I agreed to a formal wedding only to satisfy your father's need to pander to the social crowd."

"I believe he was thinking of you, also," Amanda said. "Without a gala affair, gossip would run rampant. I doubt such talk would serve you well."

He laughed. "I have never worried what others thought of me. I don't need their approval. Your entire family concerns itself far too much with the wagging tongues of Rochester society. I have succeeded in spite of them. And you, my dear, will learn they are of little import once we are married. Let them attend the wedding, but that shall be the end of such nonsense."

She wanted to ask if he planned to keep her away from her family, but she feared his response. "Then I may continue to make all of the arrangements without seeking your approval?"

He pulled her close. His dark eyes bore down on her like a vulture prepared to attack. "The only thing that interests me is our wedding night. Make certain you prepare for that event."

Amanda squared her shoulders but didn't fight his hold. "You know that I am an innocent woman. Why must you speak to me in such a manner? I may be trained in various medical procedures, but I have never been with a man." She surprised them both with her bold statement.

His harsh laughter cut through the morning breeze and echoed through the treetops. In spite of her best effort to remain calm, she shuddered. Ellert pinched her chin between his thumb and forefinger. "I'm pleased to hear that you are innocent, but in truth your fear already betrayed that fact. And I find it exciting. Fear enhances everything, don't you think?"

"Don't you mean *desire* enhances everything? Shouldn't both a man and a woman look forward to their wedding and their life together? Fear has such a negative connotation. I fear things I don't understand—destructive, mean, evil things." She raised a brow. "Surely you would not have me think thus of you. Are there not more benefits—more loyalty and respect—if I should honestly and completely love you?"

He looked at her for a moment. It was clear he was taken off guard by her comment. He softened his hold and let his fingers skim her cheek. Amanda took the opportunity to continue.

"I know the arrangement you've made with my father. Whatever hard feelings and ill will that lay between you two needn't come between us. I am willing to help my family in the demanded manner, despite the fact that my loved ones and friends think me mad. However, I would much rather have a husband to whom I could look up to and respect, love, and obey, as you once mentioned, with a glad and willing heart."

He pulled back as if her skin had suddenly burned him. Ellert looked at her oddly for a moment, and then his features hardened. "I thought you a woman of intelligence, but I can see you hold the same nonsensical beliefs as the rest of your gender. I care nothing about your desires or love. I demand your respect and obedience, and I find that fear is often the best way to get both. You will learn quickly just how cruel and hard I can be, both in public and private, when I am crossed or otherwise made to look the fool."

His words and behavior appalled Amanda, but she fought to remain calm. She must attempt to find some common ground with this man if she was to spend the rest of her life with him. Perhaps it would help if she could discover his interests. Amanda forced herself to take hold of his arm. "Let us continue our walk. Tell me of your business ventures. What interests you the most?"

"Anything that will make me money. I don't give in to the whims of what I might like or dislike. If it is a venture that will add to my holdings, I am interested. Although I abhor the boorish stupidity and the silly games played by social elitists, I do enjoy the many comforts money can buy. And I'm not opposed to purchasing occasional trinkets for myself or for those who show me loyalty."

Amanda was quite certain he didn't frown upon worldly possessions, at least for himself. The servants had been quick to tell her that Mr. Jackson had arrived with seven huge trunks filled with tailor-made suits and more shoes than had been brought by any other guest who'd ever visited Broadmoor Island—male or female. Amanda had been keeping a close watch, and as yet she hadn't seen him wear the same pair of shoes more than once. No doubt he was a man who would take a great deal of understanding, but becoming better acquainted with Ellert Jackson was proving most difficult.

She watched a boat pass by carrying a group of sightseers pointing at various islands. They appeared carefree and happy. She wondered if they'd enjoy a picnic lunch later in the day. Ellert remained a short distance from the edge of the bluff, and she turned to wave him forward. "There is a particularly lovely view from this vantage point."

"I've never been overly fond of the water. The view is fine from here."

His words affirmed his earlier comment. If he didn't enjoy the water, he would never buy one of the islands. She had hoped he might consider a summer home so that she could visit with Fanny and Sophie each year. Of course, he'd not yet said where they would make their permanent home. The thought of life without her cousins close by spurred her to ask, "Where we will make our home once we are married?"

"In New York City. I purchased an estate when I first moved to the city. It was constructed more than a century ago, but it has been well maintained and has been furnished with all of the modern amenities found in your Rochester mansion. I believe it is far superior to any home in Rochester." He crooked his finger and beckoned her to his side.

Though she would have preferred to maintain the distance between them, she did as he bid. If she hoped to persuade him to change his mind, she'd need to appear malleable. "I had hoped we might live in Rochester, at least part of the year. I've always been surrounded by family members. I'm sure you understand my desire to remain close to them."

"If you remain near your home and family, you'll never become reliant upon me." He pulled her close in an ironlike grip. "I don't want your family involved in my life—only you, dear Amanda." He chuckled at her frown. "You'd be rushing home to cry on your mother's shoulder every time you were unhappy. Then your father would pay me a visit and plead with me to behave like a good husband." Ellert shook his head. "I don't want interference in my business ventures or in my home."

"But they won't interfere. I wouldn't allow for it."

"Don't whine at me. I've seen some of the things you're capable of, my dear. I know now that I must put you fully in your place or we might never know a moment's peace." His face contorted, and it was almost as if he became someone else. "I won't tolerate you putting others between us."

"I would never do such a thing if only you will agree to

live in Rochester. I can't bear to think of losing the companionship of my cousins. I have lived in Rochester my entire life, and my family is of great importance to me. Won't you please reconsider?" When he didn't respond, she decided to plead her case a bit further. "You are aware I've been working with the impoverished in Rochester, and I truly desire to continue my work. I have begun my training to become a physician and realize it is my life's calling. I love medicine and want to continue. You have often commented that I might do exactly that and—"

He yanked her forward and pushed her against a nearby tree with a ferocity that knocked the wind from her lungs. His transformation from gentleman to monster was complete. Unable to speak, Amanda stared at him in disbelief. He bared his teeth like a mad dog.

"I know exactly how much you love medicine—I saw you along the shore of Round Island with Dr. Carstead. Tell me, what medical procedure was he teaching you when I saw you locked in his embrace?"

She cowered as he leaned even closer, his hot breath on her face. With his free hand he yanked her hair until her head tipped back against the tree.

"Look at me when I speak to you!"

Hands trembling, she forced herself to meet his hardened stare. "I'm sorry," she whispered.

"*Sorry?* If you know what is good for you, you will heed my words. In the future there will be severe consequences for such behavior. As I said, I will not tolerate being made the fool, and I will punish betrayal. If our wedding were not close at hand, I'd show you what punishment you can expect in the future. You can count yourself fortunate that I don't want you marked up for our *blessed nuptials.*"

Her scalp throbbed with pain when he finally released her hair, but she didn't want to give him the satisfaction of seeing her massage her head. She thought he'd finished with her, but when she attempted to take a sideward step, he pushed her back.

"You will move when I tell you to move! Your life with me will be as I direct. The only decision you will make is to follow my instruction. You will not come or go without my approval, and you will see no one unless I've given my consent. On the other hand, you will likely hear the servants whisper about consorts who will visit my bedchamber from time to time. I tire of women easily, and I'm certain you'll be no different than any other. You should prepare yourself to become accustomed to my habits."

"Then why marry me?" The question slipped from her mouth before she'd given thought to his reaction.

He drew back his hand as if to slap her and then stopped only inches from her face. "You are slow to learn, aren't you? I am the one who asks the questions." A cruel smirk played on his lips. "However, this one time I shall answer you because you are a silly woman with naïve beliefs about men and women. My marriage to you is nothing more than a means of repaying your father for the cruelty he heaped upon me when I was a young man. I must admit there is the added benefit of causing other members of your family a great deal of pain." He shrugged. "Besides, the marriage will require nothing of me. I will continue to live in the same fashion I've always enjoyed, but I shall have a pretty young wife on my arm and in my bed whenever I choose. And she's a Broadmoor. All of society will bow at my feet for the chance to share such an auspicious connection." He pinched her cheek until she was afraid it had turned bloodred. "I have told you how I enjoy inflicting pain, haven't I?"

She didn't know if she should answer, but when he arched his brows, she said, "Yes, you've told me several times."

"Good. I'm pleased to see there's something you remember. I can play whatever part I need to in order to accomplish what I desire. If you dare to tell anyone of this encounter, I will merely appear as gentle as a lamb, with such tenderness and concern for you that your friends and family will immediately believe you mad. You would do well to hone your own acting skills and portray in public the obedient and desirable little wife that I intend you to be." He let her go, and Amanda immediately put her hand to her cheek.

"Don't worry, it won't bruise. But please remember this. Should you do anything more to betray me—should you mention this incident—should you so much as tell your father that you do not wish to be married, I will find a way to hurt you more deeply than you can possibly imagine. It wouldn't be all that hard to create an accident for your dear Dr. Carstead."

"No!" Amanda couldn't even try to pretend his threat hadn't hit her hard. "Don't hurt him."

He grinned at her coldly. "I see it must be true love for you to react in such a near hysterical manner. At least we both know now exactly how to keep you in line."

Amanda didn't respond. There was no need. Finding any hint of goodness in this man would be impossible. Life as she had known it would end on the nineteenth day of August.

❖

*Friday, July 28, 1899*
*Rochester, New York*

Blake ignored the knock at his front door. He was unable to offer aid to anyone at the moment. Since his return to Rochester, he'd been rendered completely useless. Each day had been consumed with endless thoughts of how he could rescue Amanda from Ellert Jackson. He didn't consider himself a poor man, yet he was far from wealthy. There was no way he could raise enough money to save Amanda. With only his small house and his medical instruments for collateral, any banker would laugh at a request for a sizable loan. His thoughts continued to race to and fro as the incessant knocking continued.

"Blake! Answer the door. It's Paul Medford. I need to speak to you."

"I can't see any patients today."

"I haven't come about a patient. We need to talk. I'm willing to shout through the window, but I don't think you want the entire neighborhood listening to our conversation, do you?"

Blake raked his fingers through his uncombed hair and plodded across the kitchen and through the parlor to the front hallway. Twisting the key, he unlocked the door and pulled it open. He met Paul's startled expression. "Well, what is it that's so important?"

"You look like death itself, Blake. Have you had any sleep or considered some hot water and a razor?"

Blake rubbed his palm across the stubble on his jaw. "Ever since my return from the island, I've been consumed with—"

"Helping Amanda. I told Quincy I assumed that was the case. But locking yourself in the house is not going to help. Quincy wants to speak with you. Perhaps the three of us can put our heads together and come up with an idea. Besides, you look like you could use a good meal."

Blake took a backward step and shook his head. "I don't want to be around anyone right now. I'm in no condition to lend aid to the sick. I can't even help myself right now."

"Please come with me, Blake. We don't expect you to care

for anyone. Just come and talk with us. You need some fresh air and a different perspective." Paul clasped Blake's shoulder and pulled him forward. "Come along. You'll feel better. I promise."

Blake considered shoving Paul out the door and retreating back into the kitchen, but he knew such an idea was foolhardy. He could see the determination in Paul's eyes. The man would not be deterred. "I won't stay long."

Paul didn't argue or say much of anything except to comment on the warm weather until they'd arrived at the Home and were settled in Quincy's office. "It's just as I thought. He's dejected over Amanda's approaching marriage."

Quincy frowned. "You don't look good, Blake. I know you love Amanda and had hoped to convince her to set aside her marriage plans, but you can't permit her rejection to ruin your life. You have your work, and there are many eligible young ladies who would be delighted to have you as a suitor. Believe me, I know whereof I speak. Isn't that true, Paul?"

Paul nodded his agreement. "He's absolutely correct. Only yesterday Lila Harkness was asking about you. I believe she's hoping that you'll come calling."

Blake massaged his forehead. What were these men thinking? "I don't believe you understand my dilemma."

"Of course we do, my boy." Quincy patted his shoulder. "We've all gone through the ups and downs of love and rejection. If Amanda has decided she wants to marry Ellert Jackson, then you must determine to move forward with your own life. It's simply the way of things."

"But she didn't reject me," Blake said. Before either of the men could interrupt him again, he explained what had occurred when Amanda had come to Round Island. "We love each other, but her father is forcing her to marry Ellert in order to save himself from financial ruin."

Mouth agape, Quincy sat up straight. "Jonas has bargained away his own daughter? How could he?"

"I'm sure you know him better than I do, but it seems that money and social status are the driving force behind his decision. I've tried to come up with a solution that would resolve this entire matter, but money is the only answer. And I don't have access to enough money to be of assistance."

Quincy hunched forward and rested his arms across his thighs. "I don't want to believe my brother would lower himself to such an arrangement, but I don't doubt your word, Blake. There is nothing left but for me to do but return to the island and speak to Jonas. I knew he had business dealings with Ellert years ago, but I didn't know they'd recently entered into any business contracts. Then again, Jonas seldom confides in me. I must find out exactly what agreement he's made with Ellert." He shook his head. "None of this makes sense."

"When will you go?" Blake asked.

Quincy appeared dazed when he looked up. "I think I should catch the next train to Clayton. If things are as you say, we will need as much time as possible to get this all straightened out."

For the first time since he'd talked to Amanda, Blake felt a glimmer of hope. "If you have no objection, Quincy, I'd like to accompany you to Broadmoor Island."

## 22

*Broadmoor Island*

Quincy could barely wait for the boat to pull alongside the dock before he stepped onto the wooden pier. He extended his hand to Blake. "You may not be welcome, you know."

Blake nodded. "I understand, but even if your brother orders me off the island, I had to come."

Quincy grinned. "The last I knew, I still owned a portion of this island, so I don't think he has the authority to order you to leave. On the other hand, your presence may lead to an uncomfortable confrontation, and I'd like to speak to Ellert and my brother before they're overly displeased with me." He nodded toward the boathouse. "I see Fanny and Michael are over at the boathouse. Why don't you ask Fanny if she can arrange a meeting between you and Amanda while I go up to the house?"

Blake sighed. "That sounds like an excellent plan. I was afraid I might be forced to return home without an opportunity to speak to Amanda. I'm certain Fanny will help."

Quincy patted the young man's shoulder and then turned to the path that led to the house. Both his brother and Ellert appeared surprised to see him when he topped the hill and neared the veranda. He offered an affable greeting to them, but if their frowns were a gauge of their feelings, neither was particularly pleased to see him.

Nearing his brother's chair, he said, "I'd like to speak to you and Mr. Jackson in the library." Without giving them an opportunity to object, Quincy continued into the house. He'd never been assertive with his older brother, and he hoped curiosity would force the two men away from their game of cards.

He sat down in one of the leather chairs. When several minutes passed without the arrival of either man, Quincy drummed his fingers atop the massive desk in nervous fashion. Finally he heard the faint creak of the screen door as it opened and closed. He ceased drumming and folded his hands in his lap. He wanted to appear calm and composed when he spoke to his brother and Mr. Jackson.

"If this turns out to be another one of your brother's woeful tales that he needs money to help the poor and ailing, I'll walk out."

Quincy clenched his folded hands as the comment drifted into the library.

"Don't concern yourself, Ellert. I can handle my brother."

He felt a momentary sense of satisfaction that today's meeting would have nothing to do with requests for his charitable organizations. Both of these men would learn a thing or two today. They thought him lacking in business acumen, but today they would discover he wasn't quite so laughable.

Quincy remained seated when Jonas and Ellert entered the room. "Thank you for accepting my invitation," he said.

"Invitation?" Ellert said with a frown. "It sounded like a command to me. And for future reference, Quincy, I do not take orders. I give them. Had Jonas not persuaded me to humor you, I'd still be on the veranda playing cards."

Quincy gritted his teeth. He'd be dealing with two pompous men, not an easy task under the best of circumstances, and what he had to say would likely make matters even more difficult. He waited until they had settled in their chairs.

Jonas rested his arms across his wide girth. "Well, speak up. We didn't come in here to sit and stare at one another. What is so important that you've arrived unexpectedly and called us away from a private discussion?"

"Discussion? I thought you were playing cards." His brother scowled and Quincy turned serious. "I have recently been informed of the ill-conceived plan the two of you have entered into, and I have come here in the hope that we can set things aright before it is too late."

Ellert chuckled. "Ill-conceived plan? I don't know what you're talking about. And how *you* think you could possibly help me with anything is beyond my imagination."

"Let's don't mince words, gentlemen. I know that Amanda is being forced to marry Mr. Jackson in exchange for a sum of money. It's a bargain I find unconscionable."

Ellert's eyes turned dark, and he shook his head. "Who told you this? Amanda? You've been misinformed, Quincy. To be sure, the marriage has been arranged by your brother and me, but I did not pay for Amanda's hand in marriage. I loaned your brother some money, which he will be required to repay even though Amanda and I will be husband and wife."

Quincy straightened and threw a glance at Jonas. "Amanda said nothing to me, but I can see that the situation is as I've been led to believe. I can read it on my brother's face."

"So Jonas has been complaining of his situation? Is that it?"

"I've said nothing, Jackson. You know full well that I wouldn't."

"Then where has your brother gotten such ideas?" Ellert shot Jonas a hard look.

"Look, I know how to do business as well as you do."

"Ha! If that were the case, you would never have found yourself in such a bind," Ellert countered.

Jonas and Ellert continued to spar until they realized Quincy knew what had transpired between them. When the truth was finally spread out before them, Quincy leaned toward his brother. "Why didn't you come and speak to me, Jonas?"

"For what reason? So you could revel in the news that your brother has made a mess of the family finances?"

"Is that what you think of me? That I would gloat over your misfortune? Surely you know me better than that. Did you think I wouldn't offer aid?"

Jonas sneered. "What aid? I needed money, Quincy. You're the one who has spent these past years begging and pleading with others to give *you* money for your charities. What would you have done? Arranged another benefit and asked for pledges to pay your brother's debts?"

The sarcasm dripped from Jonas's words. His brother held him in greater disdain than he'd imagined. "If that's what it took. I have friends who would no doubt help."

Jonas jerked away as if Quincy had slapped him. "And let

the entire world know that the Broadmoors were in financial crisis? We would be the laughingstock of Rochester. Society would turn its back and never allow a Broadmoor to darken its doorstep." He shook his head. "You would quickly find that we have no friends."

Ellert guffawed and pointed an unlit cigar at Quincy. "You have no idea the sum of money I've loaned your brother. Your miserable friends and their donations wouldn't be enough to sway me in the least."

Quincy scooted forward on his chair. "Can we come to an agreement, Mr. Jackson? Surely you do not want to impose marriage on an innocent young woman. She had nothing to do with causing the bad feelings between you and Jonas."

Ellert slammed his hand on the desk. "The only agreement I'm willing to make is the one I have already secured. I want your brother to suffer as much as I did. I want to take the only thing away from him that truly matters—his family's respect."

The remark caused a stab of pain, and Quincy gave his brother a sideward glance before returning his attention to Ellert.

"But it's unfair to punish Amanda for her father's offenses."

"Members of my family were hurt by your brother. That was unfair, also." Ellert shrugged. "I've learned that life isn't fair, and therefore I seek my own methods in order to repay those who have wronged me."

" 'Avenge not yourselves, but rather give place unto wrath: for it is written, Vengeance is mine; I will repay, saith the Lord.' Romans 12:19."

"No need to quote the Bible to me, Quincy. I have no interest in what your Lord has to say about those who have wronged me or how I choose to retaliate. I don't look to God for help, and I don't plan to wait on Him to mete out His vengeance. I prefer my own methods."

Quincy bowed his head and considered a response. He couldn't permit Ellert's statement to go unchallenged, yet he didn't want the man to storm out of the room before they'd arrived at a better solution. He looked up at the man. His features had hardened into an angry sneer. "None of us is perfect, Ellert. We've all sinned and come short of the glory of God. You, me, Jonas—everyone who has ever lived. And we've all been hurt by others. But freedom from the pain of injustice doesn't come by inflicting misery upon others. You may feel some fleeting pleasure when you force Amanda into marriage, but you'll gain no permanent relief by hurting her. Forgiveness is what heals wounds. Just as Jesus forgives our sins, we must forgive one another."

Ellert held out his palm as if to stave off the words. "Enough! I said I don't want to hear your Bible verses, and I don't want a sermon, either. I have no desire to forgive or forget. My wounds are as fresh as the day your brother inflicted them, and that's exactly the way I want them. Pain is what makes people remember they are alive."

Quincy shuddered. "Surely you do not truly believe what you're saying. It is love and kindness that—"

"If you will not heed my admonition, this meeting is over."

"Wait." Quincy reached for Ellert's arm. "I promise I'll say nothing more about forgiveness or the Bible, but please remain a few moments longer."

❖

Fearful he might be detected before he could speak with Amanda, Blake silently followed Fanny up a steep path she'd declared safer than the main trail. She waved him to a halt as they neared the top. "Wait beside this tree and watch for me to wave you forward," she instructed. "Many of the windows are open, and I want to be sure no one will see you and call your name."

Blake nodded and stationed himself between two half-grown fir trees that would keep him well hidden. He inhaled shallow breaths while he awaited her signal. When he heard a faint whistle, he stepped out of his hiding place and topped the hill.

"This way," she said, waving him close to the house. "Keep low so you're not spotted if someone should look out one of the windows."

He was surprised by Fanny's stealthy maneuvers until he recalled the stories Amanda had told him of the three cousins and their escapades around the island as well as in the city of Rochester that still remained a secret. They'd obviously learned many useful tricks. He wondered what any family members might think if they should see the two of them creeping beneath the window ledges as they circled the house. He pushed aside the thought. Fanny would likely tell them it was a game they were playing with her cousins. And they just might believe her.

As they edged toward the rear of the house, Blake could hear an angry exchange taking place inside. He recognized Quincy's voice and then heard a heated response. What if Mr. Jackson stormed out of the meeting before Blake could speak to Amanda? His mouth went dry at the thought, and he pushed Fanny forward.

"Hurry. I think the meeting is going to end."

Fanny turned and placed her index finger against her pursed lips. Her searing look was enough to silence him. She motioned for him to remain hidden behind a small bush while she checked the kitchen. A moment later she waved him forward and pointed to the rear stairs. They crossed the kitchen on tiptoe and then hurried up the steps. After passing several bedrooms, she lightly tapped on a closed door and turned the knob, not waiting for an answer. With her free hand she grasped Blake's wrist and yanked him into the room.

Shock registered in Amanda's eyes when she looked up. The book she'd been reading clattered to the floor, and Fanny lunged forward and clapped her palm against Amanda's lips. "Remain quiet and I'll remove my hand."

Amanda bobbed her head, and Fanny slowly released her hold. "You two don't have long to talk. I'll wait outside the door and keep watch."

"It might be best if the door remains ajar. I don't want any accusations of impropriety," Blake replied.

The moment Fanny stepped outside the door, Blake clasped Amanda's hands in a firm grip. "I have wonderful news." He stroked the back of her hand while he explained Quincy's hopes to put an end to the forced wedding. "Quincy believes he can solicit the help of old family friends and raise enough money to see this matter dealt with. I can't imagine Mr. Jackson will refuse. I believe he loves money above all else, don't you?"

Amanda bowed her head. "No."

"No? You believe he truly loves you?"

"No, of course not. But Ellert will not agree to take the money. He has already told me that his greatest pleasure is inflicting pain upon others. No matter what Uncle Quincy offers, he'll never agree." She withdrew her hand from Blake's grasp and caressed his face in her palm. "You will never know how grateful I am that you are attempting to help, but neither you nor my uncle Quincy will convince Ellert to change his mind. He is cruel and evil. His deepest desire is to punish both my father and me."

"I don't understand why he would want to punish you. The financial transaction took place when you were a young girl. You had nothing to do with it."

A tear slipped down her cheek. "He saw us," she whispered.

"What do you mean?"

"At Round Island—he saw us kissing. He was in a skiff out on the river—he'd come looking for me."

She shivered, and he longed to pull her into his arms.

"He has threatened to harm me if I ever disobey him or if he should receive a report of me seeing any other man."

"I'll not stand for this. How dare he threaten you! I'm going downstairs and confront him. I'll not stand for—"

Amanda clutched his arm. "No, please. You'll only make everything worse. He means to harm . . ." She fell silent. "There truly is no means of escape for me. I've resigned myself to a future as his wife. Ellert has been clear—my life will be lived according to his dictates." She released her hold on his sleeve and looked deeply into his eyes. "You must not continue these attempts to save me from Ellert, but please remember that no matter what happens, I will always love you. That must be enough."

"Until you are his wife, I will not accept this arrangement your father has made. Somehow, we must find a way." He leaned forward to kiss her, but she took a backward step.

"I can't . . ." she whispered.

Blake turned on his heel and trudged across the room with the weight of defeat hanging over him like a shroud. He hoped that Quincy had met with greater success than he had. Fanny was sitting outside the door at her self-appointed post. She smiled up at him as he offered his hand to pull her to her feet.

"You don't appear very happy," she whispered. "Didn't your talk go well?"

"She has resigned herself to the marriage." He shook his head. "She seems to have no will to fight against it. Even though she's asked me to make no further attempt to save her from the marriage, I refuse to give up. Perhaps you can talk some sense into her."

Fanny glanced toward the room. "Wait here and give me a few minutes. Then we'll return to the boathouse."

Blake took up Fanny's position outside the door, and from his vantage point he watched Jonas and Quincy walk through the front foyer and exit the house. He glanced at the bedroom door. Fanny might be in there for some time. His curiosity attacked him with an intensity that wouldn't be stilled. He hadn't heard anyone downstairs since the men departed. With one final glance at the bedroom door, he walked down the front steps.

Ellert stared at the library ceiling while he finished his cigar. He'd felt a sense of relief when Jonas and Quincy left. Let the two of them wander around their island and commiserate over their misfortune and wallow in their sorrow. The thought gave him great pleasure. In fact, the entire meeting had provided a great deal of entertainment. Simply watching Jonas go pale at Quincy's suggestion that they employ the help of old friends had been quite amusing. Jonas couldn't bear falling into social obscurity. He knew it would forever damage any hopes for business dealings—at least lucrative ones.

Ellert chuckled. In time Jonas would come to realize that his position as a reigning leader of Rochester had come to an end. He could only imagine what Quincy and Jonas would do and say now that they were alone. Quincy was likely quoting Scripture to Jonas. Ellert grinned. Perhaps Jonas and his pretentious wife could take up residence in Quincy's Home for the Friendless when all was said and done. He chuckled at the idea.

With the same harshness that permeated his thoughts, Ellert stubbed out his cigar and blew one final puff of smoke into the room. The air had grown warm and dank. He looked out the far windows. A bank of clouds had turned dark and appeared to be rolling in toward the island. The breeze would surely prove cooler outdoors. He pushed himself up from the chair and ambled toward the library door. He'd made his way only a short distance down the hallway when he heard muffled footfalls on the carpeted stairs. He stopped midstep. *Blake Carstead!*

With his fingers curled into his palms, he formed two tight fists and remained motionless until Blake disappeared into the darkness. Only then did he take four long strides and look up toward the second-floor balcony. Amanda stood looking down at the front door. Anger welled in his chest until he thought it might explode. No one had mentioned Blake had come to the island. When and how had he gotten here? *Quincy.* He must have arrived on the boat with Quincy. He clenched his jaw. The entire time the three of them had been meeting in the library, Blake had been upstairs dallying with Amanda. How *dare* he? How dare *she?*

A fire raged in Ellert's belly. "That young man will pay for this. Something must happen to him—and soon," he hissed from between clenched teeth.

## 23

*Friday, August 4, 1899*

Victoria sat at her dressing table pulling the brush through her hair, the gray streaks more noticeable with each passing day—or so she thought. She lifted the top layer of hair and examined the strands that lay beneath and then leaned closer to the mirror. The roots were definitely gray. She'd be completely gray before long. And little wonder. Few women would have survived a marriage to Jonas without turning completely gray long ago. Unfortunately, the mere thought of her husband had seemed all that was necessary to propel him into their bedroom.

He crossed the room and dropped into one of the upholstered chairs that flanked the double door leading from their bedroom to the upper veranda. While Victoria continued to brush her hair, he sighed and leaned back to rest his head against the soft upholstery. "This has been a most trying day."

Victoria remained silent.

A few moments later, he said, "There was something or someone to create disharmony at every turn."

If Jonas expected her pity and comfort, he would be sadly mistaken. She stared at her own reflection and continued her ministrations. She could feel his stare boring through her until she finally turned to meet his annoyed look in the mirror. Yet she said nothing. Her piercing look should be enough to speak volumes.

"I will not tolerate this silent treatment of yours any longer, Victoria. I had no choice but to agree to Ellert Jackson's terms." He hunched forward in his chair and continued to stare at her in the mirror. "That's what this is about, isn't it? I wouldn't want to misinterpret what has caused your ire."

Victoria gathered her dressing gown in one hand and twisted around on the chair. She gave a slight nod before turning back to the mirror to braid her faded hair.

"Nothing will be resolved between us if you refuse to speak to me."

The single braid swung forward when she lurched from the chair and bent toward him, anger flashing in her eyes. "Nothing was resolved when we *were* speaking. I have told you over and over again that I do not want my daughter relegated to a loveless marriage. She is precious to me—she deserves more, even if you don't think so. I've come to realize that none of us means as much to you as your bank account."

"Don't you judge me, Victoria. When there is no money to purchase new gowns or pay servants' wages, you'll think the money every bit as important as I do. Worse still, when society turns its back on you and all the doors close to those glorious homes you frequent, you'll certainly begin to understand. I have made it abundantly clear that I had no other choice. Everyone else has accepted the arrangement. Even Amanda has come to terms with the wedding. I don't know why you can't do the same."

Victoria seized her brush from the dressing table and pointed it at her husband. "*Why?* I'll tell you why, Jonas. Ellert is a deceptive man who will do harm to our daughter, and yet you insist that she marry him. I was momentarily charmed by him, but after spending time with him here on the island, it's become apparent that he's far more than he pretends to be. You found a means to settle your mistakes, and Amanda is the one who will suffer. You made the wrong choices, yet you expect someone else to pay the price." No doubt she'd overstepped proper boundaries, for Jonas appeared stunned into silence.

Soon, however, he regained his former pomp. "What happened to my prim and proper wife who vowed to obey her husband?"

"I believe she went the way of her husband, who vowed to love and honor his wife and family." The fact that Jonas continued to deflect all wrongdoing from himself only fueled Victoria's anger. She'd not sit back and watch Amanda's life destroyed without a fight. "What would your father think of what you are doing?" She clasped a palm to her bodice. "Worse yet, what would your mother think? Family—not society—was the centerpiece of their lives. Not only did they teach you that principle, but they also lived it. How can you so easily discard what they've taught you?"

Sadness invaded her spirit. "If you permit this marriage, I don't know how you can ever again hold your head high. Besides ruining your daughter's life, your behavior shames the entire family."

Her husband's jaw twitched. Instead of softening his heart, she'd angered him further.

"I will not listen to—"

Dropping her hairbrush atop the vanity, Victoria jumped to her feet. "No need." Before Jonas could say another word she rushed from the room. Now what? As she glanced down the hallway, her focus settled on Amanda's bedroom door. Hastening to the door, she tapped lightly and waited only a moment before turning the knob. She didn't want Jonas coming into the hallway and creating a scene that would be whispered about among the servants come morning.

She glanced over her shoulder to be certain all remained quiet before she closed the door behind her. Moonlight shone through the window and splashed across the room. Amanda pushed herself upward and leaned against the pillows. "Mother! What are you doing here at this time of night? Are you ill?"

"I'm fine—at least physically. However, I cannot say the same regarding my mental state." She sat down on the edge of the bed and clutched Amanda's hand within her own. "I simply cannot bear the idea of having you wed to Ellert Jackson. I have spoken to your father at length, but he refuses to listen." Victoria continued to pour out her heart. Above all, she wanted to save Amanda from this horrid mistake.

"You can do nothing, Mother." Amanda held her mother's hand against her cheek. "There is nothing any of us can do. The agreement has been made. Ellert won't hesitate to use every means available to ruin the family."

"Let the family suffer financial ruination. I love you far too much to stand by while your father signs away your future." Victoria scooted closer. "I have a plan," she whispered.

Amanda fixed her with a wide-eyed stare. "Truly?" Amanda

drew her legs to her chest and leaned forward until her chin rested upon her bended knees. "Tell me!"

"We will run away. If we dress now and hurry, Mr. Atwell can deliver us to Clayton. We can board the first train of the morning before anyone misses us. Once we're in Rochester, we'll gather the remainder of our belongings, take the train to New York City, purchase passage on the first available vessel, and sail for Europe. We can make our home abroad."

When Amanda didn't immediately answer, Victoria continued. "My plan will work. I know it will. We have friends enough in England and France who will help us once they learn of our need."

"I'll admit the idea is tempting, but too many people would suffer in the wake of such a decision." Amanda shook her head. "No. I couldn't. What about George and Jefferson? And what of William and Grayson and their families? And what about Father? I know you are angry with him, but he is your husband. What if he did harm to himself because of our decision to leave? Neither of us could ever forgive ourselves if such a thing would happen."

Victoria hadn't considered Jonas taking his life. He loved himself far too much to do such a thing—didn't he? Yet her daughter's questions haunted her. Could she bear the thought of alienating the rest of her family? What if none of them ever wanted to see her again? Unbidden tears rolled down Victoria's cheeks, and Amanda pulled her into an embrace.

They clung together until Victoria's tears were spent. She dabbed her eyes one final time and then glanced toward the door. "Your father is likely asleep by now. I should probably go back to our bedroom."

Amanda nodded. "Thank you for your deep concern and love. We must not lose hope."

Victoria smiled and kissed Amanda's cheek. The young woman had maturity far beyond her years.

Once her mother left the room, Amanda leaned back against the pillows. Strange that she should be betrothed to a man who possessed money enough to ease the suffering of many. Yet he chose to hoard and increase his own finances while those around him suffered. "He's completely oblivious to anyone's needs or wants except his own," Amanda muttered. She plumped the pillow behind her and reached for her Bible. How is it that the Lord blessed the likes of Ellert Jackson? she wondered. Shouldn't God Almighty strike him down instead? It seemed that Ellert's life was one of charmed existence. At least it had been for many years. Granted, he'd likely suffered in his early life, but shouldn't that give him more reason to help those in need?

There was little doubt she'd be married to one of the wealthiest men in the country. Some said his fortune rivaled John D. Rockefeller, though Amanda found such assertions difficult to believe. Would a man of such wealth bother with the petty rivalry that he had displayed over the past months? Surely not. At any rate, Ellert's finances would be of little concern to her. He was not a man who would be convinced to turn loose of his money unless he could even a score or gain a profit. Helping the poor wouldn't qualify on either account. She hugged the Bible to her chest and closed her eyes. "You must help me, Lord, for there is no one else who will be with me. I earnestly pray that I won't be forced to marry him, but if there is no other way, I pray that you will grant me peace and acceptance."

Still holding the Bible in a firm grip, she closed her eyes and drifted to sleep.

## 24

*Saturday, August 5, 1899*

Walking downstairs the following morning, Amanda clenched her fingers into a tight fist. Ellert awaited her at the bottom of the steps. "I was beginning to wonder if you were ever going to come down for breakfast." He offered his arm and escorted her to the dining room. "You'll not be remaining abed so late once you're my wife. If I must be up and earning money, I expect every member of the household to do likewise."

"And how shall I earn money, sir?"

He scowled at her flippant reply. "You will earn your keep by properly running my estate and by warming my bed at night." He pulled a dining chair away from the table and bid her sit down. Once she was seated, he leaned close to her ear. "Be advised that I intend to take my pleasure with you quite often."

His hot breath on her neck caused an involuntary shudder. She didn't want to think about Ellert Jackson in such a way. She didn't want to think of him at all. Ignoring his salacious remark, she signaled the servant to pour her coffee. "I have to go into Rochester with my cousins today for the final fitting of my wedding gown and their dresses." She hoped he hadn't detected her trepidation. "Please pass the cream," she added, hoping to relieve the tension. How she wished another family member would join them at the table, but they'd probably eaten earlier. She silently chided herself for remaining upstairs until this late hour.

He handed her the silver cream pitcher. "I think not."

She turned to face him. "A final fitting is required, or the gown will not be completed in time for the wedding. I can only imagine what the social column would say. *Ellert Jackson marries Amanda Blake on August 19. The bride's gown was an ill-fitting dress of white satin with an unfinished hem and wide sleeves that drooped beyond the bride's fingertips.*" She stabbed a piece of ham and dropped it onto her plate.

"Do you think I truly care what the newspaper writes about me—or you, for that matter? What I do or say is not controlled by newspapers or the old dowagers who consider themselves authorities on proper social etiquette. However, I do want you beautifully clothed when we are married, for I look forward to removing every article that you will wear."

She felt dirty beneath his leering stare and turned away. "If you want my gown completed, I must go to Rochester."

"And I said that you will not. Do you truly believe I would permit you to go to Rochester and visit your wonderful Dr. Carstead?" He pinched her chin between his thumb and forefinger. "Do you think I'm so stupid that I don't realize your true intent? You don't care about your wedding gown or your cousins' dresses. The only thing you care about is another secret meeting with that doctor."

She twisted her head and freed herself from Ellert's grasp. "Believe what you wish, but my only reason for going to Rochester is to keep my appointment with the seamstress."

"I'll send word to the owner of the shop. They can send seamstresses here to the island. I doubt the owner will refuse the amount of money I offer for special services."

Amanda didn't argue. It would be of little use. "Then I suppose you'd best send your message soon, or there won't be sufficient time." She pushed away from the table. "If you'll excuse me, I've lost my appetite."

Amanda had expected Ellert would bark an objection when she hastened from the room, but he surprised her and remained silent. She breathed a sigh of relief once she'd made it outdoors.

Fanny rounded the side of the house with a carefree spring to her step and waved at Amanda. "There you are. We missed you at breakfast. I was going to come and waken you, but your mother said I should permit you the extra sleep." She drew closer, her eyebrows furrowed in concern. "Are you not feeling well?"

Before she could respond, Sophie bustled out the door and joined them. "Elizabeth is taking her morning nap. What time are we to leave for Rochester?"

Amanda shook her head. "We're not going. Ellert has decreed that he will make arrangements with the shop owner to have seamstresses delivered to the island to fit my gown." She hesitated a moment. "To fit all of our dresses."

"But why?" Sophie demanded. "This is our final fitting, and it has been scheduled since the very first day you ordered our dresses. Why did you agree? Tell him you're withdrawing your consent, and we are going to Rochester."

Amanda struggled to keep her tears at bay. "I can't. Ellert has made it clear that it would be in my best interest to do as he says."

"He has made you his prisoner, and you're not yet wed to him." Sophie cupped Amanda's face between her palms and stared into her eyes. "Listen to me—you cannot marry this man. Do you not realize what your life will be like?"

At the sound of footsteps approaching the door, Amanda freed herself from Sophie's hold. If Ellert was watching them, she'd be quizzed about the conversation. "Why don't the three of us walk down to the boathouse, where we can speak freely?" She hurried toward the path without awaiting a response from either of her cousins.

Once they were on the path, Sophie came alongside Amanda and grasped her hand. "I am at a complete loss, dear Cousin. At first I thought you'd agreed to this marriage simply to create some jealousy on Blake's part. It's obvious you've succeeded on that account, yet you still continue with your plans to marry this dreadful man. I know it cannot be Mr. Jackson's wealth, for you know your father would never let you suffer from want."

An unbidden frantic laughter escaped Amanda's throat. She clasped a hand to her mouth to hold back the hysterical sounds that echoed through the trees.

Wide-eyed, Sophie grasped Amanda by the shoulders. "What has come over you?"

"She'll explain once we're at the boathouse," Fanny said. She turned to Amanda. "You should tell Sophie."

"That's not fair. The two of you have been keeping secrets from me." Sophie came to a halt and glared at them like a petulant child.

"Do cease your prickly behavior, Sophie. This is much more important than your bruised feelings. Once you hear the full extent of what has happened, your sympathies will be directed toward Amanda rather than yourself. Come along, now," Fanny said, grasping Sophie's hand and pulling her forward.

Although the door to the boathouse creaked in protest, the river's familiar scent seemed to bid them come inside. Water slapped along the sides of the moored boats and swayed them in a peaceful rhythm that created a calming effect. Fanny pointed to the wooden chairs along the back wall.

"Let's move them close to the window that overlooks the path. We want to be able to see anyone who might be coming in this direction," Fanny said.

They formed the chairs in a semicircle. Once they'd each taken a seat, Sophie folded her hands in her lap and arched her brows. "I'm waiting."

Amanda smiled at her cousin. Dear, dear Sophie. She was obviously doing her best to overcome her wounded feelings, but her tone of voice indicated she'd met with little success. "My intent was never to hurt your feelings by withholding information from you, Sophie. But my time alone with you has been limited since Ellert's arrival on the island. And you are busy with Elizabeth and Paul. That is as it should be," she quickly added.

Although relating the details of all that had occurred proved more taxing than Amanda had contemplated, she explained the agreement her father and Ellert had devised, as well as the fact that he had observed her with Blake when they'd gone to Round Island.

Sophie clasped her palm to her mouth at the revelation. "You mean while Paul and I were sitting on the porch of the Frontenac Hotel, Ellert was in a skiff on the river?"

Amanda nodded. "Yes. He saw us kiss, and though I can't be certain, I believe he knows Blake visited with me upstairs in my room after he arrived with Uncle Quincy."

"Blake visited you in your bedroom?" Sophie giggled. "I can't believe my prim and proper cousin would entertain a man in her bedroom. I can only imagine what occurred during that visit."

"Sophie!" Fanny's scolding tone was enough to halt Sophie's laughter. "I can attest to the fact that nothing happened. The door was left ajar, and I sat outside until he departed."

"It's all right, Fanny. I know Sophie was merely jesting. Because Ellert believes I'll go and visit Blake, he won't permit me to leave the island. To make matters worse, he insists we must live in New York City. I doubt he'll grant me permission to visit you, but I'm hopeful that he will become more lenient with me once we are married."

"I wouldn't count on him loosening his stranglehold on you. I fear he'll become even more possessive once you're locked into your marriage vows," Sophie replied.

"We should be offering Amanda encouragement," Fanny said.

Sophie shrugged. "I believe it's best to be honest with her. She needs to find some way out of this wedding, for she'll never escape Mr. Jackson once they are wed."

"I know you're right, Sophie, but there is no way out." While her cousins kept a mindful watch on the path, Amanda recounted her mother's visit the previous evening.

Sophie inched forward on her chair. "What if we helped you escape without your mother? Surely Fanny and Michael have enough money to pay for your passage to Europe." Sophie looked at Fanny for confirmation.

"We do, and I know Michael would agree to give Amanda sufficient funds, but that doesn't resolve the problem."

Amanda nodded. "She's right, Sophie. Ellert has threatened to harm too many people if I refuse to go through with the marriage." She didn't feel she could share the threat Ellert had made on Blake's life, so she continued from a different angle. "My escape would leave the family in financial ruination. Although Mother thinks she could survive such a disaster, I know she could not. And though my father has brought this upon himself, I believe he would take his own life rather than face the social ostracism that would follow public knowledge of his financial ruination."

She met Fanny's surprised expression. "I know he said your father was weak and pitiable for such an action years ago, but that was before my father faced his own personal demons. I think he has amassed more insight at this point in his life and more fully understands the depth of despair that can overwhelm the mind."

"I hope he will never meet such an end, for there is always hope when we look to the Lord for guidance. Mrs. Atwell has helped me to understand that there is no problem that cannot be conquered with God's help."

Sophie nibbled her lip. "Then why don't we have an answer for Amanda's dilemma?"

Fanny sighed. "I'm not certain, but I continue to pray and trust that when the time is right, she will be delivered from this situation. To that end we must all remain diligent in our prayers."

"Agreed," Amanda replied.

Fanny and Amanda stared at Sophie.

"Agreed," Sophie muttered. "But God had better hurry

up, or you're going to be in New York City before the end of the month."

❖

Not only did a seamstress and helper arrive at the island, but Mrs. Smithfield, the owner of the dress shop, came along to oversee the fittings. Though Amanda couldn't be certain, she guessed that Ellert had paid dearly for the service. Much to Amanda's relief, Mrs. Smithfield insisted he remain far away from the upstairs guest room that the servants had converted into a fitting room. The furniture had been moved to one side of the room or shoved into the hallway to provide adequate space for the seamstresses to complete their assigned tasks.

The time with her cousins proved to be a mixture of joy and sorrow. They laughed and reminisced about their very first grown-up dresses and many of the dresses they'd worn since that time. Yet beneath the laughter remained the foreboding that this might be last time they would be permitted to enjoy the company of one another. When Mrs. Smithfield finally announced that their task had been completed and she would return with the finished gowns the day before the wedding, Amanda longed to summon her back and insist upon one more fitting. Anything to prolong this time with her cousins and away from Ellert's watchful eye.

Amanda remained in the room while the seamstresses followed Mrs. Smithfield like chicks scurrying after a mother hen. How she wished she could follow them to Rochester and go back to her work at the Home for the Friendless and to the warmth of Blake's arms.

A short time later she trudged down the rear stairs, through the kitchen, down the hallway, and into the library in search of a book that might take her mind off of the approaching wedding and her future with Ellert. Slowly she traced her fingers along the leather spines, hoping one of the titles would capture her interest.

The sound of the approaching footsteps caused her to glance over her shoulder. "Good afternoon, Father. I'm looking for a book."

"I've been looking for you ever since the seamstresses departed. Please come and sit down." He closed the door and drew a deep breath.

Her father's somber appearance and the fact that he had closed the door weren't good signs. Had he been seeking her out to deliver additional bad news? She truly didn't know if she could withstand anything further, yet it appeared there was little choice but to hear him out. She trudged toward the chair, her feet growing heavier with each step.

He waved her onward with a waning smile. When she'd dropped into the chair beside him, he leaned toward her. "I owe you a deep apology for what I've done to you, and I want you to know how much I regret the decision I made with Ellert Jackson. If I could withdraw from my contract with him, I would do so. I truly never meant for things to come to this. My greed and desire for power have proved to be my undoing and created a tragic circumstance for the entire family—but more than any other, I have inflicted tragedy upon you."

She was taken aback by the sight of tears forming in his eyes. Never had she seen her father cry. The idea that he could feel such sadness disarmed her. "Father, I . . ."

He shook his head. "Let me finish while I have the courage." It seemed he could not look at her. Instead, he stared at his highly polished shoes. "Throughout my life, I have prided myself in the fact that I could control every situation. Now I find myself up against something that surpasses my own abilities. I can find no way out of this disaster I've created."

She spied a single teardrop on his shoe. If he noticed, he made no move to wipe it away. How had their lives come to this? Her father weak and defeated—the rest of the family suffering the pain of his decisions. This was a time that should be filled with joy and happiness. Instead, they were all overcome by grief and despair. She reached out and rested her hand on her father's thick arm. "Please don't continue to berate yourself. Although I doubt I will ever be happy with Ellert Jackson, I am resigned to my role as his wife, and I forgive you for what you've done. I pray you will never consider committing such a misdeed again, but I cannot leave home holding this against you."

He reached forward and cupped her face between his palms, then kissed her on the forehead. "I am forever grateful and over-whelmed by your compassion. I don't deserve such a daughter as you."

## 25

*Friday, August 18, 1899*

Amanda stood on the dock holding Ellert's arm while members of the wedding party boarded the *New Island Wanderer* for their brief journey to Round Island for the wedding rehearsal. Ellert had chartered Captain Visegar's boat for the entire weekend. It was a silly and unnecessary expense, as far as Amanda was concerned. She hoped Mr. Atwell hadn't been offended by Ellert's arrangement, for the *DaisyBee* would have proved more than adequate for their needs throughout the weekend.

"I believe that's everyone," Ellert said.

"No," Amanda replied, pulling from his hold. "Sophie and Paul haven't arrived." As if on cue, Sophie scuttled down the path, her skirts hiked above her ankles.

Ellert curled his lip in a look of disgust. "Your cousin will be late to her own funeral."

"She has a baby who requires her time and attention. Besides, she's not late. She's exactly on time." Amanda didn't give Ellert an opportunity to refute the comment before she hastened to greet Sophie.

"I'm sorry if I've kept you waiting. Elizabeth sensed I was leaving her with the nanny and continued clinging to me. Paul is going to stay with her until she goes to sleep; then he'll have Mr. Atwell bring him over on the *DaisyBee*."

"No apology necessary, Sophie. Come sit by me." Amanda noted Ellert's glare when she sat down between Fanny and Sophie. He'd expected her to remain at his side. For a man who boasted he didn't care what others thought, he certainly appeared intent upon making an impression throughout the weekend.

"A wedding in Rochester would have proved much simpler," Sophie whispered.

"Indeed. However, the plans are made, and there's no need lamenting what is past," Amanda replied.

Sophie leaned closer. "Are you speaking of the wedding location or the fact that you are going to marry this man? Fanny and I can still help you escape."

"I do appreciate your loyalty, dear Sophie. But I have accepted that this marriage is going to take place and my future is with Ellert in New York City."

"And I have continued to pray that a miracle will occur and he will release you from the marriage. I fear you will be completely miserable with him, and once he moves you to New York, we'll never see you again."

"I'm determined that won't happen. We are family, and

somehow I will find a way to visit you and Fanny. You must write me often and tell me about Elizabeth and her achievements."

After clanging the bell of the *New Island Wanderer*, Captain Visegar maneuvered the boat away from the dock. The water churned in seeming protest, but moments later the engine prevailed. Soon they were on their way.

Ellert signaled for her to join him, but Amanda averted her gaze and remained between her cousins. She'd likely hear of his displeasure later in the day, but for now she'd enjoy her cousins' company. Once they were well under way, she managed a glance at Ellert. He'd taken a seat beside her father, and the two of them were in the midst of a discussion. She hoped their conversation revolved around something other than her.

When the boat docked at Round Island a short time later, Amanda's father jumped to his feet and darted to her side. "Ellert is displeased that you chose to sit with your cousins rather than with him. He's known to exhibit an unpleasant temper, Amanda. I understand your desire to visit with Fanny and Sophie, but I wouldn't intentionally provoke him."

One look at Ellert was enough to confirm he had prompted the admonition. Amanda stepped forward and grasped his arm. "Do lead the way, Mr. Jackson."

"My pleasure, Amanda. Once we're married, you'll follow only my lead." He leaned close, and his lips brushed her ear.

She attempted to stifle the involuntary shudder that coursed through her body at the touch of his lips. How could she ever learn to love this loathsome man? Stepping into the waiting carriage, she determined to remain silent throughout the short journey to the church. She had nothing to say to him. Ellert seemed impervious to her silence, for he stared out the carriage window and made no attempt to engage her.

Smiling broadly, the preacher stood in the doorway of the

steepled church and waved them forward upon their arrival. He appeared to be the only one who bore some semblance of joy. He held his Bible in one hand and shook hands with each of the men before directing them to their respective positions inside the church. "You ladies will use this room off the foyer," he said, walking with them into the room, "so that you may enter the church without being observed prior to the ceremony."

Amanda smiled and nodded as the preacher offered each directive. She cared little if Ellert saw her before she walked down the aisle. The entire marriage was a charade, yet there was no way the solemn minister could know. She covered her mouth to withhold a sudden burst of laughter, but it escaped her lips like an overflowing brook. Soon she slipped into a fit of uncontrollable laughter. Tears blurred her vision when she finally caught sight of the preacher, who appeared confounded by the situation. She did her best to stop, but each attempt proved a miserable failure.

"I believe you may have developed a case of nervous agitation, Miss Broadmoor. This sometimes happens prior to marriage. If you'll breathe deeply and exhale slowly, I'll fetch you a glass of water." He hesitated. "If that doesn't work, perhaps we should seek medical assistance for you."

Amanda giggled and shook her head. "No. I don't think a doctor will be necessary."

"Unless you could arrange for a doctor from Rochester," Sophie whispered.

She nudged Sophie in the side, but the reminder of Blake proved enough to turn Amanda's convulsive laughter to tears.

Mouth agape, the minister pushed a chair behind her. "Sit down, Miss Broadmoor. I believe you've moved from nervous agitation to wedding hysteria. I will see if I can locate smelling salts."

Those unwelcome words were enough to stop both her laughter and her tears. Amanda straightened in her chair and pointed at the man. "Don't you dare try to treat me with smelling salts." The preacher took a backward step. "I apologize for my sharp retort, but I cannot abide the use of smelling salts." She took his timid smile and nod as his agreement. "I will be fine if you'll give me a moment to compose myself."

"We will begin when you are ready," he said.

After several slow breaths, Amanda gave a slight nod. If she waited until she was truly ready, they would never begin. Soon after the minister's departure, the three of them exited the small room. In the foyer they were greeted by her father and her two older brothers, Grayson and William. Her younger brothers, Jefferson and George, stood near the doors to the sanctuary. They would act as ushers. Both had privately stated they'd prefer to take a beating rather than see her marry Ellert Jackson. She'd refrained from revealing the details of the arranged marriage to either Jefferson or George, and she wondered if they'd feel the same way if they knew the truth. Would they be willing to give up their lives of affluence and social standing for her sake? Perhaps. However, her older brothers and their wives wouldn't be so sympathetic. None of them would want their lives disrupted in any manner. Jefferson and George had attended college, and although they enjoyed living well, Amanda didn't think her younger brothers were interested in hard work—or *any* work, for that matter.

The chords of the piano sounded, and Fanny glanced over her shoulder. "An organ would have been better, don't you think?"

"Or a piano that had been tuned," Sophie suggested with a giggle.

Amanda clung to her father's arm as they walked down the aisle. After he turned her over to Ellert and retreated to her mother's side in one of the front pews, the remainder of the rehearsal proceeded in a blur. Once they'd practiced to the minister's satisfaction, they were dismissed with final instructions for the following day.

"This wedding is going to be the highlight of the summer." The preacher propelled Ellert's arm up and down as though priming a pump. "Thank you for choosing our little church for this magnificent event."

"If Amanda has not already offered an invitation," Ellert told the preacher, "you and your wife are invited to join us at the Frontenac Hotel this evening, where we'll be enjoying dinner and an evening of festivities beginning at seven o'clock." Ellert attempted to wrest himself free of the man's hold.

Amanda nearly laughed at the remark. An evening of festivities? More likely an evening of mourning. This would be her last evening to enjoy with her cousins and family before she became Ellert's wife.

❖

Ellert remained close to Amanda throughout the day and didn't even consider leaving her alone until they'd finished dinner at the hotel.

"I'm going out on the veranda for a cigar. I'm certain you'd prefer to remain inside with your cousins."

"I would."

He nodded. "I'll return before the dancing begins. Do not permit anyone to sign your dance card. Do I make myself clear?"

"Abundantly."

His eyes narrowed. "I sincerely hope so."

The warm August air was heavy with the scent of rain, and Ellert glanced at the sky as he bounded down the front steps of the hotel and strode toward a distant stand of trees. Amanda's clamoring friends and relatives were enough to send a sane man into turmoil. He much preferred solitude. This wedding was enough to reinforce his plans to avoid Amanda's family once they were married. Until after the wedding ceremony, she could believe that he'd permit occasional visits to Rochester or that he'd extend an invitation for her family to come to New York on holiday. Tomorrow, he'd abruptly put an end to those fantasies.

He struck a match to the tip of his cigar, leaned against the tree, and stared at the moonlight reflecting upon the water. Everything was falling into place just as he had planned. By tomorrow he'd be married to Amanda Broadmoor, and the Broadmoor family would be at his mercy. He took a deep draw on the cigar and considered the many possibilities.

"Strange that a prospective bridegroom would be hiding out here by himself."

Ellert wheeled around. Anger seized him as he came face-to-face with Dr. Carstead. "What are you doing here? I know your name isn't on the invitation list."

Blake shrugged. "This is a public hotel. I am a paying guest and am here to enjoy the pleasure of a weekend in the Thousand Islands. To my knowledge, an invitation is not necessary."

Ellert fought to gain control of his seething rage. How dare Blake Carstead come here and cause trouble. "We both know the only reason you're here is to interfere with my marriage to Amanda. You have no reason to be here." He spewed the words from between clenched teeth.

"Quite the contrary. You know that Amanda doesn't love you, and I don't believe you love her, either. I've come here to see if we can reach an agreement so that Amanda is free to marry me."

The young man had courage—Ellert would give him that much. And he obviously loved Amanda, or he wouldn't continue his attempts to interfere. Love truly was for fools—for those willing to step outside the realm of reasonable contemplation. He was glad he would never have to count himself among such foolish people.

"If you know what is good for you, you'll go back to Rochester and forget Amanda. I'm certain any number of young ladies would be pleased to become your wife." He gripped Blake's shoulder in a tight hold. "The circumstances surrounding my marriage to Amanda are none of your business. And they are far beyond your understanding, Dr. Carstead."

Blake twisted free of Ellert's hold and pinned him with a defiant glare. "You're wrong. I know exactly what has transpired between you and Jonas Broadmoor."

Ellert inwardly raged while he listened to Blake recount detailed information of his agreement with Jonas. Obviously Amanda and the young doctor had been doing more than kissing the morning he spotted them together on this very island. Like one of those old dowagers who whiled away the afternoon with tea and gossip, Amanda had passed along her arsenal of information. Just like her father! A genuine fool. She'd take more training than he'd thought.

When Blake had finally completed his onslaught, Ellert tossed his cigar to the ground and crushed it with the sole of his shoe. "I've heard enough." He took a step closer and grasped Blake's arm. "Now, you listen to me, Dr. Carstead. Either you put aside any thought of marriage to Amanda and forget all of what you've been told, or I'll have to see that your handsome face receives a bit of damage. Those pretty girls in Rochester might not be nearly as interested in you once you've met with an *accident*. Do I make myself clear?"

"You don't frighten me." Eyes flashing with anger, Blake pulled free from his grasp. "I can take care of myself."

"I might not frighten you, but I do frighten Amanda." He smiled. "The fact is, you cannot take care of yourself. Not against the men that I will send to pay you a visit. And if a beating doesn't do the trick, it is easy enough to have you killed." Ellert snapped his thumb and forefinger together. "It takes only money and the snap of a finger."

"You can try whatever you like, but I'll not be deterred by your threats. If I can't have Amanda, it matters little what you or your bullies do to me."

Ellert studied the young man for a moment. Blake's words rang with sincerity, and that fact alone was enough to stir Ellert to action. He straightened his shoulders and looked directly into Blake's eyes. "You listen to me, and you listen very carefully. I don't doubt what you've just said. You would likely die for your lady fair, so you leave me no alternative."

"What is that supposed to mean?" Blake curled his fingers into tight fists.

Ellert knew the young doctor longed to punch him between the eyes. He'd likely take great pleasure in pummeling him to death. But Ellert knew that wouldn't happen. Blake was a doctor. A man dedicated to saving lives, not taking them.

"I mean that unless you return to Rochester and forget Amanda, I'll be required to punish *her* rather than you. If you take any action to stop this wedding, you may rest assured that she will suffer dearly—all because of you."

Blake raised a fist and punched the air. "Only a coward

would do such a thing. I cannot believe you would hide behind Amanda's skirts."

"Don't be foolish. I'm not hiding behind anyone. I'm simply telling you what will happen: You either disappear from Amanda's life or know that she will suffer for your refusal. It is your choice, dear boy." Ellert turned and walked away. He would leave the young doctor to dwell upon his choices.

❖

*Broadmoor Island*

The boat ride back to Broadmoor Island was done in silence. Amanda sat rigidly beside Ellert but said nothing, and he seemed just as glad for her lack of words. When they disembarked and everyone went their separate ways, Ellert didn't attempt to control Amanda. She found it strange but was greatly relieved to make her exit.

Amanda had just begun to change for bed when, without warning, Fanny and Sophie bounded into her room. Veda continued to unbutton Amanda's dress as Sophie dropped onto the bed. Fanny stepped forward. "I'll do that, Veda. You can go on to bed."

The maid frowned and shook her head. "I know what will happen if I leave. The three of you will stay up late talking, and Miss Amanda will be all puffy-eyed for her wedding. She needs a good night of sleep before her wedding day."

Amanda smiled at the servant. "I promise we won't stay up much longer, Veda. You go ahead. Fanny will help me out of my dress." When Veda didn't make a move, Amanda lightly touched her shoulder. "You have my word."

The maid trudged toward the bedroom door, her reluctant steps evidence she wasn't completely convinced. With one final warning look, she closed the door behind her. The three girls sighed in unison and then giggled.

"Goodness, but she's become the protective mother hen these past few days," Sophie said. "We're either sidestepping Ellert for a few minutes of your time or staving off the servants with promises of proper behavior. What happened to those days when we used to gather in our rooms and talk for hours on end? Nobody cared in the least back then."

Fanny laughed as she unfastened the final button. "They were pleased to have us contained in one room instead of carrying out one of our many pranks. I do believe we were a greater threat than Jefferson and George." She met Amanda's brown-eyed gaze in the mirror. "Don't you agree?"

"Absolutely! Those two were never our match, though they still remind me of the whitewash incident."

"I can still see your father covered with that pail of whitewash. I'm not certain who was more surprised." Sophie rolled back on the bed and convulsed in laughter.

"It is a pleasant memory," Amanda admitted.

"Oh, and do you recall the first time we attended a dance at the Frontenac Hotel?" Fanny glanced over her shoulder while she carried Amanda's dress across the room to the wardrobe. "The three of us in our party dresses thinking the young fellows would die for an opportunity to dance with each one of us." She hung up the dress and turned around. "As I recall, they did flock around the two of you. I was the only one left standing by the punch bowl."

"I received my first real kiss that night," Sophie recalled.

"You *didn't*!" Fanny joined them on the bed. "You never told us." She looked at Amanda. "Did she tell you?"

"No! You've been keeping secrets from us!" Amanda pointed at Sophie. "What else do you need to confess?"

"Nothing. I promise," Sophie said, turning serious. "We shall miss you, Amanda. You must remember that though we are separated by distance, you will always be in our hearts and in our prayers."

"Yes, always," Fanny added. "And if you should need us, you must send word, and we'll hurry to your aid. Promise that you will write us the truth of how you are faring so that we may know how to pray for you."

"You have my word that I will do everything in my power to visit and to write as often as possible. We may be apart, but our love and our memories will keep us together always."

"Agreed," Fanny said. "I suppose we'd best leave. I don't want Veda to hold us accountable if Amanda should have puffy eyes for the wedding." She leaned forward and kissed Amanda's cheek. "Good night, dear Amanda. I hope you are able to sleep well."

Sophie added her wishes for a peaceful night before embracing Amanda and bidding her good-night. "We'll be with you through every step tomorrow."

"Thank you both. I don't know how I would have managed throughout these past weeks without the two of you." Amanda stood at her bedroom door for a moment and watched her cousins walk hand in hand down the hallway.

After crossing the room, Amanda slipped into bed. How she would miss Fanny and Sophie. Once she departed for New York, the opportunity for friendship with other women would likely disappear. She feared everything she held dear would vanish once she married Ellert Jackson. As a tear slipped down her cheek, she uttered a silent prayer for strength to face the unknown fearful future that lay ahead of her. She must remain strong.

❖

*Saturday, August 19, 1899*

"Miss Amanda, come on now and wake up." Veda's appeal was soon followed by a tug on the sheet. "No time to dawdle. This is going to be the most hectic day of your life."

Amanda rolled over and sat up on the edge of the bed. It had been close to dawn before she'd fallen asleep, and even that brief time had been filled with ghoulish nightmares.

"Look at those eyes. I knew you three wouldn't keep your promise," Veda said as she strode across the room and opened the windows.

A damp breeze wafted into the room, and Amanda glanced out the window. The dismal overcast skies predicted an impending storm—a perfect reflection of the dismal future awaiting her.

## 26

The sky was still dark and foreboding by the time Captain Visegar docked the *New Island Wanderer* at the Broadmoor boathouse. He would provide transportation to Round Island for all the family and friends attending the wedding. He and Ellert had detailed the plans for pickup of wedding guests from several of the many islands.

Ellert had also reserved the rooms at the Frontenac Hotel without Amanda's knowledge or consent. However, she was now grateful for a place where she could prepare for the ceremony and avoid contact with Ellert until time for the wedding. These final hours before the exchange of vows would be the last when she could at least partially consider herself a free woman. Certainly she'd always been subject to the dictates of her father, but life under Mr. Jackson's roof would undoubtedly prove much more restrictive. She closed her eyes and inhaled a deep breath. How she longed to lift her eyelids and discover this was merely a bad dream. Unfortunately, the pitching boat and the mist that dampened her cheeks were enough to prove this nightmare was real.

❖

Once they arrived at Round Island and she and her cousins were alone in the small suite of rooms, Amanda beckoned Sophie forward. "I'd prefer to eat lunch here in the room by ourselves rather than go downstairs and join the others. Do you think you could convince the chef to have our meal sent upstairs?"

Sophie winked. "Of course. You can count on me. I'll even go downstairs shortly before lunch and explain to Ellert that you won't be joining him. He probably won't be happy, but you can count on me to explain."

After her cousin left the room, Amanda signaled Fanny closer. "I have questions . . . about the wedding night. Mother has avoided all talk of what I might expect, and Sophie would likely laugh at me for asking. As you can expect, my knowledge is nonexistent. Would you be willing to enlighten me as to what I should anticipate?"

A faint blush colored Fanny's cheeks as she drew near and sat down beside Amanda. "I can only tell you that for me, the wedding night was very special because of the deep love Michael and I share. From my observation of Mr. Jackson, I fear he may not be kind or gentle with you."

Amanda swallowed hard and forced back the threatening tears. "Whatever shall I do? Many of his comments make me believe he won't be easily deterred. I had thought to feign a headache or stomach ailment if I couldn't abide his attentions, but . . ." She shrugged her shoulders and looked to Fanny for an alternative suggestion.

"He will undoubtedly take any attempt to discourage his advances as an affront. You don't want to anger him. I do fear Mr. Jackson would become unduly cruel if incensed. Perhaps you should simply plead the truth: You are a woman of virtue and would appreciate that he show patience with you."

Amanda removed her handkerchief from her pocket and dabbed a tear from her eye and nodded agreement. "I'll try what you've suggested." She forced a smile. There was no need for further discussion, for neither of them had an answer. She knew that pleading her virtue would have little impact upon Ellert. He cared only about himself and probably would take great pleasure in causing her pain. Hadn't he said as much in the past weeks?

Before Fanny could respond, Amanda's mother bustled into the room with two of the servants and several trunks in tow. She pointed and issued directions and then shooed the servants from the room. "Send Veda up here immediately," she called after them.

"I don't need Veda yet, Mother. I'm not going to dress this early in the day."

Wagging her finger as a warning, Amanda's mother continued across the room. "Nonsense. You must dress for the luncheon. Ellert has arranged a lovely affair—or so the chef tells me."

Amanda grimaced. "I plan to eat here in my rooms. I want to reserve all of my energy for the wedding festivities. Besides, Ellert and his guests will want time to visit prior to the wedding. What better time than at the luncheon he has arranged?"

"Ellert tells me that he will have only one guest attending the wedding. His lawyer, Leighton Craig, has arrived."

Fanny arched her brows. "None of his friends or family responded?"

Her aunt grimaced. "He has no family—at least none that he invited. His friends were either otherwise obligated or out of the city. This is, after all, August. Many of them are traveling abroad or enjoying themselves at their summer homes." As if to indicate such an occurrence was a normal and expected happenstance, her aunt gave an affirmative nod.

"Still, it would seem he would have at least a few friends and business acquaintances who would be willing to return for such an important event," Fanny said. "Many of the Broadmoor family friends are returning from their—"

"Mr. Jackson is aware his guests are unable to attend, and he appears quite content with the arrangement. He is the one who insisted upon an August wedding," her aunt replied. "If I'd had my way, this wedding would not even—"

Amanda reached forward and grasped her mother's hand. "Mother, please. There's no need to fret. Sophie is going to make my excuses to Ellert. He can visit with Father and Uncle Quincy."

Her mother squeezed her hand. "Of course. You girls enjoy this final bit of time together. I'll preside over the luncheon and do my best to assure Ellert you are using the additional time to make certain you are prepared for the ceremony."

Amanda leaned forward and kissed her mother on the cheek. "Thank you."

"It's the least I can do. I fear I'm sending you into a lion's den without any form of defense," she whispered into Amanda's ear.

"I'll be fine. You worry overmuch."

Her mother's eyes had turned as dull as the gray skies. "I pray you're correct."

"That's what we must all do," Fanny said, drawing near her aunt and cousin. "We must pray that God will keep Amanda in His constant care and protection."

"Yes. You're correct, Fanny. We must pray for Amanda without fail. And we should begin at this very moment."

With their heads bowed, Amanda's mother prayed for her well-being and for God's direction. Though Amanda was thankful for her mother's prayer, the somber plea did little to alleviate her fear.

❖

After the men had been transported to the church, the carriage returned to the Frontenac Hotel for the ladies. Preceded by Fanny and Sophie, Amanda descended the wide staircase of the hotel with Minnie clucking orders and draping the flowing train over one arm. Veda followed close behind with the veil and headpiece while Amanda's mother directed them outside.

"Do hurry before it begins to rain. I think you should have dressed at the church, Amanda. Your gown will be ruined if—"

Amanda touched a finger to her lips. Thankfully, her mother took the cue. The gown was of little concern. Even if she walked down the aisle soaking wet, Ellert wouldn't be deterred. He was determined to punish the Broadmoor family, and he would soon achieve his goal.

The ride to the church was over much too soon. Veda and Minnie whisked Amanda into the small anteroom, arranged her headpiece and veil, and pronounced her beautiful. The minute the two maids had completed their ministrations, Sophie and Fanny entered the room and added their enthusiastic approval. The gown was of the finest quality. Ellert had paid the seamstresses well, and they'd produced a gown befitting royalty. Embellished with seed pearls and imported lace, the softly pleated bodice fit snug around Amanda's waist and flowed into an overstated train that had been delicately edged with the same pearls and lace. Had she been walking down the aisle to marry Blake, she would have been delighted with the overall effect of the gown and headpiece. Instead, she cared not a whit.

The piano chords sounded like a death knell as she followed Fanny and Sophie from the room. Attired in a frock coat, double-breasted vest, and striped trousers, her father paced the narrow vestibule like a caged animal. Careful to avoid tripping on the hem of her gown, Amanda stepped to her father's side. She reached up and straightened his tie.

"You look beautiful," he whispered. "I'm so sorry this mus—"

"No more apologies, Father." She grasped his arm, and the two of them stood just beyond the sanctuary doors while Fanny and Sophie preceded them down the aisle.

At the minister's nod her father patted her hand. Together they walked toward the front of the church, where Ellert stood waiting. She shivered at the sight of him and wondered what he would do if she broke loose and ran from the church. Would he run after her, or would he simply announce to all of those present that her father was a thief and a scoundrel of the worst possible sort? She heightened her resolve and took the final halting steps toward her ill-fated marriage.

The minister's words echoed in the distance. Though she heard everything being said, she remained oddly detached. She heard Ellert repeat his vows and affirm that he wished to take her as his wife. Now the minister was staring at her, waiting for her corresponding response. Ellert grasped her fingers and squeezed until she flinched in pain.

"I do," she croaked, her hoarse whisper barely audible.

"Louder," Ellert hissed.

"I do." This time the words were crisp, clear, and loud enough to be heard by the congregation of family and friends.

At the preacher's signal Ellert crushed her mouth in a possessive and bruising kiss. When he finally released her, their guests appeared shocked or embarrassed; Amanda couldn't be sure which. But of one thing she was absolutely certain: Her life would never be the same.

# 27

A soft rain began to fall shortly after the wedding guests returned to the hotel. The light showers continued as their soup was served, but the storm that had threatened throughout the day struck with a vengeance during the main course. Although thunder clapped overhead and lightning streaked the skies, the wedding guests appeared unconcerned. They ate their fill, made several toasts, and applauded when Ellert and Amanda cut their wedding cake.

A short time later the guests followed the couple into the huge dance hall. At Ellert's signal, the musicians began the promenade march and then followed with a waltz. The moment the waltz began, Ellert crushed himself against his bride. "Look at me and smile."

Although Amanda considered ignoring his command, he tightened his hold until she thought her ribs would break. She looked up at him and forced a smile. "You've already succeeded in making me your wife. You say you care little what others think, so why must I appear to be happy?"

He leaned down until his lips were nearly touching her own. "Because I dislike dour women. Women were created to please men, and it pleases me to see you smile. Therefore, you will smile in my presence. Is that clear?"

She broadened her smile in response. He didn't appear to detect the anger that raged beneath her smile. If he had, he likely would have snapped her in two. The thought was enough to keep the smile frozen on her lips for the remainder of the dance.

Following the waltz, the musicians began to play a gallop, and Ellert shook his head. "I don't enjoy gallops or polkas." He grasped her arm and nodded toward the outer edge of the room. "You are not to dance with anyone without my approval. Is that clear?"

"Not even my father or my brothers?"

"Your father and brothers, but no one else. Do you understand?"

"Completely."

He reached forward and positioned his thumb and index finger on either side of her lips. He pushed upward, forcing her lips into a more pleasant expression. "Smile!" When she complied, he approved. "That's much better. I'm going to join my lawyer for a short visit. Make certain you behave like a good wife." He grasped her cheek in a bruising pinch before he strode off to speak with Mr. Craig.

With a sigh of relief Amanda dropped down onto one of the nearby chairs and withdrew her fan. If Ellert remained in the company of his lawyer for the rest of the evening, she would be more than pleased. Yet thoughts of the night that lay ahead wouldn't desist. What had seemed no more than a knot in her stomach during supper now felt like a boulder.

"May I have the pleasure of this dance, Mrs. Jackson?"

Amanda looked up into the dark brown eyes of her older brother Grayson. The fact that he'd addressed her as Mrs. Jackson annoyed her. Neither Jefferson nor George would have done such a thing. She stood and took his arm. "Am I now to address you as Mr. Broadmoor rather than Grayson?"

He appeared baffled. "Of course not. Why would you ask such a silly question?" He glanced heavenward. "Oh, you mean because I addressed you as Mrs. Jackson?" He chuckled. "Since the quest of every woman is to wed, I thought you would enjoy being addressed by the coveted title."

Was her brother truly so dense? Probably so, she decided. After all, his wife, Lydia, had tirelessly pursued him until he proposed marriage. And Amanda doubted her father had taken Grayson into his confidence and told him of his financial misdeeds. Yet how Grayson could think she would desire marriage to Ellert was beyond her imagination. She had never been close to Grayson, but for him to think she'd pursue such a marriage truly emphasized the lack of understanding between them.

"I don't care to be addressed as Mrs. Jackson today—or ever. And especially not by members of my own family. Don't hesitate to inform Lydia of my wishes. I'm certain she'll see that word circulates."

Grayson leaned back as they continued to circle the dance floor. "Are you saying my wife is a gossip?"

Amanda arched her brows. "Call it what you will. I'm simply saying your wife keeps little information to herself."

She'd obviously affronted her brother, for he remained silent throughout the dance. When the music stopped, he escorted her to her chair and then crossed the room and spoke to his wife. There was no doubt he'd related their conversation. Lydia looked over Grayson's shoulder with an angry glare.

The rest of the evening passed in a blur. Amanda danced with her father and brothers, as well as with Ellert and his lawyer. As Ellert's only guest, Mr. Craig had received special dispensation to dance with her. However, the podgy man had been able to circle the floor only twice before gasping for air. They'd been forced to make a prompt return to the punch table, and Mr. Craig stayed near the refreshments for the remainder of the evening.

Ellert was leading her to the dance floor when Captain Visegar approached. "Sorry to interrupt the party, Mr. Jackson, but the storm has calmed a bit. I do think it would be wise to head back to Broadmoor Island as soon as possible. There's no telling how long we'll have before the storm will strike again."

"Then again, perhaps the weather has cleared for the evening," Ellert said.

The old sailor shook his head. "No chance of that. I know the skies and the river. We're in for more bad weather this night."

"I'll go upstairs and change while you inform our guests," Amanda said. When Ellert didn't object, Amanda signaled to Fanny. "Would you come upstairs and help me with my dress? Captain Visegar says we should return to Broadmoor Castle as soon as possible."

"Of course. Go along upstairs, and I'll tell Michael to wait for me while I assist you."

Hiking her gown off the floor, Amanda hurried up the stairs and into the suite. Her embroidered peach gown lay across the bed in readiness, but she took no pleasure in the beauty of the dress. She removed her headpiece and veil and wondered if she would ever again find joy in anything.

The door opened and Fanny hurried across the room. "Let me help you with those buttons," she said. Without awaiting a response, her fingers moved deftly down the row. "Remember that I will be praying for you all night long," Fanny said as she gathered the yards of satin skirt into her arms. "Hold on to the bedpost and step to your left. That way you won't step on the dress."

Amanda did as instructed, though she cared not at all if she stepped on the gown; the dress was a symbol of a marriage that was no more than a mockery. Before she could express her opinion, the door burst open and Ellert entered the room.

Fanny gasped. "You should knock before entering a lady's dressing room, Mr. Jackson."

Ellert glared at her. "Get out of here." When Fanny didn't move, he leaned toward her. "Now," he growled in a menacing voice.

Amanda touched her cousin's arm. "Go on," she urged. "I'll be fine."

Fanny dropped the wedding gown across the bed and scurried toward the door. She edged around Ellert, careful to give him a wide berth.

Amanda reached for her robe, but Ellert slapped her hand. "I prefer you uncovered," he said. "Turn around so I may admire your beauty."

She did as he said, but when she'd completed the pirouette, he clenched her cheeks. "I told you to *smile*. You have a short memory, Amanda. It seems you're going to need to be punished. Perhaps then you'll remember to do as you're told."

She forced a smile to her puckered lips, and he finally

released his hold. "I promise I'll remember in the future," she whispered.

He pulled her closer. "I'm starting to think we should remain here at the hotel and let the others return to Broadmoor Island. You are, after all, nearly undressed."

"I beg of you, please let me return to Broadmoor for this one final night. I won't request any other concessions during our wedding trip, and I'll do as I'm told. I promise." Her lips remained fixed in a tight smile.

"We'll return to Broadmoor Castle, but not because of your pleading. I have papers at the house, and I'll need them before we depart in the morning."

She didn't mention that a servant could secure the items and bring them to the hotel. Ellert was surely aware of that fact. Most likely he didn't trust the Broadmoor servants with his business papers. That was fine with her. At least she'd spend one final night on the island. She lifted her dress from the bed and stepped into the folds of the peach silk. He motioned for her to turn around and, to her surprise, buttoned the dress with ease.

"I will take much more pleasure in removing your dress this evening," he whispered before touching his lips to her neck. She wanted to pull away but feared Ellert would renege on his agreement. She clenched her hands into tight fists and didn't move a muscle. She even remembered to keep a smile on her lips while he continued to press his lips along her shoulder. He growled when a knock sounded at the door.

"Shall I respond?" she whispered.

He lifted his head and turned toward the door. "Who is it?"

"Jonas."

Ellert stalked across the room and yanked open the door. "What is it?" he barked.

"The others have all boarded the boat. Captain Visegar is anxious to cast off. I asked him to wait for Amanda. You and I can remain behind to complete financial matters with the hotel and the orchestra. We can take a smaller boat back to the island once we've finished."

Ellert hesitated only briefly. "Give me a moment alone with my wife, and then we'll join you downstairs. You can tell the captain that Amanda will return with him."

The moment her father was gone, Ellert seized Amanda's arm in a viselike grip. "I expect you to be ready and waiting for me when I arrive. And make certain I'm not greeted by either of your cousins. Do you understand?"

"I understand," she said, careful to maintain her smile.

The moment the captain spotted the couple on the hotel steps with Jonas, he waved Amanda onward. "Hurry!" he shouted from the walkway leading to the dock. "The storm may not hold off much longer."

Although she wanted to run as fast as her feet would carry her, Amanda waited until Ellert kissed her farewell. When he finally released her, he said, "You may join the others."

Captain Visegar joined her on the path and hurried her along. She didn't need the old captain's encouragement. Short though it may be, she was thankful for this reprieve and the distance it placed between her and Ellert.

The two men stood on the hotel veranda and watched as the boat left the pier. Ellert gazed toward the horizon and shook his head. "I don't think there's any worry over another storm. There appear to be some stars in the distance. Had I noticed the clearing skies, I wouldn't have consented to Amanda's departure."

"The captain is known to be cautious. He doesn't want to jeopardize the lives of his passengers," Jonas said.

"I'd guess he's more concerned with himself than his passengers. If the skies clear, he'll have time to return to Clayton and take a group of summer visitors for a midnight cruise. He's likely thinking of the additional money he'll earn by returning the wedding guests earlier than anticipated."

Jonas shrugged. "I suppose one can never be certain." He walked alongside Ellert back into the hotel lobby. "There is another matter I wish to discuss. Why don't we sit down for a moment?"

What did Jonas want now? At every turn it seemed there was something Jonas needed to discuss. "No need to sit down. What is it you want?"

Jonas glanced over his shoulder. "You'll recall that we agreed you would sign off on part of the loan once you and Amanda had exchanged your vows. I'd like to complete that portion of our agreement before we leave the island."

"*Now?* We can transact that portion of our business when we return to Broadmoor Island."

"No. I prefer we take care of it immediately. The minister is still here, and he's agreed to act as a witness."

"You told the preacher of our arrangement?"

"No. I merely told him we needed a witness to our signatures on a contract. He need not know the content of what he witnesses." Jonas pointed toward the far end of the lobby. "He's waiting over there, and I have the papers right here."

Ellert extended his hand. "Let me look at the papers. Unlike you, Jonas, I read everything before signing my name." Once Ellert had reviewed the document, he grunted. "Although I believe this could have waited until later, I'm willing to sign now."

Both men signed the document, and the preacher added his signature without question. He'd likely been pleased with the generous sum Ellert had paid him to perform the wedding ceremony.

"Any further requests?" Ellert asked once the minister was out of earshot.

"No, I believe that's all."

Jonas had obviously failed to detect the sarcasm in Ellert's question. "I'm going to pay the orchestra leader. Why don't you make certain the hotel manager has my account prepared so we aren't unduly detained." Although Jonas immediately bustled off toward the manager's office, the accounting was not completed when Ellert arrived a short time later. In fact, Jonas was the only person in the office. "What is the problem?"

Jonas shrugged. "The man said it would take only a few moments to compile the figures, but he hasn't returned."

Ellert paced back and forth for several minutes. "I'm going to find the manager. Should he return during my absence, tell him to wait here." He leaned down and looked into Jonas's eyes. "Do you understand?"

"No need for acerbic behavior, Ellert. I was conducting business long before you closed your first contract."

"If that remark is intended to assure me of your competency, it falls short. One need only look at your dismal financial condition to realize you are a poor businessman." Ellert turned on his heel and strode toward the front desk. He stopped short when he spotted the manager entering the front door. Waving the man forward, Ellert pointed his thumb toward the office. "Mr. Broadmoor and I are waiting for a final accounting, and you are doing what, sir? Enjoying the evening breeze? I'm certain the owners of the establishment wouldn't approve of your shoddy practices."

"My apologies, Mr. Jackson, but there's another storm moving in. I wanted to ensure that all of our guests were informed."

Ellert frowned. "I would think you could dispatch other employees for such a mundane task, but I'll not argue the point. I'm anxious to pay my account and depart."

"I don't think you want to consider leaving—"

"If I want your advice, I'll ask." Ellert nodded toward the manager's office. "Now, I'd like to conclude our business." He clenched his jaw and followed the manager. No wonder businesses failed nowadays. How could any establishment be expected to succeed when the hired help required constant supervision? Another affirmation that strict control must always be maintained—both in his business and personal life. He shook his head in disgust. No one could be trusted.

After examining the account in detail, Ellert pointed out several discrepancies. "You've charged me for an extra night on one suite of rooms and sixteen extra dinners. You'll need to adjust the account, and then we'll be on our way."

The manager opened his mouth as though he might object, but Ellert pinned him with a deadly stare. He knew he was correct, and he didn't intend to argue with a sniveling hotel manager. Ellert leaned back in his chair while the man drew a line through the objectionable charges and recalculated the balance. The manager pushed the paper across the desk. Ellert gave a curt approval and paid the sum in full.

The man stood and extended his hand. "Thank you for doing business with us, Mr. Jackson. I hope you were pleased with our services."

A clap of thunder rumbled overhead, and Ellert pushed away from the desk. "Come on, Jonas. It sounds as though we need to be on our way."

"I do hope you'll reconsider your decision." The manager glanced at Jonas. "Surely you're aware these waters can be difficult to navigate once a storm moves in, Mr. Broadmoor."

"Yes, of course, but I've been around this river for years. I can handle a skiff better than most of the young fellows who navigate the river." Jonas puffed his chest and strutted across the room.

Such nonsense! Jonas was wavering on the brink of financial disaster, yet he still felt the need to impress a simple hotel employee. Ellert would never understand these men born to wealth. If they'd had to suffer poverty early in life, they'd be better equipped to handle their inherited wealth. Instead, they made poor decisions and worried over their social status.

The doorman offered them an umbrella, but Ellert refused. With the surging wind, an umbrella would provide little protection. A bolt of lightning illuminated the churning water as he and Jonas neared the river. He'd never been particularly fond of water, and the sight of whitecaps gave him pause.

Jonas cupped his hands to his mouth and shouted to a young man near the water's edge. With his head bowed against the wind and holding his raincoat between clenched fingers, the boy scurried to meet them on the dock.

"What can I do for you, Mr. Broadmoor?"

Jonas pointed to a boat alongside the dock. "I want to take that skiff to Broadmoor Island." He dug in his pocket and retrieved several coins. "I'll see that it's returned tomorrow morning."

The young man maintained a tight hold on his raincoat. "I don't think it's safe to go out in a skiff, Mr. Broadmoor. The winds are—" A rumble of thunder drowned out the rest of the young man's sentence.

Jonas stepped closer to Ellert. "What's your preference? I'm willing to take to the river if you are."

Although the journey didn't hold much appeal, thoughts of Amanda prevailed. "Let's go before it gets any worse. I don't want to keep my bride waiting."

Jonas shoved the coins into the young man's hand with instructions to untie the skiff once they were onboard. The boy shrugged. "Don't say I didn't warn ya. You're gonna be in for the ride of your life if this keeps up."

Ignoring the young man's warning, Jonas and Ellert stepped into the boat and shoved off. For a short time the winds diminished, and Jonas rowed with the vigor of a young man. They were halfway to Broadmoor Island when a low rumble sounded in the distance as if to announce impending danger. The skies had turned as black as pitch, and the wind howled with a fury that struck fear in Ellert's pounding heart. The river swelled with angry waves, pummeling the boat like hammering fists. Lightning split the heavens, and Ellert trembled at the sight of the billowing waves. A sudden shriek of wind sent the boat in a frenzied turn, and it lurched to one side.

"We're taking on water," Ellert shouted. Though he couldn't be certain Jonas heard him, he was too frightened to move. He clung to the wooden seat and hoped Jonas was in control of the boat.

The winds briefly subsided, and Ellert felt a wooden object hit his hand. "Use this and start bailing water out of the boat," Jonas hollered.

Ellert clutched the bucket in one hand while continuing to maintain a hold on his seat with the other. The rising water had reached his ankles, and he cursed the ruination of his expensive shoes.

"I'd be worried about more than my shoes if I were you,"

Jonas shouted in reply. "This storm is besting me, and you're no help."

"You're the one who said you could handle a boat in any weather," Ellert screamed. "Now I see that you are an incompetent fool in more than business matters."

Jonas heaved the oars but made no headway in the churning waves. "This has nothing to do with incompetence, Ellert. I believe this is God's retribution upon both of us for the wrongs we've committed."

Though Ellert wanted to tell Jonas he was a fool, there wasn't opportunity. The wind regained its fury, and a massive wave whipped the boat onto its side and the men into a swirling caldron of angry water. Waves and rain lashed Ellert from all sides. He grabbed for Jonas but couldn't reach him. Clinging to the side of the skiff, he gasped for air as the wind ripped the wooden support from his hands. Amid the crushing waves, he thrashed at the water and fought to remain afloat. He must breathe. He must live. Amanda was waiting for him.

## 28

*Sunday, August 20, 1899*
*Broadmoor Island*

Early the next morning, bright shards of sunshine splayed across the carpeted bedroom. A splinter of light danced across Amanda's fingers and settled on the shiny rings that now adorned her left hand. One glimpse and she sat upright in her bed. The wedding hadn't been a bad dream. She was truly married to Ellert Jackson. With a slight jerk she checked the opposite side of the bed. The covers remained undisturbed. Ellert hadn't come to her during the night. Had he returned late and gone to one of the upstairs bedrooms so as not to disturb her? Not likely.

Throwing back the covers, she slid her feet into a pair of soft slippers and padded across the room. Quietly turning the knob, she opened the door and peeked down the hallway. All was quiet. Not surprising considering the excitement of yesterday's festivities and the storm that had continued throughout most of the night. Her nieces and nephews had likely been unable to sleep. After retrieving her robe, Amanda tiptoed downstairs to the kitchen.

Mrs. Atwell looked up from the flour-sprinkled board where she was preparing morning biscuits. "Good morning, my dear. I trust you had a pleasant night."

"I slept well, thank you, but I was wondering if you've seen my father or Mr. Jackson this morning."

The older woman removed the lump of dough from the crock and shaped it into a circle. "No. You're the first family member I've seen today. I suppose you're anxious to begin your wedding trip to Europe. Fanny mentioned you'd be taking the train to New York City and then sailing for a month-long tour. Sounds as though you'll have a lovely time." Using her forearm, Mrs. Atwell brushed a strand of gray hair from her forehead. "Veda said she finished packing your trunks last night, so you have nothing to worry about. There's plenty of time for a good breakfast before you and Mr. Jackson depart for the train station in Clayton."

Amanda didn't argue. "I'm going back upstairs, Mrs. Atwell. If Mr. Jackson should appear, would you tell him I'd like a word?"

"Of course, my dear. You go on up and get dressed. Breakfast will be ready when you are."

Amanda didn't take time to explain that locating Ellert and her father was of greater import than eating breakfast. She rushed up two flights of stairs and down the hallway to her parents' bedroom.

After tapping on the door and receiving no response, she turned the knob and entered the sitting room. "Mother, may I come in?"

The swish of bedcovers in the adjacent room was followed by her mother's muffled permission. "Goodness, what time is it? I must have overslept. Why didn't Minnie waken me?"

"It's not yet eight o'clock."

Concern shone in her mother's eyes. "I do hope your wedding night wasn't dreadful." She glanced at the other side of the bed and suddenly appeared wide awake. "Your father must not have come home."

"That's why I'm here. I've not seen Ellert since we left Round Island yesterday. Do you think he and Father decided to remain at the Frontenac Hotel and wait out the storm?"

"That must be exactly what happened. We need to hurry and dress. We can have Mr. Atwell take us to Round Island and join your father and Mr. Jackson there. Then the two of you can go directly to Clayton."

Her mother rang for Minnie before she hurried across the room and pulled open the door of the wardrobe. "Let me see, what shall I wear?" She glanced over her shoulder and motioned toward the door. "Hurry along, Amanda, or you'll miss the train in Clayton. From what you've told me of Mr. Jackson, I doubt he'll be happy if that should occur."

Her mother was correct. She didn't want to suffer Ellert's wrath. He'd do more than pinch her cheek. "I'll meet you downstairs as soon as I'm dressed."

"I'll send Veda to assist you."

Before nine o'clock Amanda was dressed and downstairs, her trunks had been loaded onto the *DaisyBee,* and Mr. Atwell was waiting at the dock. Both Fanny and Sophie had joined her to bid their final farewells.

Upon receiving the news that Ellert hadn't returned to Broadmoor Island the previous night, Sophie grinned. "At least you were given a small reprieve. I do wish we could go with you, but I don't think either our husbands or Ellert would grant us permission."

Fanny giggled. "When has a lack of your husband's permission ever stopped you?"

Sophie folded her arms across her waist and tipped her head to the side. "Paul will tell you that I have become a comforting and dutiful wife. I'm doing my best to show him how much I love him."

Amanda leaned forward and kissed Sophie's cheek. "I'm very proud of the changes you're making. Paul's a wonderful man. And so is Michael," she quickly added. "Both of you are most fortunate, and I pray that God will continue to bless your marriages." She swallowed hard to keep her emotions in check. She didn't want a tearful final good-bye. "Pray that Ellert will permit me the opportunity to come home for a visit very soon. If I don't—"

"Come along, Amanda. We don't have time to tarry," her mother said as she descended the stairs. "I trust Mr. Atwell is waiting for us."

"Yes." Amanda motioned for her cousins to accompany her, but her mother shook her head. "I'm sorry, but we don't have time for prolonged good-byes. It's better if Sophie and Fanny remain behind."

"We'll be praying," Fanny whispered. "Please write."

"I promise."

After Amanda hugged Sophie one final time, her mother grasped Amanda's elbow. "Come along, dear."

❖

Amanda sat at the rear of the boat and watched until Broadmoor Island disappeared from sight. A tight knot formed in her stomach. Would she ever see this place again? She had taken her life of privilege for granted. So often she had thought herself wise and savvy to the needs of others and the miseries of the world, but there'd always been the comfort of home to ease her mind. Now that was lost to her. Just as Blake was lost to her.

While Mr. Atwell steered their course toward Round Island, she stared into the clouded water. The roiling waters appeared to have turned the riverbed upside down, leaving a murky brown waterway teeming with unwanted debris in its wake. "Much like my own life," she muttered. Ellert had stormed into her world and turned it upside down. Was the unsightly river a reflection of her future? She shivered at the thought.

Mr. Atwell cut the engine, guided the boat alongside the Frontenac Hotel's dock, and tossed a line to a young man working at the pier.

Tying off the boat, the lad offered a quick salute. "Good morning, Mr. Atwell. Anything special I can do for you today?"

"Morning, Chester. We've come for Mr. Broadmoor and Mr. Jackson. I believe they must have stayed overnight at the hotel."

The young man rubbed his jaw. "Nope. They took a skiff and left last night. Against my advice, I might add. I told 'em both they was making a mistake, but Mr. Broadmoor said he could handle the storm. I ain't seen hide nor hair of either one of 'em since they left in that skiff."

"You let them leave here in a skiff? During that storm?"

"I warned the both of 'em, but they wouldn't listen. Nobody's seen either one of them since last night?"

Mr. Atwell shook his head. "Sound the bell."

Chester hurried across the wooden planks and yanked on the rope that hung from a large warning bell at the end of the dock. The bell clanged and echoed across the island, tolling a plea for help. The response was swift. Hotel staff and guests hastened toward the dock, but it was Blake Carstead who captured Amanda's attention. Where had *he* come from? Had he been at the hotel during the reception last evening?

A group of men gathered around Mr. Atwell while he explained the need to form search parties. "Neither Jonas Broadmoor nor Ellert Jackson has been seen since they left this dock in a skiff during last night's storm. We can only guess that the boat capsized, but the men may still be alive and waiting to be rescued on one of the uninhabited islands. We need to make haste and keep a sharp lookout."

"Were they headed toward Broadmoor Island?" one of the men shouted.

"Yes, but in the storm they may have been blown off course. The Broadmoor family will greatly appreciate your assistance in the search. I plan to return Mrs. Broadmoor and her daughter to their home, and then I will join you in the search."

While Mr. Atwell continued to organize the men, Amanda edged through the crowd until she was at Blake's side. "I'm surprised to see you here. Were you here during the . . ."

He shook his head. "I was here on the island but stayed away from your wedding. I couldn't have endured watching Ellert Jackson claim you as his wife. I wanted to discuss a matter with your uncle Quincy. Because of last night's storm, I thought he'd be at the Frontenac, but the manager informed me the family had returned home during a lull in the storm."

"All except my father and Ellert," she said. "They remained to conclude some business matters and were to follow later. Mother and I thought . . ."

Her mother hastened toward them and grasped Blake's arm. "Dr. Carstead. Thank goodness you're here. Jonas may need medical attention. I fear he'll be suffering from exhaustion. He doesn't exercise much, and I'm certain the rowing was strenuous. You will come with us, won't you?"

"Yes, of course. I'll return to Broadmoor Island with you and make sure they haven't returned, then go out with Mr. Atwell to help in the search."

❖

The hours moved slowly while the family awaited word of the two missing men. Amanda's four brothers, as well as Paul and Michael, had gone out with search teams and all had now returned. Jefferson had discovered an oar and several pieces of wood floating in shallow water not far from Broadmoor Island, but they couldn't be sure the items were from the skiff that had carried Jonas and Ellert.

"I simply refuse to believe your father isn't safe and sound," Victoria told the family. "He's probably pacing back and forth on one of the islands, wondering when he's going to be rescued. I can just see him fussing and fuming, can't you?"

Amanda watched her mother search for some sign of agreement from the family. When no one responded, Amanda reached forward and grasped her mother's hand. "Why don't we go upstairs? I'll ask Minnie to bring tea to your sitting room. Afterward you can rest."

"Absolutely not. I'm going to be right here when your father walks into the house. I couldn't possibly sleep until he's home."

"Then I'll have Mrs. Atwell bring tea into the library. I don't think Father would object if you had a cup of tea."

Before she could step out of the room, her mother perked to attention. "Did I hear the front door?" Victoria jumped to her feet. "Yes! I hear voices. You see, your father *has* returned. I told you he'd be home for supper, didn't I?" She hurried to the library door but stopped mid-step when Blake and Mr. Atwell stepped into the library. "Where is my husband?"

Blake's eyes shone with sympathy. "I'm sorry, Mrs. Broadmoor, your husband has been gravely wounded. He might not live through the day. We have him on the boat and are preparing to take him to Clayton. I thought you might wish to accompany us."

After a wailing denial, her mother dashed for the door. "Mr. Atwell, take me to my husband."

Amanda looked at Blake. "Did they . . . ? What of . . . ?" She couldn't bring herself to ask.

"Ellert Jackson is dead. We found his body. We wrapped him in a blanket and are preparing to take him to the undertaker in Clayton."

Ellert was dead. Her father might well die, too. Chaos swirled around her, yet Amanda couldn't move. It was as if her feet were permanently affixed to the spot where she stood. Except for remaining frozen in place, she felt perfectly calm. Amid their concerns for her father's survival, several family members stepped forward and offered condolences for the loss of her new husband.

"Such a pity to be a widow a day after your wedding," someone said.

"You're young; you'll marry again," another remarked.

Amanda couldn't seem to comprehend all that had happened in the past twenty-four hours. It seemed like a dream.

"We need to get your father to Clayton. Come on," Blake said, pulling Amanda along.

She felt a gentle tap on her shoulder. Ellert's lawyer, Mr. Craig, stood beside her. He had accompanied the family to Broadmoor Island to await news of Ellert.

"I'll come with you."

"You don't need to do that," she replied.

He offered a sympathetic smile. "I'm afraid I must. We need to discuss how you would like to handle your husband's funeral arrangements, Mrs. Jackson."

## 29

*Monday, August 21, 1899*
*Rochester, New York*

The return journey to Rochester proved more exhausting than Amanda had expected, but she'd done her best to remain calm in the wake of her many decisions. Her choice to have Ellert laid to rest beside his deceased wife in Rochester hadn't taken long. But Mr. Craig didn't approve. He thought New York City a better place, but Amanda remained steadfast in her decision. Mr. Craig likely thought her uncaring and selfish, but no matter the location of the services, she doubted any of Ellert's business associates would appear. With the exception of Mr. Craig, none of them had been there for the wedding. Why would they attend his funeral?

"I do wish you would reconsider. I think Ellert would have

preferred New York City as his final resting place," Mr. Craig said once they'd entered the Rochester depot.

Amanda stopped and met the man's pleading look. "His final home is either heaven or hell, Mr. Craig. What truly matters is not where we bury his bodily remains but where he spends eternity. If Ellert didn't make his peace with God before he died, I imagine we both know where he is." She didn't want to seem unduly harsh, but arguing was useless. She patted the man's arm. "Besides, Ellert never mentioned a specific desire to be buried in New York City—at least not to me."

"I'm sure he didn't. Ellert thought he was indestructible."

"Then he was a foolish man. My decision stands, Mr. Craig."

"Very well. I will abide by your wishes, Mrs. Jackson. If you'd like me to accompany you to the mortuary, I would be willing to do so."

"You are most kind. I'd be pleased for your assistance. I know Ellert trusted your judgment." She would never be able to refer to Ellert as her husband, and she certainly didn't feel like a grieving widow. "If you will advise one of the porters to have the body delivered to the Ambrose Funeral Home, we can go directly there and meet with Mr. Ambrose."

Mr. Craig arched his bushy brows. "Now? Don't you think you should rest? You've been subjected to a great deal of distress. I fear the strain will be too great."

"Thank you for your concern, but I need to see the arrangements completed. After that, I will make my way to the hospital and check on my father's progress."

He shrugged. "I'm truly glad that he is recovering. I was relieved to hear they were able to bring him directly to Rochester from Clayton."

"I appreciate your concern about my father," Amanda said with a smile. "Dr. Carstead took care of everything. Father's body was quite battered by the storm, and the doctors fear he's developed pneumonia. However, the Rochester hospital is quite good. Now if you'll excuse me."

"But of course. Again, you have my condolences."

While Mr. Craig strode off to locate a porter, Amanda motioned to her cousins. Both Fanny and Sophie hurried to her side. "I'm going to the funeral home to arrange for Ellert's burial. Would you be kind enough to go to the hospital and check on Mother? Let her know that I will head over there afterwards to see Father."

"And Blake?" Sophie questioned with a slight grin. "He has been most attentive to care for your father, as I've heard Paul tell it. I suppose he hopes to charm Uncle Jonas so that he will allow you to marry him. Not that Uncle Jonas will have that much to say this time."

"Sophie!" Fanny chided.

"Well, it's true. We all know Amanda didn't love Ellert Jackson. Now she's free to marry Blake." She offered Amanda a consoling look. "I'm ever so sorry about your father nearly dying, but isn't it grand that your future isn't tied to that nasty Mr. Jackson?"

"I didn't wish Ellert dead, but I am most thankful that I am no longer his wife."

"Your next wedding will be a much happier occasion," Sophie said.

"Talk of another marriage is highly inappropriate while I'm in the midst of Ellert's funeral arrangements, but should I marry again, you may be assured it will be for love and not for money."

Fanny signaled toward the door leading to the train platform.

"We'll see to your mother. You will come home directly after the hospital, won't you?"

"Yes." She kissed each of her cousins on the cheek. "Tell Mother I'll come to the hospital as soon as I make these arrangements."

"I doubt we'll be at the mortuary for more than an hour," Mr. Craig added as he approached and offered his arm.

Once they were settled inside the coach, Mr. Craig leaned forward and clasped his hands together. "We will need to meet during the next weeks to discuss your future, Mrs. Jackson."

"My future? What do you mean?"

"You will need to advise me how you wish to proceed regarding your financial assets."

"Financial assets?"

"You are now a very wealthy woman, Mrs. Jackson. I'm not certain you know the full extent of your husband's vast holdings, but you are his only heir, and many decisions will be required." He rubbed his hands together. "I represented Ellert for many years and would be willing to act as your legal advisor. I know how difficult it is for women to understand the complexities of business matters."

"Many of us are not as obtuse as you may believe, Mr. Craig. I am willing to meet with you and review all of the documents concerning Ellert's assets. I will then decide how I wish to proceed." She hoped she had spoken with enough authority to convince Mr. Craig that she'd not be cheated. Her entire family had suffered due to the corruption and greed of lawyers and learned businessmen, her own father among them. She'd not traverse that same path. The money she received would be put to good use helping those truly in need. She would begin by using some of Ellert's money to finance a multitude of infant summer hospitals.

Bright sunlight slanted across the crisp white sheet on Jonas's hospital bed. Ellert would still be alive if there had been weather such as this on Amanda's wedding day. Or would he? *Is it true that we have an appointed time to die?* Jonas wondered. Was that why he had survived and Ellert had died? Or was it merely because he'd grown up around the water, knew how to swim, and hadn't panicked?

What if he had been the one to die and Ellert had lived? The thought gave him pause. His family's suffering would have been extreme. Ellert would have produced their contract and taken delight in seeing every Broadmoor possession sold. Victoria would have been left destitute, and Amanda would have lived the remainder of her life in a loveless marriage. He shuddered at the thought of such a legacy.

His life had been spared. What legacy would he create for his family with this second chance he'd been given? Jonas rested his arm across his forehead, and for the first time in many years, he wept. Sorrow enveloped him more tightly than the sheet the nurse had tucked around his body.

"Forgive me, Lord," he whispered. "I know I don't deserve forgiveness from you or from my family, but I beg you to hear my prayer. Teach me what I must do to make amends and heal the wounds I've caused. Amen."

He couldn't recall the last time he'd prayed. The plea hadn't eased the agonizing pain; the gnawing remorse remained lodged deep in his heart. He'd hoped to experience immediate relief, but he knew that wasn't going to happen. His decisions had cut too deeply, and that would be too easy. God's forgiveness was immediate, but a simple prayer wouldn't set things aright with his family. From this point forward, his actions must speak for him. His family would test him and expect to see changes in his life. He massaged his forehead. Could he truly change his ways? Would God help him restore his place as head of his family? Did he even deserve such a chance?

The family would likely be better off if he had drowned along with Ellert. But death hadn't come, and he must be man enough to face the consequences of his wrongdoings. "It won't be easy," he muttered before sleep once again overtook him.

Amanda slipped into her father's hospital room and marveled at how small and unimposing he looked lying there in the bed. His eyes were closed, and for a moment Amanda feared he might have passed on, but stepping closer she could hear his even breathing.

As if sensing her presence, Jonas opened his eyes and stared at her for a moment. "Amanda."

She smiled. "Hello, Father. The doctors tell me you are doing much better. That is good news."

He gave a feeble smile. "Your mother says God has given me a second chance."

Amanda nodded. "He's given all of us a second chance."

Her father's eyes filled with tears. "I . . . never meant . . . I know it was . . ."

"Hush, don't worry yourself. Everything is resolved."

"No. There is a great deal of business to attend to once I recover. I wronged so many that it's difficult to know where and how to begin making amends."

"I'm certain those you've mistreated will come to forgive you in time," Amanda said.

Jonas extended his hand, and she took hold of it. "I've done so much wrong. Money—accruing it—has ruled my life.

I have asked for God's forgiveness and prayed that our family be restored. Do you think that's possible?"

Amanda could hear the desperation in his voice. She had never seen her father like this before. She smiled and patted his hand with her gloved fingers. "If there is one thing I have learned in all of this—it's that God can do anything."

"I pray you're right."

"I am. But remember that forgiveness doesn't mean there won't be consequences. People will still have to deal with their wounds, and because of that, you will also have to deal with them."

"I will take whatever punishment I must. I deserve to be ostracized by the entire family. I can't expect everyone to simply understand and accept what I've done. I hope I can prove to them that I've become a better man. I may be required to face time in jail for what I've done." He pressed the back of his hand across his lips.

"I don't think—"

He shook his head. "I've stolen and lied, and that's merely the beginning. Those I've harmed will think it only fair that I pay the penalty for my crimes. And they're correct. It is the just and fair thing."

"This isn't about being fair," Amanda replied. "It's about grace. God has extended it to us, and we ought to extend it to one another." She leaned down and kissed him on the forehead. "I must go now. You need to rest."

Nothing she could say would ease his guilt. Even with the promise of God's forgiveness and the reassurance that she'd forgiven him, Amanda knew it would take much longer before her father was free of his own shame. Each time he looked at his family members, he would be reminded of the tragedy he'd caused among those he claimed to love the most. She prayed her father would discover that the love of God and family would eventually heal all of them.

"The doctors tell me I might return home in another few days," her father said.

Amanda smiled. "We shall all anticipate it with joy."

She walked down the hospital corridor, the smile still on her face. Amanda knew that God had completely touched her heart where her father was concerned. She held him no ill will or malice for the things he'd done, and to her surprise she found not only comfort but liberty in that knowledge.

*I'm free*, she thought. *Free of the pain and sorrow. Free from the worry of whom to blame for what. Free to forgive. I'm free, and now I can make my own choices about the future.*

She looked at the sterile hall and glanced into the rooms as she passed. The hospital had always intrigued her, even as a child, but more so now as she considered how she might reenter her training to become a doctor. Maybe even a surgeon. Now, there was a challenge.

"I hope I'm not interrupting. You seem to be daydreaming about something very pleasant."

"Blake." She whispered his name with great love.

"When did you return?"

"Just a short time ago. I escorted Ellert's body to the funeral home and arranged for his service. It won't be much. He has no friends or family. I imagine it will simply be the lawyer and me in attendance."

"I can be there if you want me."

She shook her head. "Thank you, but no. I want to lay this part of my life to rest and be done with it forever. It seems best to do that on my own."

Blake opened the door to a small room. "Come sit with me for a moment. This room will afford us a little privacy."

Amanda entered the room, took a chair, and sat rather primly on the edge. "I appreciate all of the help you've given us," she said, feeling awkward as Blake closed the door.

"It was the least I could do." He looked at her and seemed tongue-tied.

"How are things at the Home?" She disliked the silence that hung between them.

"Good. Quincy has obtained several new investors." Blake picked at a piece of lint on his trousers. "I think we'll finally get those ceilings replastered and painted."

Amanda smiled and then giggled. She relaxed and leaned toward Blake to whisper, "There are three hundred and twenty-seven places where the paint and plaster has fallen away in my recovery room."

Blake grinned. "Counted them, did you?"

"I had nothing else to do. I had the cruelest of physicians. He wouldn't let me do anything at all."

"Sounds like a very wise man."

"He wasn't acting out of wisdom."

Blake raised a brow. "Do tell."

"He was lovesick. He was mooning over me like a schoolboy. That's the only reason he wouldn't let me out of bed."

"Perhaps you were just delusional—hallucinating. Cholera can do that to a person." Blake gave her a look that suggested she challenge his comment.

Amanda got to her feet, and Blake quickly did likewise.

She shrugged. "I had considered that. I'm still not completely certain that I didn't just imagine it all."

He grabbed her unexpectedly. It was nothing like the harsh, painful manner in which Ellert had taken hold of her.

"Maybe you're just imagining this, as well." He kissed her passionately, pulling her tightly against him.

375

Amanda couldn't help but sigh.

"I didn't mean to lose control," he whispered against her ear. "I honestly didn't come here to impose myself upon you. I know it's the worst possible time."

"We both know I didn't love Ellert Jackson. He meant nothing but pain and sorrow to me. It sounds callous, but his death only served to remind me of how sin can corrupt a man to death."

Blake shook his head. "I was so afraid for you—for us. I couldn't bear to think of him touching you, holding you." He shuddered.

"Then don't think of that," Amanda countered. She touched his cheek with her hand. "Think only of us."

He put his hand over hers. "I know I should probably wait, but I can't permit you to slip away from me again. I can't bear the thought of losing you." He inhaled a deep breath and stared into her eyes.

"Exactly what are you saying, Blake?" She pulled away slightly, but Blake refused to let her go far.

"I'm saying that I need you beside me for the rest of my life. I'm saying that I love you and want you to be my wife."

She arched her brows and grinned. "Are you certain you're not merely looking for someone to help with your medical practice? Uncle Quincy said you have been rather grumpy of late."

"My grumpiness was due to losing the woman I love," he said. "That's not to say I don't miss your help with my patients, too. And I'm more than willing for you to complete your medical training if that's your wish."

She gazed into his eyes, and when he lowered his head, she willingly accepted his kiss.

"There are many things I want to teach you," he said before

pulling her close again. He covered her lips with a lingering kiss that caused her to tremble.

"I'd be pleased to learn whatever you'd like to teach me, Dr. Carstead," she whispered.

He tucked a wayward strand of her hair behind her ear while he continued to hold her close. "I know we'll have to wait until your mourning period has ended, but I don't want any misunderstanding between us. I love you and want you to be my wife. Say you'll marry me."

"Of course I'll marry you. You are the desire of my heart, and I long only for us to be together always."

## 30

*Wednesday, July 4, 1900*
*Broadmoor Island*

"I now pronounce you man and wife," the pastor declared. "You may kiss your bride."

Blake looked at Amanda and leaned forward. "We're well practiced at this, eh, Mrs. Carstead?" He covered her mouth with his before she could answer.

A cheer went up from the crowd of observers. Amanda cherished the moment. It drove out all memories of her wedding the previous year. Ellert Jackson was nothing more than a bad dream pushed aside in the light of a hopeful new day. As Blake let go his hold on her, Amanda caught sight of her mother and father. They offered her a broad smile before a swarm of well-wishers surrounded them.

"Congratulations!" Michael and Fanny were the first to

TRACIE PETERSON ❖ JUDITH MILLER

reach them. Fanny pulled Amanda away from Blake's embrace and hugged her close.

"I'm so happy for you, Amanda. I feel like I've been waiting forever for this day to come."

"You're telling me," Blake said, laughing. He received Michael's embrace and then Fanny's as other members of the family began to gather around them on the lawn of the Broadmoor Island estate.

"You treat my cousin right," Fanny admonished, "or you'll have to answer to me."

"And me," Sophie said, tapping Blake's shoulder.

Amanda laughed at their stern expressions. "We Broadmoor ladies know how to take care of our own," she reminded him.

"I can vouch for that," Paul admitted. He reached down to pick up their year-and-a-half-old daughter. Elizabeth held out several flowers she'd picked.

Amanda took the flowers and pretended to sniff their scent. "Oh, how pretty."

"Pre-ey," Elizabeth mimicked, and everyone laughed.

"I'm sorry for the interruption, Mrs. Atwell," Veda announced, bringing Fanny a bundle. "But I believe Miss Carrie is hungry."

Fanny blushed and took her whimpering daughter. "Carrie Winifred Atwell, do you not realize this is your cousin Amanda's day?"

"Oh, she is so beautiful, Fanny," Amanda declared, gently touching the baby's cheek. This only served to cause the infant to begin rooting. Carrie quickly latched on to Amanda's finger.

"Oh my!" Amanda gasped in surprise. Everyone laughed while Fanny carefully pried her daughter's mouth away.

"Come, little one. We'll give you something a bit more substantial."

"You realize, Amanda," Sophie began, "that you'll have to have a baby girl next year in order to continue the line of stair-step cousins. We're counting on you."

Amanda hadn't expected this announcement and felt her cheeks grow hot. Blake leaned down and furthered her embarrassment. "I know I shall do my part to see that legacy continued."

❖

The wedding party lasted well into the evening, with fireworks crowning the events of the day. Amanda and Blake slipped away from the crowd, anxious to escape the noise and festivities.

"I feared at times this day would never come."

Amanda nodded. She looked at her husband in the soft glow of lanterns and fireworks. She trembled at his touch, but not for the same reasons Ellert had caused her to tremble. "I'm so happy. I never thought to marry. Not really. I never felt the pressure to wed, as many women do. At least not until that disaster last year."

He put his finger to her lips. "I never want to speak of that time again."

She kissed his finger. "I feel the same. I just want you to know that you completely changed my mind about love and marriage. I truly thought I'd seek my fulfillment in being a doctor."

"And you've changed your mind now?"

She looked up at him and shook her head. "Not at all. I intend to seek it there, as well. I plan to be the best doctor in all of Rochester."

"Second best," he countered.

She pulled back and put her hands on her hips. "I beg your pardon. Are you suggesting that I can't surpass your knowledge and become an even better doctor than you?"

He laughed. "You are so competitive. Everything you know about medicine, I've taught you. Now you want to throw it back at me and suggest that you can best me?"

"How arrogant and prideful you are, Dr. Carstead. I'm not at all certain this arrangement is going to work out," she said, feigning concern. She started to walk away, but he easily caught her and lifted her in his arms.

"I can see I will have to work hard to teach you to appreciate me," he said, nuzzling her neck with a kiss.

Amanda didn't feel like challenging him any longer. "I doubt you'll have to work that hard, Dr. Carstead."

Blake laughed and headed for Broadmoor Castle. "I'm not ever going to take any chances where you're concerned. I've learned my lesson. One has to act fast when a Broadmoor is involved."

Amanda giggled and clasped her hands around Blake's neck. "I'm a Carstead now. That means I get to act obstinate, ill-tempered, and smugly superior."

He stopped mid-step and looked toward the river. "It wouldn't be hard to toss you into the water to cool off that opinionated little mouth of yours."

She tightened her grasp on him and laughed. "Where I go, you go."

He pulled her close and sighed. "That's the first reasonable thing you've said all evening. And it's a promise I give you. If I have anything to say about it, we'll be together always. Now and forever."

# More Adventure and Romance from Tracie Peterson and Judith Miller

After the unexpected death of their father, Gwen, Beth, and Lacy Gallatin carve out a life for themselves in the Montana wilds. But life for the three sisters is anything but restful, and they must face their own sets of challenges and adventures before finding their hearts' desires.

BRIDES OF GALLATIN COUNTY by Tracie Peterson
*A Promise to Believe In, A Love to Last Forever, A Dream to Call My Own*

Amid the corruption, looming strikes, and unspoken dangers lurking in 19th-century Lowell, Massachusetts, three young women strive to make a difference. But when their faith is tested, can they continue to stand strong—even if it means losing everything they hold dear?

BELLS OF LOWELL by Tracie Peterson and Judith Miller
*Daughter of the Loom, A Fragile Design, These Tangled Threads*

Jasmine Wainwright's fiery passion and devotion to what she believes transform the lives around her. But this unfaltering commitment is tested as her family splinters apart and she comes face-to-face with losing what she holds dearest.

LIGHTS OF LOWELL by Tracie Peterson and Judith Miller
*A Love Woven True, A Tapestry of Hope, The Pattern of Her Heart*

When Olivia Mott is asked to act as a rail spy, she finds that life in Pullman, Illinois, is not as picturesque as it appears...and the young man who's stolen her heart might be responsible.

POSTCARDS FROM PULLMAN by Judith Miller
*In the Company of Secrets, Whispers Along the Rails, An Uncertain Dream*